TRIPWIRE

TRIPWIRE

A Novel

Edwin W. Chamberlain III
Author of *Operation Desert Vengeance*

To Major Dan,
One of my heroes
and a true Patriot!

EW Ch[...]
COL, IN
STAKER 6

iUniverse, Inc.
New York Lincoln Shanghai

Tripwire

Copyright © 2008 by Edwin W. Chamberlain III

All rights reserved. No part of this book may be used or reproduced by any means, graphic, electronic, or mechanical, including photocopying, recording, taping or by any information storage retrieval system without the written permission of the publisher except in the case of brief quotations embodied in critical articles and reviews.

iUniverse books may be ordered through booksellers or by contacting:

iUniverse
2021 Pine Lake Road, Suite 100
Lincoln, NE 68512
www.iuniverse.com
1-800-Authors (1-800-288-4677)

Because of the dynamic nature of the Internet, any Web addresses or links contained in this book may have changed since publication and may no longer be valid.

This is a work of fiction. All of the characters, names, incidents, organizations, and dialogue in this novel are either the products of the author's imagination or are used fictitiously.

ISBN: 978-0-595-45937-7 (pbk)
ISBN: 978-0-595-90237-8 (ebk)

Printed in the United States of America

Introduction

What is told in this story could happen exactly as it is portrayed. I will frankly be surprised if it does not happen, at least in some variant, in the next three to five years.

For those readers not familiar with American military jargon or Korea, I have included in the Glossary at the end of the story the meaning of any terms used in the story that are not self-explanatory. I would recommend a quick review of the glossary by all, however, before reading this story. It is only a few pages long and may serve to enlighten, and perhaps also to entertain a bit; even veterans of this genre.

This book is dedicated to my family, and to the soldiers, both living and dead, that I have had the honor to serve with in peace and war during my thirty years in the Infantry.

E.W. Chamberlain III
Colonel, Infantry
U.S. Army (Retired)
November, 2007

0142 hours
28 October
North China Sea

Captain Sung Do Kim listened to the roar of the radial engine on the AN-2 biplane and looked out the small window to the dark sea just feet below. The AN-2 Colt was made of wood and canvas and was almost impossible to detect with modern radar. Only the engine provided a radar return. The Colt was designed and first built by the Soviets back in the early 1930's, but this plane was less than two years old. Sung knew his aircraft would get him into South Korea undetected.

Sung looked down again at the sea and shuddered. He hated the sea. His younger brother had chosen the sea, and had died in a small submarine off the coast of South Korea two years ago. Sung had chosen the air. He could not imagine what had possessed his brother to choose infiltration into a hostile land by submarine and rubber boat through the cold pounding surf when you could float down like a feather instead. Perhaps he had chosen the sea because Sung had chosen the air? Who knew? Younger brothers wish to emulate their older brothers, but only to a point. Then they must do better.

Sung knew his brother had died well from the reports in the South Korean press. It was so stupid of them to provide so much information in their media. Sung and others in North Korea followed the South Korean media very closely. It was almost as great a source of intelligence as the stay behind agents left in South Korea at the end of the first War of Liberation more than fifty years earlier. Those agents were old now, and those who did not have sons to carry on for them were dropping off the net one by one. But it didn't matter. The Second War of Liberation was beginning. Sung and his team were the lead elements of that beginning.

Sung looked around the cramped aircraft at his team. He had thirteen men counting himself. All were asleep except Sung. All were in South Korean Army uniforms. None except Sung had been to South Korea before. Sung had been to South Korea three times. Twice to kill politicians; once to kill a ROK general and his wife. Sung had infiltrated and exfiltrated through the tunnels under the DMZ for those missions. This was his first air insertion, but not the first time he and this team had jumped from this very aircraft practicing for this mission. He had lost count, but he guessed they had jumped at least fifty times.

Nothing was being left to chance. Sung had gotten his orders directly from his uncle, the Dear Leader, four months ago. The Dear Leader had explained to Sung in great detail the overall plan for the reunification of Korea. Sung had been electrified by the vision the Dear Leader had provided him. The plan was simple yet sophisticated. The outcomes were both predictable and assured. In two weeks the war would be over.

0230 hours
28 October
Camp Red Cloud, Republic of Korea

The phone rang. It rang again. Lieutenant Colonel Randy Long wanted to ignore it but the G-3 of the 2nd Infantry Division was never off duty. With a curse, Long rolled over to the phone and jerked awake when he realized the ringing phone was the STU-3 secure phone. He snatched the handset up and croaked "Long, G-3" into the mouthpiece. He expected the division commander to be on the other end but instead got the commander of the Western Area Support Group, Colonel Mark Wang.

"G-3! Johnny-Z says the North Koreans are coming tonight! You need to put the division on alert!"

Long groaned out loud. "Jesus Christ, sir! Johnny-Z says the fucking North Koreans are coming every Friday night! Why should this one be any different?"

Wang was momentarily taken aback by the intensity of the G-3's retort. He paused. Now he wasn't sure of himself. Wang was an engineer officer and totally out of his element both as the commander of the support group, and as a spymaster, which is how he chose to view himself in relation to Johnny-Z. Wang was Asian and he believed that Johnny-Z was telling him things because of his ethnicity. That Wang was of Chinese descent and the Koreans traditionally hated the Chinese for transgressions committed over the millennia didn't seem to register with Wang. His family had been in America way too long to remember such things. But Randy Long knew it, and was totally skeptical about any *intelligence* coming from somebody calling themselves Johnny-Z.

"Well, Randy, I think this time it may be for real. I really think you need to put the division on alert. I really do!" Wang said the last part almost pleadingly.

"Sir, I would have to call General Wellens and wake him up first. And just what exactly do I tell him?" Long had to fight to keep the sarcasm out of his voice. "And while we're at it, sir, who the hell *is* Johnny-Z, and how does he know the North Koreans are coming?"

Wang paused before answering. Long did not hear his reply because he said it so softly. Long said "Say again, sir, I couldn't hear you."

Wang spoke louder, "Johnny-Z is my cab driver and he says he knows people in the North who tell him things."

Long stopped himself from cursing out loud, but just barely. He took a deep breath. "Sir, you're going to need to call General Wellens yourself. I don't think I can explain all of this clearly enough to him. I'm sure he's going to have a whole bunch of questions about the source of this intelligence, the credibility of it and much, much more before he puts the division on alert. And you'd better hurry because we fly to Yong San in another three hours for the war game exercise."

Wang's voice took on almost a whine, "C'mon G-3, you know that General Wellens never listens to a thing I say. If it doesn't come from you, he won't listen."

Long barked a short laugh. "Shit, Colonel, he doesn't listen to me either!" Long stopped himself from saying more. "Sir, you're going to have to call him. You haven't given me enough to make a valid recommendation to the CG to put the Division on alert. Shit, sir, we'd be lucky if we could find half of them down in the bars and whorehouses in Tonduchon at this time of night! Sir, I need to go back to sleep here before we fly in a few hours. The CG kept us up late, uh, going over the plan for the war game so I'm all whacked out." Long was going to say 'knob dicking' the plan but caught himself in time. He liked Colonel Wang, but he needed to get some sleep before the follies with General Wellens started in earnest in a few short hours. He hoped his tone of voice conveyed all that. Wang wasn't very perceptive at times.

But Wang got it. "Okay G-3, I understand. I guess I have cried wolf a few times with Johnny-Z's information in the past. But G-3?"

"Sir?"

"Johnny-Z is gone."

"What do you mean 'gone' sir?"

"I mean exactly that. I can't find him and that's never happened before. He always answers his cell phone, day or night."

"Sir, you said Johnny-Z was a cab driver. Does he also run girls?"

Wang paused at great length ostensibly pondering the question about running whores and not wanting the G-3 to think Johnny-Z provided *him* with girls, although he did. Wang was a married man and had his reputation to consider! He responded thoughtfully, "Well, I guess he might do that. A lot of them do, I guess. I've heard that anyhow," he finished lamely.

"Then, sir, I've got a hunch that Johnny-Z is either sampling his wares or making his collections. Or has gotten into the soju and is too fucked up to answer his phone. Do you plan to call the CG?"

There it was. Wang paused. "No, G-3. I guess you're right about Johnny-Z. I'm sure he'll turn up tomorrow and feed me more bullshit about the North Koreans. Sorry to have gotten you up over this. Go back to sleep."

"Roger, sir. See you later." Long hung up the phone and rolled back over burying himself in the covers. It was cold as hell outside and the hootch he lived in hadn't been insulated when it was first built in the 1950's. After all, the US Army was only going to be in Korea for a few years so why waste money on insulation? More than half a century had passed and there was still no damned insulation! He burrowed deeper and fell asleep.

0800 hours
28 October
Headquarters, USFK/Combined Forces Command, Yongsan, Republic of Korea

Colonel Sam Sampson sat slumped in a chair in the CINC's ante room. The jet lag was kicking his ass so it wasn't nerves pushing him lower into the chair as he waited to meet with the four star general who was the overall commander in Korea. He had sat in that exact same chair numerous times waiting to brief an earlier CINC. Back then he had been the Eighth Army G-3, an important post with heavy responsibilities. Now he was just another civilian contractor working on the fringes of the army. He certainly had fewer responsibilities now, but he also had almost no authority. He was compelled as a contractor to do the bidding of any government representative regardless of rank or experience. Sampson had learned when he first started doing contract work that he could tell some of those government people straight out how to do it right as a retired colonel, and they would listen and succeed. Others flatly refused to take his advice precisely because he was a *retired* colonel and subsequently failed. And then they got to do it all over again, but this time Sampson's way. He hated the waste of his time and the army's money when that happened.

Sampson's job as a contractor was to command the enemy forces, the OPFOR, for the army's war games. He was chosen for the job because he was one of the best tacticians past or present in the army. Sampson had never lost a battle in training or war, but that had not been enough to save him from mandatory retirement from the army he loved and missed every minute of every day. Sampson was just beginning to reflect sourly for the millionth time how much being a contractor and retired from the army really sucked when the door opened and the bespectacled executive officer for the CINC came out.

"Sam, the Old Man will see you now."

Sam rose from his slump and stood up. "Thanks, Johnny. How're you doing by the way? Just so you know, you look like shit."

Johnny Raymer smiled but the smile didn't reach his eyes. He was too damned tired. He had known Sam for years and had always appreciated his bluntness like now; straight to the point, Sam said he looked like shit! Well, he felt like shit. "I'm doing okay, Sam. As well as a man can do busting his hump twenty-four seven. I think my wife and kids are still over here in Korea with me, but I'm not real sure about that lately."

Sampson laughed. "Well, I'm glad to see nothing has changed since I was here. You bust your balls at a hundred miles an hour and a hundred hours a day. Any chance of it slacking up some before the holidays?"

Raymer smiled at Sampson's description of life in the headquarters, and then turned serious. "That depends on the North Koreans. We're expecting any day now for them to rattle their sabers and put us on the defensive so they can harvest the rice crop. You know the drill and it's the same old shit every spring and fall, but we have to take it seriously."

Sampson nodded. He remembered the drill all too well. The North would make aggressive gestures every spring and fall to make the South Koreans go into a defensive posture expecting an attack, then the North Koreans would literally disband their army to do all the physical labor of planting or harvesting the rice crop. Unlike South Korea where every farmer was provided a two wheeled tractor which quintupled his rice output, the North Koreans spent all their money on weapons and still planted and harvested the rice crop by hand. The fact that North Korea continued to live in near famine most of the time seemed not to matter to Kim Jong Il, the Dear Leader. He would use his rocket and nuclear programs to leverage, or more precisely to blackmail, South Korea and its allies into providing him with food and fuel for the harsh Korean winter. This was the same old game and had been going on since the Clinton Administration brokered the first deal to buy off the North Koreans. The Dear Leader kept his rocket and nuclear programs going, and the West kept paying him in food and fuel for his empty promises to cancel those programs. Sampson shook his head. Dumb. He walked through the door into the CINC's office.

The CINC rose to meet him and offered his hand. Sampson took the hand and got a firm handshake. The CINC, General Robertson Smith had the reputation for being a soldier's soldier, something not always seen in the higher ranks of the army. Sampson had never met him before and knew him by reputation only.

"Take a seat, Sam. How's the jet lag? You figure out what day it is yet?"

Sampson laughed. "Sir, I never could figure out the International Date Line. I can't remember to this day whether you gain a day or lose a day. All I know for sure is that there's a fourteen hour time difference between here and Georgia so I think I'm supposed to be in bed right now."

Smith chuckled. "Yeah, it's a bitch and it doesn't matter which way you're going. It beats hell out of you going either way. I can't seem to get the boys in Washington to understand the time difference when they call me in the middle of the night here to discuss whatever brilliant idea they have just come up with. I've asked the secretary of defense a dozen times if he needs help getting a secure telephone line and a clock installed in his home and he just laughs. He doesn't give a shit about getting me up, and he also doesn't give a shit about this theater. That's what I need to talk to you about, Sam. I'm going to need your help on the exercise to make a few points to the secretary and his bunch. And to the ROK's while we're at it."

"Okay, sir. You're the exercise director. As the OPFOR commander I work directly for you."

"Good. Now, give me your assessment on what the North Koreans are going to do about Seoul and what you think they'll do overall."

"Sir, they're going to put just enough forces on Seoul to keep the ROK divisions pinned up and then bypass Seoul to get to the airfields. They can handle the ROK Army and what's left of the US Army over here on the ground, but they can't compete with the air power. Sir, I know you know all this but I'm going to lay it all out to make sure I'm in synch with you."

Smith nodded so Sampson continued. "The North Koreans never built a very big air force because they can't compete with ours in either technology or training. So they are planning to negate our air power with a three pronged strategy. The first is they'll use the weather because they can count on no fly weather for ground support ops about fifty percent of the time. They remember getting hammered and killed by the thousands from the air in the Korean War, and don't want another dose of that. Their second prong is the increase of shoulder fired

SAMS they have put in every infantry unit. If any of our planes or helicopters flies close enough, they're toast. Finally, they will focus their SPF on disrupting the airfields south of the Han River even before the main body crosses the DMZ. The main body will destroy or fix in place whatever ROK forces they run into, but their main objective will be to take the airfields as rapidly as possible. They know that the airfields are the only means for rapidly bringing in US forces like Stryker Brigades in the early stages of the war."

General Smith cut in, "And the airfields are how we're going to bring in the troops to man the pre-positioned equipment we have in place. Sam, you and I are seeing this exactly the same. I want you to follow that campaign plan as the OPFOR commander. We need to convince the ROK's, if we can this time, that leaving their best divisions in Seoul is the same thing as putting them in POW camps before the war even starts. But, I'm not hopeful that we'll convince them. More importantly, I need to convince the secretary that his statements to the press recently about Korea are total crap. He actually said that the press needed to understand that *less* is actually *more* in the new modern warfare." Smith shook his head in obvious frustration. "Less is just less and we're dangling out here after the last batch of troop withdrawals, but I hit a brick wall with the guy every time I bring it up. The fact that I'm the CINC in spite of his best efforts to keep me out of the job doesn't help. He forgot that the ROK's have a vote on who gets to be the CINC over here which I'm told made him very unhappy. Are we straight so far?"

"Yes, sir, but I don't think the ROK's will ever believe that the North Koreans aren't as enamored with Seoul as they are. It will be fun to see what happens this time, though. The younger officers might get a clue. But I don't think you'll get the secretary to have a clue. That's a bridge too far because you can't make chicken salad out of chicken shit, sir."

Smith barked a laugh and nodded. "No comment on the chicken salad part and that's the best I can hope for with the ROK's. I'm hoping that some of the colonels will see what's happening and take it to heart. Now, I need to talk to you about the 2nd ID in the exercise."

Sampson leaned back in his chair and looked at the general expectantly. The general seemed to be searching for the right words to use. Finally he said, "You know Bobby Wellens don't you?"

"Yes, sir. We were company mates at West Point. Bobby's two years behind me." Sampson cut it off there. Smith waited and Sampson waited too. Sampson thought he knew where this was going, but he wasn't going to go there first.

Smith finally broke the silence with a sigh. "Okay, I need you to be careful with the 2nd ID, Sam. The ROK's look up to the 2nd ID, and if they get hammered it will do some real damage over here."

"So what are you telling me, sir? To leave the 2nd ID alone?"

The conversation was clearly making the general uncomfortable because he knew he was treading on sacred ground. Everybody was fair game in a war game exercise. That was at the very heart and soul of being able to use the exercises for analytical purposes that in turn drove budgets and war plans decisions. The general twiddled with a pencil on his desk. He put the pencil down and leaned forward. "How good a tactician is Bobby Wellens in your opinion?"

Sampson took a breath before answering. "He's totally fricking incompetent, sir, since you asked."

Smith nodded and said softly, "Yes, I asked, and yes, he is. But, we play the cards we're dealt. I've been dealt Bobby as a key player, and I can't ask you to leave the 2nd ID untouched because it's the wrong thing to do, and the ROK's would see it. I can only ask you to remember that Bobby is not terribly good at the war fighting and maneuver stuff. When you hit him, I need you to do it in such a way that he has plenty of time to come up with the right response. Can you do that and still be inside the rules for exercise credibility?"

"Sir, it's just barely inside the rules, but it's doable. Here's what's not doable. If Bobby clearly screws the pooch and puts the division in a situation where it's painfully obvious to even the most casual observer that they're screwed, I've got to take the appropriate action. The same will be true for the ROK forces. I have to be a credible OPFOR against everybody or we're just going through the motions and wasting time and money."

Smith nodded. "Fair enough and I've got it, Sam. The good news is that Bobby's got a dynamite chief of staff who has his shit together. I've told Bobby straight up to listen to his chief, but I don't think he fully understands what I'm telling him. You know Bobby well, right?"

"Oh, yes sir. I know Bobby *real* well and since we're on the subject I would like to ask you a question."

"Go ahead."

"Okay, sir. Out of all the people in the army to pick from, why the hell is Bobby Wellens a two star and in command of a forward deployed division? I mean you gotta be fucking kidding me, sir, is that the best we can do?" Sampson briefly wondered if he had gone too far, but he didn't care. He was retired and didn't need to play political games anymore, not that he had ever been very good at them.

Smith leaned back in his chair and smiled. "Well, you certainly are living up to your reputation, Sam. I was afraid that retirement had mellowed you. From what I've heard you obviously haven't changed a bit."

"So what have you heard, sir?"

"That you're very, very good but also your own worst enemy. You tell it like it is and not how others want to hear it. And ..."

"And what, sir?"

"And you may be too fond of the bottle from time to time. But I'm sure that part's exaggerated," Smith added hastily. "You have lots of admirers but lots of detractors too, I'm afraid. And they seem to be in two camps with no middle ground. They either love you or hate you, Sam."

"Sir, you haven't answered my question." Sampson didn't respond to the implied drinking problem. That was his business and his alone.

"Oh, I think I just did Sam. You and Bobby Wellens are polar opposites. Bobby has no detractors; at least none that are superior to him in rank. He works the room too hard. Rightly or wrongly, if you get along and keep the boss happy, you get ahead in this man's army. And little things like tactical savvy or troop leading abilities aren't part of the equation. How many generals have you run into who really have their shit together tactically?"

"Not many, sir. In fact, damned few now that you bring it up. But in my humble opinion, that's pretty screwed up. Not that you asked for my opinion."

Smith chuckled. "You are certainly your father's son. I can hear him saying the exact same type of words to Westmoreland in Vietnam."

"Sir, you knew my dad?"

"Yep, worked for him in Vietnam. He was the best goddamned leader and field commander I've ever seen. But he did tell Westmoreland things he didn't want to hear and paid the price. The fact that he was right didn't matter. I'm glad to see the apple really doesn't fall too far from the tree. And speaking of the tree, don't let us get treed by pissants on all this, Sam. Make it work, and come to me quickly if it's coming off the rails. I see Johnny sticking his eye at the peephole which means I've got to move us along. Sam, I look forward to working with you. You've got total latitude to handle the OPFOR as you see fit, but keep in mind what we chatted about. As to the rest of your question on Bobby, sometime when we have a chance I'll explain the Theory of Tens to you over a beer." Smith stood up and offered his hand.

Sampson shook the CINC's hand and gave him a puzzled look. Theory of Tens, sir? Never heard of it."

"Later, Sam. Later. Over a beer when the exercise is over. Don't forget to remind me, okay?" Raymer had walked into the office with a folder in his hand; it was time to move along.

"Will do, sir. And, sir, make sure you're hammering the shit out of this worthless fellow you picked for an executive officer. He's a lazy bastard and bears watching at all times!" All three men laughed and Sampson jabbed the exec's shoulder on the way past him to the door. Johnny Raymer winced in mock pain.

0845 hours
28 October
In the Hills North of Seoul

Captain Sung finished his cigarette and threw the butt away. He spit. He rose from his squat and walked over to his sergeant. The sergeant was sitting with his back against a tree with his legs spread out in front of him. Sung could see the bone protrude through the skin on one leg. It was yellow and the blood accentuated the color. There wasn't much blood, though. It was cold and the wound had coagulated already.

It had been a long night. They had parachuted in from their AN-2 Colt using the German parachutes. The parachutes had three small canopies and allowed jumps from as low as 150 feet. Sung had selected exactly that altitude for his insertion. There was no reserve parachute and from that altitude it didn't matter. There was no time for a reserve to deploy. The sergeant's parachute had only one of the three canopies open and he fell hard, too hard onto the ground. It had taken the team several hours to find the injured sergeant lying unconscious in the dark hills.

"How does it go, Comrade Sergeant?"

The sergeant looked up at Sung. They had been together for over a dozen years now and injuries like this were all part of the rough life of an NKPA special purpose forces soldier. The sergeant smiled. If he felt any pain from the compound fracture of his lower leg he did not show it. "It goes well, Comrade Captain. This is only a minor inconvenience. I will be able to do my duty."

Sung said with a shrug, "Then we must go now, Comrade Sergeant. It is time to do our mission." Sung watched the older man try to get to his feet. Sung did not move to help him. The sergeant got to his feet by pulling himself up the tree trunk, and stood on his one good leg. He did not try to take a step. Sung backed up and gestured to the sergeant. "Come, Comrade Sergeant, we must go." The sergeant took a hop on his one good leg, put his weight on his broken leg and fell to the ground soundlessly. He rolled over onto his back with a grunt and faced Sung.

"It would appear, Comrade Captain that it does not go as well as I thought. I will not be able to keep up."

Sung squatted down and gave the sergeant a cigarette and lit it for him. The sergeant dragged deeply on the cigarette. "This American tobacco is so good, Comrade Captain. Do you think the Americans will still sell us their tobacco when we have liberated the people of the south?"

Sung smiled. "Yes, Comrade Sergeant, I am sure they will. Money is more important than honor or virtue to them. That is the lesson our cousins in the south have learned too, which is why we must liberate them. The Dear Leader and the State are what is important. More important than any of us. Is that not so?"

The sergeant nodded. It was so. He finished his cigarette but held the butt in his fingers. He looked up at Sung. He made eye contact with Sung and nodded his head. Sung pulled the trigger on his .45 and the echo of the shot reverberated through the cold, empty hills. The cigarette butt fell from the sergeant's fingers. Sung holstered the pistol and walked over to the rest of his team and gave the signal to move out. They started down the hill towards the highway far below in single file. Nobody looked back at the body of the sergeant.

The sergeant was the only other member of the team who knew the mission requirements; a necessary precaution in case it had been Sung who was incapacitated on the jump. The sergeant would have terminated Sung if the roles had been reversed, and Sung would have accepted that just as the sergeant had. The sergeant had been a damned good man, though, Sung reflected briefly.

Sung did not dwell on any of this for long. He led his team down the hill and looked for the dirt road in the draw that he knew from aerial photos was off to the east of the highway and just north of the bridge. Sung carried no maps. He had committed all of his mission locations to memory.

Sung finally saw the road below and silently signaled his team to spread out and approach the draw from two directions. Sung and his men moved cautiously. If they had been betrayed, this would be the place of betrayal. This was the only part of the operation Sung was uncomfortable with because he had to rely on somebody else. In this case, he didn't know this other man and was very skeptical of him based upon his name alone—Johnny-Z. It sounded too American and therefore too untrustworthy.

Sung got to a vantage point behind an outcropping of boulders, and looked down into the draw. There was a taxi cab and three jeeps with trailers parked below. Sung could see a man and a woman sitting in the taxi cab with the heater apparently going full blast. The windows were foggy but Sung could see the two people clearly enough. Sung's team on the other side of the draw signaled the all clear, and Sung climbed down the steep hill and entered the draw. The man in the cab saw him and hastily opened his door and got out. The woman remained seated and was staring fixedly down into her lap. She did not look at Sung or the other soldiers as they came down from the hills.

The taxi driver smiled and nodded his head obsequiously at Sung. "Major, I am here and with the vehicles as you directed! It is a glorious day for us! You have come to free us from oppression!"

Sung was dressed in the uniform of a major in the South Korean MP's, so the man's salutation was correct. But the rest of the man's greeting told Sung that he knew who they really were. The man was supposed to have been told that this was a ROK MP exercise to test local security measures. Sung smiled at the man.

"Johnny-Z, you have done well! And who is the attractive lady with you? Why is she here?" The woman continued to stare at her lap and did not respond to Sung's bantering tone.

"Oh, Major! She is a trusted friend of mine! I could not bring the vehicles here by myself, so she followed me in the cab after I dropped each one off. It was too far to walk, Major. Much too far for me."

Sung nodded and turned to face the taxi driver. "But your instructions were to do this alone. Did you perhaps not understand your instructions?" Sung asked the question softly. He was concerned about who the woman might have told about their little exercise. Still it didn't matter. He smiled again at Johnny-Z who visibly relaxed. "But comrade, it doesn't matter. It was a long way to walk. Perhaps too long as you say. Come with me over here to my rucksack and I will pay you as was agreed upon. The jeeps are full of fuel?"

"Oh yes, sir! And the gas cans on the back are also full!" The two men walked away from the vehicles. Several of the soldiers manned the jeeps and started them up. Others walked over to the taxi cab. Johnny-Z did not see them and Sung kept him occupied by rummaging in the depths of his rucksack for the gold that Johnny-Z had been promised. Johnny-Z fidgeted. How hard was it to find a gold brick weighing one kilogram in a rucksack, he wondered?

Sung's hand finally came out of the rucksack, but it held a pistol instead of gold. Johnny-Z lost control of his bladder as the pistol was calmly pointed at his head. Sung grasped Johnny-Z's shoulder and firmly turned him back towards the taxi cab. He kept the pistol lightly pressed against the back of Johnny-Z's head as he prodded him back to the cab. The engine of the cab had been turned off, and a soldier threw the keys into the brush far up on the hillside.

Johnny-Z stumbled on rubbery legs back to the cab. Sung pushed him down into the driver's seat, and swung the car door shut. The woman had not uttered a sound and was still staring at her lap. "Is it ready?"

"Yes, Comrade Captain. They will not be able to get out. We have jammed the locks and removed the window handles."

Sung nodded and then swung his pistol up and hit the soldier who had answered him squarely in the face with the heavy pistol. The soldier fell to the ground without a sound but was still conscious. Sung hissed, "All of you listen to me! The next time I will kill you if you make this mistake again. We are *South Korean soldiers* and no longer *comrade* this or that. Am I clear?" They all nodded their heads. "And you must call me *major*. Is that clear?" Again, the heads nodded. Sung looked at the man he had knocked down and snapped at him, "Do the gasoline and catch up with us."

The man scrambled to his feet. For the first time the woman looked up from her lap. The terror instantly etched onto her face was shocking to behold, but none of the soldiers noticed. Nor would they have cared if they had looked at her. She began to scream. Johnny-Z began to scream too.

Sung got into the first jeep and it pulled smoothly away from the draw, the little four cylinder engine whining. Sung heard the "whump" sound of gasoline igniting. He could faintly hear the higher pitched screams of Johnny-Z and his whore as they frantically tried to get out of the burning cab. The screams quickly faded away in the distance and the only sound was that of the jeep engine. The jeeps stopped long enough to pick up the soldier who had set the fire, and then turned south towards Seoul. They sped down the highway with their blue MP lights flashing but with no sirens on. They had to hurry. There was much to do.

0900 hours
28 October
Simulation Center, Yongsan, Republic of Korea

"Hey, sir. There's a captain here to see you. Says he's somebody's aide."

"Okay, Gunny. Send him in." Sampson was going through the OPFOR positioning on the computer in preparation for the start of the exercise. He switched off the monitor so nobody who wasn't part of the OPFOR could just kind of get a sneak peek. The ROK's were forever trying to get in to do just that. A captain came into the room with a big smile on his face and his hand outstretched. Sampson didn't know him but took the hand. He got a firm handshake and an elbow squeeze with the captain's left hand in return. Very general officer-like Sampson thought sourly. So far he wasn't impressed with the captain.

"Sir, I'm Captain Glen Stover, General Wellens' aide. He sent me over here to see if you could stop by and see him a minute before the exercise kicks off this afternoon. Sir, come this way please." The captain wasn't giving Sampson a chance to decline the invitation from so august a personage. Sam followed him out the door and across the parking lot to the 2nd ID TOC. The MP's waved them through the security checkpoint.

"Sir, I know your son really well. He was in my company before I became General Wellens' aide. What a fine young man he is!"

Sampson didn't respond to the remark and reflected back on what his son had said about his previous company commander—very political and very smooth. Sampson had to admit the boy was right on target. The word 'smarmy' came to mind. Then they were inside the office, and Bobby Wellens came forward to greet Sampson with a big smile, a big hand shake and a big elbow squeeze. Sampson knew when he was about to be schmoozed.

"Hi, Bobby. How are you?" It was a rhetorical question. Sampson really didn't care how Bobby Wellens was.

"Well, now that we've got ourselves a little shooting war, I couldn't be better Sam! God, how I look forward to this, even if it is just an exercise!"

Sampson was a little taken aback by this boundless enthusiasm for an event that he knew put Wellens very much outside his comfort zone. He could only respond with, "Really?"

Bobby nodded his head vigorously. "Yeah, I've missed all the other times to be in combat because I was just in the wrong job at the wrong time, but now I'm sitting pretty. They can't take this one away from me!"

"It's only an exercise, Bobby. This ain't the real deal," Sampson said dryly.

"Yeah, well I've told all my guys that they need to get their heads in the game and I want them to believe, really believe that they are really at war as we do this! All my computer operators will be in full field gear. That's how serious I am about this. If you're going to do something, do it right I always say!"

Sampson didn't respond. He knew for a fact that Wellens had ducked Desert Storm and hidden out in a speech writer's job in the Pentagon. And all the other times Wellens just seemed to be on some high ranking general's staff and not available to get shot at like the rest of his peers. He wore an Expert Infantryman's Badge, a peacetime award instead of a Combat Infantryman's Badge on his uniform, and had no combat patch on his right shoulder. As busy as the army had been over the last thirty years, Wellens had to work it hard not to have been shot at somewhere along the way.

The lack of a response from Sampson seemed to finally register with Wellens. He took a seat and waved to one across from him for Sampson. "Sam, I need your help and I know you'd never deny a fellow West Pointer and a company mate at that. I won't mince words, I want you to come back on active duty temporarily and be my chief of staff. Or I'll hire you as a civilian contractor to do the job. Either way I need you as my strong right hand man. If you want to do it as a contractor, name your price. So what do you say? It would be just like old times again."

This was so much bullshit! There never had been any 'old times' with Wellens. Sampson had known Wellens as an underclassman for two years at the Academy, and had always thought him to be too eager to please and too soft around the edges. They had never really served together because Sampson always chose duty with troops whenever the opportunity presented itself. Unlike Wellens, Sampson had fought to be with troops, and he had hated his tours of duty on the higher headquarters staff. Sampson stalled, "Where's your current chief of staff?"

Wellens grimaced. "Well, he had to go back to the States. Something about family problems. I told him his family was much more important than any stupid war game exercise, so he certainly had my blessings."

Sampson nodded, but not because he agreed with what Wellens had just said, but because Wellens hadn't changed a bit. The word on the street that Sampson had heard just minutes after leaving the CINC's office was that the chief of staff had quit after being verbally savaged by Wellens in front of the staff and commanders during the initial exercise briefing that very morning. Wellens, like a lot of incompetent men, was a bully and a tyrant with his subordinates, but always out of the sight and hearing of his superiors. In front of his superiors, Bobby Wellens always played the kind and forgiving affectionate father figure with his subordinates. He would do what the army expected of its senior leaders and underwrite their honest mistakes and help them grow professionally. But that charade was only performed in front of Bobby's superiors, and once they were out of sight, the forgiveness always turned into ugly and often personal retribution. Sampson had heard over the years that this was how Bobby Wellens really operated, so he was not surprised about what had happened that morning to the chief of staff. He wondered if it had gotten all the way up to the CINC's level yet.

Wellens mistook the nod. "So you'll do it! Capital! I knew you would! Good old Sam!" Wellens was going to gush on, but he stopped as Sampson raised his hand palm outward in the stop signal.

Sampson thought to himself, Christ! Who says 'capital' anyhow? Stupid bastard. He said, "Bobby, I can't be your chief. I'm already past mandatory retirement and it takes a national emergency and damn near an act of Congress to bring me back on active duty. And I can't do it as a contractor because it's against the law. But more to the point, as your company mate, I'll tell you to your face when you're screwed up and I know you can't take that. I can't possibly imagine why you're asking me this, other than you are looking for someone to stick it on if this exercise gets hosed up."

Wellens smiled. "Sam, you are still such a babe in the woods. It doesn't matter how it turns out, I'll still get promoted. I know I'm not the best there is at being a tactical wizard like you, but that's not what being a general is all about." The words 'tactical wizard' were just slightly tinged with sarcasm. "Here's the bottom line. Everybody knows we're dangling out here without enough combat power to be anything more than a presence. That was not my doing and how it turns out in the game won't be my fault either. But we need to plan for success and not failure I always say. That means I need to know what's going to happen with the OPFOR and as my chief of staff, you'd be able to tell me since you put all this together. But let's do this instead, and it's a better idea now that I think about it. It's less obvious. You stay as the OPFOR commander for the exercise but you keep me in the loop on what's going on, you know, before it happens. I know you can do that for me."

Sampson was at a loss for words. This division commander without mincing words had just asked him to cheat! "Well, Bobby, just why the hell would I do that?"

Smoothly, glibly, and without a beat Wellens answered, "So the Americans don't look bad in front of the ROK's. That's why. This is bigger than you or me, Sam. The secdef and I discussed this very issue an hour ago. He told me it was imperative not to scare the ROK's. He also gave me full authority to resolve any problems as I saw fit. So I guess you could say I'm actually ordering you to keep me informed, and it's by order of the secretary of defense since he's delegated that authority to me. See? So no problemo, senor! No problemo!" The attempt at humor fell flat.

"Okay, Bobby. Here's what you need to do then. I work for the CINC in this exercise, so I have to go with his guidance. You need to get *him* to tell me to keep you informed. Oh, and it'll need to be in writing since it's a violation of my contract. Or is that a problemo as you put it?"

Wellens' face went red. "Goddamn it, Sampson! Why can't you just go along for once? Why do you always have to rock the boat? If you don't do this as I have ordered you to, your contractor days are over! I'll make sure you never work again! God help me I will!"

Sampson smiled. "Willy, you haven't changed a bit and you never will. You were a fricking weasel as a cadet and you're still a fricking weasel." Wellens reddened even further at the name Willy, a sobriquet he had earned as a cadet for being caught by the upper classmen masturbating in the showers after Taps.

"Do what you're told, Colonel Sampson. That's an order from a superior officer."

"Well, for the record Willy, that's Colonel Sampson, US Army, *Retired*, and fuck you, Willy. See ya." Sampson got up and walked out of the office. He noticed that Glen, the smarmy aide, had listened to every word. Sampson wondered if he'd ask Wellens about the nickname Willy. Sam Sampson laughed softly to himself as he walked back to the simulation center. What bullshit. Sometimes it was good to be retired after all!

**0900 hours
28 October
Seoul, South Korea**

"Mother, I don't want to bring a lunch today! Why do you still make it for me?" Private Choe So Park just shook his head. His mother did not understand at all. He was too fed up to eat when he was with the army! It was all so stupid. He wondered for the thousandth time why his father would not buy him a position in the KATUSA's so he could be with the Americans and get good food and be able to practice his English.

Choe's mother looked at her son and smiled. She had heard all this before. She said patiently, "I make it for you because I know the army will not feed you and you don't want it now, you bad boy, but you will want it later today. You wait and see if Mother is not right!"

"Mother," Choe started with a whine in his voice, "can't you talk to papa about making me a KATUSA? Why would that be so bad?" Choe decided to add some tears to his eyes to further play on the sympathies of his already too sympathetic mother. Like all Korean mothers, she had shamelessly spoiled her only son. Choe, like all Korean boys, knew that the son was everything and played his role well. Mothers, and any daughters unfortunate enough to be born into a family with sons, were there only to serve the demands of the father and the sons. A son could tell even an older sister to do something for him, and she must obey. Choe actually shed a tear for his mother to see.

Yes, the son was everything and Choe's mother had argued bitterly with her husband over the boy having to serve in the ROK Army instead of with the Americans. The compromise had been that her son was assigned to a ROK reserve division that was actually a commuter division. The soldiers got on buses from home five days a week and went to their units. They would train for the day, eating the lunches they had brought, and then go home each night. The army didn't feed them. In the summer they would go to the field for a week and then, and only then, the army would begrudgingly feed them, but only for the days they were in the field.

Choe had constantly complained about the training to his mother but never in front of his father. He told her that the stupid sergeants would call off a stupid task and the soldiers must respond in unison over and over again the stupid steps of the stupid task. They would not *do* the task, but only call off its steps! The whole thing was a joke as far as Choe was concerned. Choe knew from some of his American friends that they also thought the ROK reserve divisions were a joke.

His mother answered him finally with a sigh, "Your father wants you to follow in his footsteps and be a great politician. You cannot do that these days if you are not in our army. Your father is wise and he knows what is best for you." She said the words but was not so sure of them. She saw how much her son suffered each day in the army that wasn't a real army. He felt demeaned and foolish as he called off the steps each day, and every day was the same. He had joked once about buying a parrot to send in his place one day to call out the steps. He swore the sergeants wouldn't notice. She had smiled and said nothing. It was probably true.

She continued, "Besides, you have already done one year and only have one more to go before you can go back to the university and your studies. How terrible could that be?" She handed him his lunch sack and walked him to the door. "Do not stop off at the university to see your friends tonight when you get back from the army, my son. Tonight is your father's birthday and we must honor him."

Choe nodded. He had forgotten. He left the penthouse and took the elevator down to the street and the waiting bus. He sighed. Boring, boring, boring as his American friends would say. And shit! They would say that, too. Shit!

**0940 hours
28 October
MP Checkpoint, North of Seoul**

The bus pulled up to the MP checkpoint and eased off the road. The driver swore. He was already late waiting for these spoiled brats to get their asses down to his bus on time and now this. Fucking MP's! He hated the MP's. They were the last vestige of the bad old days when discipline in the ROK Army had been both iron hard and physical. Sometimes the fucking MP's forgot that the Republic of Korea was a true democracy now with real elected officials instead of generals in charge. The driver swore again before he opened the door for the MP major standing outside, and then quickly put a smile on his face. If he played it right, they would still get to the barracks on time, and he wouldn't have to explain to the stupid sergeant major why it wasn't his fault yet again that he was late and the stupid sergeant major ought to ask the damned brats about it and not him! He smiled hard.

Captain Sung in his ROK MP uniform stepped on board the bus and shot the driver in his smiling face. Just like that, no words, just a shot to the head. Everybody on the bus jerked with the shot, and one soldier in the front started to get up from his seat. Sung shot him in the head too. The soldier flopped back dead onto the seat, his brains spattering the soldiers behind him. One other soldier started to get up in a reflex action, then caught himself and threw himself back into his seat. Sung only smiled and nodded. They understood now. Sung leaned back against the front dash of the bus and one of his MP's jumped on the bus and threw the driver's body into the aisle. He sat down at the steering wheel and smoothly started the bus back onto the road. Two of the MP jeeps fell in behind the bus, but the third one continued to keep traffic stopped well back from the check point, and out of hearing range of the shots.

Choe sat frozen in shock in the very last seat of the bus. His mind whirled. This must be a joke or some type of drill! He couldn't believe the bullets were real and kept looking around to see who would start laughing to acknowledge the joke, elaborate as it was. Nobody laughed. Several of the soldiers were crying. That was no joke. The realization came to Choe slowly that what he had just seen was very much real. He felt his stomach turn over as he looked at the dead driver and saw several of the soldiers at the front of the bus trying to wipe the spattered brains off their faces and clothes. The MP major seemed not to notice their efforts, or at least not to care.

Choe remembered his cell phone in his pocket. They were not supposed to have them, but the sergeants never really checked too carefully after the first couple of months of training. Choe pretended to be looking down in terror while actually entering a text message to his girl friend. He hoped she would take it seriously. He keyed in over and over again, *this is no joke*, but he was always joking with her. He prayed she would take it seriously and get word to his father that the MP's were killing soldiers! It could only mean that the generals had finally gotten tired of democracy and were staging a coup like they had done so many times in the past. His father had told him about those days and the years he had spent in prison because he had opposed the generals. His father would certainly be arrested or even killed by the generals if this really was a coup. He was second only to the president in political power in South Korea. But it had to be a coup! What else could it be?

Sung seemed not to notice the highly agitated young soldier starring intently down into his lap in the back of the bus, but he did smile again. That was something.

0442 hours
29 October
Simulation Center, Yongsan, Republic of Korea

"Colonel! Wake up, Colonel! Colonel Sampson!"

"Jesus, Gunny! What the hell do you want now? I just got in bed." Sampson groaned.

Marine Gunnery Sergeant Gaddis flipped on the lights in the small sleeping quarters. Sampson winced and pulled the covers over his head. The sergeant noticed the empty liquor bottle and cigar butts littering the one small table in the room. He shook his head and said, "Sir, I came to tell you that the North Koreans have crossed the DMZ!"

Sampson mumbled, "Yeah, I know. I ordered that move to begin when I left the simulation center last night. I can't believe you woke me up to tell me this shit instead of just letting me get it at the morning update."

The gunny sighed. Officers could be so dumb sometimes, particularly if they had been drinking. "Sir, I mean the no shit *real* North Koreans have no shit crossed the no shit *real* DMZ. I'm not talking about your simulation OPFOR guys. As they say in the movies, this is not a drill."

Sampson sat up with a jerk. "Are you shitting me, Gunny? You gotta be shitting me! How the hell did you hear this?"

"Sir, my wife's people live up in the Chorwon Valley. They called her and told her the NKPA was all over the damn place and forcing people onto the roads, but without their cars. They called her again on their cell phone to tell her they are headed here walking along with every other South Korean civilian north of the Han River. I went over to the ops center to check it out, and it's going fucking nuts over there so I knew it was the real deal. So there you have it."

"Holy shit, Gunny! Holy shit!"

"Yes, sir, Colonel. Holy shit."

1100 hours
29 October
The Chorwon Valley, Republic of Korea

Sung looked up the road and saw the civilians filling the road as they fled on foot southward to Seoul and hopefully safety. They completely filled the road in a slow moving noisy mass made up of the old, the young and everybody and everything in between. There were chickens in crates balanced on heads, and dogs on leashes, and cows being herded along and children clutched to mother's breasts, and old men and young men pushing farm carts piled high with the few prized possessions they could grab before being hustled down the road by the NKPA soldiers in the darkest hours of the night. Further forward progress by the bus would be clearly impossible. Sung nodded to his driver and the driver eased the bus off the road and stopped.

The bus had only been moving about thirty minutes. The ROK soldiers on the bus had spent the remainder of the previous day and last night shivering in the cold after the bus had pulled off the road and parked by a fire gutted car which smelled strangely of burnt pork. They had been allowed to eat their food and use empty soda cans to urinate in and pour out the window, but they had not been allowed off the bus, or to talk. Throughout that time Sung had stayed at the front of the bus and didn't seem to notice the cold or need to eat or urinate himself. He never spoke. Sung spoke to the ROK soldiers on the bus for the first time now. He said simply, "Get off the bus."

The soldiers got up and silently filed off the bus, stepping gingerly over the dead driver still laying in the aisle with his eyes wide open and a neat hole in the center of his forehead. His coagulated blood had spread unevenly into the grooves of the rubber matting covering the aisle of the bus, and had dried to a shiny black.

Sung did not even look at the soldiers as they passed closely by him. As they exited the bus, his team put them into two ranks and told them to stand at attention with their eyes to the front. All of them did as they were told.

The civilians, upon seeing the soldiers, stopped in the road. They were unsure of what to do, and they were instinctively afraid of the soldiers and their jeeps with machine guns mounted on them. They couldn't help but notice that those machine guns were pointed at them.

At Sung's signal, the ROK soldiers were marched as a group towards the civilians. They were halted about twenty feet away and ordered to spread out facing the civilians who were clearly starting to become agitated. Several of the civilians in the very front of the crowd nearest the soldiers tried to turn back into the crowd to get away, but nobody further back was willing to be pushed to the front. A shoving impasse ensued and the screaming and yelling echoed from the hills hemming the road in.

One of Sung's soldiers gave rifles to several of the ROK soldiers who seemed not to know how to even hold them they were so frightened. After a punch or two and some swearing, the few ROK soldiers with rifles were pointing them at the civilians. This caused a frantic increase in the efforts of the civilians in the front to press back into the crowd. Children were being knocked from their mother's arms and were being trampled on the hard road. Frantic mothers dropping to the ground to protect their children added to the crush as people tripped over them and also fell to the roadway.

The machine guns opened fire and the bullets ripped through the civilians, men, women and children alike. One of the ROK soldiers with a rifle turned to the machine gunners and aimed his rifle at them. He pulled the trigger but the rifle was unloaded. The closest machine gunner laughed at the look on the soldier's face, and then swung his gun and cut him and all of the other ROK soldiers down in a long burst. All but one of the ROK soldiers were cut down in the space of only a few seconds.

Choe stood as if in a trance as he watched the bullets slam into his fellow soldiers and tumble them to the ground. Some fell soundlessly and some fell screaming, but they were all knocked down by the stream of bullets. Choe waited for the bullets to hit him but they didn't come. He remained untouched, and stood frozen in place.

Choe turned his head and stared at the bodies of the dead and wounded civilians littering the road. He turned his head again and watched dumbly as the ROK MP major fired his pistol calmly into the head of each ROK soldier, fifteen in all. Sung had to insert a fresh ammunition clip into his pistol twice which he did calmly and efficiently with no wasted motion. Choe jumped at the sound of each shot.

Sung finally came and stood in front of Choe. He smiled. "Do you see Private Choe So Park?" He nodded towards the civilians and dead soldiers. "The civilians die because they are not doing what the law requires. In times of emergency, they are required to stay in their homes. The soldiers die because they cannot be trusted by the real army, the Hanna Army. Go home and tell your father that Hanna will save our nation, but we will also rule our nation as we did before. We have been attacked because he and the other politicians have made us weak."

Sung turned on his heel and walked to his jeep. He got into the passenger seat and the three vehicles drove off towards the south.

Choe had not moved an inch after being placed by an MP sergeant right behind the line of ROK soldiers facing the refugees. He still did not move and could only stare as the MP major and his detachment drove away.

Hanna! Choe had not heard that name for years! In Hangul it meant *one* or *first*; in the history of South Korea it meant the secret society of officers who had all graduated from the Korean Military Academy. Hanna had held all power in South Korea after President Syngman Rhee had been overthrown by the military in 1960. The president was always the most powerful general, and changes in presidents were effected by military coup d'état and not elections. It had remained that way until the first real elections were held in 1992.

Choe suddenly realized that he still had his cell phone in his pocket. He finally moved. Several of the wounded civilians were moaning and calling out to him for help, but he did not hear them. He could only think to call his father. If the generals really had decided to take charge of the government again, his father was in extreme danger! But why were the civilians on the road? And what did the MP major mean 'we have been attacked'?

Choe fumbled and dropped the phone twice in his fear and his haste to call his father as he turned his back on the moaning civilians and started walking south. His pace picked up once he reached his father and described what he had seen and heard. The tears streamed down Choe's face as he started to run, and he ran away from the horror of the dead and wounded civilians in the road, and from the war his father had just told him was starting right behind him!

2200 hours
29 October
USFK/Combined Forces Command Field CP, Republic of Korea

Sam Sampson eased his way into the back of the briefing room and found an empty chair. He sank into it gratefully. He was bone tired and felt like he hadn't been to bed in days, although he had only been without sleep for a little over a day. He and his son had stayed up almost all night sharing cigars and a good bottle of port. He had just fallen asleep when the gunny woke him up to tell him the North Koreans had attacked. When he was in his prime, he had gone without sleep for up to seventy-two hours without missing a beat. He sighed. Yeah, that was then and this is now and he was tired. He was also worried about his son who was an infantry officer in the 2nd Infantry Division. The officers in the room stirred and some started to rise. The CINC, General Robertson Smith, waved them back down.

Smith said, "Keep your seats gentlemen. Now, Johnny, give me the real story on what's going on up north. I just got the ROK version and we're doing swimmingly it seems." Only US officers attended this meeting and some of the officers smiled. It was legendary how the ROK's would never give bad news to their superiors and would instead fabricate whatever their bosses wanted to hear. If you asked them why and they were honest with you, they would say it was because their bosses would lose face if things they were responsible for did not go well. Not losing face in Korea was much more important than the truth.

Johnny Raymer started in a brisk and confident voice, "Okay, sir. Our liaison teams out with the ROK's have all called in except the team attached to the ROK 1st Division. We haven't heard from them, but the team with the 3d ROK Division on their right flank reported that the 1st Division is holding its ground."

"What about the others? According to the ROK brief I just got all the divisions on the DMZ are holding their ground."

Johnny Raymer shook his head. "None of them are in the western corridor, sir. They have all been pushed back. Some of them all the way to the outskirts of Seoul, already. We can't tell just how bad it is yet because the liaison teams are up to their asses in keeping up with the ROK's as they fall back. They report that the roads are packed with civilian refugees and the military can't control them."

"So much for the stay at home policy the ROK's have assured us the people would obey in time of war," Smith said sarcastically. "Christ, what a mess! How are the ROK's doing on mobilizing their reserve forces and securing the LOC's to Pusan?"

"Again, sir, not good news. We just don't know the status of mobilization because those liaison teams are reservists who come in from the States when we go to Defcon 2. We never got a chance to execute the Defcon sequence so we're uncovered there right now. As to the LOC's, the NKPA SPF have apparently taken control of all the bridges on the major highways and have cut the railroad line in multiple places. We're also getting reports from 9th Air Force that their security forces are fighting their asses off around the air bases. Not that anybody can fly."

Smith nodded. The weather sucked. A cold front had come in from Manchuria and mixed with the warmer ocean water, so the entire Korean peninsula was wrapped in a cloak of fog. The air force wasn't going to be a factor anytime soon based on the most current meteorological reports.

"Sir, one other thing the liaison teams reported I think you need to know about. They say the North Koreans are forcing the civilian population out of their homes and putting them on the roads, but they are doing it gently, if such a thing is possible. It's out of character for the NKPA and doesn't make any sense to us."

Smith took this in with a frown. It didn't make sense to him either. The civilians on the road impeding military operations made sense, but being nice about it did not. He turned in his chair. "Sam, you're the OPFOR expert. What's going on?"

Sampson felt every set of eyes in the room turn to him. Now he knew why Smith had sent a runner to tell him to get on a helicopter heading to the jump CP earlier in the day. He looked back at Smith. "Sir, they are doing it for two reasons. The first one is obvious. It's to screw up the ROK forces trying to use the roads. You know the terrain up there, you either go by road or you're humping over the mountains. As to why they're being gentle about it as Johnny says, my guess is they are looking ahead to their war termination criteria."

"Meaning?"

Sampson answered evenly, "Sir, this war like the last one in 1950 is to unify the Korean people into one nation. Kim Il Sung tried to do it by killing all those who were opposed to him, which was pretty much everybody in South Korea. Kim Jong Il is smarter than his father. Once he wins in the field, and the people were treated well in the process, he knows they'll sign up for the new deal. Johnny, you said they held the bridges down south. Have they blown any of them up?"

"No, Sam. We haven't gotten any reports of bridges being blown."

Sampson nodded. "That's what I thought. What they're doing, sir, is kicking the shit out of the ROK Army without breaking anything they don't have to. Kim is looking ahead and would rather unify a viable, fully functioning country than one that has been devastated. He won't touch the factories and he won't break the infrastructure any more than he has to. His goal right now is to defeat the South Korean Army, and to kick the gringos off the peninsula."

"Meaning us?"

"Yes, sir, meaning us."

Smith turned around in his seat back towards the front and said, "Well, shit. Okay Johnny, speaking of the gringos, what's going on with the 2nd ID? How are they doing?"

"Sir, they haven't been in contact with the NKPA yet, and General Wellens has asked repeatedly when the units will arrive to fall in on the pre-positioned stocks. He somehow thinks that is going to happen in computer war game time rather than real time. When I asked him if the division was at its assembly area yet, he never really answered me. So, sir, I can't give you an accurate picture on the division. We just don't know."

Smith audibly sighed. "Okay, I'll call Bobby when we're done here. George?" Smith turned in his chair again looking for George Bates in the crowd. Bates raised his hand from the back of the room.

"I'm here, sir."

"Good. How's the NEO going? Are the families getting out of Kimpo yet?"

George Bates shifted uneasily in his chair. "No, sir, they're not. We got some of them out with the aircraft that were at the airport when the balloon went up, but the ROK's have refused to allow any other aircraft in. They say they're afraid that will open the door to more SPF coming in. Right now they don't trust anybody, anywhere about anything. All the families are at the departure gates at Kimpo and the ROK security forces seem to be holding their own against the SPF that were inserted. My ROK counterpart assures me the suspension of flights is only temporary, but I just don't know, sir. This isn't at all what we had agreed upon in all our exercises. If I didn't know better, I'd think we were being slow rolled by the ROK's."

Smith leaned back in his chair and hunched his shoulders at the news of this very unwelcome turn of events. He needed the families off the Peninsula and out of harm's way. He asked gravely, "Any idea why they would do that, George?"

"The only thing I can think of, sir, is that they may want our families to stay so we won't run out on them. I know it's far fetched but I'll be damned if I can think of another reason. If our families are here, it gives us the incentive to stay the course is what I'm saying I guess."

Smith took that in. He hoped it wasn't true, but he also knew the South Koreans remembered the final days of South Vietnam like it was just yesterday. The US had pulled out of there, and the South Koreans didn't want a dose of the same. "Okay, I'll talk to their chairman and even their president if I have to. We've got to get the families out. If we do nothing else right over here, we have to get that right. George, keep Johnny posted on the situation at Kimpo."

"Yes, sir."

"Okay, that's about all the good news I can take at one sitting. I know you're all tired, but I want you to know that you're doing a great job. Make sure you get some sleep when you can and keep me informed." General Smith again waved everybody back into their seats and left the room.

0900 hours EST
29 October
The White House Situation Room

The secretary of defense looked calm. He always did. It was part of his persona. The chairman of the Joint Chiefs didn't appear nearly as calm, but wasn't openly agitated either. All the men in the room and the one woman present stared fixedly at the door waiting for the president. Any conversation they engaged in was without substance. They couldn't talk substance and stay focused on the door at the same time. Most fidgeted nervously. The president was famous for his temper out of the public view, and all of them except the secretary and the chairman had felt his white hot wrath on more than one occasion. And that was before this new war in Korea. That was when the US had been pretty much calling the shots and having it their own way. None of them could even guess how the president was going to react to the situation in Korea. The nervous tension in the room was palpable.

"Gentlemen, the President of the United States." The aide made the announcement and quickly stepped aside. The few people who had been seated quickly stood up. The president swept into the room and flopped into his chair. He seemed tired. He waved his hand and the group sat down. Without preamble he turned to the secretary of defense, "So Ralph, what do we have?"

Ralph Brooks pulled at his bow tie once, his only show of nervousness, and then launched into his reply. "Mister President, it is clear to us now that the North Koreans have attacked in force across the DMZ. At first we thought this might be a demonstration of force to gain more leverage at the talks in China next week, but we now know it's for real. This is not a raid."

The president nodded but said nothing.

Brooks continued, "The reports are the ROK's are holding their own, but the South Korean government has already formally requested immediate reinforcements from us, particularly for ground troops, air power and ammunition. We're reviewing our options to honor those requests, but we think they might be premature."

"Why?"

"Sir, because we believe the North Korean attack will collapse upon itself once the North Korean soldiers push beyond the DMZ. We believe this because those soldiers will see the wealth and prosperity of the South Koreans below the DMZ, and then turn on their leaders for lying to them and keeping them near starvation while the south is living in comparative luxury. My staff tells me it's all about loss of face in the Asian culture." The secretary chuckled, "I guess I'd be pretty pissed off too in their shoes."

The president didn't smile. "What if that doesn't happen? I mean it sounds reasonable and I'm sure the *experts* came up with it, but what's our fall back position? How many troops can we get in there and how long will it take? That's what I want to know, and I'm already tired of the bastards over in Congress calling me this morning asking that very question. So what's the answer?" The president's voice hardened and went up several notches in intensity at the end as he asked the question.

"Sir, I'll let the chairman answer that question, if I may?" The president nodded and turned his eyes to the Chairman of the Joint Chiefs of Staff, General Pat Goodman, US Air Force.

The chairman cleared his throat. "Pardon me, sir. Sir, we are reviewing our options right now and earmarking forces to deploy to Korea, if needed. We've put the brigade of the 82nd Airborne Division that's still at Fort Bragg on alert, and we've given warning orders to several other brigades to be prepared to move. We have also issued warning orders to several air force fighter wings to prepare to self-deploy to Korea. We've placed the marine forces in Okinawa on alert and have ordered CINCPAC to divert a carrier battle group from the Indian Ocean to Korean waters. That carrier battle group will be off shore in six days."

The president visibly relaxed. "Okay, that sounds like we're doing something. Jerry, did you get all that?"

Jerry, the president's head speech writer nodded while scribbling furiously on his pad and murmuring into his voice piece to the speech writers several floors above. The president was going to speak to the country immediately after this meeting in a televised address, and Jerry had to have the words ready. They had all learned that if the president didn't have the exact right words in front of him, he was prone to say stupid and even unintelligible things. Jerry continued to write and murmur.

The president turned back to the chairman. "Pat, what if we can't get these forces in place in time. What then?"

The question surprised both Brooks and Goodman, and caught them off balance. President Preston had never asked them a question about second and third order effects before, and they weren't mentally prepared to take the leap. Preston looked at them both, clearly impatient for an answer. He started to drum his fingers on the table top.

Brooks spoke first, which was just as well because the chairman wasn't empowered to give the only logical response. "Sir, we may have to go nuclear." He hastened on, "We would restrict ourselves to only tactical nukes, and we would not use any of them in populated areas or inside North Korea itself. We will only target North Korean forces that are in South Korea. It will be seen as a reasonable self-defense measure considering the fact that the North Koreans attacked South Korea without provocation." Brooks spoke with quiet assurance and he could see that the president agreed with his logic.

Preston said with a smirk, "Well, I wouldn't mind nuking some of those little fuckers if it comes to that, Ralph!" Everybody, to include the one woman in the room, laughed. "Okay, we've got this sucker nailed! Ralph, I'll want you and Pat to stand behind me when I talk to the country in a few minutes. Jerry, you got my shit ready to go? I don't want you guys screwing me up again with poorly written crap that you expect me to make sense out of for the Great American Public."

"Yes, Mister President, we're ready."

"Good! Let's do it!" Preston rose as did the others. Time to talk to the people and give them assurances that just like fighting the War on Terrorism, this president and his team had their stuff together. Kim Jong Il was going to be a sorry little bastard for messing with this president. Yes, indeed, he was!

Nobody seemed to notice that the president hadn't asked how the war was going, or if the American civilians, which there were plenty of in South Korea, were safe. And nobody dared to bring it up if the president didn't. He had told them before, there was one agenda and one agenda only; his. If he wanted unsolicited advice, he'd ask for it. Nobody seemed to really get the joke, but they all dutifully laughed when he said it. Yes, indeed, they did.

**0630 hour
30 October
US/ROK Army Airfield, Yongsan, Republic of Korea**

The two CH-47 Chinook helicopters sat like huge dragon flies with their rotors slowly turning. Even before they had revved up to flying speed, the choppers' huge rotors were blowing dirt up and were noisy as hell. The back cargo ramps were down for loading. Major Steve Young struggled to hold the large map board he was lugging against the rotor wash as he headed towards his assigned chopper. Steve was one of the planners for the US Eighth Army staff in Yongsan, and he was headed south along with the rest of that staff to set up their headquarters near Pusan. Their job was to coordinate and control the flow of reinforcements into the peninsula. They had rehearsed this move and their subsequent staff actions at least twice a year for the two years Steve had already been in Korea. Steve was only supposed to be in Korea for one year but he had extended for a second year.

Steve Young had talked it over with his wife, and both agreed that he was better off in Korea for a second year instead of going back to Iraq for his third combat tour in the space of five years. Steve was thankful he had not brought his family to Korea for that second year which his tour extension had entitled him to do. They would be sitting at Kimpo Airport just south of Seoul with the rest of the families right now. The staff had all just been told the families were still not getting out yet. The guilt they all felt as they were leaving to head south and away from their stranded families was clearly evident in their faces.

Steve felt a hand on his back and turned around to see who it was. Major Rebecca Scholes waved Steve back from the ramp and away from the chopper. He followed her far enough away so she could yell in his ear.

"Colonel Mangel wants you to switch to his bird and give me the map board. I'm going on your bird."

Steve could barely hear her as she yelled from only inches away. The Chinooks were winding up for lift off. "Why does he want me on his bird?"

"He said he has new information and will need you to do some work on the way down to Pusan."

Steve heard her and gave her the map board. She grabbed it and ran to the waiting chopper. The crew chief was signaling her to hurry up, and he was already raising the ramp. Steve raced for his own chopper and scrambled in just as the bird was lifting. The crew chief gave him a hand to steady him before he could negotiate the crowded aisle to where Colonel Mangel, the G3, was waiting for him.

Colonel Mangel handed Steve a headset and started talking even before Steve could get the set fully on his head. "... so it doesn't look like the TPFDD we worked on for the last fifty goddamn years is going to work worth a shit, Steve. The lead units on the list are all in Iraq, or just back from Iraq or headed to Iraq, so we get two Boy Scout troops from the air force and a carrier battle group due in six more days. The only available unit to be flown-in for the next seventy-two hours is a brigade from the 82nd, and it's short one battalion which is in Afghanistan. You're a mechanized infantry guy, Steve, how long would it take to train a bunch of paratroopers to use Bradley's and M1 tanks?"

Steve Young just shook his head. He keyed his microphone, "Sir, we could teach them how to drive them and maybe even shoot them some, but the NKPA would eat their lunch in an armored brawl. They know how to maneuver and shoot their tanks damn well. The 82nd guys would be outclassed pretty quick. It would end up being a waste of good men and probably, just as important right now, irreplaceable equipment. We couldn't hope to get another set of tanks and Brads in anything less than four to six months about now."

Mangel nodded but didn't answer at first. It was all too true. The war in Iraq had left the Army with no reserves of equipment to draw from. "Okay, Steve, you're right. I was going to have you draw up a training plan for the 82d guys on our way down there, but I guess it would just be a waste of time. Sorry for jerking you around at the last minute."

"No sweat, sir. One bird's as good as another." Mangel nodded in response.

The trip to Pusan was a two hour flight so most of the staff had settled themselves as best they could on the web seats and tried to doze off. The choppers were flying low just below the cloud cover that had socked the peninsula in. At times the two choppers had to dip as low as one hundred feet above the ground to stay out of the clouds.

As Steve was just dozing off he felt the chopper swing wildly to the left and then jerk rapidly upward as the pilot put on full pitch and full power. Everybody in the chopper jerked awake with the sudden maneuver. Steve looked out the window and saw a fireball with two wildly spinning rotor blades falling onto the side of a hill where it exploded into an even bigger fireball. He caught just a glimpse before they were into the clouds, but he knew from his combat experiences in Iraq what he had just seen. It was the second time Steve Young had been pulled from a doomed chopper at the last minute. Once in Iraq, and once now. He shuddered and his thoughts briefly flashed to his family, and then his mind raced to guilt as he thought about Rebecca Scholes on the other bird in his place. He turned and looked at Colonel Mangel whose face had turned ashen.

Mangel slowly said to the pilot over his intercom headset, "Please tell me that wasn't our other bird!"

There was no response from the flight deck as the chopper flew a gyrating evasive course through the impenetrable layer of clouds. The chopper rose, fell, turned and twisted with a corkscrewing motion that caused several people in the back to start heaving their guts up. After about three minutes, the chopper settled onto a straight course and Mangel got his answer.

"Yeah, Colonel. That was our other bird. He was in front of us and then we saw a butt load of SAM's come from the ground and go into both his rotors. He never had a chance. I'm just glad somebody screwed the pooch and they didn't take us out too. Looks like the report about SPF being on the ground but not having SAM's is pure bullshit. I'm staying in the clouds until we get to Pusan and then I'll try to find a hole to climb down through. I'm just hoping the SAM's they do have require a visual to lock on. And, sir?"

"Yes."

"There was no way in hell anybody got out of that other chopper. I've already told the SAR's guys not to chance it. They were going to scramble out of Osan, but I put them on hold until I could talk to you first."

"But what if there are survivors?"

"Sir, we don't need to lose more guys and another bird looking for bodies. The way this shit is going, I think we're all going to get lots of chances to die, so it might as well be for a good reason."

Steve Young who was monitoring all this cut in, "Sir, I saw the other bird go in. There are no survivors. It blew up on impact."

Mangel sighed. "Okay, you guys are right. Tell the SAR's guys to stand down and pass to Osan tower the grid where the chopper went down for graves registration when we get a chance to go back in there. I'll need all the names for the battle loss report once we get to Pusan. Shit, I hate this!"

The pilot responded, "Roger, sir. Me too."

The chopper thundered south as blind as a bat in the clouds, but hopefully also protected by the clouds. They wouldn't know if they actually were safe in the clouds until they either landed or a SAM slammed into a rotor.

2100 hours
30 October
East of Uijombu, Republic of Korea

Captain Sung watched the trucks coming down the highway with their lights on. He instantly noted that none of the guns mounted on the rings over the passenger side of the cabs were manned. It would have been very cold standing up at the machine gun and the cab of the truck was so much warmer. He shrugged. The Americans were proving to be too easy. He was professionally disappointed in their lack of security as a soldier, but he was infinitely pleased as an enemy. He spoke briefly into his radio and two MP jeeps pulled out onto the highway in front of the lead American vehicle which was a hummer. The MP jeeps turned on their rotating blue beacons. The hummer slowed and then stopped.

The passenger in the hummer got out and walked purposefully towards the MP road block. He was a big black man and was clearly angry at this interruption of his logistics convoy. As he neared the jeeps and was just getting ready to speak, one of the soldiers shot him twice in the chest. He crumpled to the ground instantly dead; the second bullet having pierced his heart.

Before any of the rest of the drivers in the front of the convoy could react to the sounds of gunfire, they were shot in their cabs by Sung's team. Not a single shot was fired back at Sung's men. The driver and passenger in each of the first eight vehicles were executed before the first American vehicle tried to turn around on the narrow road to escape.

Sung walked slowly up to the ninth vehicle which had sunk its rear tires in the roadside ditch and was spinning them furiously and fruitlessly in an attempt to come unstuck. Sung walked up to the driver's door and pulled it open. The young American soldier driving the truck was alone, and was a very pretty female with blonde hair. Her blue eyes were wide as she stared in shock at the pistol in Sung's hand while still mashing the accelerator to the floor. Sung reflected briefly that had he more time, he would enjoy taking her to quench his primal urges which always soared when he was in combat. Sadly, he had no time so he shot her twice in the head. Only after she slumped over the steering wheel did he realize that the loud keening noise he was hearing as he approached the truck were her screams. They had abruptly stopped and he was glad. He watched dispassionately as the other trucks in the convoy finished executing their turns and sped away into the night. It was always good to leave some alive to tell the story and spread fear amongst the others. Sung spoke briefly into his radio and the three jeeps formed up and sped away into the night, this time headed north towards the DMZ.

**0200 hours
31 October
USFK/Combined Forces Command CP**

"General Smith, sir, I need you to wake up. I've finally gotten General Wellens on the phone."

Smith's eyes opened and he was instantly alert. "Okay, Johnny. I'll be right there." Smith rolled over on his cot and put his feet on the floor. It was times like this when he was getting little if any real sleep that he wished he was still a smoker. That jolt of nicotine would clear his brain faster than just pure air, not that the re-circulated air in the bunker was very pure or smelled all that good. It always had the pungent tang of garlic breath from the kimchee the ROK's ate which took some getting used to for a Westerner.

Smith went into his private office inside the operations room and signaled for Johnny to close the door. He didn't want the ROK's listening in on his conversation with Wellens. He instinctively knew that something was not right with the 2nd Infantry Division because it had taken Johnny over three hours to get in touch with them. Something was definitely not right.

"Bobby, General Smith here. I need to get a read out on how you guys are doing."

Wellens came back immediately and responded in a cheerful voice, "Sir, we're doing fine! We're hunkered down in our assembly area and I've got my entire force minus one log pack accounted for. I think we're in damned good shape at this point."

Smith felt the tension drain from his neck and shoulders. What Wellens was saying was the only good news he'd had since this war had started. "Bobby, that's good to hear! Are you guys in contact with the NKPA yet? I don't have a very clear picture right now on exactly how far down they have come from the DMZ. The ROK's are all reporting that they are holding on the DMZ, but our liaison teams paint a different picture."

"No, sir. We aren't in contact and we have patrols out for security. I did get one report of contact during our move of a brush with ROK MP's but it was a minor contact."

Smith instantly got a nagging feeling that something wasn't right after all. He asked slowly, "Did you say that your people had a problem with *ROK* MP's Bobby? That just doesn't sound right to me. Exactly what kind of problem was it?"

Wellens came back with total confidence in his voice, "Sir, I didn't credit the report, but I did put my acting chief of staff on it to run it to ground. We got a garbled radio transmission from some sergeant who said he was taking the survivors and their trucks south to Seoul because the road was blocked just east of Uijombu by ROK MP's who fired on them. Sir, I don't place much faith in the report, it coming from only a sergeant. Sir, not to change the subject, but how soon can I expect the reinforcing units to link up with me?" Wellens' voice went up slightly in intensity when he asked the question.

"Bobby, there's a brigade of the 82nd being flown in, but the troops for the pre-positioned equipment are not available for another thirty days. They're going to amalgamate units in the States that have just returned from Iraq to make up full units. The chairman said they might be able to shave a week off of that, but we won't see mechanized forces for at least twenty more days at the very earliest. We've got to hope the ROK's are doing better than I think they are. Right now it looks like the only ROK division still holding its ground is the 1st Division just north of your assembly area. I may send you up to reinforce them in the next twenty-four to forty-eight hours depending on the overall situation, so be prepared to execute that move when I call you."

"Yes, sir, I'll have my staff start working on that for possible execution. Sir, I don't know how to broach this next subject with you so I'll just put it out there." Wellens paused as if searching for the right words. He began slowly, "Sir, the last time I talked to Secretary Brooks he reminded me that my forces were not really in Korea for combat purposes but only to serve as a tripwire." Wellens hurried on, "He said we were to avoid direct contact with the North Koreans and preserve my force at all costs. I'm not sure I can comply with that directive from the secretary if you send me up to reinforce the ROK 1st Division, but of course, sir, I'll do whatever you direct."

Smith was absolutely taken aback by what Wellens had just told him. He asked in a harsh tone, "And just when did the secretary give you this *directive*, General Wellens?"

Wellens sounded almost apologetic in his tone as he responded, "Yesterday, sir."

Smith could feel the heat rising in his neck and face as the anger welled up inside him. He spoke slowly and deliberately. "Am I to understand, General Wellens that you were in contact with the secretary of defense yesterday, but at the same time could not get in contact with me to report your status? Please explain that to me, General. I would really like to understand just how this chain of command you're using works."

Wellens hastily responded, "Sir, the secretary called me!" Wellens paused. It was a lie, of course. "Sir, I told him that he really needed to call you to pass on his directive for no contact and force preservation. He said he would do that, but I guess with all his overwhelming responsibilities he hasn't been able to do that yet?" Another lie, but it was smoothly delivered. Wellens had in fact called the secretary and suggested that if the Americans were savaged by the North Koreans, they would lose face and never recover their position of authority and strength in that region of the world. Wellens had spent two years as the secretary's military assistant and knew exactly which buttons to push with Brooks to elicit the responses he wanted.

Smith was very much aware that Wellens and the secretary were tight, and responded coldly, "General, I insist that you stay inside your chain of command which means you talk only to me or to the ROK Corps commander your division is attached to. Is that clear?"

Wellens made his voice sound contrite, "Yes, sir! That's the way I want it too! I told the secretary that he should not call me directly just because I used to be his MA. I told him it made me feel like a spy or something. Sir, I just didn't know how to handle it, so I insisted that he call you. He did call you, didn't he, sir?"

Smith sighed. There wasn't much he could blame Wellens for if the secretary called him. "Okay, Bobby, if he calls you again I'm going to ask you not to pass anything on that you haven't cleared with me. This current war is about as screwed up as it can be without having unity of command problems and stray voltage coming out of Washington directly to combat units. I'll talk to the secretary on this and get back with you. How's the counterfire battle proceeding?"

"Sir, it's going great! We haven't taken any loses yet."

"Well, at least there is some good news. Keep me posted on your status and be prepared to move up to the DMZ on order."

"Roger, sir. Will do!"

Both generals hung up their phones and Smith told Johnny Raymer to get the secretary on the phone.

Wellens' aide asked if he had any instructions for the staff based on his talk with the CINC and Wellens said, "No, he said just to keep hunkering down here, Glen. The CINC's no dummy. He knows we can't afford to lose this division. Now go get me some coffee. I need to make a phone call." Glen Stover hustled off to do his master's bidding. Wellens hit the speed dial on his cell phone and was rewarded with an answer after only one ring. "Mister Secretary, this is Bobby and I need to warn you that you're going to get a call from General Smith ..."

**0600 hours
31 October
Firing Point Whiskey, Republic of Korea**

"Goddamnit, Radar! I know you've got targets, but we still don't have clearance to fire!" The young battery commander turned to his XO and gave him the thumbs up sign with a questioning look on his face. The XO spoke into his headset and looked back at the battery commander, then shook his head and gave the thumbs down sign. The battery commander swore, tore his headset off and threw it down disgustedly onto the field desk in front of him.

"What the shit are we doing out here if we're not going to fire! I can't believe this shit! XO, what the hell is battalion saying? Why can't we shoot? The damn radar guys say the North Koreans are not even masking their guns anymore, and are out in the open for Christ's sake!" In frustration the battery commander took the handset from his XO and spoke directly to his battalion S3. "White Fire 3, this is Aggressor 6, over."

"Aggressor 6, this is White Fire 3, send your traffic."

"Roger, I need clearance to shoot! I've got targets up the ass and they're not moving back inside their hide positions in the mountains anymore. I say again, targets are stationary and in the open!"

"Negative on clearance, Aggressor. I say again, negative on clearance. We have just received a march order. You are to move your battery to the following grid, are you prepared to copy?"

The battery commander said he was ready for the grid. The S3 sent the grid and the battery commander tried to find it on his map sheet. It wasn't on the map sheet that covered the one hundred square kilometer area they were operating in. He asked the S3 to confirm the grid and the S3 did so. The XO brought in another map sheet from the map roll and the battery commander finally found his new location. He was incredulous. He slowly keyed the radio, "Roger, White Fire 3. This is Aggressor Six, I need you to authenticate Uniform Delta."

Even though they were operating on a secure radio net, the battery commander wanted to make damn sure this order was legitimate before he pulled his battery so far away from the DMZ that they could not possibly execute the counterfire battle they had trained for every damned day of the long damned year each of them spent in Korea! He waited for a response.

"Aggressor 6, I authenticate Bravo. I say again, I authenticate Bravo." The battery commander looked at the authentication tables for the day and saw that

Bravo was the correct response. The order was legitimate. They weren't being spoofed by the North Koreans.

"Roger, what time do I execute the move?"

"Time now. I say again, time now."

The battery commander let that sink in, and asked simply, "Why?"

"We don't know but it came from Warrior 6 directly to us ten minutes ago. Notify us when you start moving, and we'll send checkpoints digitally to your CP for reporting purposes. How copy?" The order had come directly from General Wellens to the battalion skipping the artillery chain of command!

"Good copy. We'll be moving in fifteen mikes. Aggressor 6, out." Shit! They were running away from this fight! The battery commander turned to his XO who had heard the whole conversation on the speaker box of the radio. The battery commander looked thoughtful for a moment and then said, "Okay, XO. Get a hold of Top and let's move this circus. I want all the gun chiefs up here at the CP so I can give them the movement order. While I'm doing that, I want you to go to each vehicle and make sure the guys pulling security understand that they have got to be *no shit* up at the guns and ready for SPF along the way. We've got a good hundred kilometers to move and I'm not sure of anything beyond how far I can personally see about now. Any questions?"

"No, sir. I'll also make sure all the vehicles are topped off with fuel before we start. What time do you see me leaving with the quartering party?" Normally, the XO would lead a small group of specialists ahead of the battery to lay out the new gun positions and guide the battery in once it arrived in a new location.

The battery commander shook his head. "I don't see us needing gun positions that far to the south, XO. We'll be out of range of anything going on unless the North Koreans have done a damned beach assault on the east coast which ain't likely. Shit, I don't get this. It just doesn't make sense. It's like we're running away!"

The XO nodded. He felt the same way. The fighting was to the north and they were moving south.

"Get the gun chiefs up here and talk to the security troops and do the fuel. I'm going to have you lead the quartering party about a mile ahead of us so the battery doesn't get surprised along the way. Beef your party up with some of the ammo carriers so you'll have more firepower. You and I will do a map recon once you get back on likely ambush sites along the route. Any question, Andy"

"No, sir. Got it. I always wanted to be a scout platoon leader, so I guess this will be my chance!"

"Yeah, Andy. No shit. This will definitely be your chance."

**1200 hours
31 October
USFK/Combined Forces Command CP**

Sam Sampson had found a relatively quiet corner and had fallen asleep in a chair. It took him a while to realize that the insistent buzzing he was hearing was his cell phone. It had already rung almost the maximum times before the answering system kicked in so he jerked it open and barked, "Stand by!" until he could get his ear piece in. He jammed the ear piece in and said, "Sam Sampson here. Who's this?"

"Hey, Dad! It's Sean. I thought I'd give you a call to see if you got home alright and away from the bullshit going on over here. Are you home yet?"

Sampson felt an instant flood of relief to hear his son's voice. He had been worried about his son every minute since the gunny had told him the North Koreans had crossed the DMZ. His relief was evident in his voice as he responded, "Christ, Sean it's good to hear from you, son! Where the hell are you that you have time to make phone calls?"

1st Lieutenant Sean Sampson responded with a snort. "I can't tell you where we are Dad over this cell phone, but draw a line towards your last duty assignment to your house, where I hope like hell you're sitting right now, and go right 90 degrees. Then go about the distance it is from your house to Grandma's house. Now do the same thing for me from where I started and you'll have me and everybody else I'm with." Sean knew the North Koreans had the capability of monitoring cell phones so he was making sure that they would not be able to gather any worthwhile intelligence from his comments.

Sampson took all this in and said slowly, "Are you sure about your location, Sean?"

Sean laughed. "Dad, I'm the scout platoon leader now. I led the way to this place. I know *perzackely* where I am as you used to say." He turned serious. "Dad, you got out, right?"

Sampson sighed. "No, son, I didn't get out. It wasn't an option. It seems that my services were needed as an advisor of sorts."

"Aw shit, Dad! Mom will be having a cow about now with both of us over here. Have you called her?"

"Yeah, I called her and told her I was staying and she's not a happy camper. I told her I was under a bazillion tons of concrete and she still wasn't buying it. I'll be in deep shit when I get home."

Sean laughed. "Well, tell her I love her next time you call. Also tell her not to worry about me. If they didn't get me in Iraq that last tour I don't think they'll get me this time. Have you figured out where we are yet?"

Sampson had gone into the operations room and was looking at the map to follow his son's coded message of directions to his location. He traced his finger on the map and came to a point due east of Seoul almost on the east coast of South Korea. He held his finger on the map and said, "Sean, your location can't be right. I've got my finger on it and unless you can't remember how far it is to Grandma's house, you're all dicked up."

"Nope, that's where we're at. That's why I said Mom is not to worry. Do you see why now?"

Sampson whistled. "Holy shit, yeah I see why. Any idea what's going on?"

"Negative. We lowly lieutenants only do what we're told. Dad, I gotta go. I just got told to get my young ass up to the CP. Talk to you later! Love you!"

The connection broke. Sampson looked at where his finger was on the map, and swore softly to himself. This just wasn't right. He went looking for Johnny Raymer. He needed to talk to the CINC.

1200 Hours
31 October
Star News Network Broadcast

The pretty Asian anchor woman looked into the camera but not with her customary smile. She was frowning and in fact she seemed agitated. She said in a very strained voice, "We are bringing you a report from one of our free lance reporters based in South Korea. For obvious reasons our reporter chose not to have his face taped with the images you will see. I must warn you that the images you are about to see are extremely violent and graphic in nature and are not suitable for children. I have been instructed to pause for fifteen seconds to allow for the removal of any children or persons who are emotionally incapable of seeing this type of violence." The woman stared into the camera without blinking for the full fifteen seconds. She said no more and the clip started playing. It played through twice without sound or commentary. It was indeed graphic and showed the massacre of the civilians by Sung's men.

The woman finally came back on camera and said in a shaken voice, "Our reporter on the ground has informed us that he was told by surviving South Korean civilians that the massacre you have just witnessed perpetrated by their own soldiers was done to enforce the stay at home policy in effect in South Korea during the current crisis. The North Korean government in Pyongyang has protested this action as inhumane and against the Laws of Land Warfare. As you will see in this next clip, North Korea has taken immediate action to ameliorate the situation. Again, some of these scenes are still very graphic."

A clip came on showing North Korean soldiers assisting the wounded civilians. A North Korean medical unit was tenderly treating the wounded, paying particular attention to the women and children. The camera shifted to North Korean soldiers with their rifles slung across their backs gently laying the dead in rows and reverently folding their arms across their chests. Close up shots showed the blood from the multiple bullet holes in each victim.

A North Korean general was interviewed next in English by the free lance reporter who remained off camera.

"General Kim, what was your reaction when you came across this murder scene?"

In prefect English, General Kim responded grimly, "We were stunned! We were absolutely stunned! My soldiers were in tears and they said now they knew why we were in the south. To save our brothers from a government that does not care about the average man. I know that sounds like propaganda, but that is what my soldiers are really saying."

"General, why are you attacking South Korea?"

"The answer everybody expects me to say is that we are all Koreans and an arbitrary line made by the super powers at the end of World War Two should not separate our people. We have always been against this separation. We have family in the south and they have family in the north. Families are very important to Koreans and families should be together. *All* Korean families should be together. But that is not why we are here. We did not come to unify Korea."

"But it *looks* like you are trying to use force of arms to achieve unification, General! That is what it looks like to everybody. Although you deny it, that is what everybody believes to be true. Why doesn't North Korea just abandon the demilitarized zone and open the way for all the families to reunite if that is your real purpose? Why use force of arms?"

"We would have wished for that, of course, but the government in Seoul has refused our offers to peacefully reunite, and has in fact taken very provocative steps with the Americans to directly threaten North Korea."

The reporter sounded skeptical when he said, "Oh, come now, General! That sounds really far fetched to me. The Americans have in fact been drawing down their forces in South Korea and couldn't possibly pose a threat to you. I have also seen no indications of any provocation on the part of the South Koreans. Isn't it true that the North has attacked the South solely to force a reunification on its own terms? I will say it again, that's certainly what the world at large thinks."

"No, no that is just not true! I talked to the Dear Leader before this interview to make sure he approved what I will now say. We did not anticipate this interview and our representative to the United Nations will make this same statement later today. So you will be the first to air the truth of this war."

General Kim continued somberly, "We are attacking South Korea as a defensive measure in order to force the Americans and their South Korean puppet government that clearly cares nothing for their people …" the general paused and waved his hands toward the dead and wounded civilians as the camera panned to his hand motions, and then the camera panned back to General Kim and he continued, "… to cease their provocative steps towards war. Specifically, we insist that the Americans remove the nuclear missiles they have smuggled into South Korea in response to our successful nuclear tests in 2006. We are attacking only to force that removal or to capture those missiles." The general held up his hand towards the camera and said, "And before you tell me that this is just propaganda, our United Nations representative will show photos to prove the presence of those missiles. They are satellite photos we have obtained from the French and Russians and as you media people say, photos don't lie." The general actually smiled at his last remark.

General Kim dropped the smile and said gravely, "We have asked the Americans in secret negotiations to remove these missiles, but they have refused. We have also asked the South Korean government to force the Americans to remove these missiles and they also have refused. Just as the Americans were ready to go to war and invade Cuba to remove the Russian missiles there, we too are following that same precedent. We fervently hoped the American and South Korean governments would back down like the Russians did in Cuba, but they would not. We have no choice now except to continue this action until the missiles are removed or captured."

The intelligence agencies would pick up on the fact that the off camera reporter didn't evidence the least surprise at this statement about nuclear missiles, but the average viewer in the world-wide audience did not notice. "How many missiles are we talking about General Kim? A couple? More than a couple?"

"We have direct photographic evidence of at least thirty. We assume there may be more, but we will not know for sure until we have over run the missile sites. We will not stop our attack until we have done so. We cannot afford to."

"Where are these missiles, General, if you can tell me?"

"We do not keep any secrets. The missiles are around Pusan and Osan, and we are waiting verification from our intelligence analysts that there may be a site on the east coast of South Korea as well."

"General, I know you're busy but I have to ask one more question and if you chose not to answer based upon operational security needs, I will understand. General, will the North Korean forces attack Seoul?"

The general seemed to reflect seriously on the question and seemed unsure about how to answer it. He finally shrugged his shoulders and said, "We will attack Seoul if that is necessary to bring the South Korean government to the negotiating table. We most sincerely hope that will not be necessary because we feel the collateral damage to civilians and their property would be horrendous. All we want to do is to remove the American nuclear threat from the Korean Peninsula. If the Republic of Korea soldiers would stand aside and give us free access to the sites I've mentioned, we would gladly take advantage of that opportunity."

"But General, earlier you mentioned reunification. What about that? Would North Korean forces withdraw once the missiles are destroyed?"

"Yes, they would. The Dear Leader is most emphatic on this point. He wishes with all his heart for reunification as do all Koreans north and south, but he knows that it must be mutually agreed upon and not done through force of arms. We are only here to remove the threat to *all* Koreans that the Americans have instigated by bringing their nuclear missiles to our homeland. Once the missiles are gone, we will withdraw. But we must physically verify their departure. We frankly do not trust the Americans to be very honest or straightforward in their dealings on this issue now that they have been exposed. The Dear Leader will ask the United Nations to supervise and verify the removal if they are willing to do so. I believe I must get back to my men now. Goodbye." The general turned and walked towards his soldiers who were still tenderly treating the wounded civilians.

The clip ended and the commentators immediately started to discuss the implications of the interview. All were agreed that the Americans had really overstepped their bounds by bringing nuclear missiles into South Korea! They also agreed that the Americans were very heavy handed in their approach to foreign policy. The invasion and continued occupation of Iraq was brought up as it always was, and condemned soundly as it always was, which played very well with the several hundred million Muslims who watched the Star TV broadcasts almost as much as al-Jazira. Al-Jazira quickly picked up the broadcast feeds from Star TV and immediately translated the interview into Arabic. It played to a ready audience around the world as just another example of American perfidy.

Captain Sung, still in his ROK MP uniform, approached the general. Sung had remained off camera for obvious reasons. Several of the wounded civilians might have recognized him but since they were being transported to hospitals in North Korea, and therefore isolation, it did not matter. "Comrade General, how did the interview go?"

The general turned around and faced Sung. He smiled. "Comrade Colonel, it went exceptionally well! Ah, I see by your face that you did not know the Dear Leader has promoted you today for your fine work! Congratulations, Colonel!" The two men shook hands. Sung did not do his duty for rewards but he was immensely pleased with this recognition from the Dear Leader just the same.

"Comrade Colonel, are you prepared for the next part of your mission?"

Sung nodded. "Yes, Comrade General. We are ready. We have loaded the equipment you brought to us in your trucks."

"Very well. The Dear Leader wants you to attack the ROK 1st Division. All the others have sensibly given way and have pulled back towards Seoul, but that division stubbornly holds on. You must break them. Do you understand the Dear Leader's orders in this regard?"

Sung clearly understood his orders. "Yes, Comrade General, I understand. Please tell the Dear Leader he honors me both by this mission and by my promotion which I truly do not deserve. I will not fail him."

The general smiled. He knew Colonel Sung would not fail.

1208 hours
31 October
USFK/Combined Forces Command CP

Johnny Raymer showed Sampson into the CINC's private office just in time to see the last two minutes of the Star network broadcast of their interview with General Kim. Sampson heard the reference to American nuclear missiles and breathed in sharply. That was news to him. It was also news to the CINC.

Smith exploded. "Son-of-a-bitch! That lying bastard! We don't have any goddamned missiles on this peninsula other than conventional missiles. Son-of-a-bitch!"

Sampson took an empty chair beside Smith who was grinding his teeth and muttering the foulest language possible against both General Kim and the Star News Network. Sampson reached over and touched his arm to get his attention. General Smith finally looked over at Sampson. His face calmed to its normal demeanor.

"Sorry, Sam, but these bastards have really got us by the balls with that interview. We can deny all we want that there aren't any missiles here and nobody outside of the Continental United States will believe a damn word of it. Christ, we are in a bind now!"

"Yes, sir, I understand. Sir, do you know exactly where the 2nd Infantry Division is right now?"

Smith seemed puzzled by the question but responded promptly, "Yes, they are in their assembly area just north of Uijombu. I talked to Bobby Wellens just a couple of hours ago. Why do you ask?"

"Sir, I just got a phone call from my son who is in the 2ID, and they are in fact over to the south and east by Pyongtek."

Smith was clearly surprised by this piece of information. "Sam that just can't be! How the hell could they be all the way over there? Better yet, *why* the hell would they be all the way over there? It just doesn't make any sense. Who did you say told you this?"

"Sir, my son called me on his cell phone. He gave me a coded description of his location in case the NKPA is monitoring calls, and I couldn't believe it either when I saw the map, but he assured me that's where they are. He's the scout platoon leader in the infantry battalion and he led the move for the entire division. Sir, no shit, that's where they are."

Smith was stunned and could not say a word for almost a full minute. Finally he said, "Sam, if the 2nd ID is where you say they are, they are completely out of the picture. There is no way in hell they can contribute to the current defense plan. Did your son say why they were there?"

"No, sir. He said he was just told to lead the way to the new assembly area. As he put it, lowly lieutenants only do what they're told."

Smith grimaced. "Well, he's not the only one who is in the dark on this one. Johnny, get General Wellens for me. I obviously didn't understand what he was telling me in our last conversation. Also, have you been able to run down the secretary for me or is he still in *conference*?" Smith finished sarcastically.

"Sir, I'll try the secretary again but they were supposed to call us back when he was available. Who do you want to talk to first?"

"Get me Wellens, that's the nearest alligator, and then see if I can talk to His Highness sometime this century before the NKPA knocks on the doors to this bunker."

"Roger, sir." Raymer hurried out of the room. Sampson and Smith both sat back in their chairs thinking their own thoughts which were pretty much the same. So far, this war was not going as played out in all the war games. It wasn't even close.

**0700 hours, EST
31 October.
The Oval Office, the White House,**

"Mister President, the prime minister is on line one."

Preston grimaced before he answered, "Okay, Carol, I've got it." He picked up the phone and said, "Peter! Good of you to call. What's up?"

The prime minister from Great Britain did not expect the president to be so ebullient, so he hesitated slightly. "Well, Tom, I was wondering if you had seen the report from the Star News Network yet? I must say it's already causing quite a stir over here! We did not know that you had deployed nuclear missiles to Korea." There was just the slightest hint of an accusatory tone in the prime minister's voice.

"Peter, Peter, Peter. We would never deploy those missiles to Korea without consulting your government first. This is just more North Korean bullshit. I'm surprised they took you in on this frankly. We know each other better than that."

"Tom, I believe you but I'll tell you bluntly that the opposition party here believes it to be totally true. I have already taken the liberty of denying the accusation, but frankly neither the press nor the opposition believes me. I'm calling you so that I can say I've spoken with you and this is absolutely not true."

"Well, it's not true! I can promise you that! We don't even have those types of missiles anymore! Nobody in their right mind would believe any of this crap!"

"Tom, I can't speak to people being in their right minds, but I will tell you that our somewhat large Muslim community believes every word of it. I don't think the opposition party actually believes any of this nonsense, but it does provide them a convenient excuse to challenge me directly as your ally. Which brings up a problem, as it were." The prime minister paused and said nothing further.

Finally Preston spoke, "And what problem would that be, Peter?"

"We may not be able to support you in the Security Council vote tomorrow at the United Nations." The prime minister hastened on, "But the point is probably moot since we have heard that the Chinese, the Russians and the French will also oppose the vote to take action in Korea. The best I can offer, old boy, is that we will abstain from the vote. I'm frightfully sorry about all this, but the opposition party is making noises about a vote of no confidence in Parliament. We just don't have the political strength right now with Iraq and Afghanistan going on to hold up during a general election. I'm sure you understand my position, Tom?"

Preston sighed out loud. "Yes, Peter. I understand completely. I have members of my own Congress who are howling for my blood already for something I clearly didn't do. I have to ask you, though. If we have to go nuclear, will you support me?"

There was a long silence on the line. Finally the prime minister said, "Tom, I cannot make such a promise at this time. It would very much depend on the circumstances. Frankly, I can't see where such an action would be justified."

"We have been considering using them if and when the North Koreans use nukes," Preston lied smoothly.

"Ah, well that would certainly be different then. I believe I could get Parliament to back your response should the need arise. But I must warn you, I will totally fail in getting their support if you use nuclear weapons first. And I know the rest of the Security Council will also not support such a move. I must be adamant on that point, Tom. I have already heard from the Russian president today on this, and he claimed to be speaking for the other two members of the Security Council."

Preston frowned. "I completely understand, Peter. I think the same would possibly be true here in the States if we used them first." Preston didn't believe that for a minute, but he could tell he had rattled his ally with the question of nukes. He continued in a reassuring voice, "We'll just have to wait and see what our options are." Preston brightened. "We have heard from the South Korean ambassador that they are holding the North Koreans on the DMZ, so it may not be as bad as Star and al-Jazira are making it out to be. That at least is good news, wouldn't you say?"

"Tom, you need to read your Kipling about believing reports from Easterners. That's all I'll say at this point. I must go and address Parliament and the press, so I'll ring off here. Good luck and good hunting as they say."

The line went dead. Preston sat for a few moments reflecting on the conversation and gathering his thoughts. He mashed the intercom button on his phone and barked out, "Carol, tell the secretary of defense that I want him and the chairman in my office as soon as they can shag their sorry asses over here!" He unmashed the button before his secretary could respond.

Christ, he felt like he was being slammed into a corner and that wasn't supposed to happen to the most powerful man on earth! Particularly not by the machinations of some tin pot, pissant, third world, nothing country! Goddamnit but they had to get this shit under control and right damn now!

**1400 hours
31 October
USFK/Combined Forces Command CP**

Smith took the phone from Raymer and said without preamble, "Bobby, I need to know the exact location and status of your division."

Wellens answered quickly, "Sir, we're in the assembly area I told you about earlier. As to status we still have no contact with the North Koreans, but I've got my security out aggressively patrolling." Wellens pretended to be genuinely surprised at the CINC's question and put that surprise in his voice.

"Okay, Bobby. I had gotten a report that your division was not in your assembly area and was in fact much further to the south and east." Smith chuckled. "In fact the report said you were all the way over by Pyongtek!" The chuckle choked off with Wellens' response.

"Yes, sir. That's where my assembly area is. I thought you understood that when we talked earlier this morning." Wellens said nothing more.

Smith paused long enough to rub his face with his free hand, and then held the phone closer to his ear. "Bobby, I have to tell you I would've believed you were on the goddamn moon before I would believe that you have withdrawn your entire division completely out of the zone of action. Why in god's name are you all the way down there, and who the hell told you to go there?" There was no mistaking the anger or intensity in Smith's voice.

Wellens seemed not to notice the anger and spoke confidently, "Sir, I was following the orders I had gotten from the secretary as I told you this morning. I assume that by now he has clarified those orders with you so we are on the same sheet of music?"

Smith came back harshly and sarcastically, "No, Bobby I have not heard from the secretary. He is apparently avoiding my phone calls. I did talk to the chairman and he gave me some double speak about avoiding excessive American casualties, but he knew nothing of the secretary's conversation with you, and he damn sure did not know about any orders *directly* to you from the secretary, and neither did I until just now. You told me this morning that the Secretary was giving you *guidance*. Are you now saying he gave you *an order* to move your division to Pyongtek?"

"Yes, sir. That is exactly what I am saying. I thought I made that clear this morning, but apparently you misunderstood me. He also told me that I am no longer under the operational control of the ROK Army and to withdraw my counterfire forces. They should be closing in on the assembly area at any moment now and we'll report when that move is complete."

Smith flipped the switch to put the phone on speakerphone and spoke very slowly and clearly, "So what you're telling me, General Wellens is that you have removed all American ground forces from the current war with North Korea on the orders of the secretary of defense, and your current position is near Pyongtek which is well south and east of Seoul?" Smith looked at Raymer and Sampson to make sure they understood they were to listen as witnesses to this conversation. Both men solemnly nodded their heads.

"Yes, General Smith, that's precisely what I'm saying. The secretary has also given me the latitude to refuse any and all orders that would clearly place my division in jeopardy."

"To include orders from me?" Smith asked incredulously.

"Yes, if they pose a clear and present danger to this division." Smith and the other two men listening did not miss the change in Wellens' demeanor. He spoke to Smith, a four star general, as if he were an equal. Two star generals just never did that if they ever hoped to get promoted again. But they all knew that Wellens would get promoted on the sole recommendation of the secretary, and his military abilities and performance in the current crisis were immaterial. Wellens knew it too when he said, "General Smith, do you have anything further for me? I have my staff waiting for me to go over the current situation so I can give them guidance." Wellens didn't wait for an answer and broke the connection. The dial tone buzzed angrily until Johnny Raymer leaned over and switched the speakerphone off.

Smith slowly replaced the phone in its cradle. He said nothing for a full minute or more, then looked at Raymer and Sampson. "I need you both to write up an MFR and bring it back to me. Johnny after you do that, I want you to call the White House. If I can't talk to the secretary to figure out what the hell is going on, I'll damn sure talk to the president as my commander in chief."

0745 hours, EST
31 October
The Oval Office, the White House

Preston looked up from his hunched position at his desk at Ralph Brooks who was standing in the doorway. He impatiently waved his hand for the secretary and the chairman to come into the office. He did not wave them to sit down. He frowned as he listened on the phone. Finally he leaned back in his chair. "General Smith, I'm sure there has been some misunderstanding in all this. I know that

Secretary Brooks would not give orders directly to one of our units in the field. Nobody on the face of this green earth would be so goddamned dumb." Preston stared at Brooks who would not meet his eyes but instead looked at the floor. Preston nodded. Somebody was that goddamned dumb after all. Christ what a mess!

Smith answered, "Mister President, the ROK's are all over me demanding that the 2nd Infantry Division execute a counterattack. I've been stonewalling them for the last hour, but I've got to give them an answer. I'm sorry to be blunt, but do I have command and control of the 2nd Infantry Division or not?"

Preston answered smoothly, "General Smith, I have the secretary coming over for a meeting in another two hours, so I'm going to have to wait to see what's going on before I answer that question. I know you need an answer right now, but I'm not helping you if I give you the wrong answer. I'll call you back once I have a clearer picture on this end. Tell the ROK's you've spoken directly to me on this matter and are waiting for my decision. That should shut them up for the time being. How are they holding up? Their ambassador says they are holding strong on the DMZ."

Smith responded tiredly, "Sir, we reported to JCS several hours ago that we can only confirm one ROK division holding their positions on the DMZ near Seoul. It's the ROK 1st Division which is their best. We have every indication that the other divisions have withdrawn towards Seoul, and the divisions in the far eastern DMZ have had no serious contact." Smith paused, "Sir, I'm also getting queries from the ROK JCS on the nuclear missiles we supposedly have on the Peninsula. I keep telling them that we don't have any, but they don't believe me. They've been hinting that it may be time to use those missiles. Sir, I'm going to ask you bluntly, are there in fact missiles on the Peninsula that I am unaware of?" After being circumvented in his control of the 2nd Infantry Division by Washington, Smith was now clearly wondering what else he didn't know about.

Preston repeated Smith's question out loud, "You're asking if there are any nuclear missiles in South Korea that you don't know about, General Smith?" Preston gave Brooks a hard look, and Brooks met his eyes this time and emphatically shook his head no. The chairman did the same. "No, I can assure you Robertson, there are no nuclear missiles in Korea that you don't know about. I would never allow such a clear violation of the agreements we have with the Russians and Chinese to ever occur on my watch as president." He glared at Brooks and Goodman as he made this last statement. Both men dropped their eyes to the floor again.

"Thank you, Mister President. I'll tell the ROK's I got this directly from you. You'll probably get a call from President Hyun once I tell their JCS the truth about the missiles."

"Yes, President Hyun has called here repeatedly since the interview with the North Korean general was aired. I frankly have not been able to get to him just yet. I have a few other fish to fry here as you can probably imagine!" Preston chuckled and Smith did too. At least Smith's response was genuine.

"Yes, sir. I know you're busy as hell. Thanks for talking to me and clarifying the missile status. Do you want me to call back on the status of the 2nd Infantry Division or wait for you to call?"

"Robertson, you'll have to wait for me on that one. Give me a few hours and I'll get back to you. How are you holding up? How's your morale?"

"Sir, thanks for asking. I'm fine. We're all just a little tired right now."

President Preston was no longer listening but said the right words. "Good. Well I'm personally counting on you. You know you have my full support. Robertson, I have to go now. I've got a call coming in from the British Prime Minister."

"Goodbye, sir."

Preston slammed the phone down and turned to his secretary of defense. "Ralph, why in the hell are you talking directly to a division commander? I've never been in the military, and even I know better than that! Jesus man! What were you thinking?"

Ralph Brooks nervously fingered his bowtie. He put his hand down and answered, "Mister President, I talked directly to the division commander because he is Bobby Wellens. You remember Bobby, he was my MA until he went to Korea last year?"

Preston nodded. He remembered Wellens.

Brooks hastened on, "I knew I could talk to Bobby and get a straight answer on what's really going on over there. Bobby painted a very grim picture, and it seemed to me that we can't afford to take a lot of American casualties in the very early stages of this thing. I told Bobby that his first priority was to preserve his forces until we can get reinforcements over there. I felt it was a prudent course of action to take, and I still do." What he didn't tell the president was that Wellens had actually suggested that course of action.

Preston looked at Goodman. "Do you agree, General?"

Goodman nodded his head vigorously. "Yes, sir. I agree." It was the first he had heard of any of this but he wasn't about to tell the president that! His job right now as he saw it was to support his boss.

Preston relaxed and finally waved the two men to seats facing his desk. They both sat down. "Ralph, why didn't you pass your orders on to General Smith, or have Pat here do that? I know how thorough you are, so that surprises me some."

"Mister President, this is very awkward to say, but General Smith may not be fully under our control right now."

Preston frowned and leaned forward. "What exactly are you saying, Ralph? How could one of our generals not be under our control? Are you saying he's gone off the deep end or is some sort of traitor? I refuse to believe that!"

"No, sir! No, sir! I'm not saying that at all. What I'm saying is that General Smith wears several hats over in Korea. I know you recall the trouble Harry Truman had with General MacArthur during the Korean War?"

Preston nodded. He wasn't much of a history buff, but he did remember reading about that!

"Well, the same circumstances are still in effect today. General Smith is the commander in chief of Combined Forces Command which is all the ROK and US forces on the Peninsula. He answers to you and President Hyun under that hat. He is also at the same time commander in chief of United Nations Command for all UN forces on the Peninsula. He answers to the Secretary General and the Security Council under that hat. Finally, he is combatant commander of US Forces Command Korea which is all US Army, Navy, Air Force and Marines that will reinforce the Peninsula. He answers only to you under that hat, unless those forces are brought in as part of a United Nations effort."

Brooks paused to make sure the president had followed him so far. It *was* complicated, and Brooks knew Preston wasn't the brightest bulb in the box sometimes. But Preston nodded his understanding, so Brooks continued, "So you see, sir, it's a bit complicated. The 2nd Infantry Division is technically part of Combined Forces Command, and General Smith would have to consult with the ROK's before he pulled the division back to a secure location. Clearly there was no time for that and the ROK's would never have agreed to it."

When Preston remained silent, Brooks continued, "Sir, in that regard, I'm having General Goodman issue an order putting the 2nd Infantry Division solely under US Forces Korea Command to clean this up a bit. The order will include the proviso that the division is not to be used without *your* permission. That will effectively remove them from any ROK control and keep General Smith from tossing them into the fray unnecessarily. If the ROK Army is doing as badly as Bobby Wellens says they are, they will be desperate to throw the 2nd Infantry Division into the fight. We just can't afford to lose them because the ROK's are panicking."

Preston frowned again. "Are they panicking, Ralph? Do we have any fucking idea what is really going on over there? General Smith said the Koreans are reporting that they are holding, but he seriously doubts it. And, before I forget gentlemen, your earlier thoughts on going nuclear are totally out the window. My *dear friend* the British Prime Minister has informed me that we will have no support from any member of the Security Council, to include Britain, if we are the first to use nukes," he finished sarcastically.

Brooks and Goodman were visibly very surprised by Preston's statement. Neither had contemplated seeking *permission* from another country before they used their own weapons. What was the sense of having the damn things if you had to go through a *Mother may I* process to use them! Preston knew what they were thinking for he had already had the same thoughts.

He said harshly, his voice grating, "You see, gents, we are caught by our own stated policy on this. We have maintained for decades that we would never be guilty of the first use of nuclear weapons. That has been our moral high ground against the Soviet Union and others during the Cold War and the all the way up to the present. I'm not saying that things don't change, but I am saying we'll need to make a damned good case before we use them. Speaking of them, what's our response to the accusation that we have nuclear missiles in Korea?"

Brooks spoke as usual. The Chairman of the United States Joint Chiefs of Staff only spoke when spoken to. "Mister President, we simply tell the truth. There are no missiles. I'm having a meeting with the press in the Pentagon in an hour to say exactly that with your permission."

Preston said sourly, "You know Ralph, I believe you but how do you convince people you don't have something? How do you prove the negative? That slick ass North Korean general is using the same approach that was used on Saddam Hussein. Everybody accused Saddam of having weapons of mass destruction, and he couldn't prove he didn't have what he didn't have, so down he went! You're going to need a hell of a lot more than just your denial to back this up. I'm not sure our own media will even go along with this."

"Okay, sir, then do I have your permission to offer the IAEA access to our nuclear stockpiles to confirm that all our weapons are accounted for?"

"How long would that take?"

"Probably six weeks, Mister President."

"Okay, do it. Tell the press I have directed this action in the interests of world peace and as part of our policy of openness in regards to nuclear weapons. I'll follow up over here later today with a press conference. Six weeks will buy us plenty of time. What's the status of reinforcements to Korea, Ralph? I know some fucking reporter will ask me."

Brooks had anticipated the question and answered glibly, "Sir, the first unit from the 82nd Airborne Division lifted off from Pope Air Force Base at 0430

Eastern Standard Time. There will be planes departing every thirty minutes until the whole unit is deployed."

"How big a unit are we talking about?"

"Sir, a brigade headquarters, two infantry battalions and an artillery battalion."

"Sounds like a lot. How many soldiers are we talking about?"

"Sir, upwards of three thousand."

"Three thousand! Are you shitting me, Ralph? Our immediate response is only three thousand soldiers? Or is this just the first load? Please tell me this is just the first load!"

The chairman spoke. He felt he had been spoken to. "Sir, we are projecting a further force flow after this first immediate response force. Due to our commitments in Iraq and Afghanistan, we are rearranging the TPFDD as necessary."

Preston asked caustically, "What the shit is a *tip fid,* General?"

General Goodman blushed at the rebuke. "I'm sorry, sir. It's the Time Phased Force Deployment Document. It's nothing more than a list of forces available for each of our contingency plans at any given time. My staff is adjusting it as we speak."

"Bottom line. How many troops and when, General?"

"Two full brigades, or roughly nine thousand troops within twenty to thirty days, Mister President." Goodman hastened on, "We'll have a steady flow of roughly a thousand soldiers a day after that, but we'll need to activate Army and Air National Guard units starting immediately to give them time to gear up for deployment. Sir, we'll need your authorization to federalize the guard units."

Preston stared at Goodman who held his gaze, and didn't flinch. Preston did not like bad news and this bastard of a general was giving him nothing but bad news! He asked evenly, "How many guard units are we talking about, and from what states?"

"Sir, all of them. And from every state."

"Shit!" Preston put his face in his hands and leaned forward with his elbows on his desk. He finally waved a hand towards the door and the two men hastily departed. Neither was bold enough to ask if the explicative was the approval to activate the guard units.

**1700 hours
31 October
USFK/Combined Forces Command CP**

General Smith walked into the conference room exactly on time. He was known never to keep people waiting unlike a lot of generals who seemed to always be late. Smith paused in the doorway of the conference room. It was time for the daily update or the 'Five O'clock Follies' as it had been dubbed by the press in the Vietnam War, and the room was usually packed to capacity with ROK generals and colonels. It was a status thing with the ROK's to be important enough to sit in on any briefings to the CINC. They gained great face among their peers and subordinates once they were elevated to attendance status. The room was almost empty except for the normal contingent of American officers and a sprinkling of ROK colonels. "Johnny, am I early?"

Johnny Raymer answered, "No, sir. You're right on time. We haven't been able to find any of the ROK generals, sir. They're no longer in the command post. I've personally gone to all their offices looking for them."

Raymer's answer clearly puzzled Smith as he looked around the nearly empty conference room. Sam Sampson standing in the far corner caught Smith's eye and raised his hand but said nothing. Smith motioned Sampson to come over to him. Sampson came over and nodded towards the door. He wanted to talk to Smith outside of the hearing of the few ROK colonels present in the room. Smith preceded him out the door back into the hallway and Sampson closed the door behind him.

Sampson said, "Sir, I had a ROK colonel tell me out in the smoking area that all the generals were summoned to the Blue House for a meeting with President Hyun about three hours ago. He thought they would all be back by now. He called his boss on his cell phone to remind him of this meeting and it was answered by the security police. He's shitting bricks right now because he thinks his boss has been arrested and now they'll come after him once they trace his cell phone number."

"Who's his boss?"

"Sir, it's General Yoon, the C-3."

"My god, Sam! Why would anyone possibly arrest General Yoon? He's one of the best officers they have!"

"Sir, it may be a bit far fetched, but when I was over here in the 90's, the ROK president fired every ROK general above the rank of two stars one Monday morning because they had once been members of Hanna. We thought the generals would stage a coup in response, and we went on alert. Instead they accepted it. The bottom line is that these guys have been gone for three hours and nobody can reach them. You know as well as I do the ROK colonels won't step up and take responsibility for their staff sections if the generals don't come back."

Smith winced at Sampson's last remark. He knew it was true. You didn't become a general in the ROK Army by making any decisions not directly approved by your superiors. "Sam, I haven't heard anybody even mention Hanna in over fifteen years! I can't believe that President Hyun would remove his generals in the middle of a war for survival even if they were once members of Hanna years ago."

Sampson nodded his agreement. "Sir, can you call President Hyun at the Blue House and see what's going on then? The only input for your update is what little we got from our liaison teams. We've gotten absolutely zip from the ROK's because their bosses aren't here to approve it first before we get it. You know the drill."

It was Smith's turn to nod his agreement. Sampson was right. "Okay, Sam, I need to go back in to the 'Follies' and get what information they have for me so it looks like it's business as usual and nothing's out of the ordinary. Pull Johnny out once we go back in and have him start working my call to the Blue House."

"Roger, sir."

The two men reentered the conference room, Smith smiling at the assembled officers as he told them to please take their seats, and Sampson quietly saying a few words to Johnny Raymer who discretely left the room.

The young American major from the C-3 Combined Operations section began the briefing. Each staff section took the podium in turn and gave the CINC in PowerPoint slides and words the current situation as they knew it for their areas of responsibility. Normally the staff sections would alternate between US and ROK briefing officers. This time there were only Americans briefing, but Smith pretended not to notice. The sprinkling of ROK colonels in the room would not make eye contact with any of the Americans. The absence of their generals and no ROK briefing officers was causing them to lose face with the Americans; or so they felt.

Colonel George Bates got up last to brief the status on the non-combatant evacuation plan. He had one PowerPoint slide that had the total number already evacuated and the total number waiting to be evacuated with a projection of how many would go out in the next twenty-four hours. The total already gone was less than two hundred, the total waiting was more than three thousand and the projection for the next twenty-four hours was an oversized zero with an exclamation mark.

Bates began, "Sir, as you can see, we're dead in the water. I had a meeting with my counterpart just before driving over here, and he's no longer pretending that the delay is temporary. He told me flat out that he can't get our people out." There was a stirring in the room. Every married officer in that room who was an American had family waiting at Kimpo International Airport waiting to get out. It was one thing for the officers to be in a war zone because that was their duty. It was totally unacceptable to them to have their families in a war zone too.

Smith asked calmly, "Did he tell you why, George?"

"What he said, sir, is that he is waiting for permission from President Hyun at the Blue House. I asked him if he called anybody at the Blue House to get that permission and he told me they would call him. It was not his place to call the Blue House. He refused to let me use his phone to call the Blue House myself. Sir, I think you need to talk to President Hyun ASAP. We still have plenty of food and water but the rest of the airport is pretty much deserted right now so none of the shops are open and the families are bored out of their minds. The wives with young kids are having the hardest time because the kids don't understand why they have to stay in just the one area."

Smith nodded his head. He had once had young children himself and couldn't imagine keeping them cooped up in an airport lounge for what had already been two days.

Bates continued, "Sir, they all saw the North Korean general's interview on the Star Network on the monitors in the waiting areas and several have asked me about the missiles. Is there anything I can tell them?"

"Yes, George. I'm glad you brought that up. I was going to cover that at the end of this briefing, but I'll do it now. I spoke personally with President Preston, and he has absolutely assured me that *there are no nuclear missiles* on the Korean Peninsula." General Smith looked at the ROK officers in the room and said, "I want you colonels to tell your bosses when they get back from their meeting that I have made this statement. Colonel Kim, do you understand me?"

Colonel Kim, who was in the C-3 and a graduate of the US Army's Staff College, finally looked at the CINC once he was called by name. "Yes, sir. I understand."

"Then please translate what I have just said into Hangul for your peers. This is too important to be misunderstood by anybody, and I know some of them are not as familiar with English as you are. Please translate."

Colonel Kim started speaking in Hangul and all the ROK colonels looked at him. Kim had just gotten huge face by the CINC singling him out as his interpreter. They all listened and one asked a question to challenge Kim and have him lose face if he did not know the answer. Kim answered him quickly and angrily with a raised voice and the other colonel dropped his eyes. Kim was the dominant one; information was power. Smith, because he was *the CINC* had given him face and the others could not take it away! Kim turned back to Smith. "Sir, I have informed them of the truth you told me."

"Thank you, Colonel Kim. I know I can always rely on you to help me," Smith replied. The CINC had just given Kim even more face with his compliment, and Colonel Kim smiled and nodded his head in agreement. The CINC could rely upon him for help unless his ROK superiors disagreed, then the CINC was on his own. Smith knew all this and would give Colonel Kim even more face and therefore power for possible later uses. "So I will recap the situation, and Colonel Kim, please translate again for me so we are all clear on the current situation and your peers can pass it on to their bosses once they're done at the Blue House." Smith paused and Kim started translating what Smith had already said. All the ROK officers looked at Kim.

Smith continued, "Our reports from the liaison teams indicate that all ROK divisions west of the Chorwon Valley have withdrawn from the DMZ to their defensive positions around Seoul to protect the capital." Smith chose his words carefully because the plan never called for this abandonment of the prepared positions on the DMZ; positions that had been improved and strengthened for over fifty years. Colonel Kim translated while Smith paused for him to do so.

"The ROK 1st Division continues to defend on the DMZ north of the Chorwon Valley against heavy North Korean attack, and the divisions to the east of the Chorwon Valley have only had light contact." He paused again. The ROK officers smiled when they heard about the ROK 1st Division fighting so well. Smith continued, "The 2nd US Infantry Division is in their assembly area in the vicinity of Pyongtek as the theater reserve force under my direct control." Kim looked puzzled but translated anyhow. Smith had just subtly explained away the 2nd Infantry Division's shameless retrograde operation out of the fight and made it look like it was all part of the plan. Just like the ROK divisions pulling back to Seoul being a part of the plan. Face worked both ways. The ROK officers nodded. It sounded okay to them.

"A brigade combat team from the 82nd Airborne Division will start arriving in country at Pusan by air tomorrow morning." Kim translated and some of his peers smiled. They didn't realize just how small of a force that really was, and

Smith wasn't going to enlighten them any. "Follow on forces from the United States will start arriving in theater no later than D plus thirty, and possibly as early as D plus twenty." Again, the ROK's smiled and nodded. That sounded good, but it really meant thirty more days and twenty more days respectively. That was a long damn time to hold the line, and Smith and the other American officers in the room clearly understood that even if their counterparts apparently did not.

"A navy carrier battle group will be off the Peninsula in another ninety-six hours, and two wings of F-22 fighter aircraft are self-deploying to the Peninsula in the next forty-eight hours." All this sounded good to the ROK's too, but Smith knew neither force could directly influence the ground campaign significantly unless the weather changed for the better. Smith paused again for Kim to translate.

"And finally, I will reiterate again, *there are no US nuclear missiles anywhere on the Korean Peninsula.*" Several of the ROK officers wrote this last statement down on their note pads. "Gentlemen, that will be all for now. Colonel Kim, I must speak to President Hyun and I would like for you to translate for me."

Colonel Kim had just gotten his last and largest dose of face in front of his peers! He could not help smiling as he followed Smith out of the room as the other officers rose from their chairs and came to attention. Smith called back over his shoulder as he departed, "Sam, I'll want you there too." Sampson didn't need any face but got it anyhow as he followed Smith out of the room.

0100 Hours
1 November
ROK 1st Division MP Checkpoint, South of the DMZ

Newly promoted Colonel Sung got out of his jeep at the barrier that blocked the road and stretched his back nonchalantly as if he was loosening his back after a long ride. He stretched his arms too and seemed not to notice the two MP's wearing the patch of the ROK 1st Division as they approached the barrier. Both men kept their rifles trained on Sung. Even though Sung was to all appearances a ROK MP major, they had gotten multiple reports of SPF being in the area. They had not seen or heard any SPF so far, but still, it paid to be careful.

One of the MP's stopped to cover Sung while the other got closer. He whispered the challenge and Sung responded in a whisper the correct password. The MP visibly relaxed and lowered his rifle while signaling his partner to come forward and help lift the heavy barrier across the road. Sung stepped forward and helped the two men as he reflected wryly on how easy it was to buy the challenge and passwords from the army of a capitalist country! He casually asked one of the soldiers who was a sergeant exactly where the division command post was located. The sergeant seemed to hesitate and Sung told him that he was from the Capital Division and they were scheduled to relieve the 1st Division on the DMZ tomorrow. Sung had come ahead to coordinate the relief.

The sergeant then readily told Sung how to get to the division headquarters. Everybody knew the Capital Division was the premier division in the entire ROK army, and the thought of being relieved from combat loosened his tongue immediately. Sung asked a few questions for clarification, and specifically asked where the other MP checkpoints were since his MP's would be relieving them as part of the overall relief. The sergeant told him everything, and even offered to call ahead to tell the other checkpoints who he was so they would speed him on his way! Sung told the sergeant that he was very impressed with him and that he might want to transfer him later to the Capital Division. Sung asked his name and the sergeant positively beamed as he answered.

The Capital Division! Sitting around Seoul, extra pay, better food, women, soju! The sergeant could see it all in his mind's eye. Sung thanked him and returned to his jeep. The three jeeps and their trailers pulled through the checkpoint and the MP's waved to them. Sung's men waved back and the two MP's lowered the heavy barrier back across the road.

As promised, the MP sergeant had called ahead to the other checkpoints and the MP's there were enthusiastic as they waved Sung's group through the series of checkpoints. They were not about to hold up the major who said he was coming to coordinate their relief tomorrow!

Once Sung got close to the area where the division command post was located, he had the driver slow down and pull off the road. Sung got out and walked up and down the road until he found what he was looking for which was a small trail leading from the main road to a rice paddy. Every rice paddy in Korea had such a road that had been worn down by centuries of use by the two wheeled carts the rice farmer took to and from his paddies. If he was a rich farmer, he had a bullock to pull the cart. If he wasn't, he usually had his wife pull it.

Sung walked back and got into the jeep. He told the driver where to turn and they slowly moved down the narrow trail. Sung told the driver to stop when they reached the rice paddy. The others jeeps stopped close behind him. Sung went to the last jeep in the line and told two soldiers to set up a security point a hundred meters back towards the main road. The soldiers jogged off into the dark to do his bidding. The other soldiers had gotten out of their jeeps and were pulling the tarpaulins off the jeep trailers. They waited by the trailers for Sung to tell them what to do.

Sung went to the first trailer and pointed to the heavy metal container in it. The soldiers grabbed it and grunted with its weight. They followed Sung to the end of the trail and gently put the box down. Sung waved them back while he opened the box and fiddled with its contents. He made several adjustments with a wrench, and then walked back to the second trailer. The men picked that box up and again followed Sung. No words were spoken. Sung indicated a spot on the ground next to the first box. They put the box down and again left Sung alone. Sung made several electrical connections between the two boxes. He tested each one with a small circuit tester he pulled from his field jacket pocket. Sung walked back to the trailer his jeep was pulling.

The final container was the heaviest of them all and every man, to include Sung, had to struggle to carry it the short distance up the trail to the other two. Sung told them to put it down and rest for a minute. On his signal, they all lifted together and placed the box on top of the other two. Sung waved them back and they returned to the jeeps. Sung made one final electrical connection with the third container and checked it three times with his circuit tester. Satisfied that the connection was good, Sung closed the access panels and pulled three locks from his pocket. The locks secured the access panels and also locked the three containers together. They were special locks that would require a blow torch and several hours of hard effort to break. Sung looked at the stack of containers one final time, and then walked back to his jeep.

Sung told his driver to turn the jeep around which the driver did quickly and efficiently in spite of the narrowness of the trail. The others followed suit and started back towards the main road. All three jeeps stopped before entering the main road. Sung got out of his jeep and walked over to the two men pulling security. He said in a low whisper, "Do you understand your duties?"

The taller of the two men leaned close to Sung and whispered back, "Yes, Comrade Colonel. We understand. We will not fail you."

Sung did not rebuke the man for using his new rank or the comrade word. He knew his troops had found out about his promotion from the Dear Leader and were immensely proud of him. It was also somehow appropriate for this soldier to call him Comrade Colonel right now. Sung whispered back so both would hear, "You have my word that I will personally take care of your families if you do not make it back across the DMZ. If I also do not make it back, the Dear Leader knows of your mission and he will see to their welfare. I have personally spoken to him in this regard before we left Pyongyang."

Both soldiers whispered back, "Thank you, Comrade Colonel." Neither soldier was married, but both had elderly parents that they had been struggling to support in the near famine conditions in North Korea. At least now the parents would get better food and better housing if their sons died on this mission. It was a small price to pay, and both soldiers were more than willing to pay it in order to take care of their parents. A son's duty to take care of his parents was one of the strongest elements in the Korean culture. The old were to be comforted and cared for, and not to be put in homes to die like the Americans practiced. The soldiers had heard in their political education classes how the Americans treated their elderly and were appalled. These two soldiers knew what their duties were to both country and family.

Sung embraced each of the soldiers and walked back to his jeep. He led the way down the highway back towards the checkpoints going south and away from the DMZ. He stopped at the first checkpoint to tell them he was done with his coordination meeting and needed to return to Seoul to bring the Capital Division forward. Again, the MP checkpoints were all opened when he got to them and the MP's waved and smiled. Sung and his men waved and smiled back. Sung looked at his watch. It was 0315. They were doing well on time. He told his driver to turn left at the next intersection so that they could head east.

0520 Hours
1 November
1st Battalion, 57th Infantry Regiment CP

Lieutenant Sean Sampson was totally beat. He had been on constant patrols with his scout platoon for the last seventy-two hours. He tried to count up the number of hours of sleep he had in that time and gave it up. He was too tired to remember but he knew it was less than six hours total. He slowly walked over to the TOC tent and entered through the double layers of canvas into the brightly lit TOC. The light hurt his eyes and he took a minute to adjust before looking around for the S-3 or the battalion commander. He saw both men over in a corner looking at a map.

Sean walked over to the two men and said, "Sir, we've just completed our last sweep." He paused, waiting for his battalion commander to respond. Lieutenant Colonel Bob Easley looked up from his map and could tell at a glance that Sean was bone tired.

"Sean, grab that stool over there and take a load off. Pull it up to the table and show me and the S-3 what you saw." Sean grabbed the stool and set it up at the table. It felt good to sit down, but the weariness didn't abate any.

"Sir, we didn't make contact with the ROK 52nd Division." Sean pointed out on the map where they were supposed to be. "We crisscrossed the entire area and couldn't find any South Korean soldiers or even civilians anywhere in the area where they are reported to be. The only ROK unit we saw was an MP detachment setting up on the main east-west road just before we got here. Their commander didn't speak any English so I had to rely on my KATUSA who speaks damn little English. From what I got out of them other than they knew the challenge and password was that they were setting up to facilitate traffic flow for units being relieved on the DMZ. They hadn't seen the 52nd Division either."

"Well, it's going to be damned hard to tie into them if they ain't there," the S-3 reflected sourly.

The battalion commander nodded his agreement. He turned to the S-3, "Robb, you need to pass this on to brigade so the Old Man can get it at his morning update at 0600." The S-3 stood up, yawned and stretched and went to make the radio call to brigade. This was a very strange war so far. No enemy and no allies to be found. He'd be damned if he understood any of it.

"Sir, it probably doesn't mean anything, but my KATUSA was scared shitless by the ROK MP's. You know the ROK soldiers don't like KATUSA's because they think they're all getting over, which they are, but usually they'll at least try to get the KATUSA to trade MRE's for ROK rations. These guys wouldn't even talk to my KATUSA when we first came up and he was asking where their leader was. They just pointed and turned their backs on us."

"Did you notice anything else about them? Could they have been SPF in ROK uniforms?"

"Sir, I thought about that, but if they were, they would have capped us rather than talk to us. Their detachment commander was very friendly even if he didn't speak English. He said he was the deputy provost marshal for the ROK 14th Division, and that the war was going very well for the ROK Army. The guy was very upbeat."

Easley snorted. "Shit, well at least somebody seems to know what the hell is going on. I hope he's right. So far from my foxhole we're in the middle of nowhere with nothing to do. This damned sure isn't what we always visualized a war with North Korea to be like. You know Sean, it's almost spooky."

"Yes, sir. I expected to be up to my ass in alligators about now instead of wandering the Korean countryside looking for signs of life. Sir, do you need anything else from me and the scout platoon?"

"No, Sean. I want you to take the scout platoon and bed everybody down for a good six hours. Stay inside the TOC perimeter so you don't need guys up pulling security. I know your guys are whacked out, so get some rest. I'll send for you when I need another patrol run."

"Thanks, sir! Six hours! Holy shit!" Sean Sampson bolted for the TOC door. The clock was ticking and he could not waste a minute. Six whole hours of continuous on your back damn sleep was better than winning the lottery!

0600 hours
1 November
USFK/Combined Forces Command CP

"Sir, we finally have the Blue House on the phone. President Hyun will talk to you now." Johnny Raymer was standing in the doorway to the CINC's private office. General Smith looked up from the document he was reading.

"Do you have Colonel Kim to translate for me?"

"Yes, sir. He's standing by."

"Okay, send him in and let's get this going. The fact that they wouldn't talk to us all night doesn't look good to me, Johnny. I'll want you and Sam to sit in and take notes. We'll need to send a back channel to the secretary and chairman on what was said." Raymer left to get Kim and his notepad, and Sampson quietly entered the office and sat down.

Colonel Kim looked distinctly uncomfortable to be in the CINC's private office and to be his translator. The generals had still not come back to the command post and Kim was feeling out of his element. He desperately needed his own general to tell him to perform this duty. Smith pointed to a chair and a headset and Kim gingerly sat down and just a gingerly put the headset on.

Smith started, "This is General Smith, the Commander in Chief for United Nations Command and Combined Forces Command. I am ready to talk to President Hyun at his convenience. Would you please let him know I am calling?"

Smith was surprised when a voice he recognized as President Hyun's immediately responded to his opening salutation. President Hyun rattled off a long dissertation in Hangul and Colonel Kim frantically wrote notes. Smith was finally able to interject when Hyun barely paused for breath, "Mister President! Sir! Please let my translator tell me what you have just said. I don't wish to miss anything that you're telling me because it is so important to both our nations right now."

Smith turned to Colonel Kim and waited expectantly for the translation. Kim said nothing and looked down at the floor. Smith finally said, "Colonel Kim, please translate what President Hyun has just said to me." Kim continued to look at the floor and did not acknowledge Smith's order. Smith repeated the order with the same effect. Johnny Raymer got up from his chair and stood next to Kim.

Raymer said, "Colonel Kim, you must translate for the CINC. Please do that now."

Kim did not look at Raymer and continued to stare at the floor. President Hyun started off with another spate of Hangul at breakneck speed. Raymer grabbed Kim by the shoulder and shook him gently. Kim stared at the floor.

"Colonel Kim you must translate for the CINC. You must do that now!" Raymer shook Kim a little more forcibly.

Finally Kim looked up briefly at Raymer but did not make eye contact. He shrugged his shoulders and said, "I do not speak English anymore." Kim dropped his gaze to the floor again.

Smith was stunned by Kim's statement! How the hell could this fellow all of the sudden not speak English? What the hell was going on? Smith disgustedly motioned for Raymer to take Kim from the room. Smith listened to the rapid fire Hangul until President Hyun finally paused long enough for him to say, "President Hyun, sir, I do not have an interpreter to translate for me so I must ask you to pause for me to get one." Smith hoped like hell that the few remaining ROK officers in the headquarters who did speak English hadn't suddenly forgotten how to speak it too!

Smith was looking anxiously at the door waiting for Raymer to bring in another interpreter when he was shocked to hear President Hyun respond in near perfect English, "Yes, I know General Smith. I told your interpreter that he no longer speaks English. Unlike my generals, that man at least knows how to obey. That will probably keep him out of prison but that remains to be seen."

"Sir, are you saying *your generals are in prison?*" The shock in Smith's voice was clearly evident. He looked at Sampson who seemed just as stunned by what Hyun had just said. Sampson scribbled notes furiously as Hyun continued.

"That is exactly where those dogs are, General Smith. They attempted to stage a coup using the invasion by the North Koreans as their excuse. It is only by the grace of God that I was tipped off in time. They came to my meeting and entered through the front door of the Blue House and left by the back door in shackles. Every one of the Hanna I could lay my hands on was put in prison in the last twenty-four hours."

"Sir, we can't fight the North Koreans if all the generals are in prison!"

"I will have new generals, generals I can trust, appointed within the next forty-eight hours, General Smith. My staff is doing background checks as we speak to make sure there is no Hanna among them. We cannot fight the enemy without if we cannot trust the generals within. And General Smith, why did your country deploy nuclear missiles into my country secretly?"

The sudden change of subjects momentarily caught Smith off guard, but he recovered quickly. He said firmly, "Sir, *there are no* nuclear missiles from the United States on the Korean Peninsula."

"And how do you know this, General Smith?'

"Sir, President Preston told me that last night when I talked to him personally."

"Ah, you got to talk to your president, yet he will not speak to me although I have repeatedly tried to talk to him. Can you see where I am a little skeptical, General Smith? Your president assures *you* there are no missiles but will not assure *me*? What do I tell my people and the world? All I can say to them is *I don't know*? The American President *won't talk to me*? Where are the reinforcements we were promised? Where is the ammunition we were promised? Where is America now that South Korea is in danger? Can you answer those questions, General Smith?"

Smith started to answer the questions about reinforcements and ammunition, but he realized they were rhetorical questions. Even Hyun must realize that none of that could be forthcoming in the first few days of the conflict. The United States was fourteen time zones away from South Korea. It was as far away as you could get. He responded instead with, "Mister President, I know you are familiar enough with the war plans to know how long it will take for those things to happen. My immediate concern is that you have an army in combat with no senior leadership. With all due respect, sir, we cannot wait forty-eight hours while you find new generals. I do not believe for a minute that your generals had any plans for a coup."

"You may believe whatever you want, General Smith, but I have the proof I need. In the interim, my staff tells me that my army is still holding on the DMZ, so I am not overly concerned."

"Sir, I have received the same reports but my liaison teams tell me a different story."

"Oh, and just what do your *liaison teams* tell you, General?" Hyun asked sarcastically.

"Sir, they say that all the divisions west of the ROK 1st Division have pulled back towards Seoul. They also say the ROK 1st Division continues to hold their positions on the DMZ. The divisions east of the 1st Division have had minimal contact so far."

"And what of the US 2nd Infantry Division, General Smith? What do your *liaison teams* say about them?" Hyun was again sarcastic in his tone.

"Sir, the 2nd Infantry Division is in the vicinity of Pyongtek as the theater reserve." Smith was clearly unhappy as he made this statement.

"Oh, well, that is most *convenient* for them if there has been no action to speak of over in the east. Is that not so, General?"

All Smith could say was, "Yes, sir."

"General, I need to be blunt with you at this point. We feel very strongly based upon your forces pulling back and your president refusing to talk to me that the North Koreans may actually be justified in moving across the DMZ to find your missiles. We are engaging them in talks and they assure us that the missiles are their only concern. I must admit that at this point they seem closer to being honest with us than is your government. General Smith, will you respond to my orders for Combined Forces Command if I order a cease fire? You must tell me now."

Smith reflected on the question and responded slowly, "Mister President, I would obey your orders for ROK forces, but I could not apply that order to US or United Nations forces. I must also warn you that the North Koreans are lying about the missiles. I don't know why President Preston hasn't talked to you yet, but I *do know* there are no missiles. Finally, sir, do you really believe the North Koreans will just go home if they are able to take their army all the way to Pusan? Or a better question is, what if they don't withdraw?"

"I will have to think about that, General Smith. I assume you will inform your government of our conversation?"

"Of course, sir."

"Then tell your president I am still waiting for his call, but he may already be too late. Goodbye." The line went dead.

Smith rubbed his face with his hands. "Okay, Sam, write it up. Christ on a crutch! We're losing this son-of-a-bitch and these assholes are ahead of us every step of the way. If this could get worse, I don't know how."

0755 Hours
1 November
Vicinity of the ROK 1st Division

The young North Korean SPF soldier shook his comrade's shoulder. "We must depart now, my friend."

The sleeping soldier was instantly awake. "Is it time?"

The first soldier looked at his watch. It was cheap and not waterproof and he had their only watch because he was the senior of the two. "Yes, if this watch is still working, it is time to leave. The comrade colonel was very specific about the time. I'll take the lead." The soldier shouldered his rucksack and started towards the main road. He was still wearing the uniform of a ROK MP so he knew he would not be challenged until he got close to the actual defense positions. He could hear the artillery pounding in the near distance so he knew exactly where to go. His comrade followed him.

Both soldiers had waited through the dawn hours on the rice farmer's trail that Sung had set his boxes on. Neither had any idea as to the purpose of the boxes; both merely knew they were to keep anybody from tampering with them. The farmers had long fled to the south once the war started and nobody else had come along the trail.

The soldiers moved slowly. Any haste would make them look suspicious, but they needn't have worried. Nobody came along the road as they worked their way towards the sound of the artillery. The soldier looked at his watch again and noted that it was exactly 8:00 AM. He and his comrade heard a sharp explosion back on the trail they had guarded but before either could comment they were vaporized in a blinding flash of light. Their bodies went from bone, muscle, tissue and water to plasma in a millionth of a second. Neither of course saw the mushroom cloud rise from the huge crater where the rice paddy had been.

0815 hours
1 November
Star News Broadcast

The very pretty and normally smiling young lady who read the morning news did not smile. She was clearly in shock at what she was reading from the teleprompter.

"We have just received a report from the North Korean government that the United States has delivered a nuclear missile on the North Korean forces defending on the Demilitarized Zone northeast of Seoul. The North Korean government states that it has lost thousands of soldiers in this attack, and is formally calling upon China and Russia to protect it from further nuclear attacks by the United States." The woman paused as if waiting for more from the teleprompter which she was in fact doing. Nothing more came up on the screen. She finished lamely, "That is all we know." The camera remained fixed on the woman rather than cutting back to the show in progress. The woman stared glassy eyed at the camera. She still didn't smile.

**0820 hours
1 November
USFK/Combined Forces Command CP**

"General Smith! General Smith! Sir, you need to wake up!" Johnny Raymer was shaking Smith's shoulder none too gently and arousing him from a deep sleep, the first he'd had in over forty-eight hours.

Smith mumbled, "What the hell is it, Johnny?"

"Sir, the ROK 1st Division just took a nuke!"

Smith was instantly alert and he actually felt his heart stop at the words. He grabbed Raymer's arm to help pull himself out of his cot. He seemed unsteady on his feet so Raymer supported him briefly.

Smith turned to Raymer and asked quietly, "What's the source of that report, Johnny?" His voice was level and he had recovered from the initial shock of Raymer's words.

"Sir, it came on the Star News a few minutes ago," and Raymer continued hastily as Smith started to shake his head that he wasn't going to believe a Star News report, "and it has been confirmed by NORAD at Cheyenne Mountain."

Smith looked at Raymer and said nothing for the space of a few seconds. Finally he asked, "How big a yield was the warhead?"

"Sir, NORAD says it was somewhere between fifty and one hundred kilotons."

"Christ! So there's nothing left of the ROK 1st Division?" Smith's tone was incredulous. He couldn't imagine anybody surviving a nuclear detonation of that magnitude. "How the hell did it happen? The ROK's have got the Patriot Anti-missile system up there, so how in the hell did the North Koreans get a missile through them?"

Raymer shook his head. "Sir, we don't know any of that right now." Raymer paused.

Smith just stared at him, noting the pause. "Spit it out Johnny. What's the rest?"

"Sir, the North Koreans have announced that their troops north of the DMZ 'defending' against the ROK 1st Division were the actual target and that *we* nuked them. They have called on China and Russia for protection against further nuclear attacks by the United States."

Smith visibly paled at Raymer's words. He said slowly, "I am ninety-nine percent sure we didn't use a nuke. I am one hundred percent sure we didn't authorize one on this end. Only the President of the United States could make such a decision. It has to be a North Korean weapon. There's no other way!"

This time Raymer shook his head. "Sir, Cheyenne Mountain confirms that North Korea shot no missiles capable of carrying that warhead. They also told me that the IAEA reported that in their opinion North Korea still did not have the demonstrable technology to achieve a warhead of that magnitude. Sir, all the evidence is pointing our way."

Smith's mouth moved but no words came out initially. Finally, he took a deep breath and said, "Well, we're back to the one percent I'm not sure of. Get the chairman and the secdef on the phone ASAP, Johnny. We need to find out what the hell is going on. When I said earlier it couldn't get any worse, I guess I was just full of shit. Goddamn it all to hell!"

2130 hours EST
31 October
White House Press Room

"Mister President, is it true that the Chinese and Russians have placed their nuclear forces on full alert in response to our attack on North Korea?"

The president eyed the veteran reporter and wanted to scream at her at the top of his voice, "You stupid bitch! I told you we didn't do it!" Instead he smiled and said, "Janice, we have no such reports as of yet. And I need to reiterate, and I can't stress this enough, the United States *did not* deliver a nuclear weapon onto North Korean forces. We have no such weapons anywhere near Korea." This was a lie because several nuclear submarines were very near Korea in response to the outbreak of hostilities and they all had nuclear missiles. But that wasn't something one discussed in a press conference. Even the media knew better than that. The president turned and pointed to a hand up in the back of the crowd. He knew it belonged to Dave Sutter who was a friend of the White House. "Yes. In the back there."

Sutter stood up. "Mister President, I heard what you just said about nuclear weapons in Korea, but how do you respond to the satellite photos that North Korea's Ambassador presented to the United Nations earlier today? Sir, those photos undeniably showed what appear to be our missiles in South Korea."

Preston audibly sighed. So much for friends, he thought sourly. Dave Sutter had just punked him. "Dave, we have no idea what those photos were taken of. The claims by the French and the Russians that they are accurate and legitimate are being reviewed as we speak by the CIA. I *know* they aren't our missiles, and the South Koreans say they're not their missiles, so for the time being we are assuming that the photos are faked. It would not be the first time the North Koreans have lied about something," he finished dryly.

Dave Sutter followed up quickly with another question. "President Preston, can you tell us how the war is going in South Korea? The daily information briefs at the Pentagon are providing no details and are only saying that ROK and US forces are holding their own against the North Koreans. It seems, Mister President, that we are being kept in the dark deliberately. Would you please comment on that?"

Damn! Sutter had really punked him! He'd make sure the son-of-a-bitch never got another question answered as long as he was in the White House! The bastard! Preston smiled. "Dave, the Pentagon is telling you everything they can without tipping the North Koreans off. Even *you* must understand the concept of operational security? Well, that's it ladies and gentlemen. I have pressing business to attend to as you can well understand. Thank you for your time." Preston turned to leave and the press corps respectfully stood up as he left the room.

Sutter was fuming. That sanctimonious bastard had ducked both questions and he knew when he was being fed bullshit!

George MacCreedy from a rival news network punched Sutter lightly on the shoulder. "You asked the right questions, Dave. But you asked the wrong guy. Preston hasn't got a clue on what's happening over in Korea. He knows exactly the same crap we get out of the Pentagon. Nothing more, and possibly even less. But, the good news is you can go back to your boss and ask to be reassigned out of this nuthouse. Preston will never answer another question from you now. I hate to see you go because you're good, but I'm glad to see you go because you're good. Less competition for me!"

"Thanks, Mac," Sutter replied sourly. "Glad to hear I'm making your miserable life easier. Seriously, though, I'm worried. There's been a nuclear explosion on the DMZ and nobody seems to know anything about it. That's about as scary as it can get. If it wasn't us, and the North Koreans don't have anything that big, then who the hell was it? Was it the Chinese? The Russians? The French? The goddamn Iranians? Aren't you worried?"

"Yeah, Dave I'm worried. I got an empty feeling in my gut about all of this. Nukes are as serious as it gets, and to have one go off anonymously is absolutely unbelievable. But let me ask you this, what if it was us? I won't be scared anymore if that was true because at least we're the ones pushing the buttons. But I don't think even Preston is stupid enough to lie about something this big. It would be the end of him when it got out, and these things always get out. Nope. I'm gonna stay worried because I know it wasn't us."

Sutter nodded his agreement. He too felt like it wasn't the United States that dropped the nuke, but he damned sure wasn't going to sleep well at night until he knew who did drop it; and more importantly, how to stop them from doing it again. The lack of information coming from the Pentagon and the White House gave him a queasy feeling in his stomach. They were stonewalling the media and they would only do that if things were either going to hell or they just didn't know themselves. He wasn't sure which of the two he preferred. Both were chilling to contemplate.

1030 hours
1 November
USFK/Combined Forces Command CP

"Okay, Robert. Tell me what we know so far." Smith sat back in his chair and looked and felt years older than he had just a few short hours ago.

Major General Robert Blair, the CJ-3 cleared his throat and began to speak. He had PowerPoint slides up on the screen and had to look at them rather than Smith. He read the slides to Smith and the other officers crowded around the big conference table. Only two of the ROK colonels had opted to attend the meeting although every ROK division chief had been informed of the meeting. The ROK colonels were not going to attend anything as a group until they had generals telling them to do so again. The two that had come were visibly uncomfortable. Smith grimaced as Blair read a typo from the slide without correcting it. He sighed inwardly.

"So let me recap, Robert. We know there was a nuclear explosion near the DMZ but nobody seems to know where it came from or who did it?"

"Yes, sir."

"Do we know the status of the ROK 1st Division? How many casualties did they take and are they still combat effective?"

Blair looked at his operations colonel who just shook his head. Blair looked back at Smith. "No, sir. We don't know."

"Okay, fair enough. What are we doing to find out, Robert?'

Again, Blair looked at the colonel and Smith finally said in exasperation, "Please sit down, General Blair." Smith turned to the operations colonel that Blair kept looking at and asked his question again. He was done going through the general officer middleman who didn't know anything. Blair was another general who owed his promotion to flag rank to the secretary of defense, and Smith knew his presence deep inside his own staff was not coincidental. The fact that Blair was also an idiot didn't help matters.

The colonel responded slowly. "Sir, we have sent the liaison teams from the two divisions that were east of the 1st Division to make an assessment. They are still enroute and haven't reported yet. We hope to hear something from them soon," he finished lamely.

Smith nodded his head. That was about all that could be done at this point but he expected Blair to know something that simple. "How long ago were they ordered to go over there, Colonel?"

The colonel's face flushed. He looked at Blair who would not meet his eyes. He finally mumbled an answer that Smith couldn't hear.

"Say again, Colonel. I couldn't hear you."

The colonel spoke louder, "Sir, we ordered them to go about ten minutes ago."

Smith audibly sighed out loud this time. "Okay, this thing happened two and a half hours ago, and you just now decided to find out what the hell is the status of the only division holding the North Koreans up? You're kidding me, right?"

Blair finally spoke up when it was evident that the colonel wasn't going to answer the question. "Sir, I was in a very important meeting and my staff was not allowed to interrupt it. The decision to send the liaison teams had to wait for my approval."

Smith drummed his fingers on the table for a few seconds. Then he asked in a low voice, "And who were you meeting with, General, that took precedence over the war we are fighting?"

"Sir, the meeting I was in couldn't wait. I apologize if you think I made the wrong decision."

Smith thought it was interesting that Blair wasn't admitting he made the wrong decision, but was only apologizing because Smith apparently thought so! "General, you haven't answered my question," Smith said evenly.

"Sir, I was meeting with the regional manager from AAFES. I wanted to make sure he was able to properly report his losses in theater, and to see if he couldn't get some type of PX service over to the troops in the 2nd Infantry Division. Sir, you know I'm on the permanent AAFES advisory committee which I take very seriously, and I have important duties and obligations in that capacity." Blair said this last part almost defiantly, but not quite.

Smith didn't respond to Blair, and instead quietly asked all the officers present to leave the room except General Blair. Once the room was cleared, it was not hard to hear Smith through the closed door as he roared at Blair. The words *incompetent* and *criminally derelict* among others was clearly heard out in the hallway.

Sam Sampson just looked at Johnny Raymer and whistled. "Johnny, remind me never to piss the Old Man off," he said reverently.

Raymer shrugged. "This has been building for a while now, Sam. Blair never knows shit, and we all know he reports regularly to the secdef. Right now the Old Man feels like he's a one legged man in an ass kicking contest. We've got some good officers on the staff, but we've also got some political appointees, if you catch my drift."

Sampson knew exactly what he meant. "Yeah, I've kinda noticed that. The marine two star who's the CJ-5 looks good, though. Is he?"

"Yeah, he's really good. The CINC loves him. You can always count on the marines to send their best to a joint headquarters unlike the army. You know that, Sam. You saw it when you were here and you saw it at CENTCOM."

Sampson couldn't deny it and was about to respond when Smith came out of the conference room into the hallway. Blair remained in the conference room staring down at the table.

Smith turned to Sampson and said, "Sam, how much shit will you give me about being only a contractor if I send you up to the ROK 1st Division? I want to put you in my helicopter and get you up there as fast as I can. We've lost too much time already on this."

"Sir, I don't have a problem with it, but my wife might if I get whacked. She's still just a little put out over the Desert Vengeance thing."

Smith nodded. He knew the story. The whole army knew the story of Sampson's attack into Iraq seven years earlier and his near brush with death. "Okay, so what are you saying? You won't go?"

"No, sir. I'm saying you need to bring me back on active duty so that if I do get whacked, my family will be taken care of. Some clerk around here will have the SGLI paperwork for me to fill out, and I'll take your word that you'll take care of the rest while I'm enroute. I should be ready in about five minutes once we get the form."

Smith looked as relieved as he felt. "Okay, Sam. Fair enough. You have my word on it. What else do you need?"

"Sir, I'll need a few guys for security and a chemical corps guy with a Geiger counter. I'll bring my gunny as the NCOIC. For the record, you *asked* him to go."

Smith smiled. "Yeah, I guess I did at that." Smith looked at Sampson. He was wearing the Army's Combat Uniform but without patches or rank. He turned to Raymer. "Johnny, how about squaring Sam away with some rank for his ACU's and a patch for his shoulder."

Raymer started to turn away to comply with Smith's order, when Sampson reached over and pulled Raymer's 24th Infantry Division patch off his right shoulder. The patches and badges on the ACU's were all attached with Velcro so the patch came right off. Sampson took the American flag patch off the same side of Raymer's uniform, and then he pulled the eagle of a full colonel's rank off the front of Raymer's uniform.

"See, Johnny? I just saved you a trip," Sampson said as he applied the rank and patches to his own uniform. He and Johnny Raymer had both served in the 24th ID under General Barry McCaffrey in the Gulf War; something both men were proud of.

Raymer looked at his denuded uniform and said sarcastically, "Gee, thanks, Sam. Still always thinking of others." Raymer faced Smith and said, "Sir, I'll go get that SGLI form for Sam and get some shit back on my uniform before I get arrested as a spy. I'll also tell the chopper crew to stand by and get some of the security guys together and link them up with Sam's gunny. Sam, where do you want them to go?"

"Uh, have them come here, Johnny. I don't want them showing up and telling the gunny he's going into Indian country before I've had a chance to explain how he *volunteered* for this and all. We'll link up here in the conference room."

Smith laughed. Things may be hopelessly fouled up about now, but at least he had these two good colonels who kept their sense of humor and took all this in stride. Smith thought briefly about how good it would be to have Sampson as his CJ-3 instead of the bozo he had been given by the secretary of defense. He dismissed the thought and shrugged. You have to play the cards you're dealt.

As Sampson was walking away to find the gunny, he turned back to Raymer and said, "Hey, Johnny. I need a guy that speaks Hangul too, and no, don't send me Colonel Kim! Send me a captain or lieutenant that doesn't know any better."

Raymer hesitated, and then said, "Kim blew his brains out about an hour ago in his quarters, Sam. I got that report just before the meeting started, and haven't had a chance to tell the CINC yet." Raymer turned to Smith and said, "I'm sorry, sir. I didn't think you needed that on your plate just yet." Smith only nodded with a sad look on his face and turned away towards his office.

Sampson swore. "That poor bastard!"

Smith mentally echoed Sampson's words. If you lost too much face in Asia, sometimes there were no other options. Smith was shaking his head as he walked back to his office. As much as he admired and respected the Koreans, there were some things he would just never fully understand about them.

**1050 hours
1 November
USFK/Combined Forces Command CP**

The Blackhawk helicopter sat on the pad with its rotor slowly turning. Sampson came out of the bunker entrance and jumped on board. Gunnery Sergeant Gaddis handed him his headset as he settled into his seat and strapped his shoulder and seat belts on. The pilot didn't wait for Sampson to strap in and took off smoothly from the pad. He gained about a hundred feet in altitude and then dropped the nose of the Blackhawk as he accelerated to the southeast.

Sampson clicked his intercom microphone on, "Chief, have you figured a way to get up there without flying over any NKPA units?"

The pilot responded, "Yes, sir. We're going to swing to the southeast, then head north up the slot to the DMZ. I'm not worried about the NKPA, Colonel. I'm worried about the SPF assholes who took out one of our Chinooks. We've got no way of telling where they're located, so I'm going to keep it low and fast. Everybody needs to hang on because it'll get rough."

Sampson looked at Gaddis who just rolled his eyes.

The helicopter ride initially skimmed over several Korean villages with their cinder block houses and rusting corrugated metal roofs that always looked like they were about ready to fall down. The narrow, often twisting streets through the villages had their usual litter but were devoid of any humans. Sampson didn't even see any dogs which was equally unusual. The chopper banked steeply and headed north towards the DMZ.

The villages gave way to small farming compounds with stouter houses and walled in enclosures and to rice paddies that nestled into every available space between the hills of Korea. Rice was the number one crop in Korea and had been for thousands of years. If the rice crop failed, even in a modern era where a relatively prosperous country like South Korea could easily import rice, the people would go hungry. Sampson had been told by more than one Korean that rice grown outside of Korea was 'bad' and didn't taste right. They would rather cut back on their consumption than eat 'bad' rice. They would make and eat more kimchee to make up for the loss of rice, but they wouldn't be happy about it.

As the chopper flew north, the hills got steeper. Rice paddies were terraced and sat in echelons going up the steep hills and mountains. Sampson had learned from talking to the Korean farmers years ago that it took hundreds of years and countless hours of human labor to make a good rice paddy. The bottom of the paddy had to be layered in clay laboriously brought from the banks of streams and rivers far below the hills and mountains. After it was carted in by bullock or carried in on the farmer's back, it had to be manually packed down a layer at a time by the farmer's feet until it formed a leak proof barrier to hold the water the rice grew in. Even when it finally held water, the paddy had to be maintained every year with new layers of clay.

Sampson knew the two wheeled tractors the South Korean farmers used eased the burden of hauling the clay and the harvested rice crop to and from the paddies. The tractors were also used to pump water through hoses between paddies to keep each at its optimum growing level; something that had been done in the past a bucket at a time. For all of that, the tractors still couldn't pack the clay into the bottom of the paddy. Only the bare feet of the farmer and his family could do that. Sampson had spent a day with a rice farmer on his first tour in Korea and had participated in the whole process. It had both fascinated him and kicked his ass physically. He shook his head sadly now to see all the paddies abandoned.

Even this late in the season, the paddies were still a brilliant green that flashed to a bright blue or grey color as the chopper flew directly over them, and the water in the paddy could suddenly be seen. Sampson reflected that thankfully he couldn't smell the paddies which were fertilized with the human excrement collected daily in every village and farm. The smell only went away when the standing water in the paddies froze rock solid in the bitingly cold Korean winter.

The tops of the hills were dotted with pine trees and the shrines and tombs of the dead that the Koreans built facing east so their ancestors could face the morning sun as it rose each day. Sampson had always heard that the Korean dead were buried sitting up in their tombs facing east, but he never knew if that was really true. It was something he couldn't quite ask his Korean friends, no matter how well he felt he knew them. The troops swore it was true which always made Sampson smile when he heard them talk about it.

As Sampson watched the Korean countryside in all its beauty and strange smells flash by under the helicopter, he reflected on just how sad this war was. The Koreans worked hard, were devout Christian people and deserved every blessing that came their way. They most assuredly did not deserve to be destroyed in a war that the United States had promised them for over fifty years they would never have to fear again. Sampson really felt like the United States was letting the South Koreans down in their utmost hour of need and he was shamed by that fact.

The flight to the DMZ was uneventful except for a ROK air defense unit that swung their quad-fifty caliber machine gun onto them, loosing a burst of tracers that passed far to the rear of the chopper. The unit was obviously jittery and was practicing the old air defense adage of shoot them *all* down and sort them out on the ground. Fortunately, the gun wasn't radar controlled and the crew had never actually been able to fire it in training before, so the rounds went wild. The two door gunners did not return fire and the chopper was out of range in a flash as it hugged the terrain. Sampson had taken some wild rides in Vietnam during air assault operations, but this ride beat them all to hell for sheer sphincter tightening speed and turns!

The young Chemical Corps captain looked down at her instrument readout and occasionally reported, "Negative, negative," on radiation presence over the intercom. Abruptly, her report changed to, "Positive, barely traceable. Barely, more, more, almost to red, turn right ninety degrees, Chief!"

The pilot abruptly banked the speeding helicopter in a gut wrenching turn to the right. The Chemical Corps captain had issued everybody a dosimeter to wear on their uniform lapel and several who heard her glanced down at theirs. It wouldn't physically show anything until it was fed into the reader machine for it, but they didn't know that. They were reassured that it appeared to be unchanged.

Sampson was looking down at the ground and pushed his intercom button. "Chief, you see that group at three o'clock? We need to land as close to them as we can. It looks like a CP."

"Roger." The helicopter swung further to the right and the Chemical Corps captain reported a lighter reading for radiation. The bird settled lower to the ground, kicking up loose debris which caused a momentary brownout where the pilot could no longer see the ground. The pilot skillfully lowered the bird by inches until he felt the wheels touch down. Sampson jumped out of the bird, the gunny and the security team scrambling to get in front of him as he approached a group of ROK soldiers clustered around a few jeeps and a tent.

As Sampson got closer, he could see men lying on stretchers and some were even lying on the bare ground. Most of the men were quiet, but a few seemed to be in agony and were convulsing. Sampson hurried past them towards the tent. He turned back and called the interpreter forward. None of the ROK soldiers attending to the men on the ground paid any attention to Sampson or his group. Sampson entered the tent and momentarily stepped back in shock.

The tent was full of men whose skin was sloughing away in the worst burn cases Sampson had ever seen. A doctor was trying to bandage the loose skin back onto bared muscles while an assistant administered shots. It was clearly a futile effort. These men could not possibly ever recover from their burn injuries. The fact that they were still alive at all was amazing in itself. Sampson could hear one of his security soldiers gagging behind him. The gagging noise also caused the

ROK doctor to look up towards the door of the tent. Sampson caught his eye and motioned him out of the tent. He finished tying off the bandage he was working on and came out of the tent wiping his gore smeared hands on his uniform pants.

Sampson moved several feet away from the tent and the surrounding litters to a space under a pine tree. He turned to his interpreter and said, "Please ask this officer who he is, and tell him I'm Colonel Sampson from the CINC's staff."

Before the interpreter could speak the ROK officer responded with, "I speak English, Colonel. I went to medical school in the States. But why are you here? I asked for backup medical units from the 3d ROK Army and they send you? I do not understand."

Sampson looked at the man's nametag on his uniform and recognized the Hangul characters for Park in English. "Captain Park, I'm not here for medical support. I'm here to make an assessment for General Smith, the CINC, on the status of your division. I'm sorry. I wish I could help you in some way. Do you know where your division commander or any of his staff are right now? I need to speak with them for General Smith."

The captain sighed. He really was hoping for some help when he had heard the helicopter land. "The division commander, I think, is that man I was just treating. I think it is General Hyan because of the gold tooth he has. That is all of him I can recognize. He cannot tell you anything, and will die shortly like the rest." Park waved his hand over all the men lying on the ground. "All of them will die of radiation poisoning or burns or both in the next seventy-two hours. Those men over there will die too."

Sampson looked to where Park was pointing and noted for the first time that there was a separate group of men lying on the ground who were not being attended by any medics. Sampson could also see that their uniforms were different now that he looked more closely at them. "Are they North Koreans?"

Park nodded his head. "Yes, they are North Koreans who are as badly burned and radiated as our own soldiers. They have been coming here for hours now asking for help. It seems that their division was also obliterated in the blast. But I cannot help them. I do not have enough supplies or medicine for my own soldiers. Colonel? What is happening? I know what I am seeing, but I do not understand it. Why did the United States drop a nuclear bomb on us?"

The question caught Sampson momentarily off guard, but he responded firmly, "Captain Park, I can personally assure you that the United States did not do this. We would never do such a thing. You have been to the States. Can you imagine us doing such a thing?"

Park shook his head. "No, I cannot. I know this but the soldiers believe otherwise. They keep asking me why our ally the United States has dropped a nuclear bomb on them. I can only tell them it must have been a mistake."

"Why do they think it was the United States and not the North Koreans, Captain Park?"

Park waved towards the North Korean soldiers. His message was clear. Even North Korea wouldn't use a nuclear weapon on its own soldiers. Or so the South Korean soldiers all believed.

Sampson could not refute the proof the South Korean soldiers were seeing with their own eyes. "Captain Park, I will do what I can to get your army to send you help as soon as I get back. Can you tell me specifically what they need to send you?"

"Yes, enough morphine for me to euthanize several thousand casualties," Park said simply. He saw the look of surprise on Sampson's face. "Colonel, not one of these men can live with the mount of radiation they have absorbed into their bodies. I cannot save them; I can only ease their passing. Please help me do that," Park said pleadingly.

Sampson could only nod his acceptance of Park's request, and turned back towards the chopper. His security team followed. Once he was on board, he said to the pilot, "Chief, I need to fly around the fringes of the blast area to see how big a footprint the bomb had." The pilot clicked his intercom in acknowledgement as he lifted the chopper from the ground. "Chemo, I need you to tell the chief which way to turn as we map this thing. I also want you to generate a down wind warning message on the radiation so we can put it out ASAP."

"Roger, sir."

The rest of the flight was uneventful which Sampson thought was very odd. Several times they had flown into North Korean air space to track the footprint of the nuclear explosion and none of the helicopter's threat receivers ever went off. It was like the North Koreans were allowing or even wanting this flight to occur. The helicopter landed back at the CP helipad and the Chemical Corps captain collected the dosimeters from everybody on board and went to have them read. She would let them know if anybody needed treatment for radiation poisoning. If it wasn't too severe, there actually were treatments available. Sampson passed the request on for morphine for Captain Park to the operations center as he passed through on his way to report to the CINC.

The ROK 1st Division was gone for all intents and purposes, and the North Korean division facing them on the DMZ was also gone. Sampson had a hard time believing the North Koreans would destroy one of their own divisions, and told General Smith what he had learned from the ROK doctor. Smith had to agree with the ROK soldiers. The finger was definitely pointing at the United States.

1400 hours EST
2 November
The Oval Office, the White House

President Preston just stared at his CIA director. He finally said, "You've got to be shitting me, Joe! You mean to tell me the satellite photos of missiles in South Korea are real? How the hell could that be true!"

CIA Director Joe Montgomery fidgeted in his seat and re-crossed his legs before answering. "Sir, we have looked at the originals with the Russians and the French. Both have surprisingly opened their archives for us to do just that. My experts tell me that the photos are original, and have not been doctored or computer enhanced in any way. The photos clearly show what appear to be long range cruise missiles in our pre-positioned equipment stocks down by Pusan. The missiles are deployed in an arc facing north, and have radar and command centers placed nearby. It looks like our equipment as far as the radars and command centers are concerned. In fact, *it is* our equipment. We can't deny that."

Preston turned to the secretary of defense and the chairman of the Joint Chiefs. He stared at them for a full minute before speaking. "Gentlemen, I'll ask you the same question I asked several days ago. Do we in fact have nuclear tipped cruise missiles on the Korean Peninsula? Yes or no?"

Both men hesitated and looked at each other before Brooks said, "Sir, not that we know of."

Preston exploded. "What the hell does that mean, Ralph? Not that you know of! Sweet mother of god! Now you're going to tell me that the nuke that went off might have been ours?"

Brooks hastily answered the president, "Sir, no, sir! We know for a fact the missile wasn't ours! We have accounted for our entire nuclear stockpile. We can prove that the missile was not ours. The IAEA will be able back us up on that once they've finished their count. We just don't know who those missiles belong to or where they came from, that's what I was trying to say."

Preston responded sarcastically, "Well, godamnit Ralph, they belong to somebody because they're damn sure sitting there for all to see! How the hell do we explain this? Better yet, what the fuck are we doing to find out who owns them?" Preston glared at all three of the men in turn. None of them would return his stare, and looked nervously away.

Goodman finally spoke. "Sir, we think those photos might have been staged with the help of the South Korean workers at the pre-positioned equipment site." He stopped there.

Preston looked at him and finally said, "Go on, Pat."

"Sir, the photos were taken on July the 6th." Preston waved his hand as if to say so what? Goodman quickly continued, "That was a four day 4th of July holiday for all US forces in Korea. None of the usual soldiers or American contractors would have been in the yard that day. The South Korean workers would still be required to work, however. We think those workers might somehow have been paid off to stage these photos."

"And just why in the hell would any of them do that, General?" Preston asked coldly.

Goodman took a deep breath. He was merely speculating at this point, but he just didn't have a better answer. "Sir, the South Koreans love pranks and jokes. If somebody approached them to do this as a joke and offered to pay them as well, they would jump at it. It would not be hard to make those missiles from wood and canvas or even papier-mâché. It would take only a few minutes to set them up and take them down again. Just long enough for the satellites to pass over. Then it's easy to burn them so there is no evidence of them ever being there."

Preston nodded. This was beginning to make more sense. Goodman, encouraged by the nod continued, "Sir, my guys also noted that the radars shown in the pictures are actually air defense radars and would not be used to launch a cruise missile. In fact, those missiles have an on board guidance system and don't use radars. The command centers shown are generic and could be for anything. I think this whole thing has been staged, Mister President. Our problem will be to prove it."

The CIA director leaned forward. "Sir, we agree with General Goodman's assessment and we've got a team enroute to Korea to see if we can interrogate the workers who were working that day. It will take us at least a week to sort through this and we'll need the cooperation of President Hyun to get the access we need. Right now, we're being denied country clearance to even get the team in country. We're told the Blue House has denied the requests flat out. The ambassador told my station chief in Seoul that he also can't see or talk to Hyun, or anybody else in the ROK government for that matter."

Preston slumped back in his chair. "Well, shit, I guess I'm going to have to talk to the little bastard after all. Christ, I was hoping like hell not to do that until we had some more troops on the ground. Ralph, what's the status of that because I know Hyun will ask me?"

"Mister President, the lead elements of the brigade from the 82nd Airborne Division landed in Pusan about two hours ago. They are moving towards our pre-positioned stocks as we speak," Brooks said smugly. What he didn't know was the wrong kind of troops were being linked up with the wrong kind of equipment, but he wouldn't have cared if Goodman had bothered to tell him, which he hadn't. Goodman knew that to Brooks troops were troops and infinitely interchangeable in his mind. And infinitely replaceable, too.

Preston actually smiled. "Well, hot damn! The 82nd Airborne Division is on the ground so now I can talk to Hyun and not feel like a fucking hobo at a family picnic. Great! Ralph, what time is it over there right now?"

Brooks didn't even look at his watch. "Sir, it's around noon tomorrow or the day before yesterday or something. They're awake, I'm sure. I call Smith whenever I need to during the day here and he's always available."

Preston nodded and pushed a button on his phone. "Get President Hyun in Korea on the line." No *please*, no *thank you*, no first name salutation. This president was always too busy and important to be nice. His philosophy was if the help didn't like how he operated, they could go elsewhere. The fact that some of them had done just that after years in the White House and service to several earlier presidents seemed to have escaped his notice.

The light on the phone blinked and Preston picked it up. He said smoothly, "President Hyun, I am so glad I have finally been able to get through to you! We have had a very difficult time with our communications here at the White House. How are you, sir?"

Preston's opening gambit was met with a spate of angry Hangul. Preston pulled the phone away from his ear and stared at it. "President Hyun, I cannot understand you. This is President Preston. I asked how you were doing, sir."

President Hyun replied in Hangul again and Preston's face reddened. "President Hyun, I know you speak English and I need you to answer me now." There was silence over the phone.

Finally a voice came over the phone in English. "President Preston, President Hyun says you must have an interpreter if you want to speak to him. He also says to tell you that he does not appreciate your call in the middle of the night."

Preston was stunned and said nothing for a few seconds as his jaw worked up and down. His face had gone beet red, and a vein was angrily pulsing in his neck. The other men in the room were frozen in place until Preston waved them towards the door and gasped out, "Get me a fucking interpreter in here right goddamn now!" Preston didn't bother to cover the phone mouthpiece, and he clearly knew Hyun had heard him. He didn't care. He had never been so humiliated in his life!

The interpreter scooted into the office a few minutes later, and Preston didn't wave her to a chair. He savagely punched the button on the phone for conference call and dropped the handset with disgust. He didn't even look at the interpreter and said between clenched teeth, "Tell President Hyun that I have my interpreter and I am ready to speak with him now."

In a tremulous voice the interpreter translated. Hyun came back immediately in English. "Thank you, President Preston for giving me the courtesy of attempting to communicate to me in my own language. You may dismiss her now."

Preston was fuming and the interpreter fled the room without waiting for a signal from Preston. Preston took a deep breath and calmed himself.

"I am sorry if you misunderstood me earlier, President Hyun. I had been informed by General Smith that your English was very good."

"Ah, yes. My English is very good and I understood you perfectly before. I merely asked for an interpreter on your end to make the point that we are allies and equals. You should not automatically assume that I will abandon my own language to converse in yours. It would be equally pretentious of me to insist that you only speak Hangul to me. Do you speak Hangul, Mister President?"

"No, President Hyun, I do not speak Hangul. Now that you have made your point, can we discuss more important issues? I am calling to tell you that the missiles in the satellite photos have been faked with dummies on the ground and we need to get our interrogation team on the ground to confirm that with the workers who were there." Preston was going to continue but Hyun cut him off.

"Yes, I know about your requests to send your CIA team in, but I have personally denied those requests."

"Why, in god's name would you do that?" Preston asked heatedly.

"Because I will not subject any of my citizens to your CIA team for interrogation. You may have forgotten about Guantanomo Bay and Abu Grahaib, but we have not. It will simply not happen, Mister President. What else do we have to discuss, then? I would very much like to go back to bed now."

"But do you believe me at least that the missiles were fake and that we did not deliver the nuclear missile on the DMZ that we have been accused of?"

"Oh, yes. We know all that already."

"What the hell do you mean you know that already if we just now found out ourselves!"

Hyun chuckled. "Ah, President Preston you are such an *American*. You assume that you will always know first and know best. We have known about the faked missiles for two days now, and we don't know who the nuclear missile belonged to, but we know it wasn't yours since the missiles were not real."

"Then why the hell didn't you tell us all this!" Preston exploded.

Hyun paused for a moment, then said quietly, "If you had bothered to talk to me on any of the many times I called in the last two days, Mister President, you would have known this. Several of the workers you wanted to interrogate came forward when they saw the photos in the newspapers and explained what happened. It seems what they thought was a ROK officer wishing to pull a prank on his general paid them handsomely to stage the photos. The officer they described is not in our army. We have checked. We assume he was a North Korean officer who infiltrated the south for this purpose. Or he may have been from China or possibly even Japan. Or maybe even a Korean-American for that matter. He paid them is US dollars. We will never know who he was, but it doesn't matter."

Preston asked slowly, "Why doesn't it matter, President Hyun? It seems to me that the North Koreans were most likely behind the photos so their excuse to invade your country is a load of crap. The 82nd Airborne Division has landed in Pusan, by the way. I wanted you to know that we are coming to your aid as rapidly as we can."

"Yes, again Mister President, I know all that. I also know that those troops cannot use your pre-positioned equipment because they are not trained on it. But of course, you knew that I'm sure?" Hyun left the question out there waiting for a response from Preston.

Preston put his head in his hands and rubbed his temples slowly. He lied, "Well, I don't know who told you that, but those soldiers are trained on that equipment and will be rapidly moved up into the fight. I can personally assure you of that as their commander in chief!"

"Well, thank you President Preston, but I don't think that will be necessary. We are currently negotiating a cease fire with the North Koreans. It seems they wish to talk after the nuclear weapon devastated one of our divisions and one of theirs. I am meeting with the Dear Leader today at Panmunjon which is why I would really like to get back to bed. Is there anything else?" Hyun was clearly going to terminate the call.

Preston nearly choked and hastily croaked out, "Please, President Hyun, don't hang up! Who the hell is the Dear Leader and why are you meeting with the North Koreans without us? We're allies for god's sake! You just can't do that unilaterally. That has always been our agreement!"

"Yes, which the United States breaks when it's convenient to them as I recall. The Dear Leader is Kim Jong Il. I assumed you knew he was called that in the

North. As to why I am meeting with him, well, at least I know where I stand with him. But the real reason we are meeting is about the nuclear attack. The North has hinted very strongly that they know who launched the attack. They have even told us who they suspect and are going to prove it at our meeting. Would you like to know who it was, Mister President?"

Preston was vigorously nodding his head. All phone conversations in the White House were taped for both security and historical reasons, and Preston belatedly realized that for the sake of posterity, he needed to verbally respond. "Yes, President Hyun, I would very much like to know the answer to that question. Very much so."

"It was the Japanese, Mister President. That is who delivered a nuclear missile onto the Korean Peninsula killing thousands of Korean soldiers regardless of the uniform they were wearing." Hyun's voice seethed with anger and hatred.

"But that's impossible! The Japanese don't even have a nuclear program! Or a cruise missile program for that matter! How the hell can you say it was the Japanese!"

"Ah, there you go again, Mister President, being an American. Just because *you* don't know it, doesn't make it untrue. Goodbye." Hyun broke the connection.

Preston put his head into his hands. For the first time since he was elected, he really, really hated this job.

0715 hours
3 November
USFK/Combined Forces Command CP

General Smith looked haggard from lack of sleep. He looked up at Raymer and Sampson. "So President Hyun is going up to Panmunjon to meet with Kim Jong Il?"

Johnny Raymer nodded his head and said, "Yes, sir. At ten hundred hours."

"And we're in a cease fire until further notice? How did we confirm that, Johnny?"

"Sir, General Moon is the new ROK chairman as of zero six hundred this morning, and he personally conveyed that message in English and Hangul to the operations center. He gave the correct authentications when we requested them. Sam knows him from when he was over here and personally spoke to him on the phone."

Sampson spoke up. "Sir, he's the real deal. He and I used to play golf together when I was the G-3 and it's the right guy. He was pretty amazed to go from retired colonel to ROK Chairman of the Joint Chiefs over night! He said he 'about shit' when Hyun called him. When he said that I knew it was Moon. I had to explain to him one day on the golf course what the idiom 'I about shit' meant and it became one of his favorite sayings. The good news is, he's got his stuff together and will work with us as far as he's allowed to." Sampson left the sentence open ended.

Smith said tiredly, "Yeah, Sam, that last part says it all. As much as he will be allowed to. So far, that isn't very much. Johnny tells me all the ROK's have left the CP now. Are you seeing the same thing, Sam?"

"Yes, sir. It's like they all got a magic call simultaneously and disappeared as a group. Our only contact with the ROK Army right now is our liaison teams, and two of them have reported that they were requested to leave by their ROK commanders once the cease fire went into effect."

Smith rubbed his forehead while he thought of what all this meant. "Sam, as the OPFOR guy, what do you think is going on right now?"

"Sir, I've been giving that a lot of thought. I think what we're seeing is a very well thought out and choreographed campaign plan by the North Koreans to reunify with the South Koreans. Their plan includes an information operations phase that has been masterfully thought out and executed."

"Why do you say that, Sam?"

"Sir, because everything that has happened so far has been anticipated by the North Koreans. They are using the media to quickly get their spin on things. The massacre of the civilians in the Chorwon Valley was immediately followed up by a TV interview of a North Korean general who just happened to be there at exactly the right time, and who just happens to speak English perfectly. The same thing goes for the satellite photos and the nuke. It's all too pat and too timely. They have had announcements for the media literally minutes after shit has gone down. I feel like we're playing catch up ball."

Smith sighed. "Yeah, me too. What do you think their next step will be?"

"Sir, if I were them, I'd make a permanent cease fire conditional on all US forces being withdrawn from the Korean Peninsula. Sir, I need to ask you what the secdef told you about the nuke earlier when you ran Johnny and I out of the room? If you can't tell me, I'll understand, but I think it may help me to figure out what their next step will be if I know."

Smith didn't even hesitate before he answered. "President Hyun told President Preston that the Japanese launched the nuclear missile the other day. Part of the meeting between Hyun and Kim Jong Il is for Kim to provide proof of that to Hyun."

Sampson nodded. "Yes, sir, and that fits very neatly and nicely into the North Korean plan I was talking about. The only country South Korea fears and hates more than North Korea is Japan. If I was Kim and wanted to point the finger at somebody else for the nuke, Japan is the best choice. Even better than us."

Smith was clearly puzzled and being tired didn't help. He asked slowly, "Why even better than us, Sam?"

"Sir, because that dog may hunt for a while, but it's too easy for us to get the IAEA and others to back us up on our stockpiles being one hundred percent accounted for. Accusing us directly would only cause the focus to come back on them sooner rather than later."

"So who do you think did it, Sam? I just can't buy that the Japanese did it, but I can't deny that they certainly have the technology to produce those weapons if they wanted to. Who else would send a cruise missile with a nuke on it into Korea?"

"Sir, I don't think it was a cruise missile, and I think I have a way of verifying that."

"How?"

"Sir, if the 2nd ID had their counter battery radars up, they would have recorded a cruise missile flight. NORAD says it wasn't a North Korean No-dong missile, and NORAD wouldn't pick up any missile that doesn't break the stratosphere. A Q-37 radar would pick up a cruise missile if it passed anywhere in the radar's arc. Sir, we need to call the 2nd ID and check."

Smith nodded his agreement. "Yeah, let's give them a call and have them review their radar tapes. What if they come up empty, Sam, and didn't see a missile? What's your thought then?"

"Sir, that means it was brought in on the ground. Possibly through one of the tunnels the North Koreans have dug under the DMZ. If it wasn't a cruise missile, then that's the only means of delivery left. And that will clearly mean the North Koreans did it. I just can't see a bunch of Japanese wandering up to the DMZ with a nuke through the middle of the ROK Army and getting away undetected."

Smith snorted in agreement. "Yeah, I can't see that happening either. Let me know what the 2nd ID says."

"Roger, sir."

**1200 hours
3 November
Star News Broadcast**

The pretty young lady who read the news and always smiled was smiling again as she said, "In an historic meeting today at the Panmunjon Peace Village, the leaders of the two Koreas met for the first time ever." The film footage showed President Hyun and Kim Jong Il both smiling and shaking hands for the camera. Kim Jong Il did not look at all like the photos of him everybody had seen in the past. He no longer had the wild hair and the Mao jacket on. Instead, his hair was neatly barbered, and he wore a very expensive and well cut suit. He looked very much like the leader of a country and not like some long haired crank. The transition was startling.

The announcer continued, "Both leaders engaged in private talks for over an hour. Neither would say what they discussed, but both said the talks were productive. The two leaders are returning to their respective capitals to consult with their governments, but both pledged a continuation of the cease fire and promised to meet again later in the week."

"In a statement released from the White House, President Preston praised the two leaders and said he hoped that the talks would result in a permanent peace on the Korean Peninsula. President Preston strongly hinted in his statement that he had personally brokered the deal for this historic meeting. The White House has also announced that President Preston has delayed the arrival of a carrier task force scheduled to arrive off the coast of South Korea tomorrow in an effort to reduce the tensions on the Korean Peninsula. In a brief statement from the Pentagon, Secretary of Defense Ralph Brooks promised that the United States would continue to fully support South Korea on the field of battle should the cease fire fail."

"To recap the news of this hour …"

**1500 hours
3 November
USFK/Combined Forces Command CP**

Sampson motioned to Johnny Raymer to follow him on his way to the CINC's office. "C'mon, Johnny. I got the gouge from the 2nd ID on the radars. Let's go tell the man."

"What the shit is the *gouge*, Sam?"

"Uh, what? Oh, the gouge? That's navy talk for the *poop* in army talk. I thought you were joint staff qualified, dickhead."

Raymer laughed. "Yeah, I am but I could never pass the other services' jargon tests. So either speak army to me or speak English to me, but leave air force, marine and navy out of it or I won't get it."

"Fair enough but you're pathetic, Johnny. Just frigging pathetic." He stopped at the door to the CINC's office and knocked twice. He heard Smith tell him to come in. The two men stepped into the office. Both were surprised to see a ROK four star sitting with General Smith on the couch.

Sampson recovered first. "I About Shit! How the hell are you? You still cheating at golf?"

General Moon stood up and embraced Sampson. "Sam, my old friend! You are the one who cheats at golf. I'm too good a player to do that. And you cannot call me 'I About Shit' anymore, I'm a very important man now. Yes, a very important man," Moon finished with a big grin.

It was Sampson's turn to grin. "Yes, sir!"

General Smith motioned Raymer to close the office door and waved everybody to seats. He turned to Sampson. "Sam, what do you have?"

Sampson hesitated and Smith said, "General Moon and I have agreed that we will have absolutely no secrets from each other. Please proceed, Sam."

"Yes, sir, I understand. Sir, I just got off the phone with the DIVARTY commander in the 2nd ID, and they have confirmed one hundred percent that none of the radars picked up a cruise missile at the time of the nuclear explosion or prior to it. They had four radars cued to the north that would have picked up any missile coming in from a three hundred and sixty degree circle around ground zero. If it had happened, they would have seen it."

"So you're convinced now that it was delivered by ground?"

"Yes, sir, I am. There is no other way for the nuke to get there."

General Moon spoke, "But we believe that the explosion was far too big for a North Korean bomb. We are almost certain that they do not possess such a weapon. How can that be, Sam?"

"General Moon, I can only say that the North Koreans either did make a bomb that big or they bought one that big from China or Russia, or even Pakistan or India. We know for sure it wasn't the Japanese now. We'll never know for sure whose it was, but the only way it could get there was if the North Koreans put it there. Do you agree with my assessment on that?"

Moon pursed his lips. He said slowly, "Yes, Sam, I do agree but right now that doesn't matter."

Smith spoke, "Why is that General Moon? Why doesn't it matter?"

"Because President Hyun informed me when he returned from Panmunjon that the Japanese have done this thing. That is now the truth."

Sampson gasped. "But I have just proven that the Japanese couldn't have done it! How can you now say they did?"

Moon smiled wanly. "Sam, you must remember your time over here better than that. If I tell President Hyun he is wrong, then he loses face and I lose face for telling him. And he cannot go back to the Dear Leader and tell him he is a liar. President Hyun *knows* the Japanese didn't do it, but it is politically expedient right now to *say* that they did. And that is now the truth. It will not change. What is the saying you used to have about the hearts and minds of your opponents? I can't remember it exactly, but it fits our situation."

"If you grab them by the balls, their hearts and minds will follow?"

Moon nodded and smiled. "Yes, that is what you used to say, I remember now." Moon turned serious, "And right now the North Koreans have got us by the balls. Sam, you would always tell me that our plan to defend Seoul was wrong. Well, you were right. I have reviewed my troop dispositions, and what was it you used to say about Seoul?"

"That it would become a self-imposed POW compound for your army."

Moon was nodding as he remembered the words. "And that is what we now have. Our losses have been light but we gave up everything north of Seoul and are now firmly contained in Seoul. I have my staff working on a plan to counterattack, but I don't think President Hyun will be interested. He will particularly not be interested unless there is a sizeable US presence to assist us." Moon turned to General Smith. "What can I tell President Hyun about that force?"

Smith replied uncomfortably, "It will not be available for the foreseeable future, General Moon. We are over committed right now in Iraq and Afghanistan and have no forces readily available for Korea."

"Other than your paratroopers who are desperately trying to learn to be tankers?"

"Yes, other than them and the *Kitty Hawk* carrier battle group."

Moon smiled sadly, "Yes, and they are of not much help because they cannot take and hold ground." Moon turned back to Sampson. "So you see, Sam, my old friend, our hearts and minds will have to go pretty much where the Dear Leader says they must go. So the Japanese are responsible for the nuclear bomb. We will not announce that publicly, but it will leak out just the same. We lose nothing by accusing the Japanese; we lose everything by accusing the North Koreans."

All the men sat quietly when Moon had finished. All were wondering how this thing could have gone so badly so quickly. Other than the horrific casualties caused by the nuclear explosion, losses on both sides had been light. It just didn't seem like it had been much of a war yet to be so irretrievably lost.

0230 hours
4 November
The White House

The Secret Service agent posted outside of the president's bedroom clearly did not want to wake him up, but the officer from the communications center was insistent. The president of South Korea wanted to speak to the president. The matter was urgent. The Secret Service agent steeled himself and went through the door. He got a blast of explicative from the president just as he expected he would. The communications officer pretended not to hear. Preston came out in his bathrobe with his hair mussed and was clearly not happy to be awakened in the middle of the night. He walked to the end of the hallway to his private office in the residence and flopped into his chair. He motioned for the communications officer to set the call up which he quickly did and then scooted from the room.

"President Preston! Good morning to you! I hope I didn't wake you up. What time is it there, by the way?"

Preston was not amused and got the point of the middle of the night phone call from Hyun paying him back for a few days ago. "No, President Hyun, I was already awake." The lie didn't work because he could not get the sleep out of his voice and it came out in a croak. Preston cleared his throat. "My communications officer said your call was urgent, President Hyun. What has happened over there? Have the North Koreans attacked again?"

"Oh, no, no, no, Mister President! The war is over now! The Dear Leader and I signed a peace treaty just twenty minutes ago. I know you will be happy to hear this because we have been in a state of war with North Korea since June 25th 1950. This is indeed a momentous moment and I wanted to share it with you personally. Are you not pleased?" Hyun asked mockingly.

Preston rubbed his temples and ran his hands through his tousled hair. He replied sarcastically, "Oh, yes, President Hyun, I am very pleased for you. But what did you have to give up in order to get this treaty with the Dear Leader?" There was an unmistakable sneer in Preston's voice as he said the words Dear Leader.

"Oh, nothing much. We have agreed that we will unify our two countries, which is already long overdue. The north has many extra workers and we have much industry and are short workers, so that is nice. We also are now a nuclear power, which is nice too. We will both boycott Japanese products which we already do, and we will establish two political parties to represent the two parts of the country. The Dear Leader and I will remain the leaders of our respective parts of the country and report to a combined parliament until such time as we feel that open elections are appropriate for the people. You see? It is all very simple."

Preston couldn't contain the sarcasm in his voice as he said, "So in effect, you and Kim are co-dictators until further notice? I expected better of you, Hyun. I really did. You disappoint me."

"No, Mister President, *you* disappoint me. We have been your steadfast ally for over sixty years, and in our first moment of real need in all that time, you failed to support us. We went to Vietnam and Iraq for you, but you would not even come to *Korea* for us? What I have done is to accommodate my enemy so that my people won't suffer in a war that we cannot win. I will not have the people of South Korea die or suffer so that the United States can continue to futilely try to control events in Iraq and Afghanistan. You abandoned us and we must make our own way now. So be it. There is one other thing, President Preston." Hyun paused, waiting for a response.

Preston said, "What is it, Hyun?"

"I am asking the Secretary General of the United Nations to remove all United Nations forces from South Korea by the end of this week."

"What are you saying, Hyun? Why are you telling me this?"

"Ah, President Preston, you are more uninformed than even I thought you were which explains a lot to me. Your General Smith and his staff will have to leave South Korea."

Preston thought about that briefly. He really didn't care. That would reflect badly on the UN and not the United States. He responded, "Okay, Hyun. That's fine with us. Again, why are you telling me this?"

"Ah, again I see that you do not know what the impact of this request will be. President Preston, that also means that all United States forces must depart the Peninsula because technically they are here only under a United Nations mandate now that we are no longer officially allies. Does that paint a clearer picture for you now?"

Preston swore out loud. Hell, yes, that painted a clearer picture! The United States was being ejected from the Korean Peninsula and nobody would bother to know or care that it was a result of a United Nations mandate. Christ! This was a blow to American prestige that would have world-wide implications. Preston gasped out, "You can't do that, Hyun. You just can't do that! We need to have a series of tri-lateral discussions to discuss US withdrawal first."

"There will be no discussions and I do not have a choice, President Preston. I absolutely do not have a choice. You did not provide me the promised combat power to have a choice." Hyun's voice hardened. "The Dear Leader has made it very clear that the future of South Korea depends upon the withdrawal of all UN and US forces from the Peninsula by a week from today. And Tom?"

Preston was shocked that the usually very correct and formal Hyun had called him by his first name. He was slow to respond. He didn't know Hyun's first name and struggled to find the right salutation to respond with. Finally, he just said, "Yes, President Hyun?"

"You didn't hear this from me, but I don't think the Dear Leader is going to just allow your forces to walk away from all this. Goodbye." The line went dead.

Preston shook his head. Now what the hell did that mean? He went back to bed.

1000 hours
6 November
USFK/Combined Forces Command CP

General Smith fiddled with his pen until the men finished entering the small conference room and sat down. Raymer was the last man in and closed the door. It was a small group, and it was Americans only. None of the ROK's had come back to the headquarters. Smith began without preamble, "Okay, we've got our marching orders from the Joint Chiefs." Smith pushed the short message down the table to his J-5, General Dave Walker. "Dave, read it to everybody, please."

Walker picked the message up and began reading, "From Chairman, Joint Chiefs of Staff, Washington, D.C. to Commander in Chief, United Nations Command Korea, slash Commander, United States Forces Korea slash Former Commander in Chief, Combined Forces Command Korea." Walker paused and looked questioningly at Smith.

Smith said tonelessly, "Yeah, Dave it says former. We're no longer a combined headquarters with the ROK's. Keep reading and you'll see why."

Walker continued, "By order of the President of the United States, General Robertson L. Smith is relieved of all duties as the Commander in Chief, Combined Forces Command, Republic of South Korea. By order of the Secretary General and the Security Council of the United Nations, Commander in Chief, United Nations Command Korea will plan and execute the withdrawal of all United Nations Forces from the Republic of South Korea and the Joint Security

Agency at Panmunjon no later than twelve hundred hours, nine November. By order of the Chairman of the Joint Chiefs of Staff, Commander, United States Forces Korea will plan and execute the withdrawal of all United States Forces and equipment from the Republic of South Korea no later than twelve hundred hours, eleven November. Message ends." Walker quit reading and looked at Smith again with a puzzled expression on his face. "Sir, it's not signed."

"Yes, I know Dave. That's called plausible deniability back in the Pentagon in case there's ever an investigation into all this. I've confirmed the order verbally with the chairman and that's as good as we're going to get it." Smith turned to his J-4 logistics officer, Brigadier General Richard Dominquez. "Rich, I need you to figure out how much equipment we can remove in the time available. I've asked the chairman to get permission from the Japanese to bring it to Japan initially if we have to. Rent whatever bottoms you need locally to make that happen. My intent is to destroy whatever we can't fly or float out of here in a week, but the ROK's may try to prevent us from doing that. General Moon will be here in an hour so I can sound him out on that."

Smith paused and looked at his officers before continuing in a sober voice, "I need you guys to keep your spirits up as we go through this. Your troops need to see you being up and not down. They're going to ask you how we lost the war and I want you to tell them that we didn't lose the war. This was all politics and had nothing to do with them. They know as well as I do that we never got into this fight before it was over. I need them to keep their morale up too. We're getting kicked out of Korea, but I don't want anybody looking like a whipped dog over it. We leave with our heads up and our shoulders back. On the good news side, the NEO is finally going. The first two planes with our families departed Kimpo an hour ago. The rest of the families will all be evacuated in the next twenty-four hours."

Some of the men smiled. That was good news and it would boost everybody's morale.

Smith continued, "Rich, as ironic as it is, a Chinese fellow is coming over from their embassy to offer shipping to us. Meet with him and use them as a last resort, but use them if you have to. I'd rather be accused of using commie shipping than losing equipment to the North Koreans. Can you imagine that Report of Survey?"

The men laughed. The Report of Survey was a process used by all the services to hold someone, usually an officer, financially liable for lost or destroyed equipment. The stories that had come out from the evacuation of Vietnam about officers being held liable for equipment losses they had no control over were numerous. Most of the stories were humorous, but some were decidedly not funny at all.

Smith turned serious again. "Hal?"

Hal Loomis, the three star commander of the US Air Force in Korea said, "Yes, sir?"

"Start flying your planes out today. Coordinate for tanker support to get them to Hawaii. That's directly from the chairman by the way, so I imagine it's probably already in the can. Give me an up once it's done. Coordinate with Rich for whatever needs to be taken to the ports. Hal, if it's not permanently nailed down, I want it taken out of here."

"Got it, sir."

"Okay, last but not least, Dave I want you to generate an order for my signature that gets all this going. And yes, I will sign it," Smith finished dryly.

"Uh, sir?" General Blair raised his hand like an elementary school child asking to go to the bathroom as he spoke.

"Yes, General Blair?" Smith responded coldly.

Blair slowly lowered his hand. "Sir, shouldn't I as the CJ-3 be generating that order instead of the CJ-5?" The fact that Blair had still used the C for Combined didn't escape the notice of the other men in the room. Several shook their heads or rolled their eyes. Jesus, what a dummy!

Smith responded, "No, General Blair. I want the J-5 to put that order together. But since you asked, I have one other order from the chairman and this one is signed. I'll read it to you but I'll skip the addresses and just read the one liner below them. Quote, The Secretary of Defense has announced that Major General Robert Charliss Blair, US Army has been nominated to the grade of Lieutenant General and will proceed immediately to Washington, D.C. for duties to be determined by the Secretary. Unquote."

Smith saw the huge smile that lit up Blair's face, but Smith did not smile in return. Nor did any of the other men assembled in the room. "As I said Blair, this message is actually signed and coincidentally, for the history books apparently, it was back dated to three days ago so you technically weren't here when we *lost* the war," Smith finished sarcastically. "Please excuse me if I don't congratulate you. A car and driver are standing by to take you to Kimpo, and I want you on the next plane out of here."

The smile had disappeared from Blair's face as he took Smith's words in. "Sir, I don't understand."

"Of course you do, Blair. You engineered this whole damned thing with Ralph Brooks. You've been on the phone with him every day since this started, or is the communications officer lying to me about that?" Smith could tell from the flush that rose in Blair's face that it was true. "So, since it's only a surprise to the rest of us, I'm sure you're all packed and ready to go. The car leaves in ten minutes, General, with or without you. You are dismissed from this command."

Blair just sat there and didn't move. The other officers stared at him and couldn't understand why he didn't get the hell out of there!

A whole minute ticked off, and Smith looked at his watch. "Now you have nine minutes, Blair." He paused and then roared out in a grating voice, "Blair, you stupid bastard, get out of my goddamned headquarters!"

Smith's order hit Blair like a slap in the face, and the harsh and loud delivery were finally enough to penetrate the dense mental fog that Blair always seemed to be in. Blair jumped up like he had just taken an electric shock to his butt, knocking his chair over in the process. He literally ran red faced from the room, fumbling at the door and ineffectually pushing it to get out when it was clearly marked 'Pull to Open' in large block letters in English and Hangul. Blair finally managed it, and bolted from the room. As they watched Blair depart some of the remaining officers shook their heads and some nodded their heads, but all had the exact same thought, 'What a stupid bastard!' Nobody was sorry to see him leave, but all were absolutely appalled that he was being promoted!

Smith looked at the rest of his staff. "I'm sorry, gentlemen, for losing my temper. I hope you will forgive me." He meant it sincerely and the officers nodded their acceptance of his apology. "Sam, you're the J-3 now and I want you there when General Moon comes in. Until he gets here, I want you to take a look at how we get the 2nd ID off the peninsula. The *Kitty Hawk* carrier battle group will be available to assist. And Sam?"

"Yes, sir?"

"Figure out what happens if the 2nd ID has to evacuate under pressure. A little birdie told President Preston that he thought the North Koreans might not give the 2nd ID a free ride out of here."

"Roger, sir. Will do."

**1100 hours
6 November
USFK CP**

General Moon seemed genuinely uncomfortable as he sat in the CINC's office. Unlike the last meeting where he had been alone with the Americans, this time he had two ROK colonels with him. It was very obvious to the three American that the colonels were there to watch Moon and report back anything he said to the

Americans. Moon had apologized because neither colonel spoke English, but Sampson remembered one of the colonels from of his second tour in Korea, and knew for a fact that he spoke English very well. The look the ROK colonel gave Sampson when Moon apologized confirmed it. The colonel remembered Sampson too.

Smith spoke. "General Moon, I don't understand the problem here. Am I missing something?"

"General Smith, my orders from President Hyun are very clear. All of the officers and soldiers who are here in Korea under the United Nations mandate are to fly out of Korea from Kimpo Airport. That is also the order of the Secretary General. The others who were part of US/ROK Combined Forces Command must be moved to the 2nd Infantry Division for evacuation with them."

"But General Moon, that just doesn't make any sense to us! Why would we possibly want to do that? Isn't it President Hyun's wish that all American forces be quickly removed from the Peninsula? Or is this coming from the Dear Leader?"

The flicker in Moon's eyes answered Smith's question. "No, General Smith. This is from President Hyun." Moon could not look Smith in the eyes as he told the lie. He knew that the Americans understood where the orders were really coming from. It was not a lie if the truth was obvious. Neither of the ROK colonels seemed to notice Moon's more subtle communication with his eyes. Both were instead looking at Smith to gauge his reaction for their report.

Smith sat back into his chair. "There are only a handful of officers and soldiers here who are not part of the United Nations Command staff. The majority of the rest are already down at Pusan. Are they to be brought north to the 2nd ID also?"

Moon shook his head. "No, President Hyun understands that they should depart from there. We feel that journey would be too perilous because we cannot control the SPF teams that are still deployed along the roads in the south. The Dear Leader has agreed that it would be tragic if one of those teams could not be contacted and attacked your convoy unknowingly." Moon paused. "It is the desire of both the Dear Leader and President Hyun that all foreign forces be safely removed from the Peninsula. Both agree that it will be easier to control and safeguard the evacuation as two separate entities, the United Nations forces and the United States forces. In our minds, these are two distinct groups."

"What safeguards are going to be in place to guarantee the safety of the soldiers we send to the 2nd ID, General Moon? What about the SPF teams along that route?"

"We have the word of the Dear Leader that he can control the actions of those teams. In fact, he has ordered their withdrawal and the movement will not be allowed to begin until he feels certain the route is safe." Moon spread his hands in a gesture of what more can I say?

Smith didn't look like he was convinced but could only nod his head in response to the Dear Leader's promise. He said, "I have ordered the 2nd ID to move to the coast starting at noon today as we agreed. Has that agreement changed in light of this new requirement?"

"No, General Smith. That remains the same. ROK MP's along the route will assist in that movement. And we agree to the rules of engagement you proposed."

"That we will return fire if attacked?"

"Yes."

Smith looked over at Sampson. "Sam, do you have any questions?"

"Yes, sir, I do. General Moon, can you tell us anything about the dispositions of the North Korean Army forces in the east? Specifically have they crossed the DMZ during the cease fire? Our intel guys seem to think they have."

Again Moon's eyes flickered before he answered, "No, Colonel Sampson. They are all north of the DMZ. He looked Sampson directly in the eyes and the two ROK colonels were watching Moon closely.

Sampson nodded, apparently satisfied. "Thank you, sir. That clears that up for us. General Smith, sir, I have no further questions."

"Okay, Sam. Thanks. General Moon, how long before you think we can send the convoy of people to the 2nd ID?"

Moon answered quickly, "We think soon, General Smith. Maybe tomorrow." Moon coughed as if embarrassed. "We will want to review your lists of those going by convoy and those going by air from Kimpo, General Smith."

Smith was visibly surprised by Moon's statement. He recovered quickly and asked coldly, "And may I ask why, General?"

Moon shrugged as if to say he didn't know why. One of the ROK colonels spoke up in passable English, "Because we have promised the Dear Leader that we will not allow you to manipulate your lists and make your United States presence here seem smaller than it was. His point is to show the world that you abused your authority under the United Nations mandate to force South Korea to remain separated from their brothers in the north. Your large military presence in South Korea will be readily seen to be what it was; an occupation force."

Smith looked at the ROK colonel in surprise and asked, "Exactly who are you, Colonel? You don't sound like any ROK officer I've ever known."

"I am Colonel Lee Pok of the North Korean People's Army, General Smith. I was known as Lieutenant Colonel Lee Kim in the Republic of South Korea Army, and I was even assigned to this headquarters as a communications officer for three years before you came to Korea!" Lee said boastfully. "I will be *General* Lee Pok according to the Dear Leader in the new People's Republic of Korea Army," Lee finished smugly.

Sampson was watching Moon and could tell by his expression that he genuinely did not know that Lee was a North Korean officer.

Smith just nodded his head. He, like many Americans, had long suspected that the North Koreans had infiltrated the South Korean Army, but this was the first time it had ever been confirmed as far as he knew. Crap! He turned back to Moon who was still staring at Lee. "General Moon, I formally protest this requirement to submit lists for your review and approval. I will not take such an action until ordered to do so by my president and the United Nations Secretary General. Colonel Lee, you may inform the Dear Leader of what I have just said. Gentlemen, this meeting is concluded." Smith rose and walked stiffly from the room. Sampson and Raymer quickly followed him down the hall.

Smith turned in to his office, waving the two officers in behind him. Sampson closed the door. Smith just looked at the two men and didn't say anything. He pulled a tablet to him and scribbled out the words "we have to assume this office and this entire headquarters is bugged!" Sampson and Raymer nodded. Smith scribbled again, "don't say anything, just follow me outside." All three men quietly walked out of the office. Smith led them out of the bunker command post and past the startled American guards at the entrance. Smith put his fingers to his lips signaling the guards to be quiet. The guards silently followed Smith up the hill from the bunker and automatically set up a security perimeter around him.

Smith sat on the ground and the others did the same. He turned to Sampson. "So unless I've gone senile, Sam, the North Koreans are across the DMZ in the east?"

"Yes, sir. I don't think his two watch dogs picked up on it, but Moon really went out on a limb for us."

"Yeah. I had the same thought. Johnny, can you figure out how we can talk to Wellens without using the communications in the CP?"

"Yes, sir, I'll have it set up in about ten minutes. We'll have to assume that everything else we said previously was monitored. Do you want to call General Loomis back once we get set up?"

Smith agreed with Raymer's assessment and thought about his conversation with Hal Loomis just minutes before the meeting with General Moon. Loomis had said the ROK Air Force was refusing to let him take some of his more sensitive equipment out of Korea. Smith had told him to use any force necessary short of starting an all out shooting war to get his gear out. If it looked like he couldn't get it out, he was to destroy it. Smith shrugged. It was too late now and the North Koreans needed to understand that Smith was willing to use force if necessary to remove American equipment. He shook his head in answer to Raymer's question and turned to Sampson.

"Sam, I truly believe the 2nd ID is going to get pressed by the North Koreans as they try to evacuate. What do you think?"

Sampson nodded in agreement. "Yes, sir, I'm convinced the North Koreans will do just that."

"Well, the question I have is why would they do that? What's in it for them? They have already won this thing, so why make it hard at the end?"

"Sir, because they can. They have the power to do so right now."

"To what purpose other than spite, Sam? Again, what's in it for them?" Smith asked skeptically. "These guys never do anything unless it somehow benefits them, but I'm not seeing a benefit here."

Sampson responded slowly, "Sir, the benefit is Kim Jong Il gets to tell the rest of the world that he won the war *and* he defeated the United States Army in the field. He knows that has never been done before. We've lost a few battles in the past, but we've never lost a war in the field. He wants to inflict maximum casualties and to make sure the media gets a film of every damn piece of it. He'll also be looking to take some prisoners that he can use later on to barter with us. If this hadn't gone as he had planned, I think he was going to use the families at Kimpo for that purpose. Now that he has the 2nd ID in the bag, he can afford to let the non-combatants go."

Smith thought about what Sampson had just said and he couldn't find a flaw in Sampson's logic. "So it's all about face? The United States loses face and Kim gains face?"

Sampson only nodded in response. After a pause, Smith continued thoughtfully, "Sam, what if I just tell Wellens to abandon his equipment and get his troops off as quickly as possible to the ships in the carrier battle group? We would certainly be embarrassed to lose the equipment but we wouldn't lose any troops. Kim wouldn't get his fight."

Sampson shook his head. "Sir, it's already too late. The ROK MP's will guide Wellens' convoys along the few roads through the mountains, but I'm damned sure if we were able to get some reconnaissance over those mountains, we'll find the NKPA is already there in force. As Wellens pulls back to the coast, the NKPA will close up behind him. Kim is going to have at least four divisions if not five or even six poised to hit the 2nd ID. He's going to smash a fly with a sledgehammer as a show of force and power, and leave nothing to chance."

"Well, shit! What the hell do we do now?"

"Sir, Bobby Wellens is going to have to grab his nuts with both hands and pull off a withdrawal under pressure."

Smith groaned. "Yeah, like Bobby has a clue on how to do that, Sam! That's the hardest tactical maneuver in the book and Bobby couldn't lead a Boy Scout Troop to a damned weenie roast!"

Sampson actually smiled at the analogy. "Well, sir, the good news is I'll be with him."

Smith was surprised at Sampson's statement. "Why is that, Sam?"

"Because I'm clearly not a United Nations pogue over here and the ROK's all know it. I'll be the first one they'll challenge if I form up with the UN crowd for evacuation. If I was still just a contractor, I could go to Kimpo with the non-combatants but it's too late for that now. Besides, my son is over with the 2nd ID and I'd just as soon be with him when this thing goes down."

Smith was silent. He had forgotten that young Sean Sampson was in the 2nd ID. What Sampson was telling him was that he was going to go to the coast with the 2nd ID and take up a rifle. He paused, and then asked tentatively, "How would you fight this battle, Sam? I mean if you were calling the shots."

Sampson seemed to have anticipated the question because he answered immediately. "Sir, the first thing we have to do is set the conditions to break contact with the North Koreans. They are going to try and hug us tight and we need a way to shove them back. In the good old days we would have used napalm and naval gunfire support, but the navy no longer does that and we quit using napalm twenty years ago. That leaves the really old fashioned way where we form a detachment left in contact while the remainder make a run for the beach. We'll lose the detachment, but hopefully enough of the main body will get off to justify the losses. We'll also have to leave our vehicles and heavy equipment behind but we can try to destroy as much of it as we can."

"What about bringing in helicopters to get the troops out?"

Sampson shook his head. "Won't work, sir. The NKPA has too many shoulder fired SAMS. We have to go out by boat. We can't afford to lose a helicopter load at a time like happened to the Eighth Army staff last week."

Smith nodded his head sadly. The loss of that chopper full of officers and soldiers had hit Smith really hard.

Johnny Raymer had been listening to all this and finally said quietly, "I know where we can get napalm and naval gun fire support."

Smith and Sampson just stared at Raymer. Smith finally said, "How?"

"Sir, the ROK's have napalm stockpiled at an airbase outside of Taegue. I saw it there about a year ago and asked about it. My ROK counterpart said that it would still be used against the North Koreans when the time came even if the United States no longer believed in it. He had served in Vietnam and was a firm believer in napalm as an attention getter. As far as naval gunfire support, sir, you're going to need to talk to Secretary Brooks or maybe even President Preston."

"Okay, Johnny. What am I saying to them?"

"Sir, did you notice the one liner in the executive summary a couple of weeks ago about the completion of the navy's first DD-21 destroyer?"

"I saw it and thought to myself, well, 'whoopee for the navy.' Another damn boat they'll never use since they never seem to fight anybody anymore."

"Right, sir. I had the same thought until I remembered an article I read about the DD-21. The ship was specifically designed to provide naval gunfire support for the marines. It's been funded on again and off again because the navy isn't wildly enthusiastic about it. They think naval gunfire support is old fashioned thinking in the age of cruise missiles. It's only because the Marine Corps mafia has been able to successfully lobby Congress that it got built at all. It's done and ready to go to sea trials once the navy gets off their dead ass and sets it up. So far they haven't budged on it. It's sitting in a shipyard in Seattle waiting on the navy."

"But how long will it take the navy to crew it and do sea trials, Johnny? I need the son-of-a-bitch over here yesterday!"

"Roger, sir. We need to ask the secretary or the president to order the ship deployed immediately with the crew it has on board now."

"I thought you said the navy hadn't manned it yet?"

"They haven't, sir, but the ship is manned by retired navy guys who are all contractors now. The president can order them all back to active duty. The ship can steam at over fifty knots and could be here in three days, but we need to make it happen now, sir."

Smith stood up and dusted his trousers off. "Well, shit, why didn't you say so, Johnny? Get me those comms out here and I'll start with the secretary. If he goes stupid on me, I'll call the president."

"Sir, don't you want to call the chairman first?"

"No, Johnny. I need to talk to somebody who can make a decision. As much as I personally like Pat Goodman, he's the perfect yes man to Brooks and wouldn't make a decision like this on his own if his life depended on it. C'mon, Sam. We need to figure out how to get that napalm from the ROK's. I don't think just asking for it will work out too well."

0600 hours
7 November
On board Marine Corps C-130 Mike Lima 2

"Roger, tower, this is US Marine Corps C-130 Mike Lima Two declaring an in-flight emergency and requesting permission to land."

A voice came back on the radio, "Mike Lima Two, state your emergency."

"Roger, my outboard port engine has caught on fire and is stopped."

There were voices in Hangul arguing in the background when the tower answered with a cryptic, "Wait out."

"Roger, tower. I can't wait. My other port engine is overheating now and I need to put this bitch down!"

There was no response from the tower. The pilot looked over his shoulder at the marine captain who was the mission commander. The pilot was a major but the captain was in charge. "Okay, Skipper. Your call."

The marine captain did not even hesitate, "Put her down, Major, and taxi to the south end of the runway. My guess is we'll be leaving like our ass is on fire so keep the engines ready!" The major grinned and turned into his final approach. He had cut the power to his outboard port engine and a smoke grenade was spewing smoke from that engine. At least it should look real to the people in the tower. They all hoped so anyhow.

The plane touched down with a squeal of tires and still trailing smoke. Those on board could see activity around the tower, but the flight line was empty. A jeep sped away from the tower and followed the C-130 down the runway. The jeep was loaded with armed soldiers.

The captain shouted over the roar of the engines. "Okay, we've got company. Lock and load but take your signals from me. If we can't bullshit them, then and only then will we kill them. Got it?"

The five marines all nodded and chambered rounds into their rifles, then checked to make sure their safeties were on. As the plane slowed down, the back ramp started to lower. The marines all moved to the edge of the ramp. The plane stopped and they followed the captain out. He waved at the approaching jeep and smiled. His marines all kept their rifles on their shoulders at sling arms, but were ready to whip them down in a fraction of a second and start firing if the captain signaled them to do so.

The jeep pulled up and the ROK soldiers in it looked puzzled, but the ROK major who got out of the jeep was distinctly angry. He started yelling at the marine captain and making hand and arm gestures as if to shoo them all away. The marine captain kept smiling and said, "Hey, man. I don't speak the language. Speakee English? You speakee English?"

The ROK major got louder and more adamant in his shooing gestures. The marine captain shrugged and pointed to the stopped engine and shrugged again as if to say, "Hey, buddy. What the hell you want me to do? The sumbitch is broke!"

The ROK major yelled something at the soldiers still in the jeep and they all shook their heads no. In exasperation he climbed back into the jeep and yelled something to the Americans and sped off back towards the tower.

"Sergeant Wilfred!"

"Sir!"

"Shag your ass around that fence and tell me if you see some shit that looks like bombs."

"Aye, aye, sir!"

"Corporal Wilson, get ready to pull the dollies off the plane." Wilson slapped two of the other marines on the shoulder and led them back into the plane.

Sergeant Wilfred came back from around the fence. "Skipper, there's shit over there that looks just like bombs with no fins and they're heavy."

"Okay, Corporal Wilson, go get 'em." Wilson and his two Marines each pulled a dolly off the back ramp of the plane and disappeared around the fence. Each man had made two trips before the jeep was spotted headed back from the tower.

The marine captain shouted, "Okay, marines! Belay what you're doing, they're coming back." The men stopped and pulled the dollies out of sight behind the fence.

As the jeep pulled up, the same ROK major jumped out first followed by a ROK lieutenant. The major was firing off Hangul at a rapid clip and the lieutenant had to run to catch up with him. The lieutenant turned to the marine captain and said, "My major wants to know who you are?"

The marine captain responded with a wide grin and stepped forward with his hand outstretched to shake hands with the ROK major. "Well, I'm Captain Shawn McNulty, United States Marine Corps and I'm pleased to meet you!" The ROK major couldn't help himself and took McNulty's hand out of reflex and received a powerful handshake. McNulty turned to the lieutenant and said, "And who are you guys? It's awful nice of you to let us land here to fix our plane. When we lost that engine I'll tell you I thought we were going into the drink for sure!"

The lieutenant translated and the two ROK officers conversed briefly. The major was shaking his head vehemently. "My major says you do not have permission to land and you must leave now. We are no longer allies. He says you must leave right now. He insist."

McNulty feigned surprise. "But what if we crash? We can't just fly with three engines. That's why it has four engines, you know. I mean why would it have four engines if only three would do? I mean jeez Louise, what is he *thinking*? I can't leave until the plane is fixed, so what do we do now? I mean I don't want to be here anymore than you don't want me to be here. Ask the major what I should do, please."

McNulty's southern accent was hard for the ROK lieutenant to follow and he asked, "Please, what is Cheese Louise, Captain? I do not understand."

McNulty laughed. "Oh, she's just a girl I used to date back in Louisiana where I come from. She's not here right now so it doesn't matter." The lieutenant was clearly confused by McNulty's answer and the marines snickered. McNulty said again, "Please ask your major what I am to do. My plane is broken and I cannot leave until it is fixed. Can he get me help, like get me a mechanic or something?"

The lieutenant translated and the major became very agitated, waving his arms and shouting in Hangul. The lieutenant finally asked McNulty, "My major wants to know if you will surrender to him?"

McNulty didn't need to feign surprise this time. "Well, hell no, I won't surrender to him! What the hell is he talking about?"

The Hangul flew back and forth and the lieutenant finally said, "My major says we are no longer allies and you must surrender to him."

"Ask your major if he is declaring war on the United States of America, because that it what it sounds like to me." The lieutenant visibly paled once he translated the question in his mind from English into Hangul. He fired the question at the major who also visibly paled and shook his head no vigorously.

"I've got your major's answer. Now tell him I'm staying here until he gets me help to fix my plane, and the longer I'm here, the harder it's going to be for him to explain it to his boss. I'll wait right here until you guys get back to me." McNulty smiled and shook both officers' hands and walked them back to their jeep. He waved to them as they drove away. McNulty had served in Korea. He knew neither officer would send him help, and he also knew that both would disappear for a while hoping the problem would just go away in their absence.

"Okay, Corporal Wilson, get back to your thievery and be damned quick. These guys will be back and they'll probably bring friends next time. Hey, Major?"

"Yeah, Skipper?"

"Sir, how many of these things can we take?"

"This is a new bird, Skipper. She can take as many as you can stuff into her. Thank god those snotty bastards in the air force turned her down for being quote excess to their needs, or we'd be flying those old C-models and I'd tell you to quit loading already!"

"Shit hot! Bring 'em on, men. Bring 'em on! We need to be doing the boot scootin' boogie outta here soon." The tail end of the airplane was facing away from the tower and the body of the plane blocked any view of what was going on. McNulty could see the gleam of binoculars from the tower and waved and smiled. Nobody waved back.

1000 hours
7 November
Outside the USFK Command CP

Smith sat in the front seat of the communications hummer with the handset pressed to his ear. He was tired beyond description and it had turned colder. The heater from the hummer was on full blast and just barely managed to keep the cold out.

"Look, Mister Secretary, I understand all that, but that is not the point right now, with all due respect, sir."

"Well, General Smith, that's how we see it here in Washington. We just don't believe that the North Koreans will try to interfere with the withdrawal of American troops. Why, that would be like a declaration of war against the United States!"

Smith sighed. "Mister Secretary, we are already in a state of war with North Korea and have been in that state since June 1950. We don't have a peace treaty with the North. The South Koreans have such a treaty as of two days ago, but we're still technically at war with North Korea. What has been happening over here for the last fifty plus years is only a formal cease fire."

"Yes, yes, General Smith, I understand all that." Smith could visualize the secretary waving his hands dismissively as he was prone to do at press conferences when someone asked him a hard question he didn't know the answer to. The guys in the Pentagon called it the 'non-verbal blowing you off' gesture or the 'don't bother me with the details' gesture. Brooks used it often. "I think you're too close to the problem over there and can't see the forest for the trees. We can afford to be a bit more objective over here and we just don't see it. The North Koreans just can't afford to take us on. They know we could crush them like an ant! We are the most powerful nation on earth, General Smith. I think you're forgetting that fact. Is there anything else? I need to get going here."

Smith had finally had enough. He paused only slightly, "Okay, Secretary Brooks. You and I need to be absolutely clear on this. I am requesting support as the theater commander and you are refusing to provide that support. As far as being the most powerful nation on earth, that may be true elsewhere but we don't have crap for power in Korea right now. That's why our ass is hanging out in the wind. I will ask you one more time, Mister Secretary. Will you send me the DD-21 destroyer to support the evacuation of United States troops from the Korean Peninsula?"

There was a pause as Brooks was obviously conferring with whoever else was in the room with him. Brooks replied coldly, "No, General, I will not send that ship. You don't need it and it will just look like an act of desperation on our part. The ship hasn't even been accepted by the navy yet! Technically it doesn't belong to us. I can't help you, and I'll say this again, you are crying wolf."

"Then I will take the issue up with President Preston, Mister Secretary."

"You needn't bother, Smith. I've already had the president briefed on my decision by General Blair, and he fully supports me after General Blair was able to answer some of his questions based on his personal in-depth knowledge of the situation over there. Goodbye."

Smith swore softly to himself as he waved for the driver to get back into the relative warmth of the vehicle now that the conversation was finished. To have Blair talking to the president about anything bordered on the criminal in Smith's mind. Never mind talking about the situation in Korea! Smith knew when he had been bureaucratically out maneuvered; something Brooks was infamous for doing when he wanted things to go his way. And he always wanted thing to go only his way. Back at the Pentagon everybody knew it was his way or the highway. Dissenters got their walking papers. Smith just shook his head in frustration.

Smith turned towards Johnny Raymer in the back seat and saw him remove his headset. Raymer looked down at his notes and said, "Sir, I probably need to type these up and get you to sign them. When this thing goes to shit, Brooks will throw you to the wolves first. I'm sure there won't be any record of this conversation on their end."

"Yeah, Johnny, but don't type them up. I don't care about *later*. I'm worried about *now*. Where did Sam get off to?"

"Sir, he's over behind the trees smoking a cigar. I think he's on the cell phone with his son over in the 2nd ID."

"Okay, when he's done, have him come over, please."

"Roger, sir. Will do." Raymer went off to tell Sampson and to type the notes up anyhow. He'd be damned if he would see his boss swing because the secretary of defense was an ignorant and arrogant asshole!

Sampson leaned against a pine tree and heard Sean say, "Yeah, Dad. We're over by the coast now. It was just like a road march to the range. We didn't see anybody but the ROK MP's waving us through the mountains."

"Okay, Sean. Were you guys allowed off the roads at all?"

"Nope, it never happened. In our movement briefing we were told that the area off the road was heavily mined which sounded like bullshit to me. I told my guys to be scanning our flanks as we went along but they didn't see anything. You know, Dad, it was strange that the few villages we went through were completely deserted. No people; not even a dog or a cat. It was spooky like one of those sci-fi movies where everybody just disappears! What do you think that's all about?"

"I don't know unless the ROK government evacuated them once the war started. If I get a chance I'll ask on this end, but I haven't seen a ROK officer in two days now."

"Yeah, we noticed that the ROK MP's were not very friendly as we went along. Usually they'll smile and give us the thumbs up or just wave. They just stared at us; no smiling and no waving even when we waved first. Hey, Dad?"

"Yeah, Sean?"

"I really feel like we have totally let these guys down. I mean we have always told them we would be here for them, and then when the time came, we just weren't in it. Some of my guys are really down about it, but the others just want to get the hell out of here. I'm in both camps!"

Sampson laughed. "Yep, me too. Speaking of which I'll be coming your way tomorrow it seems."

"Hey, no shit? Why you coming over here? I mean I'll be glad to see you, but this is a long damn way from rear echelon land there in Seoul. The chow ain't that good either."

Sampson laughed again. "I'll explain all that when I get there, Sean. Have you called your mom to tell her you're okay?"

"Uh, no. Have you?"

"Yes, I talked to her a few minutes ago and I told her I'd tell you to call. So please do that."

"Uh, Dad? I gotta go. I just got told the battalion commander wants to see me. I promise I'll call Mom right after that. Love you. Bye. See you tomorrow!" The connection ended. Sampson was immensely relieved to hear his son's voice. Although he was proud that his son had chosen to follow in his footsteps, he had wished more than just a few times in the last three years that he had chosen another path. Between Iraq, Afghanistan and now Korea, being an American infantryman was probably the most dangerous profession in the world. Sampson walked down the hill to go see General Smith.

1000 hours
7 November
Marine Corps C-130 Mike Lima 2

"Hey, Skipper! I think the ROK's are coming back! And there's a bunch of them!"

Shawn McNulty looked down the runway towards the tower. There were three jeeps and two trucks moving slowly down the runway apron towards the C-130. "Shit! Okay, men. Game's over! Everybody into the plane! Major! You need to crank this bitch!"

The pilot was in the rear of the airplane helping to stow canisters and was covered in sweat in spite of the cool temperature. He glanced down the runway and then pivoted towards the cockpit. He was running by the time he jumped into his seat. He hit the start switches and the engines roared to life, all four of them.

McNulty took the rifle from his marine posted as a look out and waved him up the ramp of the plane. McNulty wrapped the sling around his biceps and took up a good standing firing position. He fired at the tires of the slowly moving vehicles and achieved the results he wanted, hitting several tires. The vehicles stopped and the solders sat frozen in them. McNulty knew their surprise at being shot at wouldn't last for long, so he turned around and dove into the plane. The ramp was already coming up and the pilot was starting to swing the plane onto the runway, engines blasting. McNulty just caught a glimpse of the South Korean soldiers jumping from their vehicles and moving towards the runway. He sprinted up to the cockpit in time to hear the pilot say, "Negative tower. We will not proceed to holding area Zulu 2. We are departing now. We no longer have an in flight emergency. Have a nice day and Mike Lima Two out!" The pilot shoved the engine throttles all the way to their stops and the C-130 leapt down the runway. He shouted, "Hang on! We're going STOL!"

McNulty could just barely hear the rifle fire from outside over the roar of the engines. He hoped to hell none of them hit a napalm canister or this was going to be one ugly son-of-a-bitch! He felt the plane hit a bump and lurch, and just had time to grab the canvas strap over his head to keep from falling backward as the nose of the plane angled sharply upward. The engines screamed and the plane lifted off in a steep climb. The pilot was mumbling, "Baby, baby, oh baby, you're my sweet fucking baby! Goddamn honey! Goddamn, you *are* the one!" The plane leveled out after making a sharp turn to the south towards the coast.

The pilot turned towards McNulty and grinned. "Now that, Skipper, just gave me a woody! Sumbitch that was great! Better'n sex! Goddamn!"

McNulty somehow couldn't get quite as excited as the pilot obviously was, but he was damn glad to be out of there. He looked into the cargo compartment to see if any of the canisters had broken loose in the take off. Everything seemed to be secure. He saw one of his marines putting a field dressing on the arm of a fellow marine so the bullets had done some damage. He called out, "Anybody else hit?"

"Negative, Skipper! Just Smitty being fucking slow again like that time in Fallujah!"

"Well, tell Smitty there's no Purple Heart this time. Those folks were supposedly friendly!"

Smitty mumbled, "Aw shit man. Took a hit for nuthin'!" The marines who heard him laughed.

McNulty turned back into the cockpit. "Hey major! Two questions. What the shit was that and what was that bump just before we took off? We hit a pothole?"

"Well, Skipper, I told you to hang on because we were going STOL. It ain't my fault if you ignorant ground pounders don't understand plain aviator talk." The pilot could see that McNulty still didn't understand so he continued, "STOL means short take off and landing. It was developed for the Vietnam War when forward runways were too damn short and ground fire was too damned plentiful. It's a good goddamn thing this is a new J-Model, or we would have ended up in a fiery damn heap at the end of the runway."

McNulty nodded. He understood now. His dad had been at Kaesong in Vietnam and had told him how the marine C-130 guys would bring in supplies and take out the wounded and dead. His dad had nothing but admiration for those guys and always stood them drinks at the reunions. Now he fully understood why. "What was the bump, though? Did we get damaged and won't be able to land back at Okie?"

The pilot feigned nonchalance, but McNulty could see in his eyes that what he had to say next was hurting him. "No, Skipper. We're fine and can land at Okinawa no sweat. The 'bump' was the ROK major you talked to. He was standing in the middle of the runway with his hand up for us to stop." The pilot shook his head. "I don't know how he could possibly have thought we weren't going to run him over at the speed we were doing." The pilot sighed. "Well, it sucks to be him I guess." He paused as the image came back through his mind again. He shrugged. "We'll be back on the ground in about three hours. You need to use the radio?"

"Yes, sir. I need to let the battalion commander know we got the goods."

"You also need to let him know you left United States Marine Corps property on the ground in the form of those dollies." The major added gleefully, "You know the Corps. That shit's coming out of your pay young captain!" The pilot snickered and the co-pilot joined in. The Marine Corps with decades of limited budgets was as miserly as it came when any of its equipment was lost.

McNulty smiled, reached inside his breast pocket and pulled a folded piece of paper out. He unfolded it and handed it to the pilot. The pilot read it and threw his head back in laughter and handed it to the co-pilot who read it and did the same. The paper was a fully filled out and approved statement of loss form for the dollies signed by McNulty's regimental commander. It relieved "Captain Shawn M. McNulty, 1st Battalion, 5th Marine Regiment, United States Marine Corps from all pecuniary liability for the loss of three, (3): Dolly, Aviation, Bomb; w/ wheels 6 each, 500 lb capacity, OD in color, Stock Number 32612-482-03/A, Serial # N/A."

The aviators were still laughing when McNulty said, "I just look dumb, Major. I just look dumb." McNulty looked out the windshield and could see the sea below. At least they were away from Korea in one piece. He called his battalion commander and reported in.

1030 hours
7 November
Outside USFK Command CP

Sampson heard everything General Smith was telling him about his conversation with the secdef and his mind was racing. He was not in the least surprised that Brooks had not helped, and in fact had cut Smith out of the loop with the president. That was classic Brooks. If it wasn't his idea, well, it wasn't a good idea.

"If the 2nd ID doesn't have naval gunfire support, Sam, can they use their own artillery to make up for it?"

Sampson shook his head. "Sir, what they got will help, but it's not the Crusader so it will only be able to do two rounds a minute instead of ten or more. They just won't have enough tubes to make up for what the gun on the DD-21 can do. And to top it off, their MLRS can't help because the range will be too short." Sampson paused. "Sir, I may have a way to get the DD-21 here anyhow."

Smith looked at Sampson, but was clearly skeptical. "If my close personal friend Ralph Brooks says he can't do it, Sam, how the hell can you do it?" Sampson grimaced. He knew the term 'close personal friend' in general officer parlance meant the exact opposite.

"Sir, you said Brooks said the navy didn't even own the ship yet?"

"Yeah, that was his excuse. So what?"

"Then we need to talk to the guys who do own it and see if they'll loan it to us."

Smith just stared at Sampson. Then he started to smile. "You know, Sam, General Buford who used to be the CINC over here asked me just last week to let him know if there was anything he could do to help us out. He's got connections up the ying yang with the defense contractors. But shit, they'd be out of their minds to go along with this." The reality of just how outrageous it would be to ask a defense contractor to send a multi-billion dollar ship into a war zone *gratis* struck Smith like a blow to the chest. He shook his head. "No, even Buford probably couldn't bullshit his way through this one. It's not going to work, Sam."

"Sir, I think it will work if General Buford uses the right argument. The guys that own the DD-21 are down to building only one ship. Brooks axed the rest of the buy because it didn't fit into his hopelessly fucked up vision about what future warfare is going to be like. You know his vision; Special Forces on horses and a smart bomb is the answer to everything. The owners would like very much to build more because they actually lost money on the first one after retooling everything to build it."

Smith was nodding in agreement with what Sampson was saying both about Brooks' warped view of future combat and the costs of producing new weapons. Start up costs in the defense industry were always horrendous for a new platform. It was never cost effective to build just one of anything.

Sampson continued, "This is a once in a lifetime opportunity for them to show what the DD-21 is supposed to do. They can run simulation war games and sea trials until they're blue in the face, and it still all remains canned and theoretical. General Buford needs to stress that this is an opportunity to fire live rounds at a live enemy, and none of the current nay-sayers, to include Brooks, will ever be able to challenge the concept again. Sir, we are running out of airspeed and altitude here. This is going to get ugly quick when we try to pull the 2nd ID out."

Smith knew that was the absolute truth. "Okay, I'll call Buford. I think he'll agree with you. I know I damn sure do. I hadn't thought of it the way you said, Sam, but it damn sure makes a lot of sense. What about a crew? What if the contractors elect not to come?"

"Shit, sir! Those guys will go nuts at the chance to bust some caps on the bad guys. I'll bet you a beer every damn one of them comes!"

Smith smiled. "Yeah, I would too in their shoes, so no bet. Do me a favor and tell Johnny I'm calling Buford and I'll want to talk to Wellens once I'm through. And Sam?"

"Yes, sir?"

"Thanks for having the balls to stand up for what you believe in. Please keep it up."

"Roger, sir. Will do." Sampson opened the hummer door and a blast of frigid air fresh in from Manchuria caused the temperature inside to plummet. Damn it was getting colder! But it also meant the skies would clear. In a few more days that was going to be critical.

0400 hours PST
7 November
Seattle Shipyard, Berth 42

The docks were deserted except for the men streaming in from the parking lot. They showed their passes to the security guards, and then were let through the gate onto the dock. The security guards didn't seem surprised to see them, but the men were clearly surprised to have been called in at such an early hour. They were also curious. None of them could even imagine why their bosses had called them about an hour ago and cryptically told them to report for work. The few that asked why were told to just do what they were told; it was important. They were all former military men and knew an order when they heard it. The last few who lived the furthest away from the shipyard were finally checking through security. Retired Navy Captain Isaiah Parker watched the final few men come on board. He turned to his bosun, "Okay, Chief. Have them all go to the mess deck."

The bosun walked towards the groups of men and quietly told them to move to the mess deck so the skipper could talk to them. Most of the men assumed he was going to tell them that the long expected lay-off was going to happen today. They all had heard the rumors after the last contract review with the Department of Defense. No more DD-21's were going to be built and this one was done. Some of them would stay on to train the navy crew once it was finally assigned to the ship, but most would have to look elsewhere for work. It was not a good situation to be in.

Captain Parker signaled for the bosun to close the hatch once the last man had filed into the mess deck. Parker looked at them and could easily see the dejection on their faces. He knew they thought the middle of the night call to work was about the lay-offs. He had the same thought when the CEO of the company had called him at two in the morning. Parker smiled and slowly some of the men smiled. The skipper wouldn't smile if it was bad news. Some of the men relaxed in their seats and the buzz in the room momentarily increased. Parker held his hand up and the room got quiet.

"Okay, this is not about lay-offs. In fact our contract has been extended for two weeks, possibly more. But," Parker paused, "there is a condition attached to it. The CEO called me two hours ago and made me an offer I couldn't refuse. I hope you'll feel the same way, but I'll tell you right now, you don't have to accept this offer and you'll still get the two weeks pay." Some of the men stirred in their seats. Why wouldn't they accept whatever the offer was? And what could it possibly be that they could turn it down and still get paid? This was about as weird as it could get.

"I'm taking the ship out for sea trials and gunnery practice. I will be departing from this berth in two hours. The ship will be deployed for up to two weeks, maybe more. Now here's the part where you need to think about whether you'll go with me or not. I'm taking the ship to the east coast of South Korea and my gunnery practice may actually be against North Korean forces. We won't know until we get there."

There was absolute silence in the room. All the men had been following the news on the war in Korea and like most everybody else in the country, they thought it was already over. Finally, one man said, "Skipper, I thought that war was over? Last I saw on CNN they have already stopped fighting and we're just pulling our forces out. According to CNN it wasn't much of a war and we were never really in it. Has something happened we don't know about?"

"Great question, Davy. I asked the CEO the same questions. He told me that the White House and the Pentagon agree with CNN, but the commander in Korea thinks they will have to fight their way off the beach. The *Kitty Hawk* will cover the evacuation but you all know she has no naval gunfire to provide to the guys ashore. That's where we come in. We were built for just that. We may get an opportunity to demonstrate once and for all exactly what this ship can do and why it's needed in the fleet. If you decide to go, you can call home to say you're going to sea for a few weeks for trials but that's all you can say. Fair enough?"

The men nodded. Parker continued, "We're going as private contractors. Our beloved secretary of defense has refused the guy on the ground's request to send us over officially." The men groaned at the mention of the secretary of defense. They all knew he was *the* one man responsible for canceling their contract. "If you decide for some reason you can't or won't go, well your two weeks pay will be contingent upon you keeping your mouth shut on what the rest of us are doing. Fair enough?"

Again the men nodded. A hand went up in the back the galley. "Yeah, Davy?"

"Hey, Skipper. I can't go! I got an appointment this afternoon with the dentist to have my teeth cleaned." This brought a roar of laughter from the men and broke the tension in the room. Davy Spicer wore a full set of dentures that he liked to click at everybody when he was clowning around and when he was lovingly attending to his guns. Davy had been a master gunners mate in the navy and was legendary for what he could do with a five inch fifty-four gun. His nickname in the fleet had been 'Pickle Barrel Spicer' because he was rumored to have put a round dead in a bunker aperture at maximum range when supporting the marines in Vietnam.

Parker laughed too. "Tell you what, Davy. We'll put your teeth in a bag and send them ashore to the dentist for you. I'll have Cookie make a shit load of mush for you to eat, or should I say gum, until we get your teeth back." There was more laughter.

"Naw, screw it skipper. I guess I'll just wait until we get back."

Parker looked around the room. There were literally thousands of years of experience represented by these men, many of whom had been in combat in Vietnam and Desert Storm. "Okay, we've got to get this show on the road. I need you to make ready to sail at zero six hundred. Once we dismiss, you can tell the bosun if you can't come along. I won't ask you to give me a show of hands on who wants to go in case somebody has other plans."

Spicer spoke up, "Naw, skipper, everybody's goin'. There ain't a swinging dick here who would pass up a chance to kill dinks again. Uh, sorry, Nguen." Spicer's face actually flushed as he looked at Nguen Tran, a Vietnamese-American who was in the engineering department.

Nguen looked at Spicer and said, "For the record, Davy, North Koreans were called *gooks* and not dinks. We dinks take a damned dim view of being confused by you white supremists as all looking alike. Not all Asians look alike, Davy."

Nguen's answer broke the room up with laughter again. Davy Spicer's wife of thirty plus years was an African-American, and you could always get Davy, who was white, fired up by mentioning any white-supremist group. Davy clicked his teeth at Nguen as everybody got up to man their stations for sailing.

Not a man jack of them went to see the bosun which didn't surprise Parker in the least. He had worked with these men over the last five years on this project, and knew he had the best crew that could possibly be gathered inside the hull of any one ship. It was probably the best, most experienced crew in all recorded naval history.

At zero six hundred hours, the DD-21 USS *Gunnery Sergeant Reuben Barnes* quietly slipped her moorings and eased away from the dock. No tug boats assisted her and she glided silently out to sea in the pre-dawn darkness. The company that still owned her would make a quiet announcement in the trade news that she had gone for additional trials and fitting before being handed over to the navy sometime next year.

Gunnery Sergeant Reuben Barnes had earned the Congressional Medal of Honor posthumously in the first Korean War for staying behind to call in naval gunfire support to cover the marines' sea withdrawal from North Korea in 1950 after the retreat from the Chosin Reservoir. The name and story of Reuben Barnes was not lost on the crew as they headed to Korea. History did just seem to have a habit of repeating itself.

Once the ship cleared Seattle harbor, Parker ordered full speed on a course of two seven zero degrees, due west. The ship heeled over to the new heading as the engines kicked her up to fifty knots, seemingly without effort. She looked like a greyhound streaking low across the water.

0600 hours
8 November
USFK Command CP

Johnny Raymer stuck his head inside the door. "Sir, General Moon is on his way down. He just came through the security checkpoint."

"Okay, Johnny. Has he got his 'assistants' in tow?" Smith put only a slight inflection on the word because he was assuming that they were still being monitored inside the bunker complex.

"Yes, sir." Raymer held up only one finger with a questioning look on his face.

Smith shrugged. He didn't know why only one watcher was coming with Moon either. He shook his head as if to say, "We'll have to wait and see." He said out loud, "Well, bring them right in when they get here, Johnny, and get Sam."

"Roger, sir. Sam's already here in my office."

Two minutes later Raymer ushered General Moon and the ROK colonel who had not spoken at their earlier meeting. Colonel Lee Pok of the North Korean People's Army was not with them. Smith stood up and shook both men's hand and waved them to chairs. Raymer and Sampson came in and also sat down. Smith pointedly looked at the empty chair and said to Moon, "I assume we will wait until your other assistant arrives, General Moon, or will that be necessary?" Smith looked around the ceilings and walls of the room in an obvious gesture that he knew the room was bugged.

Moon immediately looked embarrassed and seemed to be picking his words slowly. "No, General Smith. We may proceed. It seems Colonel Lee has been delayed in traffic. You know what rush hour is like in Seoul." It was a long standing joke that it was quicker to walk in Seoul than to drive, and there was no rush hour. The traffic was horrendous twenty-four hours a day. Moon paused. "And it is safe to talk until he gets here." Moon looked around the room as Smith had done. "Colonel Yon," Moon nodded towards the Korean officer with him, "assures me that the bugs are turned off until Lee gets here. It seems the bugs are ours and not the North Korean's, as shameful as that may be. I'm sorry to admit this to you, General Smith. I also didn't know about them until after our last meeting."

Smith sat back in his chair. He never would have guessed in a thousand years that the ROK's would bug their own headquarters. It didn't make sense to him so he asked, "Why would you bug your own headquarters, General Moon? What the hell is all that about?"

Moon was clearly still embarrassed but answered evenly, "It seems that the bugging was secretly directed by a former president as a way of monitoring the generals. You know our history of military coups, General Smith. That was its only purpose."

"So President Hyun was able to use them to prevent the Hanna take over?"

"Yes, but the tapes don't reveal any such conversations. President Hyun is no longer sure there was such a plan. He believes he may have been duped by the North Koreans."

"Then he's releasing the generals?"

"No, they are in Pyongyang now."

Smith was appalled. "Why would President Hyun do such a thing! My god, man! How could he possibly turn his generals over to the North?"

"It seems, General Smith, that the Dear Leader was very persuasive on that point. He offered President Hyun a deal he could not refuse as you Americans say. In exchange for the generals, the Dear Leader cancelled the artillery barrage he had planned for Seoul. It seems that most of his ten thousand artillery pieces were within range of Seoul by then. You can imagine the results, I think?"

Smith nodded his head. He could clearly see a rain of death from that much artillery coming into the crowded streets of Seoul; a city that contained upwards of fifteen million people. The results would have been catastrophic. "So what happens to the generals in Pyongyang? Do they get executed and everybody's happy?" Smith asked sarcastically.

Moon shook his head. "No, the Dear Leader has given his word that they will remain his guests only until the unification is complete. They will be released unharmed at a later date to be mutually agreed upon by President Hyun and the Dear Leader."

Smith snorted, "Or when hell freezes over, you mean."

Moon leaned towards General Smith and slid four black and white photographs across the desk. The photos were grainy because they had obviously been enlarged. Smith said, "What's this, General Moon?" He did not look at the photos or touch them yet.

"President Hyun has directed that I give you these. They were taken last night in the Taeback Mountains. Please look at them closely."

Smith looked at the photos and picked them up one at a time, and then handed them to Sampson. "You were right, Sam. They are across the DMZ." He turned back to Moon. "Why would President Hyun give us these photos, General Moon?"

"He said because your president does not believe in the truth of these photos. He and your secretary of defense believe that this war is over. These photos prove that it is not over."

Smith reflected on what Moon had said, and on the photos which showed long columns of NKPA soldiers marching through the mountain passes towards the coast. Several of the photos showed the columns marching past road signs denoting their location in South Korea. "Yes, but why does he care what happens to us now? The Dear Leader is clearly the senior partner in all this and is calling the shots."

Moon nodded his head in agreement. "Yes, President Hyun told me that we are in a junior position so far in the reunification. As to why he is showing you these photos, he hopes that you will keep the North Koreans from defeating you. Should they lose that battle, our position in the partnership will improve because they will have lost face."

"It's as simple as that?"

"Yes, General Smith. It's as simple as that."

Smith saw a soldier come to the doorway and signal Raymer. Raymer said, "Colonel Lee is at the security checkpoint." Sampson handed the photos back to Smith who slipped them into his desk drawer.

Moon looked at Smith and said hurriedly, "President Hyun also wanted you to know that he knows about the napalm, but the Dear Leader will not know about it. He also says to tell you that no ROK forces will attack you, even if it looks like they will. He promises you that." Moon abruptly stopped as Lee came around the corner into the outer office.

Sampson knew it would look odd to Lee that nothing was being said so he adlibbed to General Moon, "Sir, you remember that hole in one you got that day at Song Nam Golf Course?"

Moon smiled, "Yes, Colonel Sampson. That was a very lucky day for me! Ah, Colonel Lee, you are here so we may now get started." Moon looked up at the ceiling briefly. They were back on tape again.

The purpose of the meeting was to coordinate the departure of the respective groups of United Nations and United States personnel that was to begin the next day. Moon no longer insisted that rosters of personnel would be required. Colonel Lee flatly stated that they would not be necessary because the NKPA personnel who would monitor the departures along with their ROK counterparts knew who was who. Those attempting to leave in the wrong group would be detained. The question of detained for how long was met with stony silence by Lee. The meeting was brief. The men did not shake hands at its conclusion. The date established for the withdrawal of the 2nd ID was set for Veteran's Day, 11 November. The Dear Leader thought the day somehow appropriate.

After Moon and his entourage departed, Smith gestured Sampson and Raymer towards the door. They all pulled their jackets on as they walked quietly down the hallway towards the bunker entrance. The security detail silently followed them up the hill outside the bunker where the communications hummer was hidden in the trees. The three men got into the vehicle. The heater was still on full blast but it was falling behind in its efforts to combat the cold pouring in from Manchuria.

Smith handed Raymer the folder with the photos in it. "Johnny, I need you to get these to the chairman for me ASAP. I don't want them going to Brooks or that fucking idiot Blair, so figure out how to do that."

"Got it, sir. I have a guy in JCS J-5 that's an old war college buddy. I'll send them to him, and he can get them directly to the chairman. He used to be in the chairman's F-16 squadron, so he gets to pop in and shoot the shit occasionally about the good old days."

"Good. Go ahead and get that done and come right back. I'll need you to help me make some phone calls after Sam and I talk." Raymer got out of the hummer and went to the warming tent set up next to the hummer. A computer with a secure satellite connection to the internet had been set up inside the tent. Nobody trusted any of the computers in the bunker anymore.

Smith turned to Sampson and said, "Go ahead and light your cigar, Sam. In fact, give me one if you have a spare."

Sampson was clearly surprised because he had never seen Smith smoke before, but handed one over along with his cutter and lighter. Smith looked at the cigar and said, "Damn! A Cuban no less!"

"Yes, sir. It seems the ROK's don't boycott Cuba quite as hard as we do."

Smith nodded as he cut and lit his cigar. He got it drawing nicely, looked at the tip and then said reflectively to Sampson, "You remember your in-brief, Sam, when I asked you if you had ever heard of the Theory of Tens?"

"Yes, sir. I remember."

"Well, I was going to share my theory with you once our exercise was over, but that got overcome by events as they say. So, I'm going to give it to you now. It's really very simple. First of all let me say, I didn't come up with it myself. Nobody seems to know who did, but it's a great theory, all the same. On a scale of one to ten, with ten being the best, how would you rate yourself as a soldier and leader, Sam?"

Sampson paused briefly then said, "You mean purely as a soldier? Knowing the business of war fighting? Knowing troops? No politics involved?"

"Yeah. The no shit dirty end of the stick stuff, Sam. How do you rate yourself?"

"Sir, I'll be immodest as hell and say I'm a ten. I know my shit."

"Yep." Smith nodded his head in agreement. "I would agree with you. Now let me ask you this, have you worked for guys senior to you that just always seemed to be uncomfortable around you?"

Sampson smiled. "Yes, sir. That's happened more than once."

"Do you know why?"

"No, sir."

"It's because they weren't tens, Sam. You were clearly a ten and they were something less than a ten and they knew it. Were any of them generals?"

Sampson laughed. "Now that you mention it, sir, yes, several of them were generals. In fact, most of them were."

Smith nodded again. "Now doesn't it seem strange to you, Sam, that we would pick men for our highest ranks who were not tens, particularly if we had tens like you to pick from?"

Sampson nodded but did not answer. He had often wondered exactly that, but knew that politics certainly played a big part.

Smith held up his hand as if to stop Sampson's train of thought. "And I know you're thinking that politics play a part in that. I won't deny that but the biggest deciding factor on who gets selected is the Theory of Tens. One last question, and then I'll give it to you. Have you ever worked for a general who was a ten?"

"Yes, sir. I have." Sampson was thinking he was working for one right now, as a matter of fact!

"Okay, and let me say they were not uncomfortable around you, nor you around them?"

Sampson nodded. That was true.

Smith nodded too. "So here's how it works, Sam. Say one of those tens you worked for has a subordinate who is a nine or even an eight. But he brings the guy along anyhow and helps him get promoted because he really believes the guy will mature into a ten. We've all seen that happen, but sadly, most of them do not mature and now they're in a position to bring along somebody else. What kind of guys are they going to bring along? Who are they comfortable with?" Smith paused waiting for Sampson to answer.

"Sir, I guess they'd be comfortable with people of their own caliber, or …"

"Or people who are even lower than them in competence so they will feel like a ten in comparison?"

"Yes, sir. I've seen that."

"But do you see where this leads us as far as who's in charge of different parts of our army?"

"Yes, sir, I do."

"So let's talk about Bobby Wellens. Who's his daddy?"

"Sir, I don't really know."

"Okay, it's General Hubert Toller. Know him?"

"Yes, sir."

"And who was Toller's daddy?" Sampson shook his head. "It was General Schuler. Toller was his aide in Vietnam and then his exec when he was Chief of Staff of the Army. A lot of people didn't think much of Schuler, but he was either a real strong nine or a very weak ten. I was too junior at the time to know so let's say for the sake of argument he was a strong nine. Would Toller be a ten if that were true?"

No, sir. Most likely not."

"You bet. I've known Fat Hubie Toller for over forty years and I'll tell you it would be a damn stretch to say he was an eight. Toller is a passable seven at best. So he picks Wellens to bring along. Where's that put Bobby Wellens by the theory?"

"Sir, he's probably a six."

"No, I'd have to disagree. By the theory he *could* be a six or even a seven, but he's lower. From what I have personally seen of Bobby Wellens this past year, he's somewhere between a four and a five as far as overall soldier knowledge and good leadership goes. I'd put his war fighting skills even lower than that. So you see, Sam, I have a bit of a problem here. I know that Bobby Wellens is unfit to withdraw his division under fire. Those North Korean soldiers in those photos weren't headed towards the coast to sight see."

"Yes, sir. Hopefully the chairman will be able to see that too."

"Oh, he will, Sam, he will." Smith drew on his cigar. "He'll either see them how we see them or he's going to see them in the newspapers if this thing goes to shit along with a caption that he and the good secretary chose to ignore them." Smith smiled. "Brooks outmaneuvered me on the DD-21 with the president, but he will have those photos shoved right up his fat ass if he tries it again and doesn't give me what I ask for." Smith turned towards Sampson and put his cigar in his mouth and spoke around it. "Sam, I'm sending you over to take command of the 2nd ID tomorrow."

Sampson just stared at Smith. He finally said, "Sir, there's no way in hell Bobby Wellens will take orders from me or even suggestions for that matter."

"Yeah, I know. That's why you're going to go as a two star. You're going to formally relieve Wellens and take the division. That's the request Brooks is going to get and honor when I call him in a few minutes and twist his nuts. And it won't be a request, it will be a demand. What other help can I give you?"

Sampson paused, taking in what Smith had just said, then said "Well, the DD-21 would have been nice. What can I ask for? Can I ask for people who aren't here?"

"Yes, on people if you're talking one or two. We can get them to the *Kitty Hawk*." Smith stopped as the J-5 came out of the warming tent and handed him a note. Smith read the note and then looked at his J-5 and said, "Dave, if you weren't so damned ugly, I'd kiss you!"

"Well, sir, I'm glad I'm ugly then!" Walker went back to the tent.

Smith handed the note to Sampson. All it said was "CEO played ball. DD-21 will be off-shore your location NLT 0100 hours, Veteran's Day your time. Warm regards, Buford."

Sampson smiled. "Hot damn, life just got easier!"

Smith smiled too. Yes it did. But he sobered quickly. The DD-21 was only part of the equation. "What people do you want Sam, and why? I'll work that with the chairman off line. I don't want Brooks going all snotty on me and refusing other things I ask for after I force his boy Wellens out of command."

"Sir, I want two guys. I want Command Sergeant Major Top Duffy out of Iraq and Colonel Matt Baker. Baker's easy; he's commanding the 82nd brigade that came in to Pusan last week. Duffy's the sergeant major for the 4th ID in Baghdad so that may be hard."

"Okay, but answer the why part so I can get Goodman to understand the need to do this."

"Right, sir. I've met Wellens' current command sergeant major and he will be a hindrance if he stays. He's full of himself and is not shy about pretending he's a two star too, like some of these guys do these days. I know he'll work behind my back and sow enough doubt among the NCO's that they will slow roll this thing. There's going to be enough confusion on the ground and I need Top Duffy to get the sergeants and junior officers totally onboard with the plan I have. Without them acting on their own, it'll turn to shit in a heart beat."

Smith nodded. He too wasn't overly impressed with Wellens' choice for a command sergeant major when he took command a year ago. The guy was all bullshit and feathers with no substance. He asked, "Why Baker?"

"He was with me in Iraq, and there is no one I trust more to be my deputy when the shit is hitting the fan. And sir?"

"Yeah, Sam?"

"I want Baker's brigade while we're at it. Both infantry battalions, but not the support guys."

Smith didn't say anything, so Sampson continued, "And I want the 5th Marines out of Okinawa. Both battalions, and again, no support guys."

Smith finally said with a tinge of sarcasm, "And just how are we going to make that happen, Sam? And why would we want to put more troops in harm's way?"

Sampson explained, "Sir, the North Koreans have got the order of battle on what's left of the 2nd ID over here down cold. They are expecting to attack a brigade with a mech battalion and a tank battalion and then the artillery and the normal ash and trash that makes up the rest of the division. They will not expect to hit paratroopers and marines. As to how we do it, that's simple. We load the

82nd guys up in a boat at Pusan today and send them up to join the *Kitty Hawk* as she comes into theater. We do the same thing with the marines at Okinawa. The *Kitty Hawk* will pass right by them so it won't even look strange if anybody is watching, and I assume they are."

Smith nodded his agreement with this last statement. "How will you get them ashore, though? You'll be lucky if any helicopters can fly based on the SAM's those North Korean soldiers were carrying in the photos."

"Yes, sir, I saw them too, but I've got that worked out I think. The *Kitty Hawk* battle group will have some LCAC's and amphibs with their MEU in the task force, and we're going to get some mike boats from the ROK Navy at Pohang, but they don't know that yet."

"What are mike boats, Sam"?"

"Sir, they're the same type of boats we used in World War Two. You know the ones with the ramps that drop down? The ROK's still use them to train their marines. When I was the G-3 over here, they invited me over to watch an exercise. We're going to have to 'midnight requisition' the boats because if we ask the ROK's for them it will tip our hand."

"Okay. Well since we're technically still at war, the marines in Okinawa come under Dave Walker as the Commander, US Marine Forces Korea. At least until he gets kicked off the Peninsula tomorrow under his UN hat. I'll have Dave make it happen. The *Kitty Hawk* has to transit by there to pick the napalm up anyhow so what's a couple of battalions of marines among friends? The 82nd guys belong to me already. I'll get the J-4 hopping on a ship for them. But Sam, let me ask you this. Aren't you worried that you'll be adding to your evacuation problem by bringing all these guys ashore? It literally doubles the amount of people you'll need to get off the beach."

"Yes, sir, I know, but if I can't hold the North Koreans far enough back from the beaches, I won't get anybody off. At least not in one piece."

"Okay. You're the commander. Let me call Brooks and get you promoted. I'll also get Goodman to get Top Duffy here. They'll be able to get him to the *Kitty Hawk*. I hope he likes long airplane rides because this one will be a bitch!"

Sampson said innocently, "Oh, yes, sir, General. Top *love*s airplane rides." Sampson knew Duffy hated flying worse than being shot at.

**0700 hours
8 November
4th ID Headquarters, Sadr City, Baghdad.**

Command Sergeant Major Top Duffy stared at the division commander like he had two heads. "Excuse me, sir?"

The division commander looked at Duffy, and said again but slowly this time, "Sergeant Major, you are to proceed to Baghdad International Airport by the most expeditious means for deployment to Korea. The order is signed by the Chairman of the Joint Chiefs of Staff. I tried to call our four star here an hour ago, and his aide said he knew about the order and to quote, 'get on with it.' That's pretty clear to me, and no, I don't have a frigging clue why my command sergeant major is being flown half way around the world on no notice. Last I heard we were pulling the plug on Korea and everybody was coming out. Did you maybe leave some unclaimed children with mamma-san on one of your tours over there, Top; that they maybe want you to come back and sort out now?"

"Huh, what? Shit no, sir, I didn't leave *no* damn babies over there! Sir, that ain't even funny." The division commander seemed to think it was as he continued to laugh. He was losing his top soldier and best advisor on no notice. He could either laugh about it or cry about it, so he might as well laugh.

"Your hummer is waiting, Sergeant Major, and there's a convoy leaving for the airport in ten minutes. On short notice like this, I need you to tuck in with them for security." The division commander held out his hand, "Good luck, Top. They wouldn't be pulling you away from me if it wasn't important. Oh, and you're to report to Major General Sampson upon arrival. You ever heard of the guy? Didn't ring a bell with me so I'm assuming he's a marine or some air force puke."

Duffy shook his head. "My old boss was Colonel Sampson but he retired a couple of years ago. No, sir. I don't know any General Sampson. This shit gets curiouser and curiouser. Goodbye sir. I'll be back." Duffy said the last part in a pretty good imitation of the Terminator. The division commander laughed and waved him towards the door.

Duffy pulled on his body armor as he approached his hummer. Jackson was up in the turret mounting the Mark 19 grenade launcher and Withers was behind the wheel. Duffy asked as he slid into the passenger seat and closed the heavy armored door, "You guys ready to go?" Both men answered in the affirmative. "Okay, Corporal Withers, pull over there by those vehicles. Tuck in just in front of that MP hummer." The MP's who were providing security for the convoy recognized Duffy's vehicle and waved him into the column. Duffy got around the division a lot and was known for dropping in on convoys and going along. Several of the MP's called out greetings to him. Duffy heard them and waved. He loved these guys like his own kids. They knew it and loved him back for it. They all knew that if something was dicked up, they could tell Duffy and it would get fixed, if it was fixable.

The convoy pulled slowly through the serpentine jersey barriers and the lead vehicle kept the speed down until all the vehicles were through. Once the trail vehicle was clear, the convoy picked up speed as it headed for the entrance to the highway leading to the airport. Everybody in the convoy knew that the bad guys watched their every move. They just hoped that they could run the highway fast enough to get ahead of any ambushes that the insurgents would scramble to put in place. The convoy took several exits to confuse the insurgents as to their real destination instead of just plowing down the highway obviously going to the airport. Sometimes the subterfuge worked, and sometimes it didn't. There was the sound of a loud explosion towards the front of the convoy. It was immediately followed by the sounds of small arms fire.

Duffy heard the MP lieutenant at the front of the convoy on the radio reporting that his lead truck right behind him had been hit with an IED. He also reported taking fire from the fields on the right side of the road. The sound of the machine gun mounted on the lieutenant's hummer punctuated his radio transmission. The lieutenant ordered the remaining vehicles to pick up speed and bypass the burning truck on its left. He detailed one of his squad leaders to take over the convoy lead and keep moving!

Duffy hit Jackson on the leg as he stood in the gun turret and yelled up, "Look for targets on the right!" He heard Jackson yell back so knew that he had heard him. As the vehicles sped by the burning truck, Duffy could see that the MP lieutenant was in trouble. His gunner was slumped over the machine gun and the lieutenant was trying to pull him back inside the vehicle. Duffy yelled at Withers who had started to slow down to help, "Keep going!"

Duffy's hummer sped past the stricken MP vehicle. The lieutenant was still trying to get his gunner down inside the vehicle, and Duffy could see the bullets from the insurgents kicking up the dust along the roadside. Jackson let loose with the Mark 19 and its slow rate of fire sounded like a distant thumping noise. The trail MP hummer slowed down to help the lieutenant but he waved them on. He had gotten his gunner down and was manning the machine gun. He fired a steady stream of tracers back into the fields but the insurgent's fire didn't slacken. They were well dug in and the lieutenant's fire wasn't effective by itself.

Duffy yelled at Withers to slow the vehicle down. Jackson had quit firing because he couldn't see any targets. Duffy opened his window and waved the trail MP hummer to come up alongside of him. They pulled up and Duffy yelled, "Follow me!" The driver nodded. He had heard the sergeant major and immediately dropped back behind Duffy's vehicle. Duffy was staring intently at the road ahead of him and suddenly yelled at Withers, "Slow down and turn onto that trail!" Duffy pointed ahead and Withers nodded as he saw the trail which was nothing more than a goat track.

The vehicle skidded sideways as Withers made the turn. The MP hummer did the same. They couldn't see the lieutenant's hummer anymore because there was a low ridge between them and his position. Nor could they see the insurgents. Duffy stuck his arm out the window to signal a right hand turn to the vehicle behind him, and told Withers to turn right and go up the ridge. As the vehicles crested the ridge together, Duffy could see that they were behind the insurgents and because they were higher up now, they were actually looking down into their holes. Jackson immediately opened up with the grenade launcher without waiting to be told. The MP's did the same with their machine gun.

The insurgents reacted quickly and brought both hummers under fire. Jackson grunted and fell back inside the vehicle. His face and shoulder were already welling up blood. Duffy looked at him quickly and tossed him a field dressing as he unceremoniously pushed him out of the way to get into the gun turret.

Duffy was a big man and stood very tall behind the gun. He saw where the most fire was coming from, swung the gun and expertly fired three 40 millimeter grenade rounds in and around the insurgent's position. He didn't wait to see their effect before he was swinging onto other targets. Some of the insurgents got out of their holes to run but Duffy and the two MP machine gun cut them down in a vicious crossfire. In a matter of less than a minute after Duffy had signaled the right turn, the fight was over. Duffy watched dispassionately as one of the insurgents tried to crawl away trailing blood. The MP sergeant next to him fired a long burst and killed the man. He looked at Duffy almost defiantly. Duffy nodded. He was about to do the same damn thing. He called over, "See how your lieutenant is doing, will you?"

The sergeant nodded and grabbed his handset and made the call. He called back, "They're okay, Sergeant Major. One guy in the truck is dead, the other guy's pretty fucked up. The lieutenant's gunner got his bell rung with a shot to the k-pot, but he's okay. They got a medevac inbound. We're heading back, but we're going down there first to make sure these assholes are all dead. You coming, Sergeant Major?"

"No, I gotta shag ass to the airport. Tell your lieutenant he is one big damn stud muffin in my book! You guys are too!" The sergeant grinned and gave a thumbs up. Duffy looked inside the hummer at Jackson who was getting help from Withers bandaging his face. "Hey Jack, you want to catch that medevac bird?"

Jackson shook his head. "Naw, Sergeant Major. If I leave, Corporal Dumb Ass here will never find his way back from the airport. I'm okay." Withers gave an extra yank to the bandage he was tightening around Jackson's head to let him know what he thought about the 'Corporal Dumb Ass' remark. Jackson winced and grinned. Duffy nodded. 'Jesus, where do we find such men!' he thought gratefully for the millionth time.

Withers tied the bandage off and put the hummer in reverse. He turned back towards the highway. Duffy remained in the turret manning the gun.

It was only another ten minutes to the airport and Duffy directed Withers over to flight operations. Withers handed Duffy his kit bag and Duffy shook hands and hugged each of the soldiers. "You two shitheads *do not* have my permission to get killed while I'm gone. You both got that?" Both soldiers nodded their heads. "Okay, then. I'll see you when I get back." Duffy grabbed his kit bag and walked into flight operations.

A navy pilot pushed himself away from the flight operations counter as soon as he saw Duffy come in. He'd been told to be on the look out for a big guy with lots of stripes who looked like he could kick your ass any day of the week. This guy fit the description to a tee! "Are you Sergeant Duffy?"

Duffy looked at the pilot in his rumpled flight suit like he was something Duffy had stepped in. "I am Command Sergeant Major Duffy, Major. Who are you?" Duffy emphasized all three words of his rank. Sergeant, indeed!

"Well, actually I'm not a major. I'm Lieutenant Commander Dale Hobson." Hobson accentuated each of the words in his rank too, but did it humorously. Duffy smiled. The lieutenant commander held out his hand and the men shook. "You ready to go, Command Sergeant Major?"

"Uh, sir. I'm supposed to check in with flight operations to get a ride to Korea."

"Yeah, I know. I'm that ride. We need to get hopping so c'mon. You may want to take a piss before we go so I'll hold your bag while you do that. Or you can wait. We'll have piddle packs."

"Uh, Commander what kind of plane do you have that doesn't have a shitter and what the hell is a piddle pack?"

Hobson laughed but was steering Duffy out the door and onto the tarmac. He pointed to the F/A 14 Tomcat sitting in the shade of the building.

Duffy pulled back. "Keeerist, you ain't getting me into that stubby piece of shit, Major!"

"It's lieutenant commander, Command Sergeant Major. *Lieutenant commander.* Not major. Now up you go, put your foot on the ladder and wedge your fat butt into the back seat and I'll show you how to strap into your ejection seat properly. That won't matter when we take off, but it'll matter a whole damn bunch when we trap on the carrier."

Duffy's voice went to a squeak. "Ejection seat! Carrier? What damn carrier? Whadaya mean *trap on the carrier*? Holy shit, I'm hating this! Goddamn I hate to fly to begin with. C'mon Major, let me fucking go. I don't deserve this! I can barely fart this seat is so small! Whatever I did, I'm sorry. Just let me go, Major!"

Hobson just kept shaking his head and saying, "Lieutenant commander. Lieutenant commander. How hard can that be? *Lieutenant commander*, damn it!" He finished strapping Duffy in and quickly strapped himself in. They were airborne in less than two minutes, and Hobson kept the plane at just below supersonic speed as he leveled off at forty thousand feet. Once he had the altitude he wanted and the plane trimmed, he went to autopilot and spoke into his headphones. "Hey, Sergeant Major, can you reach that thermos by your right hand? It's strapped to the back of my ejection seat. See it?"

There was no answer from the back of the plane. Finally the thermos was handed up. "Thanks. You okay back there? You can press that foot button on the deck by your left foot if you want to talk on intercom." Hobson heard the intercom click once or twice as Duffy experimented with it. "Yeah, that's the one. You want some coffee? We don't tank for another forty five-minutes."

Duffy's voice came over the intercom. Yes, sir. I'll take some coffee but I think I may have shit myself. You got any handy-wipes up there?"

Hobson laughed as he handed the thermos and a cup back over the seat. "Naw, Sergeant Major, you didn't do that. Not yet anyhow."

"What's that mean, Commander. Not yet anyhow? This bastard can't possibly get any worse!"

"Oh, contraire my big army friend. Wait until we go to trap on the carrier. That bitch will look like a postage stamp in the middle of nowhere. And then when we go in, it's actually a controlled crash you know. We go in hoping to catch a wire before we slide off the end of the bitch and go into the drink if I forget to give her max juice at the exact instant we hit the deck." Hobson could hear

Duffy groaning in the back without the benefit of the intercom. He laughed again. Then he said, "But oh, I almost forgot."

"Forgot what, Commander?"

"We'll be doing it at night so we'll be lucky to even find the carrier!" Now Hobson could really hear Duffy swearing in the back seat and laughed until the tears streamed from his eyes. Forty minutes until the first tanker rendezvous. They had a long ways to go.

1050 hours
9 November
Kimpo International Airport, South Korea

"Sir, I got a problem."

Sampson turned to face Gunnery Sergeant Gaddis who had just come up to him from the terminal. Gaddis had a Korean woman and a small boy with him. "What's the problem, Gunny?"

Gaddis was clearly agitated and his jaws worked briefly before he could speak. He blurted out, "Sir, this is my wife Mae Song and my son, Jason. They won't frickin' let them go on the NEO!"

Sampson could tell that the gunny was on the edge of panic so he grabbed his shoulder and said, "Tell me what's going on, Gunny. I'm sure we can get this sorted out. Why can't they go with the other non-combatants?"

Gaddis looked Sampson squarely in the eye and said, "Because I screwed the pooch, sir. That's why. I never registered Mae Song or Jason with the NEO warden because I never planned to leave Korea. I was going to retire over here. They said Jason could go because he's on file with the embassy as an American because he's my son. I at least didn't screw that up. But shit, sir, I can't put Jason on a plane and leave Mae Song here to fend for herself. As soon as the North Koreans figure out she's married to an American, she'll just disappear into the north. Her people have told her some of the girls in Tonduchon who dated GI's have already disappeared."

"Okay, Gunny. I got it. Let me go see General Smith to see if he can do anything. You wait right here." Sampson walked into the throng of people waiting outside the terminal to see if he could find the CINC. The morning had been as hectic as they come with mix ups on times to be where, and buses getting lost and conflicting directions as to what was to occur between the ROK's and the few North Koreans on hand. Sampson hadn't seen the CINC at all today and he had several issues to nail down before they went their separate ways.

Sampson finally spotted Smith in the crowd and made his way over. He saluted and Smith returned his salute with a smile. "Ah, General Sampson, just in time!" Smith handed Sampson a pink message flimsy from the embassy. Sampson looked at it and smiled too. All it said was, "By order of the President of the United States, Colonel Sampson, William S. is hereby promoted to the temporary rank of Major General, United States Army with a date of rank of 9 November; signed Patrick R. Goodman, General, United States Air Force, Chairman, the Joint Chiefs of Staff."

"Congratulations, General!" Smith pumped his hand up and down and was followed by General Dave Walker and Johnny Raymer. Smith saw the look of concern move across Sampson's face as he remembered why he had sought Smith out, and quickly said, "Is there a problem, Sam?"

"Yes, sir. There is. It seems Gunny Gaddis never registered his wife and kid for the NEO. He never thought he would be going home to the States after he retired. He doesn't have any family back there and saw no reason to go back." Smith nodded. He knew of other Americans who had stayed on in Korea after retirement. Sampson continued, "So his son can go because he's got US citizenship but his wife can't go. And if his son goes, he's got nobody in the States to take care of him once he gets there. Do you think there is anything we can do for him?"

The CINC shook his head. "No, Sam. We've already had this discussion with the ROK's and the North Koreans. They won't budge on it because they know a lot of people would try to get out. I've even talked to the ambassador this morning and he couldn't get President Hyun to help either. They all give us assurances that it will be all right and we can sort it out later. Then they get hostile and want to know who these people are who wish to leave so badly. That's when we know it's time to shut up. They may just get lost in the shuffle after we leave, but if we keep making an issue of them, we might as well turn them over to the North Koreans now."

"Well, Mrs. Gaddis certainly isn't going to blend in too well and get lost in the shuffle with her Amer-asian son," Sampson observed wryly.

"Yes, I'd have to agree. Would it help if my wife and I took the boy with us, Sam?"

Sampson smiled. "Yes, sir I think it certainly would. Would you keep him until we get back?"

The look Smith gave Sampson was as if to say, "Well, shit no, Sam. We'll give him to the gypsies."

"Uh, sorry, sir. Dumb question, I guess." Sampson paused. "I'm going to try and bullshit my way into bringing Mrs. Gaddis with us. At least she'll have some chance of getting out of Korea that way. Sir, any final guidance before we leave? They'll want us at the buses here in a few minutes."

Smith pulled Sampson away from the others. He put his head close to Sampson and said, "I'm convinced Brooks has told Wellens you're coming, Sam. You need to take whatever actions you deem necessary to take command of that division. Here's a note with my signature directing you to take command. But Sam, if Wellens gets in the way or refuses to cooperate, you have my authority to physically remove him. The chairman agrees but wouldn't let me put that in writing. My hope is Wellens will be happy to be out of it and will gladly step aside. Am I clear on this?"

Sampson nodded his head. "Yes, sir. You're clear. I hope you're right and Bobby just moves aside. I'll get him evacuated in the first group to expedite matters. I'm not sure what the hell I'll do with him in the not quite forty-eight hours we'll have left before we're allowed to start, but I'll figure out something. Sir, were you able to get me Baker's guys and the marines? And Top Duffy?"

"Yes, Sam. Just like you requested on the troops. They'll be there. Admiral Durham from the *Kitty Hawk* knows you're calling the shots. I've known Jasper Durham for a number of years and you'll find him helpful. He won't pull any bullshit on you. I wish like hell that I could go with you." Smith paused, looking at the younger man. "Sam, good luck and Godspeed on this. I couldn't have asked for a better commander to be available to me to pull this off. Bring as many of them home as you can." The emotion in Smith's voice was palpable as he said the last part. Smith loved his troops and the loss of any of them over his long and hard career had always been painful. "Now let's get back to the others."

As Smith approached the group, he said "Johnny, do you have some stars General Sampson can put on his uniform?"

Raymer's face flushed. "Sir, General Blair's exec gave me some of his old boss's stars, but …" he let the sentence trail off. Smith was shaking his head at the thought of using anything that had belonged to that idiot Blair when Dave Walker stepped forward. He took the stars off his uniform and pinned them on Sampson.

"Here, Sam. Wear these lucky goddamn Marine Corps stars I got. You know why they're smaller than the stars you army guys wear?" The US Marine Corps stars were only about two thirds the size of US Army stars. Sampson said he didn't. Walker cackled, "It's because we got bigger dicks and don't need bigger stars for our troops to know who we are! All the men laughed, Sampson included.

Sampson shook hands all around and said to General Smith, "Sir, let me fetch your grandson for you." The puzzled looks that comment generated disappeared when Sampson immediately came back with Gunny Gaddis and his family. Sampson said, "Sir, this is Mae Song and Jason." Mae Song hugged General Smith fiercely for taking care of her son which embarrassed him hugely, his face turning red.

Smith reached his hand out to Jason who took it without hesitation. "Come on Jason. You and Grampy have a plane to catch." Jason looked back at his mother and smiled and waved. He knew he was safe with Grampy.

Sampson watched them all go, then turned back towards the group that was going to the 2nd ID by bus. There were only about one hundred of them and they looked pretty despondent as they watched the guys flying out go into the terminal. Gunny Gaddis looked at Sampson and noticed the two stars pinned on each of his collars for the first time.

"Holy shit, Colonel! Are you a general now? When the hell did that happen? Christ, I can't leave you alone for a minute and you get into trouble! They only promote screw ups to general officer you know."

"Yeah, thanks for the congratulations, Gunny. I heard the same thing about making gunnery sergeant in the Corps. Collect these guys up so I can talk to them and you're my aide-de-camp until further notice, by the way. I like my coffee very, very hot and with a teaspoon of real sugar. Don't try to slip me any of the fake shit because I'll know it." Sampson turned serious. "When the Koreans get to asking about Mae Song, I want you to let me do all the talking. For the record, you're my son and she's your wife and she's pregnant with my first grandson. Tell Mae Song what I said and say 'yes, dad' if I ask you shit in front of these people. Roger?"

"Aye, aye sir. Roger all that." The gunny moved off to bring the group together and to tell Mae Song she was pregnant.

Sampson told the group that he was in charge and would take them to link up with the 2nd Infantry Division over on the coast near Pohang. They would be evacuated with the division in two more days. He also broke them down into squads and appointed a leader in each subgroup. It was quite a mix including all the services, but there were almost no combat arms soldiers in the group. There were also no weapons allowed in the group. Both Sampson and Smith had been appalled that they would be unarmed, but the Dear Leader was said to have personally guaranteed their safety. To have weapons after such a promise would be an insult to the Dear Leader and he would lose face. The Americans had no choice but to accept the North Koreans' assurances. The South Koreans were noticeably absent from the weapons discussions.

"Hey, General. That North Korean cocksucker is standing over there. It looks like he wants to talk to you."

"Okay, Gunny. Go tell him that the general will see him now. He wants me to come to him, but you make sure the little bastard knows that generals don't come to colonels. I'll be over there." Sampson pointed over to his left away from the troops and even further away from Lee Pok.

Gaddis walked over to the North Korean colonel and saluted. He said something and Lee shook his head and pointed to the ground in front of him. Gaddis in turn shook his head and pointed over to Sampson. He held up two fingers and even at that distance Sampson could see the surprise on Lee's face. Lee shook his head again and Gaddis held up his two fingers again and shook his head too. Gaddis shrugged, saluted and walked back towards Sampson with a huge grin on his face. Lee seemed agitated and shifted his weight from one foot to the other. Sampson turned his back on Lee and lit a cigar. Sampson knew how to play the face game too.

After about three minutes had passed, Sampson heard Lee say from behind him, "I must talk with you, General Sampson. I must give you instructions."

Sampson pulled on his cigar several more times, and then slowly turned around. He said coldly, "It is customary to address general officers as *sir* and to salute them Colonel Lee, or is that not done in your army?"

Lee was clearly uncomfortable and undecided as to what he should do. He had already lost face by coming to Sampson. He was just thankful that no others were here to see it. Finally, he raised his hand in a salute. Sampson slowly returned the salute and said, "What can I do for you, Colonel? I am a very busy man."

Lee started abruptly, "You must obey my instructions to you!"

Sampson drew on the cigar and blew the smoke just past Lee's head. He looked Lee in the eyes and said nothing. He tapped the stars on his collar and raised his eyebrows.

Lee dropped his eyes and said, "General Sampson, I have instructions for you, sir."

"Ah, Colonel Lee, why did you not say so? I am ready to hear your suggestions. Do they pertain to our movement to the coast?"

Lee nodded his head. He did not miss the use of the word suggestions rather than instructions. "Yes, sir. My orders are to tell you that the buses will not stop for any reason along the route and that no Korean civilians will be allowed on the buses other than the drivers. The drivers know these rules so do not order them to violate them. Do you understand, General Sampson?"

Sampson rocked back and forth on his heels, puffing on his cigar. He nodded. "Yep, I understand Colonel Lee. There will be one exception, however."

Lee looked puzzled. He clearly did not understand. He finally said, "What exception, General Sampson?"

Sampson pointed his cigar towards Mae Song and Gunnery Sergeant Gaddis. He put the cigar back in his mouth and said casually, "That young marine sergeant over there is my son and that's his wife. She is the exception. She will be with us on the bus."

Lee was vehemently shaking his head. "No, no! She cannot go on the bus! No exception! No exception, General Sampson!"

"Then none of us are going, Colonel Lee. You can send the buses back to wherever they came from. Good day, Colonel." Sampson started to walk away, but Lee grabbed his arm in a gesture to wait.

"Sir, she just a Korean woman! Your son will find another woman when he gets home. She does not need to go. She just a Korean woman!"

"Oh, Colonel Lee! She's not just another Korean woman. She's the woman who is carrying my first grandson. The doctors told us the good news just three weeks ago. Do you really expect me to leave my first grandson behind, Colonel Lee? Would you leave *your* first grandson behind?"

Lee took that in and slowly shook his head. No, he wouldn't leave his grandson behind either. He asked suspiciously, "How do you know she is carrying your grandson and not your *granddaughter*, General Sampson?" Sampson knew that in the Korean culture, and just like much of the rest of Asia for that matter, a granddaughter was not nearly as important as a grandson. A granddaughter could easily be left behind.

Sampson puffed his cigar and said with a huge smile, "Because the sonogram clearly showed his ding-ding, Colonel Lee. Girls don't have ding-dings, now do they? Nope! It's a boy! And if he grows into that ding-ding, he's going to be one helluva big boy! You get my drift, Colonel Lee?" Sampson leered and poked Lee in the ribs with his elbow. Lee was not amused. He shrugged. It didn't matter.

"Okay, General Sampson. I give her my permission to go," Lee said officiously.

"Why, thank you Colonel Lee. That's mighty decent of you." Sampson shook his hand. Lee just shrugged again. It didn't matter.

Lee knew that Colonel Sung would ensure that none of these damned Americans, the woman or the drivers for that matter would ever get to the coast. This was all just a charade. Lee composed his face into a sneer and saluted haughtily. "Good luck, General Sampson." He turned his back on Sampson and stalked away, regaining face with every step.

Sampson murmured under his breath, "Yeah, fuck you too, Lee." To say none of this felt right to him was an understatement.

1100 hours
9 November
1st Battalion, 57th Infantry Regiment TOC

Lieutenant Sean Sampson looked at the four soldiers who would make up his patrol. They were gathered around a sand table one of them had made from a map reconnaissance of the area they were going into. He knew that the assistant patrol leader had already done all the equipment checks, so he dispensed with that portion of his patrol order. "Okay, so we go in here," Sean used a stick to point at the sand table, "link up with these guys and we come back through here." He pointed at a different spot on the sand table. They all knew that you never came back the same way you went out or you were just asking to be ambushed. "What are your questions?"

The assistant patrol leader who was a young sergeant asked, "Sir, what if they're not friendly? What's the ROE?"

"The rules of engagement are we can return fire if we get fired upon. We can't initiate fire because it would violate the cease fire agreement."

"Sir, isn't it a violation of the cease fire agreement just to go out there? I mean we've all been told we can't go beyond Phase Line Warrior." The sergeant pointed to the line of blue yarn stretched across the sand table that was marked by a three by five card with 'PL Warrior' written on it. The card was held to the ground with a small rock. The wind had been picking up and the air had been turning colder.

"Yeah, so we were told, but division thinks these guys are legit. There are supposedly three of them that want to defect. Our job is to go get them so they can evacuate with us."

"Yes, sir, I got all that in your warning order, but why don't they just come here if they want to defect? Why do we have to go get them?"

Sean Sampson nodded. He had asked the same question when the battalion commander gave him his mission. "Apparently these guys are in pretty sorry shape after walking all the way south from the DMZ. That's why Doc here gets to come along." Sampson pointed to the medic. "Doc may have to stick them and get some fluids in them before we can bring them in."

"Then what happens if they're so fucked up we gotta carry them, sir? Five guys won't get very far humpin' three guys out of the hills. Don't we need more guys for this?" the young sergeant asked nervously.

Sean sighed. He had asked all the same questions earlier so he couldn't fault the sergeant for asking them too. "Yeah, I brought that up too, Sergeant Benner, but the Old Man says division limited him to only a five man patrol to reduce our signature, whatever the shit that means. We got what we got. Any other questions?"

Nobody had any so Sean said, "Okay, let's move out then. Johnson, take the lead. You got the claymore?'

Johnson nodded and patted the bandoleer slung around his neck. "Yes, sir. Right here."

Normally a claymore was used for an ambush patrol, but Sean figured it might just come in handy if they had to break contact and run. Intel said there was nobody in the hills to their immediate front, but you never knew these days. Sean had discovered in Iraq that the intelligence people were sometimes the last guys to know something.

1245 hours
9 November
In the hills west of the 2nd ID Assembly Area

Colonel Sung looked at the captain commanding the SPF detachment that had just joined his group. They were all wearing North Korean uniforms which had not been the plan. They were supposed to be dressed like ROK MP's, like Sung and his men. Sung said quietly, "Where are your uniforms, Comrade Captain?"

The captain shrugged. "I decided we didn't need them, Comrade Colonel. We have won the war and the need for subterfuge is over, Comrade Colonel." He shrugged again and looked Sung right in his eyes. Sung had known this officer his entire career and they had often been competitors, but had never been friends. The captain clearly resented Sung's promotion and could barely keep the sarcasm out of his voice when he addressed Sung as 'comrade colonel.'

Sung said softly, "Then you are refusing to take my orders, Comrade Captain?"

The captain shook his head. "No, Comrade Colonel, I will obey your orders as long as they make sense to me. But if they do not make sense to me, well ..." The captain did not finish the sentence and shrugged again.

Sung briefly debated executing the captain out of hand but thought better of it. He wasn't sure he could rely upon the captain's soldiers to follow his orders if he killed the captain. They needed a good forty men to pull off the ambush with a one hundred percent assurance of success. The captain had only brought thirteen men instead of the thirty he was supposed to bring. Sung asked him, "Where are the rest of your soldiers, Comrade Captain? Are they on their way here now? We have very little time now to get into position because you are late."

The captain looked at Sung and sneered back, "Comrade Colonel, it is none of your business where the rest of my men are. My orders were to bring as many men as *I* saw fit. What you see is what *I* would need to do this mission. If *you* think *you* need more men to kill a few unarmed Americans riding on buses, then that's not my problem, Comrade Colonel." This time the captain did not keep the sarcasm out of his voice as he spoke.

Sung lost control of his temper, and was reaching for his pistol when one of his team members came sliding down the hill is a shower of loose soil and rocks. The noise of the soldier's approach made both Sung and the captain look up at the approaching soldier.

The soldier ran to Sung and said breathlessly, "Comrade Colonel! There is an American patrol coming into the valley!"

Sung asked sharply, "How many are in the patrol?"

The soldier said, "There are five or six, Comrade Colonel, but we can't tell if there are more behind them."

Sung turned to the captain and said sarcastically, "And now you know why I wanted more soldiers and in ROK uniforms, Comrade Captain. My team has fooled the Americans many times already, but now we must fight them instead of fooling them. But it is only a small patrol so perhaps you have brought enough men to deal with it? I hope so. Go kill the Americans and be quick about it! We have only a short time before the buses get here! If we fail, Comrade Captain, I'm sure the Dear Leader will be looking for someone's head. I've done my duty, so my head is safe. Now go!" Sung shoved the captain towards the entrance to the valley the American patrol was entering.

The captain had paled at Sung's final words. He had only brought part of his men in an attempt to have Sung lose face for demanding so many men when they were clearly not needed. He had not anticipated any interference from the American's cowering at the beach! He turned abruptly towards his men and barked out, "Follow me!" and began running towards the valley.

1305 hours
9 November
On board the buses enroute to the 2nd ID

Sampson had dozed off, and woke with a start when he heard his cell phone ring once. It didn't ring again. He flipped the phone open and saw that he didn't have a signal which wasn't a surprise since they were up in the middle of the Taeback Mountains. He would have to wait until they got out of the mountains before he could figure out who had just called. It was probably another one of those damned telemarketers he reflected sourly. It was amazing that they would call you even in Korea to try to sell you crap. He looked past the driver down the road and saw another turn coming up. The turns were sharp and the driver was barely slowing down enough to make the turns without falling off the side of the mountain. In a reflex action Sampson grabbed the strap above his seat to hold himself steady as the driver whipped around the turn with the tires squealing in protest. He yelled at the driver, "Adashi! Slow down! Slow down, goddamnit!" The driver didn't even glance back to acknowledge the order, and just grimly spun the steering wheel through the turn. Another stretch of relatively straight road was coming up and Sampson relaxed just slightly. He turned to Gunny Gaddis across the aisle.

"Hey, Gunny, ask Mae Song to ask the driver why he is driving so fast? This guy is scaring the crap out of me."

Mae Song understood the request and started speaking to the driver in Hangul. The driver did not take his eyes off the road and increased his speed even more on the straightaway. He answered Mae Song's questions and he was obviously both scared and angry. Another curve was coming up and Sampson grabbed the strap above him again. Mae Song waited until the bus had screeched its way around the turn before she told Sampson what the driver had said.

"General Sampson, the driver he say that Colonel Lee tell him he could only drive exactly the speed limit for the whole trip. The driver no trust Colonel Lee, and will go as fast as he can because Colonel Lee say not to. Do you understand?"

Sampson nodded. Yes, he understood and the driver was right not to trust Colonel Lee. Even though Lee had still been wearing his South Korean uniform, his demeanor in dealing with the drivers had been very North Korean.

The driver said something to Mae Song and she translated. "Driver say he spend twenty year in ROK Army and go to Vietnam, and he know all about all kind ambush and how they work. He also say he plan to go through as fast as he can because he may go by before they ready. You understand, General Sampson?"

"Yes, Mae Song. Thank you. Please tell the driver I am pleased to have another good soldier with us." Mae Song translated and the driver turned around just long enough to grin at Sampson, and then jerked his head back to take the next turn. The bus roared on through the mountains.

**1310 hours
9 November
In the hills beyond Phase Line Warrior**

"Sergeant Benner! What's your status?"

"Lieutenant, Benner's dead!" It was the medic answering.

"Shit! What about Tarpley?"

"Dead, sir!"

"Fuck! You okay?"

"I took a round in the leg. I can't walk."

"Okay, we'll try to come to you. Stay down. I think these assholes are getting ready to rush us. Use one of the rifles over there when they come. I don't think they give a shit that you're a non-combatant, Doc!"

"Roger, sir!"

Sean Sampson turned to Private Johnson. "Larry, give me the clacker and fix your bayonet." Sean never called his troops by their first names although he knew all their first names. He spoke to Johnson by his first name now because he knew the kid was scared shitless and he hoped to calm him some. Johnson's eyes were big as he handed the claymore detonator to Sean. He fumbled as he pulled his bayonet from its scabbard and affixed it to his rifle. Sean fixed his bayonet too.

The patrol had approached the rendezvous site cautiously and had been surprised when a detachment of North Korean SPF had come barreling up the valley firing as they came. The patrol had gone to ground and killed some of the charging North Koreans. Sean was just starting to feel like he had the situation under control when ROK MP's had come at the patrol from the flank, also firing as they came. The patrol had then scattered into the cover afforded by the large rocks littering the slope. The patrol had tried to leap frog its way back over the hill providing covering fire for each other as the two groups that the scatter had caused tried to rejoin each other and mass their fires. After over thirty minutes, they were as close to each other as they were going to get. Sean couldn't tell how many of the ROK MP's or North Koreans were left. He knew they had gotten some of them with grenades and with rifle fire, but the grenades were all gone and so was the rifle ammunition except for what was left in their magazines.

"Hey, Doc! When they come I'm going to give them the claymore and then attack down hill into them. You stay put and give us covering fire if you can."

"Got it, sir!"

Sean turned to Johnson. "Okay, Larry. Once the claymore goes, we've got to be right in there before they recover. Save your ammo if you can. Just stick anybody you see, other than me." Sean smiled and Johnson smiled wanly back. He appreciated Sean's attempt at humor at a time like this.

"Okay! Put your heads down! They're coming!"

The ROK MP's and North Koreans flowed out of the rocks below screaming and firing as they came up the hill. Sean poked his head up just briefly enough for them to see it, and they all shifted as a group to where he was. He waited briefly as their screaming got closer, and then squeezed the clacker for the claymore which went off with a thunderous roar. Sean was up and screaming himself as he charged down the hill with his bayonet fixed. He saw enemy soldiers lying in bunches where the flechettes of the claymore had slammed into the close packed group. Some of the soldiers were still alive and trying to bring their weapons to bear. Sean lunged at them with his bayonet swearing and screaming as he plunged his blade into their throats or chests. He fired his last bullet at one he couldn't reach in time, and felt the bolt lock to the rear on his empty magazine. He felt several bullets pluck at his shirt and saw Johnson fall in a heap with a bullet hole neatly centered above his left eye. Sean spun to his left and saw the ROK MP major he had met on the highway just a few days earlier aiming at him from barely three feet away. Sean screamed and lunged at the ROK major just as he felt the bullets tear into his chest through his flak jacket. Sean's momentum carried him forward and his bayonet sliced into the ROK's chest all the way to its hilt.

Both men fell to the ground and the noise of the fighting abruptly ceased. There was only silence in the valley.

1605 hours
9 November
On board the buses enroute to the 2nd ID

Sampson actually sighed in relief as the bus came down the road out of the mountains. The driver was still taking no chances and was going like a bat out of hell, but at least the road was as straight as an arrow from here to the coast.

Sampson turned to Mae Song and said, "Will you tell the driver we need to go to the schoolhouse in the village at Chong-ju, Mae Song? That's where the 2nd ID command post is." Mae Song told the driver and he nodded his head. He would find the school. He slowed the bus perceptibly. All of them were glad to be out of the mountains. Particularly after a hair-raising ride at top speed around hair pin turns! A few of the passengers on the bus had been sick as the bus corkscrewed around the turns, and the smell of vomit permeated the bus.

Several of the passengers said they thought they had heard gunfire at one point in the trip several hours ago, but Sampson never heard it. They said it sounded like it was far away from the road which was fine with Sampson, if it really was gunfire. He knew how keyed up everybody was and suspected they were hearing things. With the racing of the bus engine and the squealing of tires, Sampson highly doubted they heard anything other than their hearts pounding in the chests like his was doing. Anyhow, they had made it!

The bus slowed down as it entered the village and the driver drove directly to the schoolhouse. It was not a big village and the schoolhouse was the biggest building. The outside of the schoolhouse was festooned with triple strand concertina wire and about two dozen MP's were on duty patrolling around the building. Other MP vehicles were stationed at all the intersections leading to the schoolhouse with soldiers manning the machine guns on the vehicles. The buses were expected, so some of the MP's actually waved at them. Several of the passengers smiled and waved back. They may still be in Korea but at least they were with Americans again!

Sampson had been surprised that there was no security on the main road coming in from the mountains; the road they had just been on. He had expected to run into armor and infantry forces blocking that road since it was the main avenue of approach into the beachhead. In fact, as he looked around, the only security he saw anywhere was these MP's around the division headquarters. He looked past the school house and could see some troops playing volleyball on a net strung between two trucks. Nobody had their weapons handy and no one was wearing flak jackets or helmets. Everybody was in the 'admin' mode; a peacetime concept where the troops ceased being tactical during a training exercise. Sampson shook his head in disbelief and started to walk towards the MP checkpoint at the entrance to the CP.

"Hey, General! Wait one!" Gunny Gaddis called out to Sampson. Sampson stopped in response and turned back towards the bus. Gaddis was carrying a barracks bag and hurrying towards Sampson. He reached inside the bag as he got closer. "Here, sir. Colonel Raymer gave me this for you and I hid it in the baggage after the Koreans checked our stuff. Gaddis handed Sampson a general officer's leather belt with holster and pistol. It was the only uniform item that generals wore in the field that marked them as generals. The belt was polished black leather and the buckle was gold with an American Eagle embossed on it. Sampson was clearly surprised to see it.

"Where the hell did Johnny Raymer get one of these on short notice, Gunny?"

"Sir, he said it was General Smith's and the general wanted you to have it."

Sampson took the pistol out of the holster and did a function check on it. The magazine was loaded and the safety was on. A round was in the chamber. Satisfied that the weapon was safe he put it back in the holster, and then and only then, did he take the belt and holster from Gaddis. He put it around his waist and buckled it. "Well, I guess I look like the real deal now, Gunny. Thanks. Now follow me in and act like my aide, or is that too hard for you?"

"No, dad."

Sampson looked at Gaddis and smiled. "No, Gunny you were supposed to call me that in front of the Koreans. Now you're demoted back out of the family to just another dumb ass marine. And how do I want my coffee once we get in there, aide-de-camp?"

"Sir, the general likes his coffee very, very hot with one teaspoon of real sugar and don't give him any of that fake shit because he'll know it."

Sampson nodded as he turned towards the CP. "Let the games begin," he mumbled under his breath. The MP's came to attention and saluted when he approached. They obviously knew he was coming and didn't ask for identification, so the CINC had probably been right that Brooks had tipped off Bobby Wellens. Sampson passed through the checkpoint and said, "The gunny is with me." The MP's waved Gaddis through too.

As Sampson entered the building he could hear a very heated exchange punctuated with profanity coming from one of the classrooms. He glanced through the glass of the closed door, and saw two officers standing at a map pinned to the wall. One was pointing at the map and jabbing his finger on it. Sampson realized the second officer was the G-3, and he was shaking his head vehemently in denial. Sampson passed on towards the door marked Command Group. He guessed he would have to see what that was all about once he met with Wellens and took command.

Sampson pushed the door to the command group open, and Captain Glen Stover stood up from behind his desk. He did not smile and he did not offer to shake Samson's hand and squeeze his elbow like he had done a few weeks earlier in Yongsan. The sour expression on the captain's face told Sampson that Brooks had definitely spilled the beans to Wellens. Stover said woodenly, "Sir, General Wellens has been expecting you and will see you now." Stover led the way to the door separating his office from the commanding general's private office. Sampson idly noted that this set of offices must have been for the school's headmaster and his secretary.

Stover opened the door and said, "Sir, Major General Sampson to see you, sir."

Wellens looked up from a folder he was studying and said, "Very well, Glen. Have him come in."

Stover moved aside and Sampson entered the room. Wellens had gone back to studying the folder and did not acknowledge Sampson's presence. Stover had entered the room behind Sampson and had pointedly closed the door before Gunny Gaddis could also enter. Gaddis started to open the door, but thought better of it. If Sampson wanted him in there, he'd tell him. He wandered off in search of very, very hot coffee with one teaspoon of real sugar and don't give me any of that fake shit because I'll know it.

Sampson was just about to speak when Wellens dropped the folder on his desk and said, "Well, I'm glad you made it here safely, Sam. Congratulations on the promotion, but I understand it's just temporary. But congratulations anyhow, I guess. Now what can I do for you, or is this just a social call?" Wellens was very confident in his demeanor. He was still very much in charge, obviously.

Warning bells were going off in Sampson's mind. This guy had to know he was being relieved of his command! Being relieved before your tour of command was completed was always embarrassing because it denoted failure. Being relieved in a combat situation was the ultimate disgrace for a commander at any level. Sampson unfolded the typed and signed letter formally relieving Wellens from command and handed it to him.

Wellens immediately took it. He said, "Yes, I have heard about this order." He seemed to study it for a few seconds, and then tossed it onto the desk. "General Smith is no longer the commander in chief of US Forces in Korea. He is only the commander in chief of United Nations Command which," Wellens paused and handed Sampson a message flimsy, "you can see that the 2nd Infantry Division is no longer a part of. I'm afraid your order relieving me is not valid, General. Is there anything else you would like to discuss or can I get on with my busy day?"

Sampson looked at the message flimsy. It was an order from the secretary of defense detaching the US 2nd Infantry Division from the United Nations Command effective upon the withdrawal from South Korea of General Robertson L. Smith and his United Nations staff. Both men knew that Smith and his staff had departed South Korea several hours ago. The message was not authenticated by the chairman of the Joint Chiefs, which was unusual but not unheard of with Defense Secretary Ralph Brooks.

Sampson looked at Wellens and started to speak but Wellens preempted him. "It would actually appear now that Smith is gone, that I am in fact the commander in chief of US forces in Korea right now, General Sampson. I believe my date of rank to major general predates your date of rank? Oh, and you're date of rank would be just today, wouldn't it?" Wellens finished sarcastically.

Sampson nodded but before he could speak Gunny Gaddis came through the door with a canteen cup of coffee. Both Wellens and Stover seemed startled by the intrusion and Stover started to move towards Gaddis. Gaddis said "Get the fuck out of the way captain, this cup is hotter than a motherfucker!" Gaddis gingerly turned the cup around by its wire handle so Sampson could grab the handle and not touch the body of the metal cup. The cup, based on the steam rising out of it, was indeed hot.

"Thanks, Gunny. Why don't you and Captain Stover wait outside for us."

Gaddis started to shepherd Stover out the door when Wellens barked out, "My aide stays! I need him to witness all this."

Sampson looked at Wellens, took a sip of his coffee and then sat down in the chair across from the desk. The captain and the gunnery sergeant were both motionless. Sampson took another sip, and then fished in his pocket for a cigar. He pulled it out and lit it. He sipped his coffee again, and pulled on his cigar as the three men in the room seemed spellbound by his actions. Wellens started to get red in the face and opened his mouth. Sampson said, "Willy, I don't think your aide is cleared for what I'm about to say. He's not in the compartment. Neither are you for that matter, but I'm empowered to bring you in, which I will do once these two gentlemen have departed the room. Or, if you wish we can talk about the good old days and how you got the name Willy."

Wellens had gone beet red in the face at the use of his cadet nickname and choked out, "You two get out." Stover hesitated still but Gaddis grabbed his arm and physically pulled him through the door, kicking it shut with his foot as he went out.

"How dare you insult me like that, Sampson! How goddamn dare you! We may temporarily be the same rank but I'm still your senior by about three fucking years. You'll do what you're goddamned well told! I have the full authority of the secretary of defense behind me, you son-of-a-bitch!"

Sampson didn't say anything but just looked at Wellens and puffed on his cigar. Finally he said, "You want one of these cigars, Willy? They're Cuban. There's none better in the world. I'll be glad when that old bastard Castro dies so we can start importing them into the States again. I had to come all the way to Korea to buy these."

Wellens was shaking his head no. He finally said, "Don't call me Willy, Sampson. It's disrespectful and you know it. You may only be a temporary general but you need to act like one as long as you are playing the part."

Sampson nodded his head. "Yeah, you're right. Let me ask you a question, General. Why isn't there any security posted up in the hills and along the road? And why are the troops running around like this is just some type of exercise?"

Wellens looked at Sampson and said sarcastically, "Well, not that I need to explain myself to you, Sampson, but why in the hell should I put security out and scare the shit out of the troops when we're just waiting to embark in two days? And don't you think taking an aggressive posture might just be deemed provocative by the North Koreans?" Wellens waved away what Sampson was going to say next and finished caustically, "And yes, I've seen the photos General Smith got from the ROK's. I agree with Secretary Brooks that they were staged to scare us to make sure we're leaving."

"So the division is just sitting here waiting for the *Kitty Hawk*?"

"Yes." Wellens didn't elaborate further.

Sampson continued, "So why all the security around the CP here, Willy? If there's no threat, why are you sitting behind all this concertina wire and sandbags with an army of MP's running around?"

Wellens said haughtily, "Because we have had reports of snipers possibly being in the area. The North Koreans have said they pulled all their SPF teams out of the area, but we have no way of verifying that. I'm not about to give them a present of a dead American general to add to their other laurels. I'm the only important target left on the Korean Peninsula now." Wellens said this with absolute conviction and without the least hint of modesty.

Sampson reflected on the answer briefly and puffed his cigar slowly. He looked at the cigar tip and asked quietly, "Will you obey the written order from General Smith, Bobby?"

"No, I will not! That order has been superceded by Secretary Brooks."

"Okay, then we need to go outside." Sampson pointed to the door behind Wellens that led out into the school yard.

"Why do we need to go outside, Sampson?"

"Have you had this room checked for bugs, Bobby?"

"Well, hell no! Why would I?"

"Because we found out that the entire CP back in Seoul was bugged. The North Koreans knew you would use this building once they directed you here because it's the biggest building in the village and one of the few with running water and real plumbing. We have to assume that they bugged the place and what

I have to say is compartmented and for your ears only." Sampson rose and started for the door. He placed his finger to his lips and motioned with his head for Wellens to follow. Wellens nodded and followed him outside.

Sampson quietly closed the door, and put his arm around Wellens to whisper his message.

1608 hours
9 November
Combat Command and Control Center, USS *Kitty Hawk*

"Admiral, the *Scorpion* is reporting intermittent sonar contacts in front of the task force. Bearing is zero three zero degrees."

Admiral Jasper Durham looked at his watch officer, Commander Burnes. "Okay, Burney. Tell the *Scorpion* we don't need a repeat of the China fiasco. He needs to keep on it and ask for help if he needs it."

Burnes nodded. The China fiasco had happened a few years earlier when the *Kitty Hawk* was making a port of call on the Chinese as a show of friendship. A Chinese diesel powered submarine had penetrated the destroyer picket line around the carrier and had surfaced within two hundred yards of the carrier undetected. The message at the time was clear. If the two nations had been at war, the *Kitty Hawk* would have gone down to Chinese torpedoes.

The incident had caused the Navy to rethink its approach to detecting diesel powered boats which were almost totally silent when they ran on their batteries. The result was a combination of new detection equipment using super computers to instantly analyze sounds, and magnometers that detected the slightest shift in magnetic fields. The only draw back was the relatively short range of the new detection equipment. The range for the magnometer in most water conditions was just barely over a mile, and sometimes even shorter.

Durham turned in his swivel chair and faced back into the command center. "Plot, how long until we reach the beachhead?"

"Six hours and twenty minutes, Admiral."

"Thanks." Durham made a decision and said, "Okay, Burney, shift the destroyer screen all to our front in support of the *Scorpion*. The North Koreans know we're coming and they know pretty much from where. We can expect them to vector in from the coast of Korea if they are going to try and interdict us. Plot, can we get any more speed out of the task force?"

"No, sir. If we sprint to our capacity, we'll leave the support ships behind. Sir, that includes the *Julius Montdale*. She's still three hours out at this speed." The

Montdale was the ship carrying the marines from Okinawa, and almost as importantly, the napalm.

Durham thought for a few minutes doing the math in his head. The *Montdale* had suffered a catastrophic failure in her propulsion system and had been delayed for six hours which was why she was trailing the task force. The task force had slowed its own forward progress to help her close the gap quicker. Durham wasn't comfortable with the slower speed if they started running into North Korean submarines. "Okay Plot, give me a course back to the *Montdale*. Burney?"

"Yes, sir?"

"Tell Captain Enright he's in command of the escort screen, and he's to clear ahead of us and leave picket ships to pick us up when we come back through. I'm taking the main body of the task force back to link up with the marines. The North Koreans won't expect us to split our forces and leave the carrier unprotected, so they'll vector in on the destroyer screen. Have Captain Enright array the screen to look like the task force with his ship in the center. CAG, you need to double the air patrols until we're done hanging out here on our own."

The commander of the air group, Captain Mark Richland, said, "Aye, aye, sir" and called down to the pilot's ready room to get the birds launched.

Now Jasper Durham would see just how aggressive the North Koreans were going to be. Like his friend Robby Smith, he was sure they weren't going to get a freebee pulling the 2nd Infantry Division out of Korea. No, it was going to be as painful as the Dear Leader could make it. Durham could feel the *Kitty Hawk* lean slightly as she made her turn back to the south.

1622 hours
9 November
2nd ID CP, Chong-ju, South Korea

Everybody heard the shot but no one could tell where it came from. The soldiers playing volleyball scrambled to find their helmets, flak jackets and weapons. The ball was in mid-air when the shot was heard and fell to the ground, rolling under one of the trucks. The soldiers it was served to were already gone.

Gunny Gaddis and Captain Stover rushed back into the CG's office just as Sampson was coming through the outside door. His face was ashen and he seemed stunned. He didn't say anything and just stared at the two men who were frozen in place. Sampson finally stammered out, "My god, General Wellens has been killed by a sniper!"

Captain Stover made a movement towards the door and Sampson held him up.

"Trust me Captain, he's dead. We'll take care of his body once we get the sniper. Go get the G-3 so we can get some security going. We need to nail this guy before he gets anybody else. Gunny, get a blanket or something to cover General Wellens, but keep your head below the wall out there."

Gunny Gaddis was the first to react. He said, "Aye, aye, sir!" and went to find a blanket or a poncho. Stover was slower to react. He was clearly in shock. Sampson shook him gently. "Glen, go get the G-3. We need to secure the area. The North Koreans didn't kill Wellens by accident. They were obviously waiting for him. Has he been out on that veranda before?"

Stover shook his head. "No, sir. General Wellens never left this building since we got here."

Sampson nodded. That was the Bobby Wellens he had known; never going out to see how the troops were doing. Bobby had never liked soldiers. It wasn't part of his job description as he saw it.

"Go get the G-3, Glen, and the chief of staff. I need to tell them what happened and to get us in a defensive posture." Sampson pushed Stover towards the door.

The G-3, chief of staff and another lieutenant colonel quickly came into the room once Stover had told them what had happened. Stover followed them in. Sampson looked at the G-3. He had observed Randy Long during the train up for the exercise several weeks ago and was fairly impressed with him. He didn't know the colonel who was obviously the acting chief of staff. He also didn't know the lieutenant colonel but saw his name tag and knew he was his son's battalion commander, Lieutenant Colonel Bob Easley. "Lieutenant Colonel Easley, why are you here?"

Sir, I'm your son's battalion commander. I'm here because I'm trying to convince the G-3 to let me take a combat patrol out beyond Phase Line Warrior to find out what happened to my patrol that went out five hours ago." Easley was clearly agitated.

Sampson looked at Long and the chief of staff and both men shook their heads. Long said, "Sir, we don't know anything about a patrol going out. It didn't come from the G-3 shop."

Easley said heatedly, "Randy, I've told you before, your goddamned operations office personally called me and gave me the patrol order. I really don't give a shit *where* it came from, I need to go get my men back!"

Long started to speak and Sampson held up his hand. "Gentlemen, we'll come back to that. Chief of Staff, here are my orders to assume command of this division. I need you to go get the word out that I am in command and I want all battalion commanders and above here at the CP in one hour for orders. Any questions?"

"No, sir. I'll make it happen." The chief of staff left the room.

Sampson said, "Okay, G-3, I need you to draw up a plan to push the security of the division out past this CP and all the way to Phase Line Warrior. Bring me the map and we'll work it together. We need to do this ASAP; we're dangling in the wind right now. Go get the map and come right back. Captain Stover, go with the G-3." Stover obviously wanted to stay and listen to what Easley was going to say to Sampson, but the look he got from Sampson didn't look like it was negotiable. As Stover turned to leave, Sampson said, "And send me the G-3 Operations Officer."

Easley looked like he was going to say something when the other men left the room but Sampson preempted him. "My son is leading that patrol, isn't he?"

Easley nodded, clearly uncomfortable. "Yes, sir. It was supposed to be a short patrol to pick up three North Korean defectors and bring them into our lines."

"When were they due back?"

"Sir, they were due back at the latest two hours ago. We haven't been able to raise them on the radio and I have already sent a couple of patrols out to Phase Line Warrior. Sir, I'm going to need permission to take the whole battalion because the North Koreans are definitely in the hills. My patrols spotted them, but they would move further to the west away from my patrols when they saw us."

The G-3 Operations Officer came in the room with Captain Stover. Sampson turned to him. "Major, did you give a patrol order to Lieutenant Colonel Easley for a patrol out past Phase Line Warrior to pick up defectors?"

The major cast his eyes to the floor and mumbled, "No, sir."

Easley's face flushed bright red. "You goddamned sure did, Major! What kind of shit are you pulling?"

The major flinched at the words and oddly, looked at Stover as if for support. Stover shook his head almost imperceptibly. Sampson caught the signal. "Captain Stover, leave the room."

"No, sir! I'm your aide-de-camp and I should stay here," Stover said stubbornly.

"Why?"

"Sir, in case you need a witness. General Wellens always had me sit in meetings for that purpose."

"Okay. I'm not General Wellens and I don't need you, now leave the room and close the door behind you." Stover still hesitated and was staring hard at the operations major. He finally said, "Yes, sir" and left the room.

Sampson turned to the major and said evenly, "Okay, Major, now tell me the truth."

The major looked Sampson in the eye and said, "Yes, sir. I called Colonel Easley and gave him the patrol order."

"Then why did you lie about it?"

"Sir, because the order was from General Wellens personally and was compartmented. I wasn't allowed to tell anybody. Not even my boss, the G-3."

"Then why are you telling me now? How do you know I'm in the compartment?"

"Sir, I don't think there is any compartment! I think that little shit aide set me up! He was squeezing my nuts all the way in here about not breaking General Wellens' confidence, particularly now that he's been killed in the line of duty."

Easley had gone pale and Sampson felt a cold knot in his guts. The door opened and the G-3 came in with the situation map. He spread it on the table. Stover tried to get back into the room and Sampson just pointed towards the door. Stover sullenly went back out the door.

Sampson looked at the map and said, "Show me on the map where this patrol was supposed to link up with the defectors."

The major pointed to a spot on the ground and his finger shook. "Right there, sir."

Sampson looked at the spot on the map and saw a large red star drawn on the map very near that point that was labeled, 'NKPA SPF 40+!' He knew why the major's finger was shaking. He turned and faced the major. "You're telling me you sent a patrol to a known enemy location?" he asked harshly.

The major was shaking his head violently. "No, sir, Captain Stover told me that General Wellens personally said the report was bullshit and there weren't any SPF there! It was just more ROK bullshit to spook us! I swear to god I asked him exactly that question!"

"This report came from the ROK's?"

"Yes, sir. A ROK colonel came into the CP about six hours ago and gave us the report. He said he had confirmed intelligence that the SPF were there."

"Where's this colonel now?"

"Sir, I don't know. He was called into General Wellens' office. That was the last we saw of him. That's why I thought Stover was telling me the truth. General Wellens had personally talked to the guy."

Sampson felt the knot in his guts get bigger. "Did General Wellens give any guidance as to the composition of this patrol?"

"Yes, sir, he did. He said the scout platoon leader was to personally lead the patrol and he could take no more than three men and a medic. He said that was because we were violating the cease fire and he wanted the patrol to be low profile and under competent leadership."

"You heard this from General Wellens?"

"No, sir. Captain Stover brought me the general's guidance."

Sampson nodded. That was Bobby Wellens all over. Never get your hands dirty if you could get somebody else to do it for you. That the orders came from Wellens was without a doubt the truth. Sampson never would have guessed in a thousand years that even Bobby Wellens would be cold blooded enough to send American soldiers into what could only be a death trap. That he would personally and vindictively send Sampson's son was absolutely incredible! Sampson shook his head as if to clear it. Jesus, his boy was probably dead and Wellens had deliberately done it! He felt the grief start to well up in him as he thought about Sean, and turned his back to the others. He stood motionless for about a minute, and then turned back to the waiting officers. His face was set in a grim visage.

"Okay, Major. You're dismissed. Send Captain Stover and Gunny Gaddis in on your way out." The major fled the room.

"Lieutenant Colonel Easley, I can't let you take your battalion out. I know the North Koreans are in the hills too, and I can't afford a fire fight with them yet. I need you to return to your battalion and move them into a defensive line along this ridge." Long handed Sampson a map marker and he drew Easley's battle position on the map. "Start moving now and tell your brigade commander what you're doing. I want your guys dug in with turret defilade for your vehicles and overhead cover for the troops by midnight tonight. I'll tie the rest of the division into you. The tank battalion will be on your right blocking the highway coming into the beachhead from the west. I need your battalion to tie into them on your right, and then tie into the rest of the units I'll send up on your left. You're my anchor to set this up. Any questions?"

"No, sir. I've got it, but sir …"

Sampson held up his hand. He knew what Easley was going to say. "Bob, I would have done the same thing in your shoes. You got an order from legitimate authority and we all have to assume that those orders are given for a good and valid purpose. If we can't trust each other in the Army, then this whole thing comes apart. I'll be up to your positions later and we'll talk more. Right now I need you to get your guys up there before the North Koreans take the high ground first."

"Yes, sir." Easley put his helmet on and left the room.

Sampson turned to the G-3. "Randy, take the rest of our combat power and extend the line from Bob's battalion as far as you can along the hills to the south." Sampson drew a line on the map. "Grab whatever other units are available like the MP's and support troops and put them in positions as well. I want the frontage of the division to be as far as you can make it. Everybody to include the headquarters troops are to be used. Any questions?"

"Yes, sir. Shouldn't we be trying to defend in depth instead of all spread out? We won't be strong anywhere."

"And that's exactly the picture I want the North Koreans to get."

"Uh, sir. May I ask why?"

"Yes, but not right now. I need you to get these guys moving before it gets dark. Stand by a minute, G-3." Sampson turned to face Gaddis and Stover who were standing just inside the door. "Captain Stover, you are relieved of your duties in this headquarters, and you're under open arrest. You will face court martial charges for conspiracy to commit murder when we get back to the States. For now, you will report to Lieutenant Colonel Easley for his use as he sees fit."

Stover's face had gone completely white at Sampson's words and he opened his mouth several times like a fish. Sampson's voice came out like a cracking whip, "Just shut your mouth, Stover and pray to god my son and his soldiers are holed up somewhere safe! Now where is the ROK colonel?"

Stover looked at the floor and didn't answer. Sampson hissed out, "You're only hope of living long enough to go to prison, Captain, will probably depend on what this ROK colonel knows. Did Wellens have him killed too?"

Stover mumbled, "No, sir. The MP's have him. General Wellens said he was a spy." Stover looked up pleadingly, "Sir, I didn't know what General Wellens was doing! Honest I didn't! You need me here as your aide. I can help you!"

Sampson said coldly, "No, Captain, I don't need your fucking help. Leave now before I have the MP's arrest you."

Stover turned abruptly and left the room, slamming the door behind him. Sampson didn't even notice the defiant gesture. "G-3, get me the ROK colonel from the MP's right after you put the warning order out. Gunny, I need you to get the division command sergeant major and bring him to me. He's got a reputation for being a real pussy chaser, so go wherever the most female soldiers are here in the beachhead. If he doesn't want to come, I'll count on you to persuade him to do so."

Gaddis smiled. "Aye, aye, sir!" There was nothing in life that he would like to do more than thump some fat army sergeant major!

"Go, gentlemen. We are running out of time." The two men saluted and left the room, Gaddis quietly closing the door behind him.

Sampson sat behind the desk and pulled his cell phone out of his jacket pocket. He had heard the chime earlier when he was outside with Wellens signaling that he had a signal again and then a second chime that he had a message. He slowly flipped the cover up and saw that the message was from his son's cell phone number. His fingers trembled as he hit the keys to retrieve the message. He put the phone up to his ear.

"Hey, Dad! It's Sean." His son's voice was breathless like he had been running. "I just called to say I love you and Mom and to thank you for always being there." Sampson could hear firing in the background. "I also called to say goodbye. I got me and one guy left and a shit load of ROK MP's and North Koreans to my front. I'm doing the great grand pappy thing here in a minute. I thought I would be scared, but I'm not. I'm just mad. Well, gotta go. Looks like the bad guys are coming! Love you!" Sampson heard more firing and the message ended.

Sean Sampson had grown up on the stories of his great grandfather Erasmus Sampson leading a desperate bayonet charge as a battalion commander of regulars in the Civil War. Erasmus had received the Congressional Medal of Honor for his actions; but he had gotten it posthumously. Sampson put his face in his hands and wept.

1900 hours
9 November
USS *Gunnery Sergeant Reuben Barnes* at Sea

"XO, how long before we rendezvous with the *Kitty Hawk*?"

"Skipper, that looks like it's going to slip a few hours. The *Kitty Hawk* has turned south again to pick up the marines from Okinawa. Their ship had a catastrophic propulsion failure and missed their rendezvous. One other thing, Skipper."

"Yes?"

"The sub and destroyer screen think they're in contact with some diesel boats, but they don't know whose they are yet. They're off the south coast of Korea in international waters so they could be Chinese or North Korean. The screen commander has requested permission to engage, but that's being decided at the White House."

"Well, crap! So CINCPAC doesn't have the authority to grant authorization? It's been pulled up to the White House? Like those bastards are even awake at this time of night back there?"

"Yes, sir. That about sums it up. The big question the White House staff asked was how do you know they're hostile? Admiral Durham sent a zinger back saying they wouldn't be closing in on his task force if they were just sightseeing!"

"And what response did he get?"

"The White House said, 'We'll get back to you.'"

"Well, crap again! XO, you'd think these guys would learn the damn lesson that you can't fight a war in real time while you wait for decisions to be made personally by the president. The only thing that has ever achieved is more casualties! Crap! How long before we rendezvous with the new time schedule?"

"At our current speed, we'll be there before the *Kitty Hawk*. It will be about an hour after daybreak."

"Is Admiral Durham okay with that?"

"Yeah, Skipper. We're to link up with the destroyer screen. We'll look like just another part of that in case anybody is looking. The intel guys believe we haven't been detected yet, but once we get closer to Korea, they think the Russians and French may still be providing satellite coverage of that area to North Korea. We'll be bringing the daylight with us so their satellites will see it all."

Parker nodded his head. It made sense to him. His ship looked just like another destroyer but with a gun turret instead of missile pods. In fact it looked more like an old fashioned destroyer so it might just escape notice altogether. "We'll need to slow this baby down when we get closer, XO. Even the French might question a destroyer with a mile long wake!"

The XO smiled at the reference to French competence. "Aye, aye, sir. We'll bleed some speed off about fifty miles out. I'll let the *Kitty Hawk* know we'll be a few minutes later than we projected earlier."

"Okay. You've got the con. I'm going below to get some sleep. Tomorrow promises to be exciting if there are diesel boats in the area. Get our sonar guys going full up once we're about six hundred nautical miles out. That's about the max range of the North Korean boats if I remember right. Confirm that with the intel guys. I'll relieve you in four hours."

"Aye, aye, Skipper."

**2312 hours
9 November
USS *Scorpion***

"Bridge, Sonar. We've just lost contact again."

"Same bearing?"

"Negative. This one was at zero seven two degrees."

"Shit!" Commander George Findley looked at his plot board as the sonar operator keyed in the latest location. He could see that he had intermittent contacts on both sides of the *Scorpion* now. He turned to his exec, "Bob, what kind of torpedoes are these guys going to have if they're North Korean?"

"Skipper, we have to assume that they'll have whatever the Chinese have."

"So pretty much everything out there?" The exec nodded. "Sonar, on your last plot, was it sound or magnometer?"

"Magnometer, Bridge."

"Shit! All stop. XO, dampen all noise down."

"Aye, aye, sir."

The *Scorpion* had been creeping along like a blind man trying to feel his way through a furniture store. They had had intermittent contacts with at least two if not three submarines over the last four hours. The contacts were getting progressively closer and were easily inside torpedo range now. The magnometer was only good out to a mile, so the last contact told Findley they were at least that close.

"XO, what's our weapons status from the *Kitty Hawk*? Any change?"

"Negative, Skipper. We're still at weapons hold. We can't shoot first."

Findley was going to say 'shit' again but let it go. There was absolute silence on board the *Scorpion*. Her forward movement through the water had stopped so even the limited noise of water passing along her hull was gone. Findley looked at the plot board again. He was the skipper of a fast attack nuclear submarine, the best submarine in the world and he was being played with by boats that used World War One technology for their propulsion! What kind of crap was that? They didn't have the range or underwater speed and endurance of the *Scorpion*, but then again, they didn't need to.

Findley made his decision. "Con, I want all ahead full on a bearing of zero seven two degrees. Push her as fast as she'll go. Do it!"

"Con, aye!"

"Sonar, when you pick them up again on this heading, give me a correction dead at them."

"Sonar, aye!"

The *Scorpion* picked up speed as she turned onto the new heading. The movement was almost imperceptible to the men in the boat.

"Torpedo Room standby! Decoys stand by!" Findley barked into the 1MC.

"Bridge, Sonar! We have a fish in the water, bearing zero six nine degrees!"

"Con, go to zero six nine degrees."

"Con, zero six nine degrees, aye!"

"Sonar, let me know when you have a bearing to the shooter."

"Sonar, aye." There was a short pause, "Bridge bearing to target is one one two degrees, range three thousand yards. Range to torpedo is two thousand yards, on our nose. Target is on sonar now and picking up speed. It sounds like he may be surfacing."

"Bridge, aye. XO, put the decoys out. Torpedo Room, fire one."

"Torpedo Room, aye, one fired!"

The men on the bridge could feel just the slightest jolt as the torpedo left the tube in a burst of compressed air. The torpedo would do all of its own guidance. It had been fed the sonar noise pattern and would now seek that pattern until it found it. If the pattern changed, the on board computer would adjust accordingly and keep the torpedo on the target. Hundreds of millions of noise patterns and every conceivable possibility for their adjustments or change were stored in a very small microchip in the torpedo's computer.

"Decoys deployed!"

"Con, turn to one eight zero degrees."

"Con, one eight zero degrees, aye."

"Sonar, status of inbound torpedo?"

"Bridge, it's breaking towards the decoy. Sonar contact one eight two degrees, range fifteen hundred yards! Fish in the water!"

Findley said calmly, "Bridge, aye. XO, put the next decoy out. Torpedo Room, fire two."

"Torpedo Room, two fired!"

"Decoy deployed!"

Findley had guessed right that the enemy submarines were trying to put him in a box. He had suspected that the two on his flanks would have a buddy sneaking up behind him. "Con, turn to two seven zero degrees and go to full emergency power."

"Con, two seven zero degrees, full emergency power, aye." This time the men inside the boat could feel the surge as the reactor kicked an extra ten knots to their speed. The *Scorpion* was slicing through the waters at over forty knots.

"Sonar, I'm looking for the guy to our front now." Before Findley could continue two thunderous explosions were heard through the hull.

"Bridge, Sonar! Hit Target on One! Hit on Decoy One!"

"Bridge, aye on hits. Sonar I need you to focus on the guy ahead of us. Let the torpedoes take care of themselves."

"Sonar, aye. Negative contact to our front." In the excitement of real shooting after so many years of training, the chief petty officer in charge of the sonar section couldn't help but get excited! He leaned over and looked at the two scopes his operators were watching intently. Two more explosions were heard through the hull. Since they were all still alive, he stopped himself from reporting the obvious to the bridge. He tapped the operator on his left, put a finger on the very edge of the screen and said "Neck that down." The operator tapped a few keys on his keyboard and the image centered on the screen and became sharper. "Bridge, magnometer contact, two three two degrees, range twelve hundred yards!"

Findley swore. The bastard had shifted further to his rear while he was going after the other two. It had moved too far and too fast to be a diesel boat on batteries. "Con, maintain this heading, all stop." There was no way Findley could turn in a tight enough radius at this speed to be head on to the new contact. "Sonar, let me know when he shoots. Torpedo Room, stand by."

"Torpedo Room, aye."

Again there was absolute silence in the boat. Findley waited and nothing happened. A full three minutes ticked off. "Sonar, do you still have contact?"

"Sonar, aye, Skipper, but he's moving off. We've got him on sonar too now."

If they had him on sonar they should be able to tell what type of boat it was from the sound pattern it emanated. Every type of submarine had its own distinct sound pattern.

"What is he, Sonar?"

There was a pause, and then sonar reported slowly, "Skipper, he's a Russian Alpha Class boat, and he's moving away. He's kicked it up to max speed and doesn't seem to care how much noise he's making."

Findley took that all in. He instantly realized that the Russian wanted to make damn sure the Americans knew who he was and wouldn't shoot. But it was damned strange for a Russian nuclear powered sub to be hanging around with North Korean diesel boats.

"Torpedo Room stand down. Sonar, Bravo Zulu! Con, all ahead slow, heading zero four five degrees." All the departments responded to Findley's orders in sequence. The sonar guys were giving each other high fives for the Bravo Zulu which was navy talk for good job!

Findley turned to his exec. "Bob, what the hell do you make of the Alpha Class being here?"

"I don't know, Skipper. The only thing I can think of is that he might have been helping the North Koreans with keeping track of us. They've got a good propulsion system with the diesel and battery combination, but I can't believe their underwater detection capability would be very good. They use these boats to infiltrate the South. They weren't designed for blue water fighting."

That was the only reason Findley could think of too. Trust the Russians to not take sides openly but to sell their services for cold hard cash whenever the opportunity arose. "Okay, put a sitrep together for the *Kitty Hawk* to let them know all this." The exec smirked. Findley raised his eyebrows. "Did I say something funny?"

"No, Skipper. I was just thinking how I'll word our little maneuver towards the North Korean boats. Somehow 'playing chicken' with them just doesn't seem to do it justice. I think I'll call the maneuver the 'Classic and infinitely memorable Findley in your face' maneuver.

"Let's just call it the 'turn towards the enemy to close the range' maneuver, XO and leave it at that," Findley said dryly.

Findley knew that two North Korean boats were out of the picture for sure, but neither Findley nor anybody else knew how many more there were, or if the Russians would continue to play. He also knew the Russians would never allow themselves to get spooked and fire off a torpedo. They would be very hard to kill if they decided to play hardball in this game.

1900 hours EST
9 November
The White House

The president had been handed a note during the middle of the state dinner he was hosting for a Saudi Arabian prince. He had excused himself and left the dining room. He thrust the note into the secretary of defense's face and snarled, "Ralph, what the hell does it mean that we 'have engaged and destroyed two submarines, presumed to be North Korean'? Just what in the hell does that mean? I didn't authorize any action by the navy! What the hell are they doing?"

"Mister President, the navy fired in self-defense. They have their own authority to do that." Brooks was clearly upset because the president was so upset.

Preston snorted and said sarcastically, "Yeah, I'll just bet they were firing in self-defense, Ralph. I'll be goddamned if I will allow them to disobey my explicit orders, Ralph. I want whoever is responsible fired on the damn spot, Ralph, and I want it done now! Right goddamned now, you hear me?"

Brooks sighed audibly. "Mister President I have personally reviewed the tapes the navy sent of the submarine commander's orders and the tape of the sonar contacts. They are all legitimate. They're like an airplane's black box. They can't be tampered with. The submarine commander had no choice but to shoot. Otherwise, I'd be standing here telling you we lost a nuclear sub off the coast of South Korea."

That statement penetrated Preston's anger. The magnitude of having to face the press and answer questions about the loss of a multi-billion dollar submarine made Preston shudder at the thought. He did not even think about the loss of the crew. He had never been in the military and didn't have a very high opinion of those who had. The military was where you went if you were born poor and didn't have any other options. Or if you screwed up and got caught, and the judge said 'it's either the army or jail, son.'

"Then you're saying the North Koreans shot first? You have confirmed that?"

"Yes, sir, I have." Brooks nodded his head in affirmation of his words.

"Were we in North Korean waters? Is that why they shot at us?"

"No, Mister President, we were not in their waters. I have also confirmed that fact. We were actually in international waters south and east of the Korean Peninsula."

"Then why the hell would they shoot at us, Ralph? What the hell is in it for them? We've already agreed to evacuate the remainder of American troops from the damned Peninsula once the carrier gets there. What more could these bastards want?"

Brooks' body language was that of a man who was decidedly uncomfortable. He hesitated before he finally spoke. He chose his words carefully. "Sir, a few of my advisors now believe that the reported threat to our forces in Korea may have some substance to it." The look of incredulity that sprang onto Preston's face at these words caused Brooks to continue hastily, "However, Mister President, I'm still not sure I personally believe those reports. As you said a moment ago, there's nothing in it for them to take us on."

Preston was now obviously confused by Brooks' remarks. "If you still have your doubts Ralph, then why bring it up? You sound like you're trying to play both sides of the fence here." Preston looked at his secretary of defense closely, and then asked perceptively, "And just who are the *few advisors*, Ralph? Is Goodman one of them?"

The secretary of defense nodded his head uncomfortably and murmured, "Yes, Mister President."

"And who else, Ralph?"

"General Smith."

Preston asked impatiently in a harsh voice, "And who else, Ralph?"

Ralph Brooks sighed, shrugged and said, "Pretty much all the military people, Mister President."

Preston shook his head at the response and said, "Jesus, Ralph! You can be such a fucking idiot, sometimes!" Brooks looked devastated at the president's remark. He knew it was being taped and someday would be released to the public. The president knew that too and didn't care. The Secret Service agent standing a few feet away also heard it but studiously kept his eyes to the front. "So what the hell were we going to say if this whole thing went to shit, Ralph? Tell me that!"

"Sir, we would just tell the truth. Sometimes you just don't know what you just don't know."

Preston groaned and swore. He said with intense sarcasm, "Oh, yeah, Ralph. That would look just great for the *New York Times* headlines. I'd fucking sound like President Yogi Berra! Get Goodman over here and we'd better figure some shit out quick, or we're going to be hosed by the media if this goes down ugly." Preston snapped his fingers at the Secret Service agent who came over to him immediately. "Go back in there and tell my wife to tell the raghead prince whatever his fucking name is that I've been called away for an emergency."

The president didn't know the agent's name. He only knew a handful of their names and got most of those wrong. The agents would defend his life with their own if need be, but that didn't mean they needed to like the man, which none of them did. He treated them like part of the furniture. The agent nodded and went into the dining room to convey the message.

2330 hours
9 November
2nd ID CP, Chong-ju, South Korea

Sampson had just returned to the command post from visiting all the units up on the line. The combat units were well advanced on their fighting positions and the support units were not. Sampson directed the combat units to send over soldiers to help supervise the support units' efforts. Randy Long who had gone with him had already proven himself to be invaluable. Sampson was glad he was on the team he had inherited. As he entered his office, he glanced at the back door. He knew that Wellens' body had been removed in his absence and taken to the graves registration unit, but he looked anyhow. As he flopped down wearily in his chair, Gunny Gaddis brought in a steaming canteen cup of coffee.

"Here, sir. You're gonna need this. I finally found Sergeant Major Fat Ass and he's waiting to see you." Sampson took the cup gratefully. He needed the caffeine jolt about now. He had almost forgotten how hard it was to operate with no sleep and lots of pressure and not enough time.

"Thanks, Gunny. Bring him in and you stay in here too."

"Aye, aye, sir."

Gaddis ushered the command sergeant major of the 2nd Infantry Division into the office and closed the door behind him. Command Sergeant Major Rudolph Rheinhart came into the room and stood nonchalantly in front of Sampson's desk. He had a black eye that was beginning to swell up. Sampson waited. Rheinhart looked around the room and then moved towards a chair with the obvious intent of sitting down. Sampson's voice stopped him cold.

"Report, Command Sergeant Major."

Rheinhart seemed confused. "Uh, report what, General?" Rheinhart started moving towards the chair again, and again Sampson's voice stopped him.

"I want you to stand in front of my desk at attention, salute and report to your new division commander, Sergeant Major. You know, just like we do in the army and have done for about two hundred and fifty years now."

Rheinhart was clearly flabbergasted. "General, we don't do that shit anymore! I'm equal to you, and not some damned subordinate!"

Sampson smiled grimly. He had heard this crap before and it was the single biggest reason why much of the senior non-commissioned officer corps of the army had become so politicized that it was just another old boys club like the general officer ranks; and about as useful in Sampson's opinion. Senior non-commissioned officers now took up as much manpower, energy and resources for their entourages as generals did. Sampson shook his head at Rheinhart. "And who told you that, Sergeant Major? That you were equal to a two star?"

"We were taught that at the Sergeant Major's Academy." Rheinhart responded with a challenge in his voice.

"Okay, Sergeant Major. I'll ask you two questions and then we'll go from there. First question, what's your rank? What rank is on your leave and earning statement each month? Does it say Major General O-8, or Sergeant E-9?"

Rheinhart mumbled, "Sergeant E-9."

"Second question. Please give me the Army Regulation that states that a Sergeant E-9 is equal to a Major General O-8 in rank and authority."

Rheinhart shook his head. There was no such regulation.

"Okay, it doesn't matter. You're relieved of your duties as division command sergeant major."

Rheinhart's face instantly flushed red. "You don't have the authority to do that, goddamnit!"

Sampson looked at Rheinhart and said evenly, "Come to attention, Sergeant Major." Rheinhart looked as if he didn't understand Sampson's order. Sampson said again, "Come to attention, Sergeant Major when you address me, or I will charge you with insubordination. Or do I need the gunny here to help you come to attention?"

Rheinhart flinched and sprang to the position of attention. Sampson knew exactly where the black eye had come from and wasn't surprised when Rheinhart quickly came to the position of attention.

"Very good, Sergeant Major. You are relieved of your duties and will report to the DIVARTY Commander. He is expecting you and will use you in his CP. You will have the authority of a staff sergeant major, nothing more."

"Sir, as I said earlier, you don't have the authority to relieve me as a command sergeant major. That takes at least a three star and I ain't seen one of them around here lately!" Rheinhart finished smugly.

"Of course I do, Sergeant Major. We're at war and I have every authority over you short of having you shot. I could probably even make a case for that if you disobey my orders. Gunny, where did you find *Staff* Sergeant Major Rheinhart, by the way?"

"Sir, he was shacked up with his female driver in one of the houses in the ville."

"Ah, and I see by the ring on your finger, Sergeant Major, that you're a married man?" Rheinhart nodded glumly. "Then I think that alone is sufficient to remove you from your duties as division command sergeant major. Gunny, please write a statement up to the effect of what you saw."

"Aye, aye, sir!"

Rheinhart blurted out, "This man struck me!" and he pointed a shaking finger towards Gunny Gaddis.

Sampson seemed to weigh the accusation seriously. He asked slowly, "Gunnery Sergeant Gaddis, did you strike Staff Sergeant Major Rheinhart?"

"Yes, sir, I did."

"Why did you strike him?"

"Sir, he refused to obey the order from you to report to you immediately."

"Did he say anything else?"

"Yes, sir. He said you could quote just kiss his bare white fucking ass, unquote."

"Well, make sure you include that in your written report, Gunny, for the court martial."

Rheinhart paled. Sampson said, "Now get out of my office Sergeant Rheinhart before I have the MP's put you in handcuffs." Rheinhart let out a grunt like he had been physically hit in the stomach and stumbled from the room.

Sampson turned to Gaddis. "Call DIVARTY in about thirty minutes to make sure that son-of-a-bitch gets there, Gunny. Did they find the ROK colonel yet?"

"Yes, sir. You want him in here?"

"Yeah, Gunny."

"You want me to stay when he comes?"

"No, Gunny. This guy will be a friend. I could use more coffee though, and I bet he could too."

"Aye, aye, sir. Can do."

The ROK colonel came into the room somewhat hesitantly. He had not been treated terribly well by the Americans the last time he had come into that particular office. He was clearly surprised to see Sampson and not Wellens. Sampson stood up from behind his desk and came forward with his hand outstretched. He was smiling. The colonel took his hand numbly, clearly confused.

"Colonel, I'm Major General Sampson, the new division commander."

They shook hands and the colonel asked, "Where is General Wellens, sir? I spoke to him before."

Sampson looked at the colonel's nametag and replied, "Colonel Han, General Wellens was sadly killed by a sniper earlier this afternoon. Please, have a seat here." Sampson waved towards a chair and Gunny Gaddis brought in two canteen cups of coffee. Sampson sat down in a chair beside Han. "Colonel, I was told that you had brought information to General Wellens. I need you to tell me what it was. He and I did not get a chance to discuss that before he was killed."

Han hesitated. The last time he had told the Americans something he had been handcuffed and dragged out the back door of the headquarters. Sampson saw the hesitation and said reassuringly, "Colonel Han, I know you're not a spy and I know you're here to help us, so please tell me what you know."

Han started slowly in very good English, "Sir, I was sent here by General Moon. I was to warn the 2nd Infantry Division about an ambush on the highway to kill the Americans coming from Seoul." Han hung his head in shame. "I could not convince General Wellens, so the Americans all died."

Sampson would have been stunned by this statement but he already knew what Wellens had done. He had sent his son to the ambush site, but not with enough combat power to change the outcome. Wellens, if he had ever been called to task for not responding to the warning, would glibly say he had responded to the report using his best professional judgment based upon the unconfirmed report he had received from some *renegade* ROK colonel. Sampson could hear Wellens saying the words and closed his eyes briefly. On further reflection, Sampson realized that Bobby Wellens had expertly hidden his surprise at seeing Sampson alive and well earlier in the day. He shook his head, and he felt a grim satisfaction that Wellens was dead. Sampson shook his head again to clear his thoughts of Wellens and what he had done.

Sampson reached across and touched Han's arm. "No, Colonel Han. I led that group from Seoul. We arrived here safely. You were successful in your mission."

Han looked up and was clearly surprised. "But General Moon said there were to be forty or more in the ambush team! Our intelligence people heard Colonel Lee Pok talking on his cell phone about it!"

Sampson nodded. "Yes, but one of our patrols engaged them and prevented the ambush."

Han sighed in relief. He sat back in his chair and sipped his coffee for the first time. "That is good to know, General. I am to tell you from General Moon two more things. The first is to say that no ROK forces will act against you. General Moon says it's very important for you to understand that." Han paused and looked at Sampson who nodded his understanding. "And I'm to tell you that I will stay with you and be evacuated."

The last statement clearly surprised Sampson. "Why, Colonel Han?"

Han shrugged as if what he was about to say was of no consequence. "I must go with you because I'm a graduate of your military academy at West Point. General Moon knows that I will be arrested and sent north for reeducation at the hands of the communists if I remain in Korea. General Moon was a friend of my father, and has been like a second father to me since his passing."

"Are you married? Where's your family, Colonel Han?"

"Sir, my family is already in Hawaii. They were visiting family there for Chusok, the Korean Thanksgiving. They were scheduled to come home the day the war started but had plane trouble and were delayed, thank God!" Han like many South Koreans was a devout Christian. Sampson knew his thanks to God for delivering his family were not just empty words.

"Then you are more than welcome to come along with us, Colonel Han. I understand the problem now. Do you know anybody over at Pohang Naval Base, by the way?"

Han smiled. "Yes, sir! My second cousin on my mother's side of the family is in command there. He came to Seoul to play golf with me just last month. But why do you ask, sir?" Han's earlier enthusiasm rapidly waned as he realized the question couldn't just be casual.

"I need to borrow some boats from your cousin. How agreeable do you think he would be to that?"

Han sucked in his breath through his teeth, a typically Korean gesture of doubt that the Americans jokingly referred to as the 'four molar suck.' If you got the 'eight molar suck,' what you were asking was not only impossible but also laughable. Sampson noted the four instead of the eight and pressed, "We would have to make it look like he had no choice, of course. But if we're going to get off the Peninsula in one piece, Colonel Han, we need those boats."

Han nodded. He had been to Pohang and seen the small fleet of landing craft there. He didn't know the exact numbers but felt sure there were at least forty if not more. "How many do you need, sir?"

"All of them." This time Sampson got the full eight molar suck as Han shook his head. It would not be possible to take them all. The North Koreans would kill his cousin if that were to happen.

Sampson saw the doubt in Han's face and offered, "We can bring your cousin and his family out with us, if that would help."

Han brightened. "Yes, that would help!" But his enthusiasm flagged again rapidly. "But who will operate these boats, General? We cannot possibly ask my cousin to order his sailors to do that. We are all under the strictest orders from the Dear Leader to not help you in any way."

Sampson had already thought about that and Gunny Gaddis had spent the evening rounding up every soldier in the division who had ever operated anything as small as an outboard motor. Gaddis had told Sampson how he had been surprised at the numbers of soldiers in the support battalion who had actually operated mike boats for the army in the Transportation Corps. Gaddis hadn't known that the army had a fleet of small boats that was actually larger than the navy's small boat fleet, and that there were soldiers whose normal duties were to actually be sailors in that fleet. He said it had made his head hurt to find all that out, but he had gathered more than enough to man the boats, and the soldiers who were really sailors had been instructing the others throughout the night on how to operate the mike boats. Sampson explained all that to Colonel Han who smiled.

Han asked a final question. "General Sampson, if some of my cousin's men want to come, what do I say to them?"

"If they are single men, they may come with you. I cannot afford to have a lot of civilians in the beachhead, Colonel Han, because it's going to get very dangerous. You will go tomorrow night at first dark to get the boats and your cousin. I will get his family out to the carrier along with any other civilians we have at that point. Colonel, I'm glad to have you with us. Thank you for all your help."

Han beamed at Sampson's words.

0200 hours
10 November
USS *Gunnery Sergeant Reuben Barnes* at Sea

"Well, I'll be damned!" Parker scribbled his initials on the message form and handed the clipboard back to the bosun. "Thanks, Chief. I'll announce it on the 1MC." Parker grabbed the handset from its mount on the bridge and hit the button to open the 1MC circuit. The bosun tweeted his whistle in the age old signal that told the entire ship that the captain was about to speak. Parker waited briefly for the sailors who were off watch to wake up and listen to what he had to say.

Parker began, "Now hear this! Now hear this! This is the captain speaking." Parker could hear his words coming over the 1MC in the other compartments away from the bridge. He continued, "We have just received communications that this ship has been federalized by order of the President of the United States. You men are now all back in the United States Navy!" A cheer went up throughout the ship. Parker smiled, paused and then said, "So your pay will revert back to your former navy pay until further notice." A huge groan went up throughout the ship punctuated with some choice swear words. The entire crew had just taken a huge pay cut! All the men understood that you couldn't be on active duty and draw contractor pay simultaneously. It was against the federal acquisition regulations.

Parker smiled. He knew the CEO would take care of his guys with a hefty Christmas bonus once this was over and they were no longer on active duty. The navigator saw the smile and was puzzled as he said, "Skipper, we're four hours out. We'll need to bleed some speed off of her when we get one hour out." Parker continued to smile as he said, "Thanks, Rafe. Put it in the log. Helm, set your clock to lower the speed three hours from now."

"Helm, aye, Skipper."

**0618 hours
10 November
USS *Scorpion*, 60 miles east of Chong-ju, South Korea**

"Bridge, Sonar. We've got the Russian back."

Findley looked at his XO. He wondered if he looked as tired as the XO did. It had been a crappy night with intermittent contact with the Alpha Class sub several times every hour. "Sonar, bearing and range?"

"Bridge, bearing is three five two degrees, range is twelve thousand." Findley watched the plot board as the new target location was put in, and the earlier plot of the Russian sub was dimmed to show its previous location. The Russian was actually leading the *Scorpion* to the rendezvous site, or he was going home to Vladivostok. They would know which in an hour or so. If the Russian stopped when they did to wait for the *Kitty Hawk*, then he clearly wasn't going home just yet.

"XO, what's the ETA on the *Kitty Hawk* now?"

"Skipper, she'll be here in fifty-eight minutes. She has just picked up the last picket ship."

Findley looked at his watch. It was just beginning to get light out there. It would be full daylight when the task force got to the rendezvous site. The good news was that the helicopters forming part of the carrier task force's anti-submarine patrol would be able to see better in the daylight. The bad news was that any North Korean submarines would be able to see better too. "Con, give me a slow turn to port, reduce speed to ahead to one third." It was time to see what the Russian was going to do.

"Con, aye. Slow turn to port, ahead one third."

Findley waited, tapping his fingers absentmindedly on his work table for what seemed an eternity. Finally the silence on the bridge was broken.

"Bridge, Sonar. The Alpha Class has started to turn with us. She has also reduced speed."

Well, so much for going home to good old Vladivostok, Findley thought sourly. If the Alpha was staying, he had to assume it was for some purpose, and the only one he could come up with again was to serve as a spotter for North Korean diesel boats. "XO, assume for a minute you were some rotten commie bastard of a bitching North Korean submarine commander. How would you go about taking the *Hawk* down?"

The XO looked startled at the question, particularly at its wording, and he furrowed his brow in thought. He replied slowly, "I would assume that you would assume that I would come in from the coast because you know my boat doesn't have much blue water range."

Findley nodded, but sixty miles out wasn't beyond the range of the diesel boats. "So you would assume that I would assume that so you would actually hit me from the open ocean?"

The XO nodded. Findley continued, "But if you knew I would assume that you would assume that I would assume that you would hit me from the open sea, what would you do?"

The XO smiled, "I would hit you from the coast while you were looking out to sea for me."

Findley grunted. Yeah, he'd do the same. Sometimes doing the obvious achieved the greatest surprise in combat.

"Con, put me on a course to the beach, all ahead full. Sonar, keep your eyes peeled for diesel boats and keep posting what my Russian friend is doing."

"Sonar, aye."

Findley went back to drumming his fingers.

0628 hours
10 November
USS *Kitty Hawk* off the coast of South Korea

"Admiral Durham, the *Scorpion* reports the Russian Alpha Class sub is staying with him in the rendezvous area. *Scorpion* is patrolling towards the beachhead. Captain Findley thinks the Russians are there to spot again for North Korean subs."

Durham said, "Thanks, XO. I think young Findley is right. That Russian bastard is obviously up to no good. They've got satellites up there that can see everything we're doing, so he's not here scouting us for his home team. CAG, how soon before we can launch the helos?"

"Another twelve minutes, sir, or they'll get there just in time to turn around and come back to refuel."

"Okay, launch them on your command, CAG."

"Aye, aye, Admiral. Launch on my command."

**0642 hours
10 November
USS *Scorpion*, 10 miles east of Chong-ju, South Korea**

"Bridge, Sonar. Contact! Magnometer hit three two six degrees, twelve hundred yards."

"Any fish in the water, Sonar?"

"Negative on fish."

Findley looked at his XO and said quietly, "Fire torpedo one, XO."

The XO knew that Findley was violating the rules of engagement that were still being hotly contested between the Pentagon and the White House staff, but he passed the order on without any hesitation. Findley had already figured out that the Russians had tipped the North Koreans off about not shooting first. They wouldn't make the same mistake twice. Findley wasn't going to wait for them this time.

"Sonar, I'm turning to port so keep looking. Tell me if that Russian bastard even farts!"

"Sonar, aye!"

Several seconds ticked off and they heard the unmistakable boom of the torpedo exploding.

"Bridge, Sonar. Hit on torpedo one."

"Bridge, aye. What's the Russian doing now?"

"Bridge, Sonar. He's turning towards us."

"Is he increasing speed?"

"Negative, Bridge. Standby! Fish in the water! The Russian has fired a torpedo!"

Findley froze for a fraction of a second, and then barked, "Sonar, range and bearing of the torpedo?"

"Range fourteen thousand yards, bearing one eight zero degrees."

Findley glanced at his plot board. Unless the Russians were guiding that torpedo manually, it would come nowhere near the *Scorpion* on that track.

"Bridge, contact on magnometer, eight hundred yards straight ahead!"

"XO, fire torpedo two! Helm, ninety degrees to starboard, full emergency power!"

"Torpedo away!"

"Helm, aye!"

The *Scorpion* actually heeled over with the violent turn and burst of speed. Several coffee cups clattered to the deck.

"Sonar, status of the Russian torpedo?"

"Bridge, the torpedo is running hot and straight on a bearing on one eight zero degrees. Bridge, third contact, three four two degrees, two thousand yards! Fish in the water!"

"XO, launch decoy one, fire torpedo three."

There was only a short pause before the XO responded, "Decoy away! Torpedo three away!"

"Helm, give me ninety degrees to port and all reverse."

"Helm, aye!"

"XO, shit me another decoy as we back the hell out of here. Make that two more! Sonar, status of the Russian torpedo?"

"Bridge, same bearing, same course; hit on torpedo two!" A few seconds later the sound wave from the explosion reached the *Scorpion*. "Miss on torpedo three, bridge!"

"Well, shit. Sonar, where's the target? You still got him? Give me a bearing so we can shoot again."

"He's surfacing, Bridge! He's blown his tanks and is heading as fast as he can to the surface!"

"Okay, but I still want to kill this bastard so give me a bearing and range, Sonar."

"Skipper, Sonar, we have sonar pods in the water! Do you still want range and bearing to Target Three?"

Findley sighed in relief, and said, "Negative, Sonar, but keep tracking it until we figure out who all the players are in this circus."

The helicopters from the task force were on station dipping their sonar pods as they went along looking for submarines beneath the waves. Findley's relief was shattered by the sounds of another explosion. "Sonar, was that the Russian torpedo?"

"Bridge, aye, but we don't know what he hit. It was below the surface. The Russian has blown his tanks and is surfacing too!"

Findley looked at his XO. "Beam us up, Scotty. We might as well see what the hell is going on up there."

The XO gave the orders to surface and the *Scorpion* was going to see the light of day for the first time in almost a month. The sub communicated its intentions to the helicopters above. By Findley's count, his would be the third submarine suddenly popping to the surface, and he didn't want the well armed anti-submarine helo crews any more confused than they surely already were!

0736 hours
10 November
USS *Kitty Hawk* at the Rendezvous Point off the coast of South Korea

"Admiral, the *Scorpion* reports link up with the Russian sub. Its skipper is coming aboard the *Scorpion* now." Admiral Durham put his binoculars to his eyes and could just make out the two submarines side by side in the distance. He turned his binoculars back towards the coast and saw the ugly gray hull of the North Korean diesel boat hunched down sullenly in the waves. The captain of the destroyer USS *Kennesaw* was talking to the North Korean skipper through a young Korean-American sailor who was translating his captain's word through a bullhorn. Durham could clearly see the North Korean skipper violently shaking his head at the words he was hearing through the bullhorn.

Durham turned to his exec. "Get the skipper of the *Kennesaw* on the horn for me, please." Durham saw the captain of the *Kennesaw* move back inside the bridge to talk to him. A few seconds later, Durham heard over the radio, "Admiral, this guy says he's in international waters and was fired upon by one of our boats. He's lodging a formal protest through his country, and insists that we grant him freedom of maneuver so he can continue to his home port. What are your instructions, sir?"

"Standby, *Kennesaw*. Captain Findley, did you monitor all that?"

Findley came back quickly over the radio, "Yes, Admiral, I did. According to the Russian skipper I have standing here; the North Korean is lying and was attempting to sink the *Kitty Hawk*."

Durham looked puzzled as he said, "And just how the hell would he know that, Captain Findley?"

Findley came back immediately so he had obviously asked the same question. "He says they have broken the North Korean naval codes and can prove what the North Koreans were up to. He brought documents over from his boat to give to me."

"Do you buy all this, Captain Findley?"

"Admiral, wait one, please." There was a short pause before Findley continued, "Sorry, Admiral. I had to have my new found Russian friend escorted to the galley so he couldn't hear what I was going to tell you. He claims he doesn't speak English but who knows with these guys? Admiral, the documents he gave us have already been translated into English, and they clearly show that the orders given to the North Korean subs were to sink the *Kitty Hawk*. That said, I also clearly know my Russian friend was acting as a spotter for the North Koreans."

"How do you know that, Captain?"

"Sir, because there is no way in hell those four diesel boats could have simultaneously vectored onto the *Scorpion* and boxed us in without help. They don't have the sonar or other detection systems good enough to do that, but the Alpha Class does."

Before Durham could respond, Findley came over the radio again, "Admiral, you also need to know that the Russian sub took out the fourth North Korean boat. We had missed it, and it was sneaking up behind us. We had already nailed two out of the four with the third one in our crosshairs when the helos showed up. We didn't know about the fourth boat, but the Russian damn sure did and took it out with a long range torpedo shot."

Durham nodded his head in agreement with Findley's assessment. The Russians had definitely been spotting for the North Koreans. Still, killing the only undetected North Korean boat didn't make sense to Durham. He keyed the radio and said, "But why would he take that sub out, Captain? Why not just leave the area?"

"Sir, because we knew the Russian Alpha Class had been here and we could prove it with our sonar tapes. He took the fourth boat out because I think he figured that one boat wasn't going to be enough to take on the task force successfully, and dead men tell no tales. There would be nobody left to rat him out, but he hadn't figured on our torpedo missing the third boat. He definitely didn't count on that third boat over there broaching and getting caught instead of going down, so he's probably shitting bricks down in the galley about now."

Durham smiled at Findley's description of the Russian skipper down in the galley of the *Scorpion*, and agreed with his analysis of the Russian's actions. He said, "*Kennesaw*? Did you monitor *Scorpion*?"

"Affirmative, Admiral. What are your instructions for the North Korean boat?"

Durham didn't even hesitate before he replied, "Tell the captain of that boat that he has five minutes to abandon ship and then we're going to sink it. If he asks to be taken aboard the *Kennesaw*, grant his request. If he doesn't, let the crew go in whatever boats they have."

"I understand, Admiral. Out here."

Durham watched through the binoculars as the captain of the *Kennesaw* came back out of the bridge onto the deck, and told his sailor translator what he wanted him to tell the North Koreans. The translator put the bullhorn to his lips and gave the message. Durham saw the North Korean skipper shake his head and fold his arms across his chest in defiance. He would not order his ship to be abandoned.

Durham keyed the radio microphone, "*Kitty Hawk* to *Kennesaw*, tell your skipper to fend the North Korean boat off."

"*Kennesaw*, aye, aye."

Durham watched as the space between the ship and the submarine widened. The North Korean skipper unfolded his arms and dropped through the conning tower hatch. The submarine started to froth water as the air was blown from her tanks. Slowly at first, and then in a rush the North Korean boat slipped under the waves. Durham turned to the CAG and said simply, "Take her down, CAG."

Within a minute, two helicopters that had been waiting with their rotors turning on the deck of the *Kitty Hawk* lifted off and vectored to where the submarine had submerged. One helicopter lowered its sonar pod into the water and the other flew around it in a wide arc. The first helicopter lifted its pod, moved a couple hundred yards closer to shore and reinserted its pod. A few seconds went by, then the second helicopter flew past the first one and dropped three cylinders into the water and turned away, flying off a couple of hundred yards and hovering. The first helicopter pulled its sonar pods out of the water and also went into a hover.

After a full minute had gone by, the sea erupted into three huge water spouts. All of them clearly contained pieces of metal, human body parts and other wreckage. An ugly brown oil slick rose to the surface along with more pieces of the submarine and its crew. Durham turned away and put his binoculars down. "Combat, tell the commander ashore that the *Kitty Hawk* battle group is at the rendezvous site and it is secure."

"Combat, aye, aye, Admiral."

"Also signal the *Scorpion* Bravo Zulu." Durham turned to his exec. "Did the *Scorpion* know about the change in the rules of engagement to weapons free, XO? Specifically, when he was nailing those North Korean subs?"

The XO paused and then shook his head. "No, sir. We got the word from the White House through the Pentagon about ten minutes after the *Scorpion's* final contact report after he engaged. Is there a problem, sir? That Findley violated the ROE?"

Durham noticed the concern in his XO's voice. A real tight ass admiral might make it a problem, but he sure as hell wouldn't! He liked officers like Findley who had balls enough to do what was right instead of what was politically correct or career enhancing. Durham smiled at his XO whose face relaxed. "Nope, no problem, XO. Bring young Findley aboard for dinner tonight. I want his first hand account about how he is now the first submarine ace in history by taking out five other submarines! Six submarines if we keep quiet about our Russian help," Durham smirked.

The XO said, "Uh, sir. I only count five even with the Russian one."

"Oh, no, XO. The *Scorpion* gets the one we just blew up too. They're the ones who drove her to the surface. But let's not haggle over particulars. Have the skipper tell the cooks that we'll want steaks tonight. In fact put that out across the task force. And steak and eggs for breakfast. And happy birthday, XO."

"Sir, it's not my birthday."

"Yeah, I know. It's the Marine Corps' birthday and tomorrow is Veteran's Day. I want every marine in the fleet to get a cold beer with his steak tonight with my compliments. Get them out of the stores and enter it into the ship's log as an order from me in case some rear echelon twerp wants to make an issue of it later."

Navy ships did not allow the consumption of alcohol in any form when deployed; a rule strictly adhered to. Durham didn't care about precedent or rules made up by bureaucrats sitting safely far, far away. He wanted to thank his marines for all that they did, and he particularly wanted to give them a good meal and a beer before they went ashore tomorrow. He was afraid that many of them would not be coming back. He hoped like hell this guy Sampson had his shit together.

0810 hours
10 November
USS *Gunnery Sergeant Reuben Barnes*

"XO, signal the flagship and ask them where we go in the task force."

"Aye, aye, Skipper." The executive officer made the radio call, wrote down their orders and turned back to Parker.

"Skipper, the admiral said to tell you welcome back to the navy, and you're to go for dinner tonight aboard the *Kitty Hawk* at seventeen thirty hours."

Parker smiled at the message. He and Jasper Durham had been shipmates on a destroyer in the old days before Jasper went off to flight school to fly over North Vietnam and Parker had continued on in surface ships supporting the marines ashore with naval gunfire. "Where does he want us in this circus, XO?"

"Sir, he said to park behind the *Kitty Hawk* inside the destroyer screen. We're the second most valuable ship in the task force now. He said we were only second because he happens to personally be on the *Kitty Hawk*."

Parker laughed. Jasper obviously hadn't changed a bit with promotion to flag rank. He looked forward to his dinner tonight. He also knew he would get the gouge on how his ship was supposed to support the army troops ashore.

0845 hours
10 November
2nd Infantry Division CP, Chong-ju, South Korea

The big navy helicopter kicked up a bunch of loose dirt as it settled onto the playground of the school. The racket of the rotor blades echoed off the walls of the school. Just as the wheels touched down, a large man jumped to the ground and ran crouched over away from the helicopter. He was passed by a Korean woman who ran to the chopper and was helped inside by the crew chief. The big man waved back at the crew chief who returned the gesture as the helicopter pulled away from the ground and headed rapidly out to sea.

The big man ran towards the only person he could see outside the building. He said breathlessly as he came up, "You Gunny Gaddis?"

The gunny broke his gaze from the departing helicopter, nodded and smiled as he shook the big man's hand. "Yeah, Sergeant Major, I'm Gaddis. Follow me." Gaddis took the kit bag from the sergeant major's hand as he led the way into the building through a back door. Gaddis seemed not to notice the pool of dried blood he stepped over on the way through the door. Duffy saw the blood, and stepped over it too.

As Gaddis opened the door he said, "Sir, Command Sergeant Major Duffy is here to see you."

Sampson got up from behind his desk and walked towards the door. "Well, it's about time you got here, Top."

Duffy stopped dead in his tracks and just stared at Sampson. He saw the white hair, the grey eyes and the scar on the chin. It damn sure *was* Sam Sampson but he was wearing two stars on his collar. They were small stars but stars all the same!

"Jesus Christ, Colonel! You're supposed to be sitting on your fat ass fishing somewhere in Georgia the last time I checked. What the shit are you doing here for god's sake?" Duffy was grinning from ear to ear as he pumped Sampson's hand vigorously in a monster handshake. "Goddamn it's good to see you, sir! Goddamn!"

"It's good to see you too, Top. And it's general and not colonel by the way." Sampson fingered his stars mockingly.

Duffy guffawed at the implied rebuke. "You ain't fooling this old Georgia boy, Colonel; I know you bought that shit at the PX or something. Naw, the army wouldn't have been that dumb. No, sir, they sure would not." Then Duffy turned serious. "Sir, what's the drill? This can only be bad news if they grabbed you again, and it's really got to be bad news if they thought enough of my sorry ass to fly me all the way out here in a navy fighter plane. And it's got to be totally butt ugly all to hell for them to promote you in the process."

Sampson waved Duffy to a chair and sat down too. He also waved Gaddis to a chair. "Top, what have you heard about what's going on over here?"

"Sir, not much. I picked some scuttlebutt up on the ship about pulling you guys off the beach tomorrow and apparently the navy had a scrap with North Korean submarines on their way up here. But as far as CNN and the rest of them are concerned, all that has happened over here is yesterday's news. They're already shifting their focus to everything but here from what I saw on the TV in the Chief's Mess. So what is going on, boss?"

"The North Koreans are going to try and take us down as we evacuate tomorrow, Top."

Duffy pursed his lips reflectively. "What've they got to do it with and better yet, what do we have to stop them with? My guess is not much on our part and too much on theirs, and that's the reason the poor old sergeant major gets shanghaied to Korea? Is that about it, sir?"

"Yeah, that's about it."

Duffy looked glumly at Sampson. "So what do you need me to do, boss?"

"Top, I need you to spend the rest of today and tonight talking to the NCO's and junior officers in each unit up on the line. We're going to execute a withdrawal under pressure and I'll need them to clearly understand how that works. We haven't even talked about this type of maneuver in the army since the Soviets went tits up on us and quit playing. I know it's still in the tactics manuals, but we quit training for it close to twenty years ago. You know the deal from the old days, one half of the crew served weapons …"

Duffy finished the sentence which he knew by heart, "… and one third of the troops under the command of the executive officer or the S-3 while the commander moves the main body back to an overwatch position to cover the subsequent withdrawal of the detachment left in contact." Duffy nodded. Yeah, he knew the drill. You learned it by rote when you were stationed in Germany during the Cold War because the plan was to trade space for time against the Russian hordes until the reinforcements came in from the States. You always hoped like hell there would be enough space and enough time if the Russians really attacked.

"Got it, sir. What else can I tell them?"

"Tell them I am arranging enough firepower for them to break contact when the time comes. Make goddamned sure they know that the North Koreans don't have an air force so they are not to shoot at any low flying planes. You need to know I'll be using napalm, but they don't need to know that in case the North Koreans get froggy and try to capture some of our guys tonight. I'll be moving around the units too, so I'll probably see you out there. Gunny has a hummer and driver and two security guys for you outside. If I don't run into you tonight, Top, come back here by first light and help me pull this off." Sampson stood up and held his hand out. "It's good to see you again, old friend. I wish it was under better circumstances."

Duffy took his hand and asked "Isn't Sean over here, boss? How's he doing?"

Duffy saw the shadow flicker behind Sampson's eyes and instantly knew something was wrong.

"Sean's MIA, Top. He took a patrol out early yesterday and they never came back." Sampson said no more.

"Shit, sir, I'm sorry to hear that. I'm sure he's okay and just holed up waiting for his chance to get back." Sampson nodded. Sampson knew better but wasn't going to burden Duffy with it right now.

Duffy quickly changed the subject. He knew Sampson well enough after thirty years to know how hard it was for him to talk about Sean right now. "Sir, what happened to General Wellens and Sergeant Major Rheinhart? Are they still around here? I'm asking because I want to know if I'm going to have to work around them. Reinhart's as fucking ignorant as they come and that don't say too much for Wellens for picking him."

Duffy saw another flicker in Sampson's eyes. Sampson said, "Wellens was killed by a sniper out there yesterday afternoon, and I relieved Rheinhart of his duties last night for boning his driver among other things." Sampson pointed out the door where Duffy had seen the dried blood.

Duffy nodded. He had seen the flicker in Sampson's eyes, so he just shrugged and gave Sampson a bear hug before he turned towards the office door. He turned back to Sampson when he got to the door and said, "See you on the high ground, boss!"

"See you there, Top." Sampson waved a hand at his friend and turned to Gaddis and said, "Gunny, go grab the G-3 and Colonel Han and come back in here. Have the G-3 bring his map."

"Aye, aye, General."

Duffy had waited in the hallway for Gaddis to tell him where his hummer was located, and although Sampson couldn't see him, he heard Duffy whisper loudly to Gaddis, "What's with the dinky Marine Corps stars and that aye, aye shit, Gunny? Are we in the Marine Corps in this outfit? If we are, I never signed on for none of that shit I'll tell you!"

Sampson heard Gaddis laugh and he smiled. It was damned good to have another good soldier he could rely upon tomorrow.

0850 hours
10 November
***Shingto Maru*, two hundred miles from the *Kitty Hawk* rendezvous site**

Colonel Matt Baker shook his head in frustration. He was not getting through to this Japanese captain. The trip had started out well enough with Baker's troops crammed on board the freighter for what was supposed to be an eight hour voyage. They had been at sea for sixteen hours already, and Baker could tell by the compass on the bridge that they were headed south and not north. He pointed to the north arrow on the compass again and said, "Captain, we must go north!"

The captain shook his head. He spoke enough English to understand Baker, but he also understood even more clearly the warning the North Koreans had put out on the maritime radio about the waters off South Korea now being a war zone. He was not about to lose his ship for this or any other American. He personally owned this ship, and although he had gladly accepted the lucrative payment the Americans offered, he was not about to put his ship and livelihood in danger. He said slowly in English, "I am not allowed to take my ship into a war zone, Colonel. My country forbids me to do that."

Baker had heard all this before. He turned to the commander of the 1st Battalion (Airborne) 504th Infantry standing behind him on the bridge and said, "Sal, escort the captain to his cabin. I'm taking command of this boat."

The captain understood the command and looked as if he wanted to resist, but Lieutenant Colonel Salvatore Maretti had been an all-American wrestler in the heavy weight division in college so the captain quickly changed his mind. Instead he shrugged and said, "My sailors will not obey you, Colonel, even if you can get them to understand what you want. None of them speak English."

It came out as 'Engrish' but Baker got the point. "We'll see about that, Captain. Sal, take him below." Baker stepped over to the helmsman and pointed to the north arrow on the compass. The man shook his head and would not make eye contact with Baker. Baker sighed. "Sergeant Major, physically remove this guy from the bridge, please." Command Sergeant Major Fletcher stepped forward and tapped the helmsman on the shoulder. He did not resist and turned away and went with the two soldiers Fletcher had with him.

Baker said, "Thanks, Fletch. Now grab that wheel thingee and let's turn this bitch around." As Fletcher gingerly turned the wheel, the ship started to turn.

Baker smiled. Now they were getting someplace! Just as he had that thought, Baker felt the ship's engine stop and the ship started to noticeably slow down. Well, shit! He could steer the bitch but he couldn't make the engines run. He was just about to find some troops and storm the damned engine room if he had to when Fletcher's voice stopped him. "Sir, we've got company."

Baker looked where Fletcher was pointing and saw a helicopter approaching from the east. Baker vaguely knew Japan was over that way somewhere, and the big Rising Sun painted on the helicopter confirmed that it was Japanese. Well, shit again, he thought. Now what?

The chopper landed on the small helipad on the fantail of the ship and about a dozen Japanese Defense Force soldiers got out. All were armed. Baker's men were also armed and both groups just stared at each other. A final figure got out of the helicopter and walked quickly towards the bridge. The Japanese soldiers moved on either side of the man obviously providing security. The man climbed the ladder to the bridge lithely and told his soldiers to wait below. He opened the hatch to the bridge and came inside.

"Are you Colonel Baker of the United States Army?" The man spoke excellent English.

Baker nodded his head. "Yes, I'm Colonel Baker. What's up?"

The man hesitated at the colloquialism and then brightened, "Ah, you are asking me what I want?"

Baker nodded again but didn't say anything.

The man smiled and held his hand out. "I am Colonel Nagama of the Japanese Defense Forces. I am pleased to meet you!" Baker took the offered hand and looked quizzically at Fletcher who just shrugged. He had no clue what the hell was going on either.

Baker mumbled "Pleased to meet you, Colonel." Then he said more clearly and slowly, "Colonel Nagama, why are you here? Why did you fly out to this ship?"

Nagama seemed puzzled, and then said slowly, "I am taking this ship over, Colonel Baker." Nagama looked around the bridge and asked in surprise, "Where is the captain? And where is the helmsman?" Nagama was truly baffled as to why those two individuals were not present on the bridge.

"Well, Colonel Nagama, I had to order them below. You see, I have already taken charge of this ship so you will not be able to do that."

Nagama seemed to be taking all that in for a minute. He shrugged and stepped past Fletcher and barked some orders to his soldiers waiting on the deck below. Baker was going to intervene when he saw the soldiers hand their weapons to their comrades and scurry below deck. A minute or two later, Baker felt the engine rumble to life again.

Colonel Nagama nodded his head in satisfaction and called to another soldier below who also handed his weapon off and came up the ladder and onto the bridge. Nagama pushed him towards the wheel and was giving him instructions as he went. The young soldier grasped the wheel thingee as Baker called it and spun it expertly. The ship turned on its new course. Baker was again going to intervene until he glanced at the compass. They were traveling due north again!

Baker turned to Colonel Nagama who was standing beside the helmsman. "Colonel Nagama, are you going to stay on this course?"

Nagama smiled. "Of course I am, Colonel Baker. My orders are to get you to your rendezvous point with the utmost speed. I told you, I was sent to take command of this ship."

"But the captain said he was not allowed by your government to take the ship north because the North Koreans had declared it a war zone, and off limits to neutral shipping!"

"The captain is a liar and a thief, Colonel Baker, and he will be severely dealt with when we get back to Japan. He was ordered by my government to proceed with all speed to your destination. The government of Japan will not permit the North Koreans to deny us use of any international waters. That is an act of war. If the North Koreans fire on this ship or any Japanese ship, it will be another act of war. Our constitution says that we may only defend ourselves; we may not make war on others first. It does not prevent us from kicking ass on the North Koreans as you Americans say, if they start it first. Did I say that right? Kicking ass?"

Baker smiled widely. "Yep, Colonel Nagama, you said that exactly right! Sir, I hereby formally relinquish the ship back to you."

Nagama smiled at the charade but said politely, "Why thank you, Colonel Baker. You are so kind," and he bowed ceremoniously to Baker.

Baker bowed back. He liked the hell out of this guy!

**1000 hours
10 November
2nd Infantry Division CP, Chong-ju, South Korea**

Sampson looked at Colonel Han and raised his eyebrows in a question. Colonel Han nodded his head, and said. "I understand, General Sampson. I will have the boats here no later than three hours before first light."

"Do you understand the night recognition signals, Colonel Han?"

Han smiled. "Yes, sir. Even a ROK colonel can do the math to make the total number come out to seven!"

Sampson barked a laugh. "Yes, I know you can, but I'm sending the gunny with you and I'm not sure a marine can do the math, so I'm relying on you."

Gaddis groaned and said, "Aw, shit."

Sampson smiled at the gunny's response and said to Han, "I'll let Admiral Durham know that your first stop will be whatever ship he designates for the families to go on. I need you to make that stop first, and make it quickly so you can be off shore three hours before daylight. We're going to need that much time to get the support folks off the beach and the MLRS on the boats and offshore again."

Sampson turned to the G-3. "Randy, how far off shore does the MLRS need to be?"

"Sir, at least six kilometers, preferably a little more."

"Okay. Got it. Any questions, gentlemen?" Sampson asked.

Nobody had any questions. Sampson stood up and the others did the same.

As the men filed from the room, an MP came and stood just outside the office door. He stepped inside the office once the last man left. "Sir, we've got a Swedish colonel outside at the checkpoint who says he needs to speak with you."

Sampson was not surprised. He had expected that the North Koreans would use one of the neutrals much earlier than now to convey their demands on how they wanted the evacuation to occur. Sampson said, "Bring him in, please." The MP turned away to get the visitor.

A minute or two later and Sampson was shaking hands with Colonel Jorgenson of the Swedish Army. Jorgenson had been part of the United Nations' forces that served at Panmunjon as a go between for the North Koreans and the South Koreans and their American allies. Sampson waved Jorgenson to a seat and looked at him expectantly.

Jorgenson seemed a little embarrassed by what he was about to say. "General Sampson, the North Koreans have asked me to convey a message to you." Jorgensen hesitated.

Sampson said, "Yes, I've been expecting to hear from them. Am I right to say that they demand that we not begin our evacuation until eleven hundred hours tomorrow?"

Jorgenson seemed surprised and nodded his head vigorously. "Yes! That is precisely what they said. But how did you know that?" Jorgenson seemed genuinely surprised that Sampson already knew the substance of the message.

"I expected them to make that demand for two reasons. The first is because it is the actual hour of the Armistice from World War One which we celebrate as Veterans Day in America. The other reason is because they will have full daylight by then to launch their attack. In fact, they will have had several hours of daylight by then to move their forces into position instead of stumbling around in unfamiliar ground in the dark."

Jorgenson was clearly appalled at what Sampson had just said. He blurted out, "But you do not really believe they will attack you!"

Sampson nodded his response and said softly, "Oh, yes, Colonel Jorgenson, that is exactly what they will do. They cannot afford to let us walk away from this. It will leave it unfinished in their eyes." Sampson knew that although Jorgenson was a neutral, he would not repeat anything of their conversation back to the North Koreans. Sweden for all its neutrality was a lot more aligned with the Americans than they could ever be with the North Koreans. Sampson continued dryly, "You must have seen that they have quite a large number of troops on hand, Colonel Jorgenson. They don't need all those troops just to watch us evacuate. No, they mean to do us great harm if they can."

"But why, General? Why not just let you go? They stand to gain nothing from attacking you, surely?"

Sampson said sadly, "Ah, you have not been in Asia long enough yet, Colonel Jorgensen and hopefully you never will. What they stand to gain is face. If they drive us forcibly from the Korean Peninsula, they will be the only power in history to have defeated the American army in the field. That will give them great face in the Third world and the rest of the world for that matter. That is what they will gain, and America will lose face. Does this make sense to you now?"

Jorgenson took on a reflective look and stared away into space. He said slowly, "Yes, General Sampson. Yes, it does. I see your logic and I can't disagree with you. It will make things very difficult for the whole world if America is seen as being weak and unable to help others. At least for the parts of the world that want peace and stability. There's a parallel you know."

Sampson nodded. "Yes, ancient Rome. Once the barbarians defeated the legions in open battle it was only a matter of time before Rome fell. Is that what you were thinking?

"Yes, General." Jorgenson nodded. "What will you do, then? What answer do you want me to give the North Koreans?"

"Well, I will not tell you what we're going to do because as a neutral that would compromise your standing if they somehow found out." Jorgenson nodded his understanding of what Sampson had just said. Sampson continued, "As to my reply, please tell them I understand their requirements."

"That is your only response?"

"Yes, you may tell them I said 'yes' to their demands."

Jorgenson was clearly confused at Sampson's answer. "If you really believe they are going to attack you, why would you agree to their demands?"

Sampson stood up and only smiled as he led Jorgenson towards the door. "Actually, Colonel Jorgenson, it doesn't matter what I say, does it? They will attack regardless of my response, so at least they cannot say I gave them provocation by refusing their demands. Just tell them I said 'yes' and for them to have a nice day."

Jorgenson seemed more confused than ever, but dutifully moved down the hall back towards the entrance to the building. He shrugged. He would convey Sampson's message exactly as given and report its content back to his UN superiors. That was all he could do.

Sampson turned back into his office and took off his general officer leather belt. He put on his web gear, grabbed his helmet and went out the back door to his waiting hummer. It was time to get out with the troops and make sure that they did in fact get off that beach.

1820 hours
10 November
USS *Kitty Hawk* off the coast of South Korea

The admiral's aide came into the wardroom and gave the admiral a message form. Durham was regaling those present with a sea story about him and Parker as young ensigns innocently lost in the bordellos of Alongopo in the Philippines many years ago. He finished the story to a round of laughter before looking at the message. He smiled once he read it. "Well, that is good news, Denny! Put the good colonel in my launch and get him ashore. I know General Sampson is eager to get Colonel Baker read in on his plan. Have the launch stand by for him to come back and get his troops. And tell Colonel Drewry from the marines to stand by to ferry the army ashore when ordered."

"Aye, aye, sir." The aide left the room and Durham began another story. The others leaned forward in anticipation. Durham had a wealth of stories, and although they always had a hidden lesson in them, they were invariably funny as hell.

2005 hours
10 November
2nd Infantry Division CP, Chong-ju, South Korea

Matt Baker grinned as he pumped Sam Sampson's hand in a vigorous hand shake. "Sir, it is just goddamned good to see you again!"

Sampson returned the grin. His affection for the younger man was clearly evident. "Matt, it's good to see you too! But I thought you would have been here hours ago?"

Baker said, "We had to stage a mutiny on that Japanese ship to get here, sir. The captain refused to come north once the North Koreans started rattling their sabers. As it was, a colonel from the Japanese Defense Force flew out to the ship and brought us up. Me and Fletch had actually already taken charge of the ship but when the engine crew quit we were literally dead in the water. The Japanese colonel arrived in the nick of time and was able to 'persuade' them to do their duty, so here we are, better late than never."

"You've got Command Sergeant Major Fletcher with you?"

"Yes, sir. He's my brigade CSM."

"Well, that's great, Matt! We can use all the good help we can get about now." Sampson turned serious and began without preamble, "Here's the deal, Matt. I've got two small battalions, one tank and one Bradley, spread thinly along this line. Neither battalion is at full strength." Sampson pointed out the positions on the map. Baker studied the map as Sampson's finger traced the positions. "The rest of the division is spread along here, but it's only for show. There's no real combat power in those units. They are there to make our line look longer and to hold the North Koreans back some."

"How many North Koreans are there, sir, and where are they, if we know?"

Sampson paused and turned to the younger man. "We think they have four of their light infantry divisions in front of us in the hills and possibly a heavy brigade or two up the highway to the west."

Baker whistled and said softly, "That would be a whole shit load of North Koreans." He seemed lost in thought for a minute then said, "Okay, sir, so what's the plan? How're we gonna kill all these assholes?"

Sampson smiled. Most other officers would be dwelling on the impossibility of the situation, but Baker wanted to know how they were going to make it work. Sampson was immensely relieved to have this officer with him again when the chips were down.

"Okay, since you asked, here's what we're going to do. At three hours before first light tomorrow, I'll have the South Korean 'Volunteer Navy' here with mike boats to take off all the division's ash and trash."

Baker interrupted, "Uh, sir. What's the South Korean Volunteer Navy?"

Sampson smiled. "We have a ROK colonel who showed up who happens to be a West Point graduate whose cousin happens to command the ROK Marine Corps base at Pohang. This cousin has agreed to bring his mike boats to help us in exchange for bringing his and some of the crews' families out of Korea. Pretty spiffy, huh?"

Baker said slowly, "Okay, sir. But what's a mike boat?"

"Oh, those are modern versions of the old World War Two assault boats you see in the movies. That's a mike boat. The ROK's still use them, and they're the best boats for taking people and equipment from a shore quickly. They come in, drop the ramp and you cram folks and shit into them until they're full, close the ramp and then head out to unload on the marine amphibs off shore. That's why we have to start at zero five hundred. That's when the tide is coming in. We've got about three hours to maximize our outflow, then the tide starts going. After that, we have to use the fishing dock in the village which will take longer."

Baker took it all in. General Sampson never ceased to amaze him! How many army guys were running around who would even think of mike boats much less know where to get some and how to use them? He just shook his head and looked at Sampson.

Sampson continued pointing to the map. "I'm going to swing the left positions in before first light. The units are going to be told to make a lot of noise and be very causal about it. The North Koreans will hear that and think we're pulling back to leave. The North Koreans have dictated that we are not to begin our debarkation until eleven hundred hours, so I don't think they'll be in position yet to react even if they hear the boats starting to take the troops off. You with me so far?"

Baker nodded. "Yes, sir. But how are you going to hold the left if you pull those guys out?"

"Well, that's where you guys and the marines come in. You can't see it on the map, but there is a long gully coming down from the hills that I will use for a blocking position. I'll put the marines in there and they'll refuse their right flank back up the hill." Sampson traced the position with his finger. "I'll put your forces over here, though." Sampson traced his finger along the highway coming through the mountains from the west. "This is where I expect their main effort to be initially and you have to hold them long enough to get the heavy units withdrawn and on to the LCAC's and mike boats."

Baker looked at Sampson, "How long do we have to hold?" he asked grimly.

"Best case is two hours, but most likely case is four to five hours."

Baker nodded. That was plain enough. "What's the terrain like over by the road?"

"Ah, well at least I have some good news for you on that. The road runs along a small ridgeline so you can occupy both sides, engage the road and not have any fratricide. There are also gullies running perpendicular to the road towards the top to secure your flanks. The North Koreans seem to be mostly infantry so far as we can tell. If they do have any armor, and it gets through the First Brigade in front of you, it'll have to come down that road. Do your guys have Javelins?"

"Yes, sir. We can deal with any armor as long as the Javelins hold out. What about fire support while this is going down, and what about breaking contact when our turn comes? All we have is mortars and not much ammo."

"Good questions. I have three things going for us. The first is we have napalm which the navy is going to bring in when I call for it. Where it goes depends on what the bad guys do. The second thing I have is a DD-21 which will provide naval gunfire support, and the last thing I have which will have to be used fairly deep, is the MLRS's firing from some of the mike boats. That's going to be an area suppression weapon because the artillery bubbas still aren't sure such a thing can be done. I do know if the MLRS stays ashore they can't help you; the range is too short." Sampson paused to put emphasis on what he was going to say next. "The key for us is going to be the DD-21, Matt. The only problem I have is finding somebody who still knows how to call in naval gunfire support. That, like using napalm, seems to be a lost art these days. Any questions so far?"

"No, sir. I've got it. Where are you going to be?"

"I'm going to start out on the left and make sure those guys get off the line in some semblance of order, then I'll be with the tanks and Brads up on the right until they pass through you, then I'll be with you or the marines until we withdraw."

"Uh, sir? You being a division commander and all now, don't you think those places might be a bit, well, exposed?"

Sampson smiled. "Yeah, but those are also the places where I can have the most impact. If they end up being a bit too 'exposed' as you so delicately put it, you are to take command, Matt. That's why I told you all this. You're my 2IC for this fight. The bottom line is we leave the Peninsula with every soldier and every piece of equipment. That includes our dead. The North Koreans have been calling the shots at every turn so far, but they won't call this one," he finished grimly. Sampson was silent for a full minute as if lost in thought. Baker waited.

"Okay, Matt. I need you to get your guys ashore and into position before first light. The navy will bring you in to a quarter mile of the beach, and then you guys will have to use the rubber boats to get the rest of the way in. The North Koreans can't see shit in the dark, but they can still hear. I've called ahead to Admiral Durham to set that up while you were enroute so your first guys ought to be landing here in a few more minutes. I still owe you a naval gunfire guy once I find one. If all else fails, talk to Captain Parker on the DD-21 direct on this frequency and he'll help you figure it out." Sampson gave Baker a piece of paper with the frequency printed on it and offered his hand. "Matt, I'm sorry to pull you into this, but I can't think of a better commander to have with me in combat. Good luck and God bless you and your soldiers. I'll see you in your positions tomorrow, God willing."

Baker took Sampson's hand and said, "Thank you, sir. And please keep your head down this time. I really don't want to be in command of this mob, if you don't mind!"

Sampson smiled. "Yeah, Matt. I'll try. Make sure you do the same."

Baker put his helmet on and went out into the night towards the beach. He had a hell of a lot to do and not much time to do it in.

0030 hours
11 November
USS *Kitty Hawk* off the coast of South Korea

A grainy black and white film flickered on the screen in the pilot's briefing room. F-4 Phantom jets passed across the screen silently tumbling napalm canisters into the jungles of Vietnam.

"Billy, freeze the film." The film stopped and Admiral Durham leaned forward from the podium with his pointer in his hand. He pointed to the F-4 frozen on the screen. "This is the perfect angle of attack for putting napalm on the bad guys. You'll see the jet has flared out just as it came out of the dive." The admiral tapped the screen. "It's hard to see, but the pilot has thrown on full flaps to slow the aircraft just before he pickles. Billy, turn it on again."

The plane dropped its napalm and went into an almost vertical climb as the canisters tumbled towards the jungle. "Billy, pause it again. Now, ladies and gentlemen, you were all watching the canisters, which is a natural reaction, but I need you to watch the plane this time. Billy, back it up about five seconds." All the pilots had their eyes glued on the jet this time as it released its canisters and then stood on its tail as it went to afterburners to gain altitude.

"Okay, that's how it's done and that was some shit hot flying you just witnessed, if I do say so myself!"

"Uh, sir. Let me guess. That was you flying, wasn't it?" This came from the commander of the air group.

"Why CAG, how could you tell? Was it the expert timing? Or was it the sheer poetry of the speed of light reactions of a true naval aviator? I mean, what gave me away?"

"Well, sir, it was actually the wobbly way the plane was climbing to altitude. It looked like it was being flown by a geriatric ward patient!" Everybody laughed in a burst of nervous energy.

The admiral pretended like he was offended and waited for the laughter to die down. "Well, CAG, that wobbly climb as you called it is part of what will ensure I eventually get to be a geriatric patient some day. This film was shot late in the war, and the bad guys had acquired very sophisticated shoulder fired SAM's from the Russians by then. We didn't have all the neat shit you've got today to help you dodge the little bastards. But your astute, if mildly offensive, observations are welcome anyhow. I need to stress two points about what you saw on this film. The first is you have got to almost kiss the deck and slow down before you pickle your napalm off, or it's not going to do anybody any good. The second point is you have got to hit the juice and run like a raped ape or you're going to get fried by the napalm, or by the SAM's, or both. Don't wait to hear a lock on for the SAM's. Go vertical and dump your chaff and your flares. We only have enough napalm for one good run, so every canister has to count. SWO, what's the forecast?"

The staff weather officer cleared his throat before he spoke. "Sir, there's a front coming through, but we don't know if we'll have ground visibility until after sunrise. We'll need the guys ashore to let us know when and if the fog clears."

The admiral nodded his head. "Okay, unless there are any questions, everybody needs to hit the rack. We go on flight alert at zero eight hundred which is sunrise. And like they say in that old TV show, ladies and gentlemen, be careful out there."

The pilots rose as one and came to attention as the admiral left the room. As soon as he was gone, the pilots broke up into small groups using their hands as all pilots do to simulate how their planes would fly. Some even made zooming noises.

0100 hours
11 November
2nd Infantry Division CP, Chong-ju, South Korea

Sampson was absolutely beat. He had just spent four hours walking the line checking on the troops. Every bone he owned ached and his head was pounding with a headache that comes from wearing a k-pot after years of being without one. He dropped his k-pot on the floor with a thud and sat down behind the desk. Gunny Gaddis came in with coffee and aspirin without being asked. Sampson had seen the gunny sitting in the outer office when he came in, so he knew the mike boats were on hand. He nodded his thanks to Gaddis for the coffee and the aspirins.

"Sir, I think you're too old for this shit, if you ask me."

"Well thanks, Gunny. That makes me feel all better now, you damned smart ass." Sampson took the three aspirin tablets and gulped the hot coffee. He continued, "What I really need Gunny, is a gun so I can shoot your insolent ass the next time you provide unsolicited advice." Sampson slapped his holstered pistol. "This goddamned thing is good in crowded elevators but not worth a shit otherwise. You think you can scare me up a decent gun? And don't bring me an M-4. It doesn't have the range or stopping power I want."

Gunny Gaddis grimaced at the use of the word 'gun' to describe a rifle. It was one of the greatest sins in the Marine Corps to refer to one's rifle as a 'gun'. The image went through his head from boot camp of the poor recruit who first committed that heresy in his training company. That poor bastard had to tell every other recruit in the company, all two hundred of them, what he had done. He had walked from man to man with his rifle in one hand and his other hand grabbing his crotch and had shouted at the top of his lungs repeatedly: "This is my *rifle*! This is my *gun*! One is for *shooting* and the other is for *fun*!" Gaddis smiled at the recollection. That sure was a long damn time ago. "Sir, I think I can square you away. Let me go check. You want more coffee?"

"No, thanks, Gunny, but see if you can find the G-3 so he can update me on the status of the airborne and marines coming ashore."

Gaddis responded with a nod and went out of the room. He thought he just might have the 'gun' problem for the general fixed.

A few minutes later the G-3 came in. He looked as tired as Sampson felt. "G-3, you look like Death taking a shit. When was the last time you slept?"

Randy Long looked confused initially at the question and was having a hard time putting his thoughts together. He finally mumbled, "Sir, I think it was about three days ago, but I'm not sure anymore."

Sampson nodded. He had been through the same drill numerous times in his earlier career before a wise old sergeant had sat him down and told him he was of absolutely no value to the unit if he was so tired that his judgment was shot. Since then, he had forced himself to stick to a rest plan. Even laying down for twenty minutes with no hope of sleep provided some rest. "Okay, I want you to give me a quick rundown on the guys coming ashore, and then I want you to go find a place to lie down for three hours. You with me?"

Long nodded his head. He felt like he was letting the Old Man down by being tired. Sampson saw the look on his face and understood it too. "I'm not mad or disappointed in you, Randy, so don't take it that way. Every one of us is replaceable. The army is set up that way. I know your staff is weak and you feel like you have to be on duty twenty-four seven, but I'm going to need you rested when the shit hits the fan later today. I'm putting you in command of the debarkation point. I've already told all the unit commanders that your word is law, and they are to do exactly what you tell them to do, and to do it exactly when you tell them to do it. How the debarkation goes is the key to this entire operation, so I'm counting on you." Sampson saw the resolve in the younger man's eyes and leaned back in his chair. He knew he could count on Randy to make it go right. "Okay, so how's the reinforcing business going?"

Long smiled. "Sir, it's going great! The marines are all ashore and in position, and Colonel Baker has all but one company ashore and has moved them up to their positions. We've got good comms with him, the marine commander and all their battalion commanders. Going to one radio net has cut out the redundancy in reports, and everybody hears what's going on at the same time. It sure cut down on the bullshit after we slapped a few units for trying to do routine radio checks and get sitreps on an hourly basis like peacetime training. Some of these guys still don't get it, sir. They act like this is just another exercise."

"Yeah, I've noticed the same thing as I was going around the division tonight, Randy. Troops were running around without their helmets and flak jackets on and some foxholes were only partly dug. They'll damn sure know it's not another exercise in a few more hours! Go get some sleep and then go down and act as my beach master. The priority for debarkation is people followed by equipment. My goal is to not leave anything to the North Koreans except empty shell casings. If you can't get some of the equipment off, it has got to be totally destroyed so when these assholes do their propaganda thing afterwards, they don't have anything to show for their troubles. Can do?"

"Roger, sir. Can do." Long got up slowly, stretched his back out and went to find a quiet place to rack out for a few hours. His body might sleep but his mind wouldn't. It was already racing through all the contingencies and problems that he would face on the beach. The United States hadn't done a debarkation under enemy pressure since the first Korean War.

0430 hours
11 November
13th NKPA Corps Headquarters, West of Chong-ju, South Korea

"Comrade General, our units report movement in the American lines. They say they are pulling back to the beach."

General Park looked up at his operations officer and smiled. "Then they are doing exactly what we want them to do, Comrade Colonel, are they not?"

The operations officer fidgeted as he looked at his corps commander and weighed his next words carefully. "Comrade General, I do not think they will be as easy to kill as we planned. I have a feeling about this," he finished hesitantly as he saw the frown grow on the corps commander's face. He was causing the corps commander to lose face by even suggesting that his plan might not work. He hung his head and did not make eye contact with Park.

General Park stared at his operations officer and debated on sending him away with a sharp rebuke for his temerity, but decided instead to see what the younger man was thinking. "What is this 'feeling' you have, Comrade Colonel?"

"Comrade General, we did not intercept the Americans who were sent over from Seoul." The corps commander nodded. He knew that and was still puzzled about what had happened to Colonel Sung and his men. He had directed patrols to go out and search for Sung, but they had found nothing so far. Some of the patrols had not reported back in yet, so they might still learn something.

"Go on, Comrade Colonel."

"Sir, our comrade in Seoul reported that an American general was on those buses. He also said this general is known to him and is reputed to be a very good soldier. I am worried that we now have an unknown factor in our plans. We knew what General Wellens would do. He would believe that he was just to leave and would take no precautions against our attack. He is a politician and not a soldier. We do not know what this new general may do, if he was sent to be in charge of the Americans. I think he is in charge and that is why they moved up to the hills."

General Park reflected briefly on what the operations officer had just said, then shrugged his shoulders. He looked up and said, "It doesn't matter what the new general will do, Comrade Colonel. The Americans do not have enough combat power to stop our attack. The worst that can happen is we lose a few more soldiers when we crush the Americans. A bloodier fight maybe, but the outcome will be the same." He shrugged his shoulders again, and then changed the subject. "Has the Swede come back yet?"

"Yes, Comrade General. He said that General Sampson has agreed to not start his evacuation until eleven hundred hours as you demanded."

"Ah, Sampson! Is that the new general's name?"

"Yes, Comrade General. Do you know of him?"

"No, Comrade Colonel, I do not know of him, but I do know of a Sampson from the Christian Bible that we were forced to learn from the missionaries before Kim Il Sung, the Great Leader, freed us from all that nonsense. As I recall, the story goes that Sampson was a very strong man and would remain so unless his hair was cut. He allowed a woman to cut his hair and he was defeated and killed. So is this man's hair cut?"

The operations officer was clearly confused by the question. "Comrade General, I do not know. Am I to find out somehow? Is it important for us to know this?"

The general smiled at the operations officer's confusion. He was a very good operations officer but had absolutely no sense of humor. "No, Comrade Colonel, you do not need to find out. If his hair is long, we shall soon cut it." Park could see that the colonel did not understand the analogy he was making. "And the weather?" he continued.

The operations officer brightened. "It is as we predicted, Comrade General. The fog will lift by midmorning. Our film crews will be able to capture every detail of our glorious battle!"

Park smiled. He looked forward to viewing that film with the Dear Leader in the very near future. The film would make him known the world over. He would be the general who had handed the Americans their greatest defeat in history. He wondered if he would be allowed to write a book about it. Would the Dear Leader approve that and maybe even a movie? He wondered who would play him in the movie. He didn't even notice that the operations officer had left the tent as he amused himself with victorious thoughts and dreams.

0910 Hours
11 November
Chong-ju, South Korea

Sampson looked on with satisfaction as the paratroopers around him improved their fighting positions. They barely spared him a glance as he walked up the slope towards the regimental CP. A few took a second look when they realized he was a general and decked out rather strangely at that. Sampson came to the CP bunker that had been hastily dug into the side of the hill. Sandbags were piled up at the entrance to provide side cover from direct fire. He stepped inside the bunker, stooping to get his head under the canvas across the top of the entrance. He saw Matt Baker on the radio and quietly waited for him to finish. He could tell by the side of the conversation that he could hear that Baker was talking to the marines. Baker signed off and handed the radio handset to a young paratrooper sitting on the ground with his back to the dirt wall. The kid looked tired.

Baker turned around and saw Sampson in the dim light of the bunker. "Hey, sir, it's good to see you up and about. Your staff said you put up your 'do not disturb' sign and went to bed, and were not to be bothered by us lesser beings. Or, words to that effect."

Sampson smiled. "Yeah, Matt. I decided to get a full night's sleep so I lay down for three hours." Sampson looked pointedly outside the bunker and continued, "I can see by all the work that has been done that you guys weren't as lucky as us rear echelon types. The positions are looking really good, Matt! This is exactly what I wanted you to do. The marines are in good shape too, I gathered from your radio transmission just now?"

Baker took his helmet off and rubbed both hands through his short cropped hair. "Yes, sir. They're all set. Sometimes I think those guys might be as good as us, you know?"

Sampson laughed. "You know, Matt, they might even be better than us sometimes. For example, my marine," Sampson gestured towards Gunny Gaddis just outside the bunker who scowled back in response to being singled out, "outfitted me with this really neat flak jacket and gun. Whaddya think?"

Baker whistled in appreciation. "Well, sir, he done you proud. Let me see. Flak jacket circa 1945, maybe even Korean War, so maybe as new as 1950; and M-1 rifle from the same time frame." Baker looked out the bunker entrance and called out to Gaddis, "Hey, Gunny! Did you rob the local museum for this shit or what?"

Gaddis just shook his head and growled something unintelligible in response to Baker's question. Baker laughed as Sampson said, "Actually, this is exactly what I wanted the gunny to get for me. The flak jacket is good enough and the rifle is damn sure good enough. You ever shoot an M-1, Matt?"

"No, sir. I grew up on the M-14 which has a tinge less stopping power. Is that why you wanted it, sir? For the stopping power?" Baker looked apprehensive as Sampson nodded his head in response.

"Yep. Exactly so."

Baker said seriously, "Sir, I'm hoping now that you're a general and all, you will be far enough out of the way to not need to stop anything. Either coming or going, if you get my drift?"

Sampson chuckled. "Yeah, I get your drift, Matt. I'll give you the same promise I gave Deidra when I called her two days ago to tell her I was coming over here. I won't go looking for trouble unless it comes looking for me. Fair enough?"

"Yes, sir. Fair enough. The marines have told me that the 2nd ID troops in front of them have all pulled back as you directed. I told their commander that he has battle handover now and everything to his front is not friendly."

"Good, Matt. Did you also remind him that all the air defense weapons are on 'Weapons Hold' until I lift it?"

"Roger, sir. He's got that. My SWO says this fog should be lifting in an hour or so at the latest. When do you see this thing cranking up, sir?"

"Probably as soon as the fog lifts. Is there anything I can do for you here, Matt? I'm going to head down to the beach and see how that's going, and then I'm going back up to be with the First Brigade up on the highway."

"No, sir. We've got about all we need. The only thing I haven't seen is the ANGLICO team from the marines for the naval gunfire support. Your guys gave me the new frequency and call sign to the boat in case they don't show up, so I guess we can figure it out on the fly. You ever use the navy guns before, sir?"

"Yeah, once in Vietnam when I was a young punk RTO. All you have to do is tell the navy where the hell you are and they do the rest as long as you give them direction and distance from your location. You can bring it in as close as twenty-five meters, Matt if you're hunkered down. Keep that in mind if it gets tight. And tell your guys to keep their mouths open if you do bring it in that close or they'll bust their eardrums with the overpressure. Okay, I'm off to the beach. I'll come back here once the First Brigade pulls back." Sampson offered his hand and Baker shook it warmly.

"Yes, sir. We'll see you then."

"Good luck, Matt!"

"You too, sir!" Sampson stooped his way out of the bunker, walked back down the hill and climbed into his hummer. Gunny Gaddis put the hummer in gear and turned towards the beach.

0940 Hours
11 November
Chong-ju, South Korea

"Randy, you have done one hell of a good job down here in just a few hours time! Goddamn this is great!"

Randy Long flushed with the praise from Sampson. He had never once gotten a kind word out of Wellens for any of his hard work and long hours. Wellens always managed to make him feel like he somehow wasn't measuring up, when he knew damn well he was! He looked at Sampson and said, "Well, sir, it's not too hard actually to get a bunch of scared young soldiers to get on boats headed the hell out of here. If anything, I had to hold them back!"

Sampson smiled. "Yeah, I can see that happening. What equipment do we still have left to get off the beach?"

"Sir, just the artillery and the tanks and Brads with the First Brigade and a few hummers still running around."

"You mean to tell me you got all that shit off the beach already?" Sampson was incredulous. "Holy shit, I figured you'd still have half or more of it to go!"

Long nodded in agreement. "Sir, so did I, but one of my young sergeants came up to me and said we were wasting 'bottoms' as he put it by loading the trucks on them. He rigged together a bunch of empty fifty-five gallon drums that were sitting in a dump across the road and lashed them to the trucks. Each mike boat towed a truck out with each lift and brought the drum hula-hoops back for the next load. I told that kid you'd give him a Bronze Star for having the balls to tell me I was all fucked up."

Sampson grinned. "Yeah, he'll get that and a Legion of Merit too. Sumbitch, I love American soldiers! All you have to do is tell the little bastards what you want done, then get the hell out of the way!" Sampson turned serious again. "Are the MLRS set offshore, Randy?"

"Yes, sir. They're all set. Most of the crews are heaving their guts up in the chop out there outside the bay, but their ready. The battalion commander wanted me to remind you that he can't reload once they fire their pods off. The remainder of his rockets are in the dump about half a mile south of here with an engineer squad set to blow it. They have a zodiac boat and some navy guys with them so they can beat feet once they set the charges. It's set for eleven hundred as you directed."

Sampson heard the report and nodded. He said, "Yeah, eleven hundred will still be good. That ammo is going to make one hell of an explosion and I'm hoping it distracts the North Koreans. It was mighty kind of them to send the Swede down here to make sure we knew when they were going to attack, wasn't it?"

Long grinned, "Yes, sir. That was most kind of them, but I don't get it, sir. Why the hell did they do that?"

"They did it out of arrogance, Randy. Sheer arrogance. They have no respect for us as soldiers. When Wellens made a run for the coast, we suffered irreparable loss of face with the NKPA. Now they think we're weak and will do what we're told. But we're going to kick the shit out of these people today, Randy, with a few good soldiers and marines." Long saw the hardness in Sampson's eyes and did not doubt for a second that what he said was the god's honest truth.

Both men were silent until Sampson spoke again. He offered his hand to Long and said, "I gotta get up to the First Brigade, Randy. Keep up the good work down here, and I'll see you when we pull back Matt Baker's guys. You'll see the First Brigade next, then the marines and then Matt's guys if this goes according to plan. If it doesn't go according to plan, use your best judgment based on the guidance I gave you last night."

"Got it, sir. See you in a few hours, then." Sampson walked back to his hummer and got in. He waved as the gunny turned the vehicle up the road towards the hills overlooking the beach. Long wondered briefly how the first part of the war would have gone if Sampson and not Wellens had been commanding the division. He knew for damn sure they wouldn't have cut and run.

1100 Hours
11 November
1st Brigade CP, west of Chong-ju, South Korea

Sampson glanced down at his watch and saw that it was exactly eleven hundred hours. He looked towards the south east and saw a sharp flash followed by a fireball that towered up a thousand feet into the air. As he watched he could see the shock wave from the explosion spread out from its epicenter. He turned his gaze to the south along the hill line and could see North Korean soldiers by the thousands crest the hills and stop dead at the sight and sound of the explosion. He nodded his head in satisfaction. To his right, he could hear tanks and Bradleys opening up on North Korean vehicles as they flooded the highway from the west. The first spot reports were already coming in over the command net. The voices were excited but controlled. He nodded his head again. That's exactly as it should be.

Sampson spoke into his handset. "*Kitty Hawk*, this is Centurion Six. It's time for your show. Your audience is massed on the hills with their thumbs up their butts but it won't last long. How copy?"

Admiral Durham answered immediately. "Roger, Centurion. First sortie is feet dry and inbound on final now. Ten seconds to splash."

"Roger, ten seconds to splash." Sampson looked to the south and saw nothing for a few seconds, and then a navy jet appeared as if by magic, slowed down, and dumped its napalm right in the middle of the North Koreans. Although Sampson was almost a mile away, he felt the heat of the napalm as it ignited. The North Koreans not in the fire envelope did not move. They were frozen in place. The first plane rocketed skyward jinking as he went but no SAMs were fired at him. The North Koreans were too stunned. The next plane missed the gun target line and dropped the napalm too far towards the beach and closer to the marines. Sampson swore. "*Kitty Hawk*, the last drop was short! I say again, the last drop was short!"

There was a pause before Durham answered. "Roger, Centurion, we've already made the correction. Next one should be pickling about now."

Sampson looked and saw the next plane come exactly onto the gun target line and drop his load. Again he felt the heat, but this time the North Koreans reacted. Several SAMs chased the plane as it streaked skyward pumping chaff and flares as it went. The North Koreans were getting over their shock faster than Sampson hoped they would. "*Kitty Hawk*, that was right on target. Have your guys go for the biggest clusters if they can, these guys are spreading out now."

"Roger, biggest clusters. We've got six more loads, then we're rounds complete. I hope like hell it's helping."

Sampson didn't answer immediately. His concentration was broken by a change in the sound of the Bradleys' firing. Their firing pattern had changed from the short three round bursts used against vehicles to the longer cannon bursts and machine gun fire used against troops. He called over to the brigade commander who had his handset mashed against his ear to hear over all the firing, "Joe, are your guys killing crunchies already?"

The brigade commander held his hand up signaling that he would answer after he had heard this latest transmission. He acknowledged the call and turned towards Sampson. "Yes, sir. They just told me that all the North Korean vehicles have been destroyed, and the North Koreans are using human wave assaults against their positions. They're pouring out of the hills, and they just keep coming!"

Sampson paused a second, then asked sharply, "Are you losing any vehicles?"

The brigade commander keyed his handset and asked the question, his face reddening because he should have asked it himself when he got the last report. "Yes, sir. Two Brads have been disabled with RPG's. Both have lost turret power but are mobile. The crews are hand cranking their turrets to stay in the fight."

"Okay, pull the Brads out now. Have the tanks cover them as they pull back. Tell the tanks to be prepared to move forward on my command."

"Move forward, sir! You mean pull back!" The brigade commander's voice almost came across as a squeak it was so high pitched with shock.

Sampson looked calmly at the brigade commander, meeting his eyes. He said slowly and decisively, "Joe, tell the Brads to pull back and the tanks to prepare to move forward on my command. The tanks are going to have to literally crush these guys before they can break contact. Do it now, Joe."

The brigade commander made the call. Sampson knew that the rest of the forces on the beach would hear the transmission and know the Brads were pulling back so there would be no confusion or fratricide. Sampson turned to Gaddis. "Come on, Gunny. Time to earn the lavish combat pay we're getting."

Sampson ran to the hummer with Gaddis right behind him. Sampson just pointed towards the firing as Gaddis started the vehicle up. The hummer sped over the top of the hill. Even Sampson was not prepared for what he saw. The valley floor was literally covered in North Korean dead and wounded, and more North Koreans were flowing out of the hills down into the valley and into the beaten zone of the tank and Bradley fires. They did not even hesitate as they climbed over the bodies of their comrades and pressed the attack against the armored vehicles, firing as they came. RPG gunners were finding whatever cover was available and firing rocket after rocket at the Americans, mostly with no effect, but they kept firing. Sampson swore at the sight and swore again as Gaddis jerked the hummer in a hard turn to avoid a collision with a Bradley thundering up the hill, its gun turned over the rear deck, and continuing to pump rounds into the masses of North Koreans.

Sampson signaled for Gaddis to stop the hummer. He picked up his radio handset and keyed the microphone, "Thunder Six, this is Centurion Six."

The tank battalion commander came back instantly. "Thunder Six, go."

"Roger, as soon as the last Brad gets over the hill, I want you to attack straight into these guys and kill every goddamned one of them. I want you to shoot them and I want you to literally crush them. How copy?"

"Roger, task and purpose?"

"Task is to inflict maximum casualties so you can break contact and buy time for the guys behind you. If this mob gets over the hill unchecked we'll be hand to hand on the beach. Go in buttoned up."

"Wilco. Thunder Six, out."

As Sampson looked up he saw a Bradley take an RPG rocket in its tracks and slew to the right as the track broke. The gunner adjusted the turret and kept firing from the stationary vehicle. Once the vehicle was stationary, one of the RPG gunners saw it and increased his fire on it to finish it off. Two RPG rounds impacted the Bradley, but its reactive armor fended them off. Sampson saw the RPG gunner calmly reloading his rocket launcher, preparing to shoot the Bradley again, but this time he would aim at the bald spots where the reactive armor had fired off. Sampson stood up in the hummer, raised his rifle and shot the gunner through the head just as he was aiming his RPG. The gunner was a good two hundred yards away. Gaddis sat with his mouth open while Sampson murmured, "Shoots a little high. I was aiming at center of mass."

An M-88 recovery vehicle crew pounded up to the stricken Bradley and hooked their chains up to tow the vehicle. Small arms fire wounded two of the M-88 crew but both managed to crawl back inside their vehicle. With a roar, the monster recovery vehicle jerked forward and dragged the thirty ton Bradley over the hill like it was a toy wagon. Sampson keyed his microphone, "Thunder Six, execute, execute, execute. Time now."

"Thunder Six, roger, execute, time now." After a pause of only a few seconds Sampson saw the tanks back out of their firing positions and turn down the hill into the valley. Several of the tank commanders were still up in their hatches firing their machine guns.

"Thunder Six, tell your people to button up. I still see commanders up."

"Jesus, Centurion! Where are you?" The tank battalion commander could not believe that the division commander was far enough forward to see his tanks. That just wasn't where division commanders were supposed to be!

"I'm up the hill about two hundred meters behind you. Button up and go like hell. Tell your drivers to run over every fucking living thing they see in front of them. I'll tell you when to withdraw. If we lose contact, use your own judgment on withdrawal but these people have to be stopped right here, right now. How copy?"

The tank battalion commander winced at the 'lose contact' remark. That meant if Sampson was killed because he was too far forward. "Roger, good copy. All tanks buttoned up, moving, time now."

Sampson watched as the tanks formed a loose line abreast and thundered down the hill into the valley. The whine of their turbine engines as they accelerated was almost enough to drown out the small arms noise, but not quite. The North Korean fire intensified as they began to realize the tanks were coming at them and not running away. Then abruptly, the fire slackened and almost stopped as the tanks roared into the nearest North Korean soldiers. The tanks had also quit firing for the most part as the crews focused on maneuvering their tanks over the North Koreans. The screams of the North Korean wounded lying in heaps on the ground as the tanks crushed them were clearly audible, even inside the roaring tanks. Several of the tanks started to slow down.

Tankers always bragged about running down crunchies to grease the treads of their tanks, but doing it for real was horrifying.

"Thunder Six, tell your people to press hard now. No stopping or slowing. I don't care if they're puking in their turrets, I want these bastards dead! How copy?" Sampson did not get an acknowledgement but saw the slowing tanks jerk forward as they continued to catch and crush running North Koreans. More machine gun fire was heard as tank crews chewed up groups of soldiers running to the flanks.

Sampson heard a retching noise and looked over as Gunny Gaddis was vomiting outside the vehicle. When he finished, he wiped his mouth and his eyes and said, "General, I've seen a lot of shit, but nothing like this!" Sampson only nodded. He felt the same but it didn't make him sick to his stomach. He knew exactly what he was doing and why. No light infantry in the world, no matter how well trained and disciplined they were could withstand a tank attack in the open that had the single minded purpose of crushing them into pulp. The Russians had taught the Germans that harsh lesson on the Eastern Front in spades.

Sampson keyed his microphone, "Thunder, Centurion. When you get to the next hill line stop, reverse and clear one more time. Have your commanders up to help observe to the flanks and engage as necessary."

"Roger."

As Sampson watched the tanks slowed and began turning back towards him. He keyed his microphone again, "Thunder, I will pull back over the hill. There are no friendlies between you and the brigade CP. Cease fire once you reach the hill in front of the CP. Your brigade commander will give you further instructions from there, over." Gaddis gunned the hummer and turned up the hill.

"Roger all, Centurion. I see your hummer now. As soon as you're clear, we'll begin." The battalion commander's voice was raw. Apparently Gaddis wasn't the only one who had gotten sick.

**1120 Hours
11 November
Admiral's Bridge, USS *Kitty Hawk***

Durham watched as the first of the birds trapped onto the carrier's flight deck. He turned to the CAG. "What were you saying, Mark?"

"Admiral, the pit crews want to know if you want the planes reloaded with dumb bombs. They're standing by ready to go."

Durham nodded. He picked up his radio telephone handset and called Sampson. When Sampson responded, Durham could hear the whine of the hummer engine and firing in the background.

Sampson came back immediately and said, "Roger, *Kitty Hawk*, go."

"We need to know if planes with dumb bombs would be of any assistance to you, over."

"Negative on dumb bombs, *Kitty Hawk*. The fur ball is too close and it's not worth losing a plane. We won't get away with a second strike. Your last bird had about thirty SAM's chasing his butt out of here."

"Well, actually it was 'her' butt, and I think she's been chased before," Durham said dryly.

Sampson laughed in response. "Roger, tell them all great job. What we're going to need next is the DD-21. The tanks and Brads are pulling back, so the next phase belongs to the marines and airborne guys."

"Break, break. This is Warrior Three, the first of the Bradleys are here and are loading on the LCAC's. The lead tanks are also in sight."

Sampson acknowledged the update from Randy Long from the beach. What he had to hope for now was that the North Koreans would focus on the close fight and not interfere with the debarkation. Their only means of doing so was to break through the marines or paratroopers, or to use artillery. He was puzzled that the North Koreans had not used any artillery or even mortars yet. He knew that normally they had an abundance of it; more than any other army in the world, man for man.

The tanks had caught up to them and the hummer was trailing the last tank down the road eating its dust. Sampson could feel the heat from the turbine engine washing over him with its stink of burning jet fuel. He signaled Gaddis to pull off to the left towards Baker's CP. Gaddis stopped the hummer about twenty feet from the CP and Sampson got out. He retained his grip on the radio handset and keyed it. "Warrior Three, Centurion Six."

Randy Long answered instantly, "Warrior Three, go."

"Roger, get the word to the gunners to get ready to shoot at the preplanned targets I gave them."

"Warrior Three, wilco."

"Centurion Six, Thunder Six, over."

"Thunder Six, go."

"Roger, need to advise you that one of my tank crews engaged and killed a film crew in the valley. And," the tank battalion commander hesitated, then rekeyed the radio and continued, "the crew was Russian. One of my lieutenants searched them for identification because they were Caucasian. They all had Russian military passports. We have secured their camera and film."

"Roger, tell the lieutenant good job. Turn the camera and film over to the navy once you get out there. *Kitty Hawk*, did you monitor?"

Durham responded immediately. "Yes, I monitored. My intel guy is sending flash traffic to CINCPAC on this as we speak. Pretty damned curious if you ask me."

Sampson grimaced. He agreed. The North Koreans were more than capable of filming their own misdeeds without Russian assistance. He wondered if they were going to see any other Russian 'help' before this was over. On a hunch he keyed his mike, "*Kitty Hawk*, you may want to increase your anti-submarine patrol, particularly around the DD-21. If the Russians are still playing, that's the target they'll want. Along with your ship that is."

Before the admiral could respond, Sampson heard a weird fluttering sound and without thinking, grabbed Gaddis and pulled him to the ground. A mortar round exploded with a roar about twenty feet away, and showered both men with rocks and dirt. Gaddis spit dirt out of his mouth and said, "Goddamnit, I hate fucking mortars!" Sampson heard more flutters and buried his face in the dirt. Several more mortar rounds impacted near the CP, and then the explosions moved off along the road towards the beach. Sampson still had the radio handset in his hand and keyed it, "Centurion Seven, this is Six, you guys getting any of this shit over there?"

There was a short pause before Top Duffy answered. He was clearly out of breath from running. "Roger, Six. Same stuff. I guess holding the low ground may have some disadvantages for us. I think the assholes can see us!" A short pause, "Over."

"Roger. Tell the marines to keep their heads down. Unless they take a direct hit in their hole, they ought to be okay."

Duffy snorted into the radio. "I don't need to tell these guys shit, Six. They already got it figured out. I was the last dumb bastard standing when the first round came in. I haven't run this goddamn fast since I left Iraq two days ago. I gotta tell you, boss, I ain't exactly self-actualizing about now. The NKPA pulled back from the napalm so I guess this means they're getting ready to try again. We got any magic to turn this shit off?" Sampson could hear several rounds impacting close to where Duffy was over the radio.

"Roger, Top. Working it. Break. Warrior Three, this is Six. You taking any hits?"

"Six, this is Three. Negative. We're just outside their range. Closest they've gotten is two hundred meters. If they move their guns forward that will change quick."

"Roger. Okay, scratch the preplanned targets I had for the gunners. Get their radar going and tell them to fire counterbattery on their command. I need them to do it fast. These guys have got observation on us and will be adjusting fire onto our young asses before too much longer!"

"Roger, Six! Break. Red Leg? Warrior Three, did you monitor?"

"This is Red Leg Six, I monitored and first rounds are on their way." Sampson looked out to sea but couldn't see the mike boats with their floating rocket batteries. As he watched, he could finally see the huge plumes of smoke as the rockets rippled out of their pods, and then he could actually see the rockets arching up into the sky.

It seemed to take forever, but Sampson heard the welcome sound of eighteen rockets with their hundreds of bomblets explode in a continuous roar punctuated by multiple and single louder explosions up in the hills. Several larger explosions followed closely as the ammunition dumps in the North Korean mortar positions were detonated by the bomblets. The mortar fire ceased as abruptly as it started. Sampson stood up and dusted the dirt off the front of his flak jacket. He keyed the handset, "Red Leg Six, Centurion Six. Good job! I need you to hold the radar and a firing platoon ready to do that again if we need it. Fire the remaining launchers on target Alpha Bravo Two. I say again, Alpha Bravo Two. How copy?"

"Good copy. Fire remaining launchers at Alpha Bravo Two, keep one platoon on standby for counterfire, over."

"Roger, do it." Sampson had looked at the map of the surrounding hills and identified several places where he expected the North Korean commander to mass his troops before assaulting down the hills. Each was the last covered and concealed area before breaking the sky line, and each was large enough to hold at least two regiments with some dispersion. They were the areas Sampson would have picked for his own use if he were conducting the attack.

Nine MLRS' launched six rockets each. Sampson could see them arching their way across the sky again. This time the roar up in the hills was longer. An entire grid square of one thousand meters was being hit with thousands of bomblets. Very few men out in the open would survive that attack untouched. Almost all of them would either be killed or wounded.

Sampson looked at his watch. It wasn't even twelve o'clock yet! Shit! He called out, "Hey, Gunny! My kingdom for a cup of coffee about now. The whole kingdom and all that's in it is yours for a mere cup of hot coffee with real sugar. No shit."

Gunny Gaddis looked at Sampson for a second and then said, "Some fucking kingdom about now, General, but I'll fly if you'll buy." Gaddis headed into the airborne CP. He had smelled the coffee when they first drove up and was on his way to mooch some when Sampson threw him to the ground. He realized that Sampson had very probably saved his life. Gaddis hadn't heard the mortar round coming. He knew you had to be at just the right angle to hear one. Usually the first indication you had that it was inbound was when the fucker blew up in your face!

1212 hours
11 November
USS *Scorpion*

"Bridge, we have contact, zero three two degrees! Moving fast."

Findley almost spilled his coffee at the suddenness of the report from Sonar. Almost, but not quite. He calmly pushed the 1MC button. "Sonar, what heading is he on, and what type of boat is it?"

"It's the Russian Alpha Class, Bridge and it looks like he's trying to penetrate the escort screen. We've got a plot on him."

Findley saw the new icon marked 'Alpha' flash on his screen that showed the location of all the ships in the task force. The task force's ships were green icons and the Alpha Class was a pulsing red icon. It was moving fast towards the task force. Findley keyed the 1MC, "Torpedo Room, stand by." Findley should have been surprised that the Russian had come back, but he wasn't. That Russian skipper had been just a little too accommodating when he handed over the information on the North Korean subs yesterday. Leopards never do really change their spots. Findley had played cat and mouse too many times with the Russians in the Cold War to ever trust any of them.

"Torpedo Room, aye!"

"Bridge, Sonar! Fish in the water! Fish in the water!" There was a short pause. "They have launched four torpedoes and are turning away. Heading on the torpedoes is towards the task force."

Findley barked "Torpedo Room, fire on the Alpha, stand by with counter measures!"

"Torpedo on the way! Standing by with counter measures, aye!"

"Con, all ahead flank, heading two seven three degrees. Sonar, can you identify the type of torpedoes?"

"Negative Bridge, but they're shifting course to match the task force's movements. On plot now."

Findley looked at the screen and saw the four torpedoes marked one through four. He could see them shifting as the task force moved. Two were going to the *Kitty Hawk* and two were clearly going to the *Reuben Barnes*. The *Scorpion* was almost directly in the path of the torpedoes. The Russian skipper either didn't know the *Scorpion* was there, or he had gotten rattled. He had also fired his torpedoes at maximum range, so they were mercifully coming at their slowest speed.

"Okay, XO, now for the fun part. We are just going to have time enough to get in front of those torpedoes. You with me so far?"

The XO looked at the skipper with wide eyes and nodded his head.

"Good. Once we're there, we'll execute counter measures to see if we can pull those torps into our decoys. Sound like a plan?" The XO still wide eyed just nodded again. "Okay, we're also going to have to see if it's possible to shoot a torpedo with a torpedo. We may not have enough decoys left to take care of four fish. The chief in the torpedo room swears it's possible with a little reprogramming. I need you to go down to the torpedo room, grab the chief and give him whatever help he needs to make it happen. We've got about fifteen to twenty minutes before those fish get to the task force. Tell me damned quick if the chief says it was all bullshit because I'll need to shit another plan. Keep me posted."

The XO still wide eyed at the thought of putting the boat directly in front of four Russian torpedoes said, "Aye, aye, sir!" and ran to the torpedo room.

"Sonar, what's the status of our fish and the Alpha?"

"He's broached, Skipper, and is running away at full speed on the surface. He'll outrun our fish. Do you want to terminate it?"

"Negative. We'll keep it going after him as long as it'll go. That should keep him from having any ideas about coming back. Torpedo Room, slow it down so it will last longer."

"Torpedo Room, aye, aye, sir."

Findley looked at the plot and saw that he was just coming into the direct path the torpedoes would have to take to get to the task force. "Con, give me ninety degrees right rudder!"

"Con, aye!"

Findley said quietly, "Torpedo Room, fire off the first decoy."

"First decoy on the way!"

Findley watched as one of the torpedoes seemed to hesitate, and then it broke to the left to follow the decoy. One down, he thought; if the little bastard didn't change its mind again. "All slow! Torpedo Room, fire the second decoy."

"Torpedo Room, aye. Decoy on the way!"

Findley watched the screen again but none of the torpedoes followed the decoy. Well shit, he thought. "Torpedo Room, fire the next decoy directly at the torpedo marked Two on plot."

"Torpedo Room, aye. Decoy on the way!"

Findley watched the screen closely again. For a moment nothing seemed to happen, and then Torpedo Two slowly started to turn towards the decoy as if it were not quite sure it should. Then it made its mind up and sheered towards the decoy and picked up speed. Two down, two to go.

"Skipper, Torpedo Room. We only have one decoy left."

"Okay, then we need to make it count. Con, give me ninety degrees right rudder and full ahead." The sailors who could see the plot board could tell that this last command would place the *Scorpion* directly in the path of the remaining torpedoes again.

"Con, aye."

Findley watched as the path of the *Scorpion* and the torpedoes converged. When the torpedoes were about two thousand yards out he commanded, "Con! Ninety degrees left rudder! All slow! Torpedo Room, fire the decoy!" Both sections responded to his orders instantly. Findley watched the last decoy streak towards the oncoming torpedoes and was rewarded by one of the torpedoes veering only slightly off course to intercept it. The resulting explosion was clearly audible inside the submarine. The last torpedo bore down on the *Scorpion*. "Con, all stop."

"Con, aye."

Every eye that could on the bridge watched the last torpedo as it moved slowly across the screen towards the *Scorpion*. "Bridge, Sonar. Thirty seconds to impact."

Findley responded in a distracted voice, "Bridge, aye." Then Findley seemed to snap out of it. "Blow all tanks! All ahead flank!"

The planes operator slammed his palm onto the button to blow the ballast tanks and the *Scorpion* shot to the surface.

Findley felt like he was in an elevator rocketing to the top floor. He keyed the intercom, "XO, if this little fucker doesn't broach with us because of our turbulence and get stupid on its guidance system, you guys need to nail it! You ready?"

"XO, aye! We're ready! You ain't gonna believe this shit!"

"Bridge, Sonar! Torpedo Four is still running hot, straight and normal! We did not break its target lock!"

"Okay, XO! Do your shit my friend!"

"XO, aye!"

Findley watched the plot as two torpedoes left the *Scorpion's* tubes chasing the Russian torpedo.

"Skipper, torpedoes away!"

"Skipper, aye. Hey, XO. You didn't let the chief touch a computer did you?"

"Uh, yeah, Skipper. He did the reprogramming."

"Are you shitting me, XO! The chief can't even figure out how to get to his navy email account!"

A burst of laughter rocked across the bridge. Chief Thompson knew more about computers than Steve Jobs and Bill Gates put together. If he had been born ten years earlier, Thompson would have invented the damn things!

The XO was clearly at a loss as to what to say, so Findley took mercy on him and finally said, "Okay, XO. Never mind. I guess it's okay this one time for the chief to touch the computer. Sonar! Status?"

A whoop came back over the 1MC from Sonar, "Hit! Hit! Our torpedo hit the Russian cocksucker!"

Findley grinned. "A little decorum, Sonar. A little decorum. Remember this shit is all taped. XO, tell the chief I never doubted him, even if I said I did about a hundred times."

"XO, aye!"

Findley grinned and looked at the plot board. The second American torpedo was swimming its way happily towards the task force. "And XO, you may want to shut down your second torpedo before it hits the *Kitty Hawk*."

"Uh, roger, Skipper. That would be a good thing to do."

"Yes, XO. A very good thing to do." There was another burst of laughter on the bridge. Although they couldn't see it, they knew the XO's face would be bright red by now for forgetting the second torpedo. Well, it was a small thing considering they had just saved the task force and all.

1220 hours
11 November
13th NKPA Corps Headquarters, West of Chong-ju, South Korea

General Park stared at his operations officer. He waited for the younger man to continue his report. Finally, when it was apparent that the operations officer would not continue, Park spoke. The words came out harshly. "What do you mean that we have lost *six* regiments of infantry and all our tanks? How could this be possible! How, Comrade Colonel? *How?*"

The operations officer hung his head. He mumbled something the general couldn't hear. All of the staff knew that the general was hard of hearing so his mumbling further enraged the corps commander. He slammed his hand onto the table. The loud noise made the operations officer jump and look up. His words came in a rush, loud enough for the corps commander to clearly hear them. "The Americans crushed the attack in the north with their tanks. They literally came out and crushed our soldiers with their tanks! The four regiments in the south were attacked by airplanes with napalm and artillery fire and were destroyed in the attack position and the assembly areas."

The general responded angrily, "They were destroyed by the American artillery that the intelligence officer said the Americans couldn't use if we grasped them by the belt buckle and held them tight? That artillery?" he finished sarcastically.

The operations officer only nodded dumbly. General Park leaned back in his chair and continued to stare at the younger man until he dropped his eyes, which he did quickly. Park said nothing and drummed his fingers on the table. He made a decision.

"Comrade Colonel, you will use our remaining regiments that I held in reserve as follows. We know the Americans are holding two positions between the hills and the beach. They cannot support each other. They are too far away from each other which is stupid but predictable. You will use two regiments to hit the American battalion in the north and you will use four regiments to hit the battalion in the south closest to the beach. I want them to destroy the Americans and capture the beach before the Americans can evacuate their armor. We must capture their tanks! The Dear Leader has ordered it so! Do you understand me so far?"

The operations officer nodded his head rapidly in agreement.

Park continued sarcastically, "I will assume that the intelligence officer was at least correct on how many American battalions are in Korea since it is not a secret, and every whore in South Korea knows the number." Again the operations officer nodded his head rapidly in agreement. "Good. And since the Americans do apparently have artillery, we must close with them quickly. The reserve regiments will not move forward and assemble. They will run from their current positions in the hills on the straightest path to the Americans. We can no longer afford the time to make this a pretty battle for the Russian film crews. It must be done quickly and violently!" Park slammed his fist on the table to emphasize his point and the operations officer again jumped at the noise while still vigorously nodding his head.

"Do you understand, Comrade Colonel?"

"Yes, Comrade General! I understand!"

"Then you must go issue the orders, and personally go forward to ensure their success."

The younger man visibly paled at this last command. He knew if the attack failed and he survived, he would be shot. He knew if he went forward in such an attack, he would probably also be killed. He looked directly into Park's eyes and hoped for a reprieve. When it was not forthcoming, he lowered his eyes and stood mute.

Park did not relent. "Go now, Comrade Colonel. I want the units moving in one hour. After you give them their orders, you will execute the intelligence officer and move to the front. Leave now!" The younger man turned and ran from the tent.

Park settled back into his chair and murmured a short prayer to God for success. The missionaries of his youth would have been both pleased and appalled. And he silently cursed the Dear Leader for denying him the use of his normal huge artillery support because it would "obscure the battlefield with all its smoke and dust and make it seem like our guns and not our brave soldiers defeated the Americans. No! I will not allow it!" Park ground his teeth as he recalled the Dear Leader's exact words. And he ground his teeth some more as he thought about how all the spies in his own headquarters had prevented him from bringing his artillery along 'just in case'.

They would win this fight, but it was going to cost a lot more than they had planned for. The film crews would have to edit a lot of the footage out showing the thousands of North Korean dead and wounded that the cameras could not help picking up as they covered the battle. Park shrugged. It would cost more, but he would still win.

1305 hours
11 November
504th PIR CP

Sampson took another sip of coffee, swilled the dregs in the bottom of the canteen cup and tossed them through the bunker door, just missing Gunny Gaddis as he was coming in. Gaddis just gave Sampson a raised eyebrow that seemed to say 'you missed me'. Sampson hadn't seen Gaddis approach the doorway. Acting as if he hadn't noticed he had almost tossed his coffee dregs on the gunny, Sampson asked innocently, "What's up, Gunny?"

"Sir, the hummer's tits up. That mortar round mangled the engine compartment. The comms work, but it's dead in the water as far as going anywhere goes."

Sampson took that in and reached over to take the radio handset from Baker. He keyed the handset, "Centurion Seven, this is Six."

Top Duffy came back immediately. "Seven, go."

"Roger, my hummer is tango uniform. I won't be coming your way."

"Roger, Six." Duffy didn't say anything more. There was nothing more to say.

"Seven, is the marine commander with you?"

"Roger, he's right here."

"Put him on the horn, over."

After a short pause, a new voice came over the net. "Centurion Six, this is Leatherneck, over."

"Roger, Leatherneck. Here's the deal. You guys are the main effort. Unless the North Korean commander is totally incompetent, he's going to hit you the hardest because you're closest to the beach. How copy?"

"This is Leatherneck, good copy. Anything further, over?"

Just like that! Sampson had just told the marine commander he was going to get hammered the hardest, and his calm response was exactly what Sampson had hoped for and wanted to hear. He didn't know this guy at all, in fact, he had not even had a chance to meet him yet, but he would certainly do! "Roger, Leatherneck. You will have the DD-21 at your command. They only have one gun, but it shoots twelve one five five rounds a minute. You'll need to use it early and often, over."

"Roger, Centurion. We have comms with the *Reuben Barnes*. They are standing by for fire missions. *Reuben Barnes* did you monitor?"

Captain Parker came back, "Roger, Leatherneck. We monitored. You have priority of fires. Centurion Six, do you see the priority of fires changing later in the fight in case we lose comms?"

Sampson appreciated the question. Parker definitely had his head in the game. If the marines got over run and went off the net, the *Reuben Barnes* needed to still influence the rest of the fight in the absence of orders. Sampson replied, "*Reuben Barnes*, use your UAV to monitor the fight. If we lose comms and you see targets, use your own best judgment. My guess is you're going to have a target rich environment, so focus on helping Leatherneck. Break. Guidons, Guidons, I will remain with the airborne guys. Break." Sampson paused to collect his thoughts before he continued. "I know I don't have to tell you guys this, but we will not leave anybody behind, whether living or dead. If we don't get all the equipment off, so be it, but we *will* get all the people off. How copy?"

Everybody on the net to include Admiral Durham acknowledged Sampson's order. It was a grim reminder that no matter how many casualties they incurred, no American soldier, sailor or marine was going to be left to the North Koreans and their film crews.

"This is Centurion Six, nothing further. Out." Sampson looked over at Matt Baker who had listened to every word of the radio conversation. Sampson looked Baker in the eye and then said, "Well, Matt, it seems I have handed you the dirty end of the stick again. Remind you of anything?"

Baker actually smiled. "Yes, General, it does. It reminds me of the last time we were together back in Iraq. But," Baker paused, "I've got faith in you, sir. It came out all right last time." Baker changed the subject, "You want more coffee, sir, before this dance begins?"

Sampson nodded his head and held out his canteen cup. He fished in the pocket of his flak jacket and pulled out two cigars, handing one to Baker. Baker hesitated, and then took the cigar. He had quit smoking, again, after his first fight in Iraq with Sampson. He had done two tours in Iraq and one in Afghanistan since then and had managed to not smoke again.

Sampson saw the hesitation and said dryly, "This is probably not the time to be worried about your long term health, Matt. Besides, it's Cuban so it's actually good for you, or so Winston Churchill claimed." Sampson cut the end of his cigar cleanly with a cutter and handed it to Baker who did the same. Baker handed the cutter back and Sampson slid it into his flak jacket pocket.

"You familiar with the DD-21, Matt?"

Baker shook his head.

"Well, it's the state of the art in stealth and firepower. You heard me tell Leatherneck it can do twelve rounds a minute?" Again Baker nodded while he drew on his cigar. "Now here's the fun part. The gun system is actually the same one on the Crusader artillery system that the US Army was developing a few years back. You've heard of that program, right?"

"Yes, sir. I heard it was too heavy and the program got cancelled."

Sampson sighed. "Yeah, it was too heavy to be brought anywhere by airplane with its ammunition carrier in the same plane. Together they weighed one hundred and ten tons fully loaded. Of course, nobody stopped to consider sending the Crusader on one plane and the ammo carrier, or actually two ammo carriers, on another plane. It would have required three planes to lift two gun systems, but our beloved former Secretary of Defense Donald Rumsfeld couldn't do the math, so he shit canned the whole program. He also said there was no place for such a system in future warfare as he envisioned it, and the army was again engaging in archaic Cold War thinking!"

Sampson paused and took a shred of loose tobacco off his lip and flicked it away. He studied his cigar reflectively, then continued, "So now here we sit in a situation Rummy said would never happen again in future warfare, and the army doesn't have any artillery that can make a real difference in this fight. We got lucky with the MLRS in the mike boats, but that was a one time shot." Sampson drew on his cigar as he watched Baker nod his head in understanding.

Sampson had not had a chance earlier to tell Baker all this, but he needed Baker to fully understand not only the current fire support set up for this fight, but also for Matt Baker to fully understand how the army had been forced by politicians with no real military experience into their current 'no shit here and now' dilemma of too much enemy and not enough artillery. If Baker survived this fight, Sampson knew he would go on to much higher rank and influence in the army, and if *General* Matt Baker didn't get to fix anything else for the army down the road, he needed to fix the army's artillery shortfall! Sampson was counting on him to do just that.

Sampson continued. "You'll have the 2nd ID artillery battalion for fires until I have to pull the plug and get them off the beach. Their rate of fire will be two rounds a minute, maybe three depending on how well trained the gun crews are. Once they expend their on board ammunition, I'll have to pull them off. We don't have time for a reload. So you're going to have about twenty to twenty-five minutes of max effort from the guns and they'll be gone." Sampson drew on his cigar again and let the smoke roll out of his mouth slowly. He looked at Baker and knew he understood the situation.

Sampson took the cigar out of his mouth and continued. "You'll need to save enough rounds to fire a TOT to break contact. It needs to be danger close and you have got to be moving as it's coming in. The troops will want to hunker down as all that shit hits the fan that close, but they have got to move, Matt. I want you to send your dee-lick back now to get set up to cover your withdrawal and hold until your main body is at the beach. I will accompany the dee-lick so I need to know where they will be. Any questions?"

Baker stared at Sampson and said slowly, "So what you're really saying to me is that you are going to command the detachment left in contact, aren't you sir?"

Sampson studied his cigar closely. He didn't say anything for almost a full minute. Finally he said without looking up, "Yep. That's exactly what I'm saying, Matt. I need you to focus on getting your troops off the beach. It's going to be a cluster fuck and you and Leatherneck know your troops and can get it unfucked. I would just be in the way."

"And that's the point, sir! You would be in the way which is why you should withdraw to the carrier once this starts up again! Jesus, sir! You're a general now! You need to quit acting like a goddamned lieutenant!"

Sampson looked up and smiled at the younger man's rebuke. "You're just pissed because you were going to command the dee-lick once the main body passed through, weren't you?"

Baker's face reddened. That was exactly what he was going to do because it would be the critical point on the battlefield at that time. He finally sighed and smiled back at Sampson. "Guilty as charged, sir. I understand where you're coming from. Just do me a favor this time and don't get your ass shot up again." Baker held out his hand and said, "Deal?"

Sampson took his hand and shook it warmly, "Yeah, Matt. Deal. I'll see you on the beach. Now where is the dee-lick forming up, and call them to let them know I'm taking charge, will you? I don't want some lieutenant getting uppity with me over it, you know."

Baker laughed. "Sergeant Major Fletcher will take you over there, sir, and I'll make sure they know I'm letting you be in charge. You taking the gunny with you?"

Sampson looked appraisingly at Gaddis as if debating the question. Then he finally said, "Yeah, I'll take his sorry ass with me so you don't have to be searching for him when you pull back and the shit is hitting the fan."

Gaddis gave a snort and followed Fletcher out of the bunker. Sampson looked at Baker and said again, "I'll see you on the beach, Matt," and left the bunker.

**1315 hours
11 November
1 Kilometer east of the 504th PIR Positions**

Sampson looked at the young soldiers arrayed in front of him. He spotted a familiar face and called out, "Jesus, Stokes! Is that you? And you're a sergeant now? The army really does have a sense of humor!"

The young soldier Sampson was singling out was grinning from ear to ear as Sampson recognized him. "Yes, sir! I'm a sergeant now! Actually I've been one three times since we were together in Iraq. I just can't seem to make them fucking stripes stick to me, I guess." The other soldiers laughed. Stokes was a legend in the 82nd Airborne Division. He had won the Congressional Medal of Honor in Operation Desert Vengeance in Iraq, but he hadn't let that keep him from living it up and raising hell in the local bars every payday! But when it came to business, there wasn't a better machine gunner in the whole division, which meant there wasn't a better one in the entire world as far as the paratroopers were concerned.

"Well, good! Come on up here, *Sergeant* Stokes. You're now in charge of the left flank of this fight." Stokes grabbed his M240G by its carrying handle and lifted the thirty pound machine gun like it was a child's toy. He came forward to Sampson. Sampson shook his hand and clapped him on the back. "Good to see you again, Jimmie!"

"Thanks, sir! Uh, good to be here, I guess?"

Sampson laughed and then turned serious. He faced the other machine gun crews. "Okay, this is not going to be how you were trained to do it. Sergeant Stokes is going to take half of you and move off about three hundred meters on the other side of the road. He's going to find the best cover he can and orient his fires back up the road. You with me so far?"

Everybody nodded their heads. Sounded same old, same old so far to them. Sampson continued, "And Sergeant, what's your name son?" Sampson asked a young NCO standing up at the front of the crowd.

"Sergeant Napier, sir."

"And Sergeant Napier is going to take the other machine gun crews off to the right flank the same distance." Napier nodded that he understood his instructions.

"Now here's the different part. You are not going to fire directly at the North Koreans as they come down the road. I know that's what you've been trained to do using six to nine round bursts, but that won't work here today. We have to go back to World War One tactics to make this thing work. Six to nine round bursts won't stop a human wave assault which is what we're going to be dealing with. There are going to be thousands of these assholes coming all at once." Sampson paused and saw several eyes widen at this last comment.

"Sergeant Stokes and Sergeant Napier, I want you to divide up your guns so that you have six of them firing at one time on a fixed azimuth that cuts across the road about five hundred meters in front of you. Your fires will cross each other at that point. The guns must fire continuously. No bursts. It has to be a steady stream of bullets out there for the enemy to get through. Use your tripods and have the fire one meter off the ground. Have your spare guns and barrels ready to switch off if a gun gets too hot or jams. Link all your ammo belts together as soon as you get into position so you're not trying to reload the guns every hundred rounds. You still with me so far?" Every head nodded in the group gathered around this very unusual general who was giving them tactical guidance on the nuts and bolts level.

"Okay, I'll be with Sergeant Stokes and we will initiate this attack by fire on my command. Once Sergeant Stokes lights them up, you join in, Sergeant Napier. We'll keep firing until we either kill them all or we are forced to withdraw to the beach. The withdrawal signal will be a green star cluster. Who's the senior officer present here?"

A young captain stepped forward from the edge of the crowd. "I am sir, Captain Maxton."

"Okay, Captain Maxton, I want you to organize the remaining troops to provide close support to the machine gun teams to take care of any leakers that get through. They'll try the flanks if they get through, so make sure you have all around security. Any questions?"

"No, sir. Got it."

Sampson could tell that the captain had his shit together just by the look in his eyes and the way he carried himself. "Okay. Here's a green star cluster. If I go down for some reason, you make the call on the withdrawal."

Sampson addressed the entire group again after giving Maxton the green star cluster. "We have got to stop these people here or we don't get off this beach. We don't leave as long as they have enough troops left to make a difference. And gentlemen," Sampson paused and looked into their eyes, "these are brave men attacking you today, but you must kill them all. We cannot lose this fight today or the United States can forget about having any say in what goes on in this part of the world for a long damn time." Heads nodded. The troops knew that this fight was about more than just getting the 2nd Infantry Division out of Korea in one piece. "And then all the prices will go up at Wal-Mart and your wives will be pissed!" Sampson finished. The troops laughed. Yeah, gotta keep momma happy or there is hell to pay!

"Okay. My call sign is Centurion Six. See you on the radio."

As incongruous as it may have seemed, the troops all came to attention and saluted when Sampson finished. They all thundered out the motto of the 82nd Airborne Division in unison as they saluted, "All the Way, Sir!" and it echoed off the hills.

Sampson felt a lump in his throat as he returned their salute and said "Airborne!"

Now it was time to get on with it. Sampson looked at his watch as the paratroopers started to jog to their positions. He could hear the officers and NCO's giving instructions as they ran. It was 1318 hours. He wondered how much longer they had before the NKPA launched their next attack. He also wondered if machine guns alone were going to be enough at the end when the DLIC took up the fight. He sure as hell hoped so. He signaled for Gaddis who was now humping a man pack radio to follow him as he headed for the left flank position.

1320 Hours
11 November
In the DLIC positions, West of Chong-ju

Gaddis handed the handset to Sampson as they walked. "Leatherneck is calling you, sir."

Sampson took the handset and pressed it to his ear. "Leatherneck, this is Centurion, go."

"Roger, Centurion. We are engaging now. They are cresting the ridge to our front in tight formations at the double time, over."

"Roger. Any idea as to how many?"

"Negative. My grand dad was at the Chosin Reservoir, so my guess is one horde, maybe two."

Sampson laughed. He too had heard the stories of the Chinese assaults during the Korean War that the troops had wryly termed 'hordes' in order to try to put a magnitude on seemingly hundreds of thousands attackers. They would say things like, "Yeah, we only got three hordes coming our way so we ought to be able to deal with it."

"Roger, Leatherneck, I copy one, possibly two hordes. Devil Six, you have any business yet?"

Matt Baker responded quickly, "Roger, Centurion. I can see what's coming at Leatherneck and two hordes is about right. We seem to be only getting one our way. Our horde is walking though, so it looks like they just want to fix us in place."

Sampson nodded as he walked. He had been right. The NKPA commander was making his main effort against the marines and the shortest route to the beach. "Roger. Okay, you guys know what to do. You've got to take them down before you pull back. Although I don't expect them to have any air power, just in case, we're now weapons free on the air defense weapons. How copy?"

"Devil Six, roger on weapons free."

"This is Leatherneck, air defense weapons free, aye."

Sampson handed the handset back to Gaddis who was puffing a bit as they walked towards the left flank position. "Hey, Gunny! You probably ought to quit smoking you know. It's bad for your health and apparently your wind. You want to take a break?"

"No, sir, I don't want to take a break. But I do want to know how I can transfer out of this chickenshit outfit and go back to my cushy desk job!"

"Well, apply in writing for a transfer and I'm sure we can look into it in a week or so. Is that good enough?"

Gaddis only grunted in reply as he heaved the radio straps higher on his shoulders to shift the weight and ease the growing pain in his lower back. You'd think with all the technology of the computer age they could make a light weight damn radio!

1332 hours
11 November
USS *Reuben Barnes*

Captain Parker pressed his earphones tighter against his head. The near continuous roar of the gun as it spewed shells towards the shore made hearing almost impossible, even on the highly sound insulated bridge. "Say again, Leatherneck. I didn't get your last!" Parker yelled into the microphone.

"Roger, we can't keep up with their movements for adjustments. The fires are having an effect but we can't really tell how much."

"Okay, I understand now. With your permission, I'm going to shift targeting to my UAV. My operator will scan the enemy from above and direct the fires. He's right here beside me so I'll be able to keep you informed. We'll also be able to tell you where their heaviest concentrations are coming into your positions. Will that work?"

"Roger, sounds like a plan! I'll also need to know when they start falling back so I can pull the plug on this side. Any indications of that yet, over?" The hope that the enemy was in fact pulling back was clearly evident in the marine commander's voice. He had read and heard about shit like this happening in the Korean War, but he damn sure never thought he would see it in person! Up close and personal, even!

Parker looked at the UAV operator's screen. It seemed to be filled with humanity from side to side across the entire screen. He shook his head. This was unbelievable to watch. "Negative, Leatherneck. They're still coming. We can see them falling all over the place but the others just run over them and keep coming. They will be in small arms range in about three minutes at their rate of advance."

"Roger. Well, keep firing. We'll take care of the guys in front once they get in our range, so you keep working the follow up hordes. That's the best I can come up with about now."

"Okay, we'll do that." Parker flipped a switch on the console and hit the 1MC button. "Chief, how's the gun holding up?"

The noise in his ears got even louder when Davy Spicer down at the gun keyed his microphone. "It's a thing of damn beauty, Skipper! She's pumping rounds like a whore pumps sailors on a Saturday night in Norfolk!"

Parker grimaced at the analogy but had to admit it did bring a vivid picture to his mind as to the efficiency of the gun. "Okay, we're going to go digital off the UAV feed. Jamison will hit the button on each target group from the UAV picture so we're no longer plugging in the data manually over the radio. We ought to be able to get more coverage. You guys ready?"

"Aye, Skipper. I just hit the switch to digital feed. Fire away!"

As the UAV operator clicked his mouse on the largest groups of enemy soldiers the gun slewed automatically to engage the designated targets. Parker watched as the fires covered more of the battlefield in just a matter of seconds. Warfare by mouse he thought wryly to himself. It was too much like a video game, but damned effective from what he was seeing.

After about six minutes of the distributed fires, Parker caught a movement out of the corner of his eye. He tapped the screen to the far left edge and said, "Jamison, shift the UAV over here a minute." Jamison pulled the joystick ever so slightly and zoomed in on the area Parker indicated. Parker looked more closely at the screen, and saw several small groups of North Korean soldiers slow down and some even seemed to stop. He saw them hesitate ever so slightly. They were not going to the rear, but they weren't advancing either. He tapped the screen on their location. "Hit these guys, Jamison."

Jamison put the cursor over the soldiers and clicked the mouse. Other rounds still in flight continued on to their targets, but after less than a minute, the first rounds on the new target started to impact. Parker could see the results immediately. The North Korean soldiers who had just begun to move forward again, stopped dead and then started running to the rear. The soldiers closest to them saw the movement and hesitated. Parker tapped the screen again over them, and Jamison clicked the mouse. Another short pause while the gun adjusted and the hesitating group had started to move forward again, but at a walk and not a run. Parker could clearly see their leaders pushing them forward. The new rounds impacted and the whole thing came apart in a flood. The North Koreans started streaming to the rear. It started in the very back and quickly worked its way forward in the mass of troops as those in front realized they had no one behind them to help them carry the attack.

Parker keyed his mike, "Okay, Leatherneck. They are breaking to the rear. We're going to keep hitting them as they go back so they don't have a change of heart."

Leatherneck's voice was clearly tinged with relief as he said, "Roger. I'll need you to bring it in close to me when I call for it so we can break contact. We probably have about a thousand of these little bastards who have gone to ground in front of us who aren't just going to let us walk away."

"Roger, tell me when you're ready and we'll shift the UAV over that way and start engaging. Centurion Six, did you monitor?"

"This is Centurion Six. Roger, I monitored. Leatherneck, go when you're ready. Devil Six, did you monitor and what's your status, over?"

The gunfire and artillery impacts were clearly audible when Baker responded. "Roger, Centurion. We're up to our butt in alligators right now. The artillery is having an effect but we're into the close fight. Red Leg tells me he's rounds complete in seven mikes and will have to pull off the beach. We'll go with our mortars then, but they won't be enough for us to break contact when the time comes. Any chance of getting the DD-21 at that point?"

"Standby Devil. *Reuben Barnes*, what's your ammo count?"

Parker responded immediately, "We have enough rounds for six more minutes of firing. We'll need three to finish these guys in front of Leatherneck. I figure it will take two more minutes to cover his withdrawal adequately so I'll have one minute left for Devil. Sorry. We have no resupply for this thing. We only have what we brought with us."

"Okay, we'll make it work. Break. Devil, tell Red Leg to save three mikes for a TOT. You'll have to use it to break contact. Supplement it with your mortars. I'm saving the last minute of the *Reuben Barnes* to cover you guys with precision fires as you pull back. How copy?"

"This is Devil. Good copy but what are you going to use if the dee-lick needs help breaking contact?" There was obvious concern in Baker's voice as he asked the question.

Sampson paused, then keyed the radio, "We're going to fall back by sections and cover each other the best we can. I'm counting on these guys to be too fucked up after losing in front of you and Leatherneck to be very combat effective after you withdraw. At least I hope they are. Anyhow, that's my story and I'm sticking to it."

All Baker could say was, "Roger. Good copy." The *Reuben Barnes* pounded away at the retreating North Koreans but slowed its rate of fire in the hopes of saving enough ammunition to help the paratroopers.

1436 hours
11 November
13th NKPA Corps Headquarters, West of Chong-ju, South Korea

Four soldiers carried the stretcher up to the general's tent and gingerly placed it on the ground. The operations officer lay mutely on the stretcher. He had been wounded and bandaged in several places and his right leg stopped abruptly just below the knee, but he did not utter a sound. He looked into the eyes of the corps commander and said simply though clenched teeth, "Comrade General, your attack has failed." He knew he was going to die either from his wounds or at the hands of the State for his failure, and he no longer cared about losing face. He did care that the responsibly for the failed attack would belong to the corps commander for all time.

The corps commander's face reddened as he realized that not only the staff officers standing around him had heard what had just been said, but so had the four soldiers carrying the litter. He briefly debated on having all who were within hearing shot, but also knew that would raise questions later on. Several of the staff officers were related by blood to the Dear Leader and their sole reason for even being on his staff was to keep the Dear Leader informed. One did not remain the Dear Leader by trusting anyone too much, particularly generals.

He salvaged what he could with his response. "Yes, my attack failed, Comrade Colonel, because you were not man enough to carry it forward as I instructed you, and the intelligence officer was again wrong about everything. Everything! And," he paused slightly, knowing that his words would be reported directly to the Dear Leader, "the Dear Leader's closest advisors failed him when they convinced him not to let me bring my artillery forward. He should have them shot!

My attack failed because I had no artillery!" There! That was a good as he could make it.

Park looked down at the operations officer who returned his stare. He debated on having him shot for his failure, but decided that he didn't want to end his suffering just yet. He would be taken care of in time, of that he was sure. He turned to his staff. "We must continue this fight. It is not over yet. I will personally go forward now and you will come with me. We must rally the troops for one final effort. We must get to the beach and catch the Americans before they all run away!" The corps commander turned and grabbed the staff of his personal flag of rank fluttering outside his tent and said while brandishing the flag, "Come! You must follow me!"

Several of the officers, notably, those related to the Dear Leader, looked decidedly unenthusiastic about the thought of going forward into the battle zone. The corps commander smiled. He knew they would slip away to make their reports before they came anywhere near the firing line. He brandished the flag again. "Come! We must go now before we are too late!"

1500 hours
11 November
504th PIR CP

"Shit!" Baker handed the handset to his RTO. He turned to his S-3. "John, call the battalions and tell them to standby to pull back." The OP's had just reported to Baker that even more of the bastards were coming down the road, and Baker knew he couldn't hold them back this time without sustained artillery support. Baker motioned for the handset for the radio that was set on the command net. "Centurion Six, this is Devil Six, over."

"This is Centurion Six, go."

"Roger, my OP's are reporting another horde coming over the hill about one klick out. They are at the double time so they ought to be here in about ten mikes. We're going to hit them with all we have, and then we'll need to pass through your position, over."

"Roger, good copy. *Reuben Barnes* did you monitor?"

"This is the *Reuben Barnes*, we're shifting the UAV your way now. We think we've got it set up now where the artillery on shore will also fire using the digital downlink on the UAV which will help focus their fires. We'll know in less than one minute. We're firing a test round. Stand by."

"Roger, standing by."

After a pause of almost half a minute, Parker came back on the air jubilantly, "Yes! We've got the link and that round plowed right into them exactly on target! We're ready, Centurion. Say the word."

"Roger. Matt, are you ready?" Sampson dispensed with the usual radio jargon. It wasn't necessary.

"Roger, Centurion. They're five hundred meters out and we're engaging with small arms and mortars. We're not making much of a dent so do what you can for us. I'm pulling the riflemen back now so just the machine guns are still up front. I'll be pulling them and the mortar crews in about one to two mikes."

Sampson looked up the hill and could see the paratroopers starting to pull back. They were calm and were carrying their wounded. They seemed totally nonchalant about the whole thing. Clearly some of the stretcher cases being carried out of the position carried dead men as the bearers didn't seem concerned about the jolts in their path as they jogged towards the beach. Sampson also looked around his position briefly and nodded with satisfaction. The machine gunners had piled up whatever loose earth and rocks they could find to provide some cover for their crews. Sampson keyed the radio, "Okay, *Reuben Barnes*, let her rip. Disperse your fires as widely as you can across Devil's front so he can finish breaking contact. We win it or lose it here."

"This is the *Reuben Barnes*, wilco!"

Sampson keyed the radio, "Roger, break. Centurion Seven, what's your status?"

"This is Centurion Seven. We're closing in on the debarkation point. We'll be there in three mikes."

"Roger, Seven. Good copy. Leatherneck lead element closing in three mikes."

"Negative, negative, Six! *Trail* element is closing in three mikes. Jesus, whaddya think I'm in the first group trying to get the hell out of here? And embarrass myself in front of all these fine marines? Over."

Sampson smiled. He should have known Top Duffy would be the last man out of the position. He probably had to arm wrestle the marine commander for the honor of being the last man to the beach. "Okay, Seven. Now that you've made the history books, I want you to load up with the marines and get out to the ships. Do not, I say again, do not wait for me at the beach. How copy?"

Sampson could tell that Duffy wanted to argue with him because it took him a good fifteen seconds before he answered. His voice was somber when he did so. "Wilco, Centurion Six. I will evacuate with Leatherneck. Good luck, sir."

Sampson said simply, "Roger, thanks. I'll see you on the high ground, Top."

Duffy came back with, "This is Centurion Seven, roger on the high ground! Nothing further, out."

Sampson turned to Gaddis who thought he was going to give him the handset back. Instead Sampson said to Gaddis, "Gunny, give me the radio and take this message to Warrior Three down on the beach. Then I want you to get on the first thing smoking out to the fleet. You've done a good job, but your part in this is done once you deliver my message." Sampson could see that Gaddis was going to argue and held up his hand.

"Gunny, I know what you're going to say and I appreciate it, but I need you to do what you're told right now." Gaddis was clearly puzzled by the order. He was even more puzzled when Sampson removed the two stars from his uniform and handed them to him. "Get these back to General Walker, and tell him I said thanks. I was honored to wear them, but I don't need them anymore. If we get over run, I'm just another soldier as far as the North Koreans are concerned." Sampson handed the folded message to Gaddis. "Go ahead and read it and make sure Lieutenant Colonel Long clearly understands what I want done. Okay?"

Gaddis read the message and understanding dawned on his face. He looked as if he was going to question the message, and then thought better of it. He held out his hand to Sampson who shook it warmly. "Take care of that wife and boy you have there, Gunny. They're both priceless. And take care of yourself." Before Gaddis could say anything Sampson shouldered the radio and moved towards Sergeant Stokes' machine gun position. Gaddis turned towards the beach and joined the steady stream of paratroopers headed that way.

1503 hours,
11 November
USS *Reuben Barnes*

"Skipper, this is Guns, we're bingo on ammo in one minute."

Parker sighed. He had hoped that his earlier conservations would have given him jut a little longer. He called on the radio, "Centurion Six, we have one minute left on ammo. We're shifting to the Time on Target grid at your command. Guns ashore did you monitor that?"

"This is Red Leg, we monitored. We will be ready to shoot the tango oscar tango in one five seconds. Going off UAV digital gun feed, time now."

Sampson shifted the heavy radio on his back and keyed the handset. "Devil, stand by to pull your remaining forces once the time on target starts. Let me know when you're ready."

Baker came back immediately. "Roger, we're ready now."

"*Reuben Barnes* and Red Leg, this is Centurion Six, fire now. I say again, fire now."

The North Koreans had mistaken the short pause when the guns stopped firing as a signal that they had won the fight. They came out of the prone positions they had been using for cover and started to move forward en masse. Their officers and sergeants yelled at them to come together and move quickly before the Americans all got away. They were just starting to bunch up when the devastating time on target fire impacted over them. The concentrated barrage had its intended effect and their attack was instantly stalled as the soldiers instinctively sought cover again. The remaining paratroopers did not jog back like the earlier group had. They came back at a dead run, knowing that they only had a very few minutes to get back through the detachment left in contact before the North Koreans recovered and pressed their attack. The North Koreans would be coming like a freight train once the artillery used up the last of its ammo on the TOT.

Sampson saw Baker and his staff loping down the road and waved Baker towards the beach when he saw Baker about to break stride to join him. Sampson keyed the radio and said, "Keep going, Matt. Get them to the beach and out to the ships." Sampson saw Baker nod and turn his eyes towards the beach. Baker kept the handset from the radio jammed against his ear while he ran. His RTO was in perfect stride with him, keeping the radio close. Sampson turned back to the soldiers around him and said loudly, "Okay, Jimmie! Time to kick some ass!" Stokes looked up from his machine gun and grinned. Sampson crouched down beside him. They waited for the North Koreans to crest the low ridge five hundred meters in front of them.

1515 hours
11 November
At the Debarkation Point, Chong-ju, South Korea

Randy Long looked up from the note. "Did the general say why he wanted this, Gunny?"

Gaddis shook his head. "No, sir. But he said to make sure you understood."

Long snorted. "What's to understand? Okay. I'm a bit short handed right now. You think you can take care of this?'

Gaddis nodded. "Aye, aye, sir." He turned and walked towards a group of soldiers waiting somewhat impatiently for their turn to get off the beach. Some were relaxed while others were clearly agitated and fidgeting. They could hear the artillery pounding behind them earlier, but they had no idea what was really happening. Seeing the marines and the paratroopers starting to come in from the hills was making the more imaginative among them decidedly uncomfortable.

1520 hours,
11 November
Detachment Left in Contact Positions, West of Chong-ju

Sampson looked to his front and still did not see any movement. He was beginning to wonder if the NKPA had finally given it up. He knew that their losses were easily ten thousand or more killed and wounded so far. Maybe even twice that number. Just as his hopes were rising he saw a solid black mass of soldiers crest the ridge. Again, they were jogging forward and not walking. Their sense of urgency was all too evident even at this distance. Sampson said quietly, "Okay, Jimmie, show the rest of them how to do it."

A split second later Stokes' machine gun opened up in a steady stream of tracers going diagonally across the front of the enemy mass. The other guns joined in from both sides of the road. A few of the guns wavered and fired directly at the enemy in short bursts as they had been trained to do, but they were quickly fixed by the NCO's. The North Korean mass jogged into the walls of bullets and started to fall like rows of rag dolls. Those behind them pressed forward into the killing zone. When the bodies started piling up, those behind climbed over them. Nobody looked for cover. They just came ahead through the fire and some of them made it through. Those that did pressed ahead, firing as they came. Although the fire was inaccurate, there was enough of it that some of the machine gun crews started taking casualties. They were quickly replaced by others in the crew, and the fires did not slacken.

Sampson looked off to the left and could see other North Koreans advancing from where the marines had vacated their positions. He ran down the firing line and oriented two of the guns towards the threat growing on the flank. Those guns could not use the steady fire technique and had to fire directly at the enemy with short bursts. They were hitting them, but Sampson wasn't sure it would be enough to stop them. This was beginning to look like Custer's Last Stand. Sampson was just wondering what the hell he was going to do now, when he felt a tug at his sleeve. He turned and Colonel Han was squatting beside him and smiling.

"Hello, General! It is good to see you again."

Sampson was more than a little surprised to see Han and was at a loss as to what to say. He finally mumbled a greeting in response. He just stared at Han.

Han kept smiling and nodding his head. Finally, he said, "I have a surprise for you."

Sampson couldn't even to begin to wonder what the hell Han was doing there, much less what kind of surprise he might have. He knew his mouth was open but nothing was coming our yet.

Han moved to the radio on Sampson's back and changed the frequency. He took the handset and immediately started rattling off in Hangul to whoever was on the other end. Sampson was too surprised to react at first, and then it hit him that Han might be talking to the North Koreans! He started to rise and Han tugged at his sleeve impatiently to stay down. Han finished his conversation and deftly put the radio back onto the command frequency. Almost immediately a voice Sampson hadn't heard before came across the net.

"Centurion Six, this is Shooting Star Flight Lead, over." When Sampson didn't answer immediately, the message was repeated.

Sampson finally keyed the radio, "Shooting Star Flight Lead, identify yourself, over."

"Roger, Centurion Six, this is Shooting Star Flight Lead. I am Colonel Ham Yon Kim of the Republic of Korea Air Force. I have come to support you as soon as you can put all air defense weapons on hold, please. You are to please put them on hold soon because I think we have very little time."

Sampson made a quick decision and made a guidons call to put all air defense weapons on hold. All stations acknowledged the order in turn. Admiral Durham confirmed that they had just picked up the Shooting Star flight on the radar. They had apparently been flying on the deck until they got confirmation that the air defense umbrella would not shoot them down. The Admiral was scrambling another fighter CAP just in case.

"Shooting Star, this is Centurion Six, all air defense weapons are on hold. What ordinance are you carrying?"

"We have napalm, Centurion. You must identify your positions so we may use it only on the enemy, I think."

"Yes, Shooting Star, that would be preferable. I am going to pop smoke in front of my positions, but I need you to hold off your attack until I can coordinate with all my elements to withdraw as you attack. I'm going to use your attack to break contact. How copy?"

It was clear to Sampson that Shooting Star did not understand what he was trying to tell him. The ROK pilot spoke 'air force' English and not 'army' English and there was a difference. Sampson turned to Han. "Do you understand what I am saying to Shooting Star, Colonel Han?" Han nodded his head. "Then I need you to explain it to him and please do it quickly, we're running out of time." Sampson keyed the radio and said briefly, "Captain Maxton and Sergeant

Napier, standby for the green star cluster. Don't go until you see it. Keep up the fires."

Han took the handset from Sampson and launched into Hangul with Shooting Star. After about a few seconds, he smiled and handed the handset back to Sampson. "Sir, Shooting Star understands now, but he needs two things before he can attack and create all kind fire tunnel for your troops."

Sampson had heard the ROK tactical phrase 'all kind fire tunnel before' so he knew it was as close as he was going to get to a common understanding. "What does he need, Colonel Han, and please hurry." Sampson glanced at the North Koreans attacking from the front and left flank, and could see more of their troops were across the beaten zone of machine gun fire now.

"He needs permission for his families to land in their C-130's at Kadina in Okinawa, and he needs fuel for his aircraft once he creates all kind fire tunnel to get to Kadina. He is defrecting to the United States!"

Sampson paused briefly to decipher "defrecting", then keyed his radio. "Admiral, this is Centurion, over."

"Roger, Centurion, go."

"Shooting Star has two requests before he bails my ass out. The first is permission for his families to land at Kadina. They are apparently inbound in C-130's. The second request is to tank his aircraft after they make their runs so they can make it to Kadina to defect to us. Can you tank air force aircraft?"

"Roger, Centurion. We can take care of both requests. Permission for the families to land is going out to Kadina Tower now, and we'll have the tank birds in the air in about ten minutes. Shooting Star Flight Lead, do you acknowledge?"

The relief in Shooting Star's voice was clearly evident as he responded. "This is Shooting Star, I roger all! We go now once Centurion Six give me smoke for all kind fire tunnel!"

The admiral wisely decided not to question what the hell an 'all kind fire tunnel' was, and instead gave Shooting Star a frequency to shift to for the tanking operation once the napalm runs were finished.

Sampson called on the net, "All elements pop smoke and stand by for the green star cluster."

Sampson waited about twenty seconds for the smoke grenades to put out enough smoke to be seen from the air, and then called Shooting Star. "Shooting Star do you confirm my smoke?"

"Shooting Star, roger on smoke."

"Okay, the gun target line is south to north and no closer than three hundred meters to my smoke. How copy?"

"Shooting Star, good copy. I'm in!"

Sampson watched as the first F-16 piloted by Colonel Ham Yon Kim peeled off from the group and nosed over into the attack. His approach was perfect and his napalm tumbled into the North Koreans and burst into a sheet of flame that spread for two hundred yards along the direction of flight. Even at a distance of over three hundred yards, the heat was intense. Sampson slammed the palm of his hand onto the bottom of the green star cluster and the rocket shot into the sky. The dense black cloud of the burning napalm accentuated the star cluster as it burst. "All elements, all elements, cease fire and withdraw. Cease fire and withdraw!" Sampson tapped Jimmie Stokes on the back and swung his arm towards the beach. Stokes didn't move and instead shifted his fires to the North Korean attack on the left flank, and started taking groups of them out with short bursts. His other gunners followed his lead, and Sampson realized Stokes was right to do so. There were more North Koreans over there than he had thought. More F-16's swooped in and extended the carnage to the front. The heat was becoming unbearable.

As Sampson looked again to his left, he knew that his group was penned. If they stopped firing, the North Koreans would be able to prevent their withdrawal to the beach unless he was willing to accept heavy casualties and leave the wounded and dead behind. Sampson was not about to do that.

"Shooting Star, this is Centurion. Can you put a bird on the enemy to my south? I need to break contact to my south. How copy?"

"Negative, Centurion. We are finished and must get fuel now. Sorry. I am very sorry for you."

Sampson actually smiled in spite of the situation. He knew that like most Koreans, Ham could really feel the need of others much more vividly than any Westerner ever could and really *was* very sorry for him. Well, shit!

"Centurion this is the *Reuben Barnes*, over."

Sampson couldn't imagine why the *Barnes* would be calling him just now so he answered somewhat distractedly as he watched Jimmie Stokes' gun teams continue to whittle the North Koreans down, but it wasn't enough. The North Koreans had gone to open order and were pressing their assault using ground cover now. They no longer ran forward en masse into the machine gun fire. Firing now was like hitting the gophers in that pop up arcade game. And the North Korean fires were getting more accurate as Sampson felt a bullet pluck at his shirt sleeve. He lowered himself closer to the ground.

"*Reuben Barnes*, go."

"We have uploaded some of the ammo that the army guys had in their ammo carriers ashore and will provide fires for you in about two minutes once we get the UAV into position. Will that help?"

Sampson was ecstatic! "*Barnes*, I owe all of you a beer and good cigar! How much can you give me?"

"We can do about two minutes, will that be enough?"

"It will have to be. Give me a heads up before you start so I can get these guys ready to pull out. We've got some wounded and one KIA coming with us."

"Roger, Centurion. UAV is one minute out. We'll call when we've got our targeting completed."

"Centurion, standing by."

"Centurion, this is the *Kitty Hawk*. Once you begin your withdrawal, we're going to use the dumb bombs we have on the CAP birds. Gun target line will be east to west. I say again east to west parallel to your withdrawal route. Do you approve, over?"

Sampson keyed the mike quickly, "Roger *Kitty Hawk*! You've got my full approval and undying love to go along with it! You guys are pretty damned good for a pickup team!"

Admiral Durham's voice came back dryly with, "Yeah, well all we can say in response is Go Navy! Beat Army!"

"Roger, and a Go Army! Beat Navy! back at you!"

The machine gunners had almost stopped firing as the North Koreans slowed their assault and went to ground. Sampson knew they were getting organized to rush the positions once they had worked in close enough. "Jimmie, tell your crews to cease firing but stay alert. These assholes are going to rush us. I want everybody ready to pour it on when they come up. I want long killing bursts like the Bradley guys do it." Stokes bent over his squad radio and put the word out and the battlefield was actually quiet enough to hear the faint screams of the North Korean wounded from the napalm attack almost a quarter a mile away. Nobody seemed to notice the screams or the smell of cooking meat that wafted down on the wind as they all focused their attention to the south.

"Centurion, this is the *Reuben Barnes*, we have the UAV on station, and be advised they are massing behind that small ridge about five hundred meters to your south. In fact here they come! Fires one minute out to impact!"

"Hit it Jimmie! I need one good minute of fires and we're the hell out of here!"

Stokes fired his gun in a steady stream using a Z-pattern from the front to rear of the enemy formation, then shifting left and right with the same pattern. The fires of the remaining three machine guns were also effective, but not effective enough. The North Koreans were closing in fast. "*Reuben Barnes*, I need it danger close! I say again danger close!"

It seemed a full lifetime or even two before the first round impacted. By the time its flight from the gun to the ground had transpired, the enemy was no longer there. They were moving too fast.

"Keep firing Jimmie!" Sampson stood up and shot an enemy soldier carrying a flag at the front of the mass. The whole formation paused briefly until another soldier picked up the flag and started forward again. Sampson shot him too, but then had to duck back down as the North Korean return fires intensified. Again he felt bullets plucking at his uniform in near misses, but had too much adrenaline flowing to even care.

The rounds from the *Reuben Barnes* had been adjusted for danger close and were impacting in the middle of the enemy formation now. Sampson noticed a slight hesitation in their forward movement and told Stokes, "Tell the other gun teams to haul ass. We'll cover them from here. Tell them to remove their bolts and leave the guns."

Within seconds the remaining gun teams were running at a low crouch towards the beach. As Sampson had hoped the North Koreans ignored them while still trying to attack the remaining machine gun as Stokes poured it into them. One of the paratroopers was carrying a wounded comrade in a fireman's carry and four others were carrying their KIA out in a poncho that they half dragged and half carried at an awkward run. Sampson knew from personal experience that there was no burden in the whole world heavier than the body of a dead buddy.

Stokes kept firing the long killing bursts and the fires from the *Reuben Barnes* seemed to intensify. It was right on target tearing huge chunks out of the North Korean formation. "Okay, Jimmie. Pull your bolt and we're out of here. Let's go!" Sampson turned and headed towards the beach. He glanced back and saw Stokes running right behind him carrying his machine gun on his shoulder. Sampson slowed and said, "Dump the damned gun, Jimmie! We've got to haul ass now!"

Stokes' response was to hold onto the gun and pass Sampson at a dead run like Sampson was standing still. "C'mon, sir! We gotta go!" Stokes pulled ahead.

Sampson swore and increased his speed to catch up but there was no way in hell his more than half-century old and highly abused body was going to catch up even with his adrenaline pumping at warp speed. He shed the twenty pound flak jacket, and the thirty pound radio, but kept a tight grip on his rifle. The fire from the North Koreans seemed to slacken as the *Reuben Barnes* kept firing. Just as the small group of soldiers crested a small rise and fell thankfully behind its cover, the jets from the *Kitty Hawk* screamed by so low that they were literally lifting the dirt off the ground with their passing as they began their bomb runs. Each jet popped up to unload its bombs and then went vertical on afterburner to escape the explosion. The troops on the ground were screaming and pumping their arms up and down in the classic arm signal to 'go like hell and kick ass and take names' at the jets as they streaked by! The noise was deafening and damned exhilarating if you weren't on the receiving end!

Sampson quickened his pace and finally caught up to Stokes who had stopped and was taking a nose count of his guys. "Godamnit, Jimmie! Why the hell didn't you do what I told you to do, and leave the damn gun behind?"

Stokes looked solemn when he responded. "Sir, this gun saved my ass in Iraq and I couldn't even think about leaving it behind. It would be like leaving one of my kids behind."

"You don't have any kids, Jimmie."

"Sir, none that you know of, none that you know of," Stokes responded with a smirk, "but Fayetteville on a payday Saturday night is still a wonderful place!"

"Okay, smart ass. Let's get these guys to the beach. My fun meter is fucking pegged about now." Sampson leaned forward and put his hands on his knees to steady himself and catch his breath which was coming in ragged gasps. "Go ahead, Jimmie. I'll be okay in a minute. Shit, I'm too old for this crap!"

Stokes laughed and gave the orders and the small group began to work its way slowly through the low ground using the folds in the ground for cover as they headed to the beach. The North Koreans were too busy trying to get out of the beaten zone of artillery shells and five hundred pound bombs to follow them.

This fight was over and the Americans had not lost any face.

1629 hours
11 November
Debarkation Point at Chong-ju, South Korea

The first person Sampson saw at the beach head was Gunny Gaddis. The second person he saw was Randy Long. He swore out loud and said to Gaddis, "I told you to get on a boat, Gunny and get the hell off the beach. What part of that didn't make it into that marine brain of yours?"

Randy Long stepped forward. "Sir, I told the gunny to stay and take care of the order you sent. He'll be on the next boat."

Sampson nodded his head in acceptance of Long's decision. "Where is he?"

Gaddis went behind a small shed and led Captain Glen Stover over to Sampson and Long. The captain was clearly unhappy and was just as clearly handcuffed with a zip tie. Even before he got to Sampson, Stover started to loudly voice his protests at his treatment. Several of the paratroopers waiting patiently in line for evacuation glanced over but soon lost interest.

Sampson spoke. "First of all, Captain, I want you to shut the hell up. You'll speak when you're spoken to. Secondly, stand at attention, godamnit!" Stover slowly pulled himself into a position of attention. "Gunny, cut that cuff off of him." Gaddis stepped forward and cut the zip tie none too gently with his combat knife. Stover flinched when he did it. "Captain Stover, you are under arrest for sending a patrol out under false pretenses into a known enemy ambush site resulting in the probable deaths or capture of American soldiers. Colonel Long, can you confirm this charge?"

"Yes, sir. I can."

"If we get back to the States, Captain Stover, you *will* stand trial for these charges. Do you understand that?" Stover nodded his head. "Answer me, godamnit!"

Stover whispered, "Yes, sir. I understand the charges, but …"

Sampson cut him off abruptly. "I don't want to hear any bullshit excuses from you, Captain. I have not read you your rights, nor am I going to, because my guess is you'll never go to trial. Make sure your canteen is full of water and get ready to move out. Gunny, escort him."

Sampson checked his rifle and inserted a fresh eight round clip into the M-1. He slowly filled the ejected clip with loose rounds and put it in his ammo pouch. He looked over at the line of paratroopers and spotted Stokes and his team waiting their turn to embark. He stepped over and said, "Jimmie, give me your grenades." Stokes pulled his grenades from their pouches and handed them to Sampson. He did not seem the least bit surprised by the request. Sampson stowed the grenades and stepped back over to Randy Long who at least was very surprised at what Sampson was doing.

Long finally blurted out, "Sir, what are you going to do? Why do you need grenades?" The answer hit Randy Long with a rush and he said incredulously, "Sir, you are not going back out there! You can't!"

Sampson remained silent while Gaddis brought Stover back from the water trailer parked by the dock. "Okay, Captain. Here's a map." Sampson thrust a map into Stover's trembling hands. "I've marked the patrol's last known location. You're going to lead me there and if you try to run away, I'll kill you. Do we understand each other?"

Randy Long looked at the last boat filling up with the paratroopers who had held the final firing line and said softly, "Sir, we need to get on board. This is the last boat." When Sampson didn't respond, Long said just a bit more loudly. "Sir, we need to get on the boat. We have won. We need to go home now. Sir, *we need to go home now.*"

Sampson finally turned to Long and said slowly, "Randy, I'm not leaving my son and his soldiers here unaccounted for. I have done everything General Smith and the National Command Authority asked me to do, but I'm done with this operation. Tell Admiral Durham we couldn't have done it without him and his people and thank him from me. You and the gunny get on board and I'll see you later, maybe." Sampson started shepherding the remaining two men towards the mike boat. They went hesitantly, but they went. Even before the boat had pulled up its ramp and started to back away from the dock, Sampson was pushing Stover in the back to get him started towards the hills to the west.

0800 hours
12 November
In the hills West of Chong-ju, South Korea

Sampson had been joined by two young ROK marines as he and Stover had started into the hills. Both had come from Pohang with the mike boats to help in the evacuation, but neither had chosen to evacuate because they could not leave their families behind. The one marine who had identified himself as Lance Corporal Chang, had studied English at Seoul University before being called up for his mandatory two years of service and spoke it fairly well.

The other young marine did not speak English at all. Chang had seen Sampson with his stars on his uniform down at the beach head before the fighting started, so when Sampson had said he was only a colonel, Chang had shook his head and persisted in calling him general. He knew what he had seen. Sampson couldn't adequately explain the temporary nature of the rank, so had given it up. It didn't matter anyhow.

The small party had taken a long detour to the south to skirt the field of battle. They had heard the moans of the North Korean wounded and had kept that sound to their right as they continued to move west when darkness fell. Around midnight, Sampson had stopped the small group and taken shelter in a small cave in the rocks. Once they had stopped, the marine explained to Sampson is whispers that he was staying behind in the hopes of reaching his family in Seoul and eventually getting out of Korea with them. He had further explained that the other young ROK marine, Private Chae, had family up in the hills that he felt obligated to return to. They were his aging grandparents and he was their only support. He told Sampson that Private Chae had wanted very much to leave with the Americans, but could not abandon his responsibilities to his family.

Sampson had reached over and shook the young marine's hand and told him he was very proud of him for putting his family ahead of himself. Lance Corporal Chang had translated and the young marine had smiled and nodded his thanks for the kind words. Chang had explained that Sampson was a great American general which had made the young marine smile all the harder.

Sampson had turned to Stover and said, "Captain, you're probably trying to figure out how to run away tonight in the dark. You just need to remember that after the trashing we gave the North Koreans today, they will not treat you kindly once they catch you, and they will catch you. My guess is they'll keep you barely alive and in as much pain as they can inflict for a month or two before they finish you off." Stover hadn't responded, and Sampson had closed his eyes and immediately fallen asleep.

The small group was moving again before first light. They no longer heard the moans of the North Korean wounded, so they started heading north towards the ambush sight. Sampson took the map from Stover and determined exactly where they were. He pointed the direction he wanted Stover to move towards. Sampson had forgotten that in the age of GPS, a lot of younger officers no longer knew how to read an old fashioned map very well, and Stover was less competent than most which was not a surprise to Sampson.

After another hour, they crested the hill into the ambush sight. Sampson saw instantly how the battle had gone based upon the empty cartridges scattered around each fighting position. Numerous dead bodies also spoke silently of the struggle. Sampson noted two Americans huddled together in one position, both dead, and both of them had clearly been wounded first. Their initial wounds had been bandaged; their final wounds had not.

Some of the dead scattered around wore the uniforms of ROK MP's, but they had clearly been killed by the Americans. And they had just as obviously killed the Americans. Sampson was just beginning to wonder if this whole fight had been a case of mistaken identity when he noticed some of the dead were wearing North Korean uniforms. His questions were further answered when he came around some rocks and spotted a ROK major lying on his back. Sampson's appearance caused a raven standing on the major's chest to reluctantly hop away a few feet, but it did not fly away. The raven called raucously at the interruption. As Sampson got closer, he could see that the raven had been busily removing the left eyeball of the ROK major. The remainder of the eyeball dangled down onto his chest connected only by the optical nerve. Stuck in the middle of the ROK major's chest was a bayonet still affixed to an M-16 rifle. There is no mistake about friend or foe once it gets down to bayonets. The major's chest was still moving in labored breaths.

Just as Sampson was getting ready to kneel down beside the wounded major a voice called out, "Don't touch that bastard! He's the one who attacked us!"

Sampson spun around and saw a young soldier sitting behind him pulled up against the backside of the rocks Sampson had just skirted around. He was holding another soldier close to his chest, and Sampson saw as his heart dropped that it was his son. He ran over to his son and the sitting soldier. The soldier had a bandage across his thigh soaked in blood and was wearing a medic's armband. The contents of his aid bag were scattered around him. Sampson saw with relief that his son, like the ROK major was still breathing, but in even shallower gasps.

Sampson asked, "How bad is he?"

"I think his left lung has collapsed. The bullets are still in him. There aren't any exit wounds. Are you here to get us out? Who are you?" The young medic spoke in a monotone and was clearly on the verge of going into shock.

"I'm his dad," Sampson said softly, "and yes, I came to get you out of here. Who are you?"

"Sir, I'm Sergeant Wilson. I've been sitting here for two days now wondering what was happening as I heard all the firing towards the coast. When it got so quiet yesterday, I thought we had been forgotten and everybody had left."

Sampson said gently, "Everybody has left, Sergeant Wilson, but I've got a small group that will move you to a safer place. We'll see what we can do about a pick up once we get there. Can you walk?"

Wilson nodded his head. "I need something for a crutch but I can walk. But we'll have to carry the lieutenant, uh, your son, sir. He's out of it."

"Has he regained consciousness at all?"

"Yes, sir. Just long enough to drink a little water, and then he drifts off again."

Sampson nodded. That was at least a good sign that Sean wasn't giving up the fight.

Sampson stood up and called over to Corporal Chang. "Corporal, we have two wounded men to get out to a safer place. Do you know where we can go?"

Corporal Chang hurried over. "Yes, General, Private Chae says you should go to his grandparent's house up in the hills. There are no roads and you will not be found there. He says it is very safe there. The North Koreans will never go there because it is of no value to them." Sergeant Wilson's eyes had widened in surprise when Chang had called Sampson 'general' but he said nothing.

"Ask my marine friend how far it is to this house."

Chang asked the question and answered, "It is not far, General, but I think we must hurry. This place is too close to the highway and the North Koreans may come here to find out what happened here." Chang waved his hands around at the dead ROK MP's and North Koreans.

Sampson could tell by where they had fallen that the ROK MP's and the North Koreans were fighting together as a unit, so this was the SPF unit Colonel Han had been sent to warn the American's about. It would be close to the highway, and the North Koreans would be looking for this team, if they hadn't done so already. They did need to move on soon.

Sampson turned and saw Stover staring at all of the North Korean dead. His face was ashen as he saw first hand what he and Bobby Wellens had done. His lips were trembling. Sampson said harshly, "Captain Stover, rig a litter for Lieutenant Sampson, and collect a dog tag and the personal effects from our three KIA's." Stover didn't move so Sampson barked out, "Stover! Rig a litter and collect the effects! Do it now, goddamnit!" Stover jumped at the harshness in Sampson's voice and stumbled towards the nearest American soldier's body to do as he was told. Corporal Chang was already taking a poncho out of a rucksack, and was making a litter with two rifles.

As Sampson turned away disgustedly from the still trembling captain, he saw the raven perched again on the ROK MP's chest and tugging at the eyeball again. The raven had one claw on the eyeball and the other wrapped around the barrel of the M-16 to gain leverage. Sampson stepped closer and the raven again hopped away protesting. The other eye fluttered open at the sound of Sampson's footsteps. It fixed on Sampson. Sampson returned the stare.

"Sir, are you going to shoot that sorry bastard?"

Sampson paused before answering; staring into Colonel Sung's remaining eye. He shook his head. "No, Sergeant Wilson. I'm going to let the raven take his other eye. And then he's going to slowly starve or freeze to death in the dark. I can tell by the look he's giving me that he very much wants me to end it for him."

Sung looked into the American's eyes and saw no pity, but no hatred either. The bayonet had severed his spinal cord and he could move only his eyes, or now only his remaining eye. Even his voice did not work. He had tried to yell at the raven but nothing had come out. He moved his remaining eye rapidly back and forth in an effort to communicate his desire to be put out of his misery, but the American just turned away. As soon as he did, the raven hopped back onto his chest and Sung squeezed his eyelids as tight as he could, but he knew the raven was hungry.

**1030 hours
17 November
Taeback Mountains, South Korea**

Sampson looked at the cell phone screen and it flickered but would not hold a steady screen. He decided that he needed to go outside in the hopes of getting a signal. With the flickering screen, he could not tell if he had any signal at all. He stood up, looked over at his son who seemed to actually be sleeping instead of unconscious, and stooped through the low door.

Sampson looked again at the flickering screen and knew his battery was about shot. He punched in the letters slowly for a text message. He wasn't used to doing it, and had to make sure he got it right. He punched in, "sn ok call gnsmth pu 2 wks sn brth hr plus kds grid 7802 plus yr met 1466 minus yr wed." Sampson had never figured out the punctuation and caps thing in text messaging, so this was as good as it was going to get. He prayed that the message would go out and more importantly, that his wife Deidra would figure out his code. He hit the send key and the screen flashed once and went completely black. He tried turning the cell phone on and off again but the battery was completely dead. He said a silent prayer and went back inside the low stone house.

Sergeant Wilson looked up from where he was helping Sean take some soup the old Korean woman had made for him. Now that Corporal Chang was gone, it was extremely difficult to communicate with the young marine and his grandparents, but they were managing. The old woman had fussed continuously over Sean in spite of the language barrier and it was clearly helping.

Wilson said, "So what do we do now, sir?"

Captain Stover also looked up at the question. His whole demeanor had changed once he had gotten to the ambush sight. He had even volunteered to make his way to the Swede to report the location of the three remaining dead Americans so their bodies could be recovered. Sampson never expected to see him again, and was surprised when he returned several days later. Sampson had figured he would try to get the Swede to get him out somehow. When Sampson had asked him why he had come back, he had said simply that it was his duty to do so. Sampson had let it go.

Sampson turned towards Sergeant Wilson and said, "We wait, Sergeant Wilson. We wait. Sean, how're you feeling, son?"

Sean Sampson looked at his dad and smiled that same crooked smile Sampson remembered from when he was a kid, and said weakly, "Like a sack of shit, dad. Just like a sack of shit."

Sampson smiled.

Epilogue

"I mean, really General Smith, do you expect us to believe that this administration is lying to the American people about what happened in Korea? I mean come on now, we all know what happened. You were the general in charge, and you failed to hold the line. Isn't that the real truth? Don't you think it's just a little cheesy on your part to call for a congressional investigation when we all know who is to blame?

General Smith actually smiled at his host. "Gosh, David. You are even dumber than they told me you were! This is great! So go ahead. I know the White House tells you what to say on this show; so go ahead and explain to me and your audience how I failed in Korea."

The host flushed and was actually disconcerted by the general's response. He was absolutely sure that Smith would get angry and lash out at him like most of the rest of his guests did when he taunted them. Instead Smith smiled and called him dumb! The host was at a loss for words and signaled a station break.

When the show came back on, the general was still smiling and the host still was not. Before the host could say anything, Smith said, "For those of you just tuning in, David here is going to explain to you the White House's fairytale on how I personally lost the war in Korea. Go ahead, David. We're waiting."

The host tried to signal for another station break but got the wave off from the producer. He tried to change the subject instead. He seemed to get control of himself as he smoothly said, "Well, we'll get back to that later, General Smith. Instead, I know a lot of people are very, very concerned about the footage that has been aired with young American soldiers being ordered to crush defenseless North Korean soldiers with their tanks. I'm sure you've seen that footage released by the secretary of defense two days ago? And while you're at it, what do the rules of fair fighting or whatever you call them say about running over wounded soldiers? Some of those Koreans in the footage were obviously wounded and unable to get out of the way. Isn't this clearly a war crime and the man behind it a war criminal?"

This time General Smith did not smile. Instead he looked directly into the camera and said, "No, it is not a war crime to run your enemy down with a tank, anymore than it is a war crime to blow them up with bombs or bullets. War is about killing, David. Or hasn't the White House told you that yet? More importantly, what the secretary neglected to mention in his statement when he released that footage was that it was taken by a *Russian* military film crew. Nor did he mention that the tactic used, as brutal as it may seem, was instrumental in saving American lives."

The host waved his hand as if to say all of this wasn't important to the issue at hand. "Yes, we all know, General, how the military likes to cover up for its own and say I vas chust following orders!" The host said the last part in a very bad imitation of a German accent. He continued, "My sources tell me that the man who gave those orders, one Colonel Sampson, is to be charged if the authorities can ever get their hands on him. My sources also tell me that he refused to be evacuated from Korea because he knew he had committed war crimes and would have to answer for them!" The host's smugness was palpable. He was fairly preening in front of the cameras.

Smith's face reddened and he sat back in his chair. He remained silent for almost a full minute. He said slowly, "First of all David, let's go ahead and establish up front that your *sources* as you call them are the White House and the secretary of defense. Secondly, the officer who gave those orders was *Major General* Sampson, and not *Colonel* Sampson. I personally received the message from the president promoting him to that rank and I personally pinned that rank on him. That the president denies that he ever authorized that order is just so much more of his bullshit and it's a disgrace. I have the original order with me right here. Would you care to see it?" Smith unfolded the message he had received on Sampson's promotion and held it towards the host who did not move to take it. Nobody had told him that the shit had been in writing for Christ's sake!

Smith paused. The host still didn't respond to him or to the message he held out, so he continued, "*General* Sampson personally saved thousands of American lives in Korea, and he is one of our greatest heroes. Thanks to him, our soldiers were able to withdraw intact from Korea rather than being killed or captured on the evacuation beach by the North Koreans. If you want to harp on something, David, why don't you harp on what the North Koreans tried to do to us?"

The host finally responded and answered Smith by saying, "Oh, General. Come on now!" in a very condescending voice.

Smith ignored him and continued angrily, "This administration is trying to make what General Sampson did on the battlefield look criminal, David. They are doing this to deflect the media's attention away from their own failures in Korea and elsewhere. I find the whole charade absolutely mind boggling. Thank god, the American people and the media are smarter than that, and know bullshit when the see it and hear it. Everybody knows that General Sampson didn't evacuate because he went back to get his son and four other soldiers who were missing in action. That alone tells you everything you need to know about what kind of soldier Sam Sampson is. What else have you got David? I'm about done here."

Although the host was pleased that he had finally angered General Smith, he was clearly not pleased with the response. He made one last effort to turn the interview around. He knew he was going to get a zinger from the White House on this show!

"Okay, General, back to the first question. Why did you lose in Korea? I mean we all thought you were better than that. And don't tell me you didn't lose because we all know you were taken down a star before you retired a few days ago. They wouldn't do that if you weren't responsible, now would they?" The smug look was back.

General Smith was silent for a moment, but his face was no longer red. "Well David, yes, I did lose a star when I retired. I know if I had played along with the White House's story on what happened and why it happened, I would have kept that star, but you know, it just wasn't important to me. They made just such an offer and I refused it, because here's what's important to me; that we *never* find ourselves in this situation again. That's why I've called upon Congress to investigate this matter fully and to finally do their job of providing a balance of power in our nation again. One man or a few men should *never* be able to put this country or its allies in jeopardy again because they think they know better than all the rest of us."

Smith did not continue and the host went for the kill. "Aha! But you haven't answered my question General! You're ducking the issue here! You were in charge and we lost! It's as simple as that! You can't deny it, can you?" he literally howled. He looked around the audience triumphantly, and there was small spattering of applause which quickly died out.

Smith leaned forward and said almost confidentially, "David, I'm going to answer your question and then I'm going to punch you right in the nose." Smith leaned back in his chair and the host smiled nervously. Surely Smith wasn't serious about punching him in the nose!

Smith continued, "David, since I know you actively ducked military service during the Vietnam War, I'll use a little analogy to explain this to you in terms that you and even the clowns in the White House will understand. Let's say you and I build a house on the side of a mountain, David. It's a steep mountain and the house has to have lots of support beams to hold it up. Now as time passes, I'm living in the house, but you have made repeated trips back to it to use the support beams elsewhere in other houses, some of which weren't even very good houses. But you took them anyhow. One at a time you took the support beams out and now there is only one little support beam left in place on my house. One day we get a little tremor on the mountain and the whole damn house crashes down the hill. That little support beam you left couldn't withstand even a minor shock. Now here's my question to you in this little scenario. Do you blame the guy living in the house or do you blame the guy who took the support beams away? What do you think a court would decide as to who is to blame? Who do you think your neighbors, who are also depending on you for support, would blame, and how much are they going to trust you in the future? They have to be asking themselves about now if their house is going to be next."

"Oh! General Smith, puuuleeze! That is such a stupid analogy! I just can't agree with that at all! It's just silly! What we had in Korea didn't need to be full support. We all know that. It only needed to be a tripwire. Why, we're the most powerful nation in the world! You had your tripwire, it got tripped and you blew it! That's the truth here!"

Smith smiled. "I guess your right, David, but the last I heard, a tripwire needed to be attached to something other than just words and empty promises in order to work properly. If there's no real combat power or deterrent tied to it, it's just another piece of useless wire lying on the ground. But I think we need to go to a commercial break here."

Puzzled, the producer signaled the commercial break on Smith's call and Lieutenant General Robertson L. Smith, US Army, Retired, did in fact punch David squarely in the nose, and the audience rose to their feet and clapped and cheered with unfeigned enthusiasm. None of them recalled seeing a thing later on when the host wanted to sue, however. Nor somehow, could the film footage of the alleged assault be found in the studio archives.

Maybe there was hope for America after all.

Glossary of Terms

2IC—Second in Command

AAAFES—Army and Air Force Exchange System. The agency that runs the military's version of Wal-Mart on all posts, camps and air bases.

Adashi—Hangul for mister, or man. Americans use it like "Hey buddy" when talking to a Korean male.

ANGLICO—Air Naval Gunfire Liaison Company. No longer in use, but formerly, Marines specially trained in calling for and adjusting naval gunfire support and close air support for other Marines in close combat ashore.

Break—used on the radio to denote a pause, and tells everybody else on the net not to acknowledge the call or start talking because the current speaker is not done yet.

CG—Commanding General. The number of stars he or she wears is dictated by the size and type of unit commanded. A division commander has two stars; a corps commander has three stars, a theater commander has four stars and may be referred to as the CG or the CINC. See next under.

CINC—Commander in Chief. Pronounced "sink". A title reserved for the senior military commander of a combatant command or theater of war; usually a four star general or admiral. Not to be confused with The Commander in Chief, the President of the United States who is never referred to as a CINC or the CINC by military personnel.

CINCPAC—Commander in Chief Pacific, usually a four star admiral responsible for all US forces in the Pacific theater except for those stationed in Korea.

Also used interchangeably to denote that admiral's headquarters based at Camp Smith, Hawaii, as in "I'm being assigned to CINPAC for duty."

CJ-5—Combined Joint 5, staff section that handles the political-military aspects of war fighting. "Combined" in a headquarters' title means a headquarters containing military elements from other countries; "Joint" in the title means a headquarters containing a mix of different US military services. The CJ-5 also assists the CJ-3(Operations) in developing future plans for execution.

CP—command post. A unit's headquarters in a field location away from their normal fixed peace time locations.

Defcon—Defense Condition. A series of steps taken to ramp up for imminent combat in a theater of war. Also used nationally during the Cold War to put bombers on alert, have units assemble at airfields for deployment, etc.

DIVARTY—Division Artillery. The headquarters commanded by an artillery colonel responsible for all artillery units in an Army division.

DLIC—Detachment left in contact; pronounced "dee-lick". A tactical formation normally composed of one half of a unit's crew served weapons (machine guns, mortars, anti-tank platforms, etc.) and one third of their riflemen. It is used to hold the line against an attacking enemy while the main body withdraws from the fight.

DMZ—De-Militarized Zone, a space between the two Koreas that is ostensibly clear of any military units or equipment as agreed upon in the 1953 Cease Fire Agreement. It's in reality actually packed with minefields and actively patrolled by both sides, occasionally resulting in firefights and casualties.

G-3—the staff officer responsible for actual combat operations in a division or corps headquarters. Titled as an S-3 at battalion and brigade levels, J-3 at a joint headquarters, and so on. Long suffering, and always over worked, but a good G-3 is key and essential to any successful military operation at division or corps levels. Usually the commander's right hand man, and also usually hand picked for the job by the commander.

Guidons, guidons—a call over a radio net for everybody on that net to hear something important simultaneously. A quick and efficient way for a commander to put out orders to all units.

Hangul—the language of Korea. Koreans do not speak "Korean". They speak Hangul, a very difficult language to learn. Americans who say to English speaking Koreans "Don't speak Korean to me, speak English!" often get puzzled looks in response.

KATUSA—Korean Augmentation to the United States Army. A program started in the Korean War to replace US combat losses temporarily with South Korean soldiers. The program has continued to this day and the South Korean soldiers are supposed to be fluent in English. Unfortunately, most are not fluent and owe their positions in the much easier disciplined and better fed US Army to political clout or money. Duty in the much harsher and extremely poorly paid South Korean Army is generally strenuously avoided by the sons of the well to do. Military service in South Korea is compulsory for all males for a two year period.

Kimchee—a staple in the Korean diet, and frequently like rice, is eaten with every meal. It is made up primarily of a concoction of cabbage, hot peppers and lots of garlic which is buried in the ground in an earthenware pot to ferment. According to American GI's, "kimchee breath" has a lethal radius of at least five meters, and can make a Westerner's eyes water even further away in enclosed spaces like command bunkers. The only known defense to kimchee breath is to also eat kimchee and join the crowd.

Klicks—kilometers, a 1000 meters, 5/8 of a mile.

K-pot—Kevlar helmet. Weighs about five pounds and is guaranteed to give excruciating headaches until the wearer gets used to it.

LCAC—Landing Craft, Air Cushioned. Used to bring men and equipment ashore. Once it gets to land, it "floats" ashore on an air cushion created by its engines, thereby negating small obstacles.

LOC—lines of communication, pronounced "lock", military parlance for open roads cleared of the enemy to bring up replacements, reinforcements and supplies, and used to evacuate wounded and dead to the rear.

MEU—Marine Expeditionary Unit. A combined arms Marine force attached to most carrier battle groups. Depending on the mission, it is battalion sized or larger and may be special operations qualified (MEU-SOC). A MEU usually has its own artillery and helicopter assets attached.

MFR—Memorandum for Record. Written to document an event or conversation and sworn to and signed by its author as to its veracity.

Midnight requisition—old Army term for stealing equipment.

Mikes—minutes in radio speak

MLRS—Multiple Launch Rocket System. A rocket system mounted on a tracked or wheeled chassis. Each system carries a pod of six rockets with varying types of munitions. A long range weapon capable of shooting 30+ kilometers (~20 miles) away.

NKPA—North Korean People's Army. The bad guys in this story and in real life! A well equipped and well trained army that is in excess of a million men according to open intelligence sources.

NEO—Non-combatant Evacuation Order. Once a NEO is announced to be in effect, all US civilians to include military family members are allowed to take only one suitcase each (and no pets), and must immediately report to collection points for transport to the nearest airfield or port for removal from the combat zone.

PIR—Parachute Infantry Regiment. An airborne command comprised of three airborne infantry battalions.

ROK—Republic of Korea or any South Korean according to American GI's. Pronounced "rock"

SAM—surface to air missile

SAR—Search and Air Rescue, highly trained and very brave helicopter crews who specialize in trying to get downed pilots and crews out of hostile fire areas.

Secdef—Secretary of Defense, pronounced "seck deff".

Sitrep—Situation Report. A unit's status at a given time. Usually couched in terms relative to the ground and enemy forces.

Soju—a clear and very potent Korean liquor made out of something indeterminate that ferments, and it rips your head off the next day. Not for the faint of heart. The North Korean version often has a dead viper floating in the bottle which speaks volumes if you think about it!

SGLI—Serviceman's Group Life Insurance. Life insurance policy for service people that does not have a war clause and is relatively cheap to buy. Premiums are paid automatically out of the serviceman's monthly pay.

SPF—Special Purpose Forces. Bad guys who are highly trained and used like our special operations forces; Green Berets, Seals, etc. North Korea has large numbers of these forces and knows how to use them effectively.

TOC—Tactical Operations Center, another name for a headquarters in the field, or the specific location inside a CP where ongoing operations are monitored and supported by the staff.

TOT—Time on Target. Pronounced "tee oh tee", or tango oscar tango phonetically over the radio. A technique used by modern artillery to put maximum rounds on a single point on the battlefield with all rounds landing nearly simultaneously. Some types of guns can fire multiple rounds at different elevations and have them all impact at the same time. A devastatingly violent artillery attack, but short in duration.

TPFDD—Time Phased Forces Deployment Document. Most people say the last D actually stands for "Dream" because it never seems to work. A series of plans constantly updated to flow forces or reinforcements into an existing theater of war or to a new theater of war like Desert Storm. (Where it didn't work!)

UAV—Unmanned aerial vehicle. A pilotless drone controlled from the ground with varying sensor arrays and occasionally weapons.

If I missed any you don't understand in the book, send me a note at billcham118@aol.com and I shall gladly enlighten you at no extra charge!

978-0-595-45937-7
0-595-45937-4